WRATH OF OLYMPUS

VOLUME 2

REALM WALKER

BRIAN TRIPP

BRIAN TRIPP

ISBN: 978-1-945567-36-0
Library of Congress: 2023915796
Cover Design: Emily's World of Design
Interior: Ruth Souther

DEDICATION

To Grandpa Heyduck, Mom, Dad, Amy, Chris, and Jane;
the most supportive family I am lucky to have.

ACKNOWLEDGMENTS

Special thanks to Karen and Chris, who never stop
encouraging me to continue my writing,
and to my friend Bjorn, who made so much of this book
possible.

CHAPTER ONE

Ashe

"The time has finally come."

A booming voice cut through the boisterous roar of the crowd. Onlookers gathered among the stands of the colosseum, as the initial rays of sunlight began to shine upon the grounds, lighting up the marble splendor of Olympus.

An intense pang of anxiety and exhilaration shot through Clotho. She ran her hands over her braided, caramel hair, making sure not even a strand was out of place. For the last two hundred years she went through an intense training regimen for the most sacred of missions. Though long for humanity, to an immortal it is but the bat of an eye. Today, her legacy would finally begin.

"One thousand years have passed since the last Weaver claimed the Tower of Fate," Zeus addressed her, drawing the crowd in with every word. "And now the tower has appeared again in the mortal realm, ready to be claimed by its next champion."

As if on cue, the "oohs" and "aahs" of the crowd picked up. Clotho ignored them. Like most things on Olympus, the interest and cheers of the crowd were superficial. All the immortals pranced and preened when the eyes of the Olympians fell upon them. They only cared about tradition so long as they looked good doing it.

Clotho never cared about the luxuries Olympus offered. From an early age she was raised to care about one thing, and one thing only: the Throne. The immortals held dominion over the mortal plane for as long as humanity existed.

To put it simply, humans are too helpless to control themselves. And while Clotho had her own opinions about the Olympians, they at least had the power necessary to lead the less fortunate in the right direction.

"I am ready, Lord Zeus," she addressed the long-bearded god.

The smell of ozone permeated the air around him, causing Clotho's skin to tingle. "For two centuries I have trained in warfare with Lord Ares. Every day I have been grilled on strategy by Lady Athena. There is not a mortal alive who can beat me to that throne."

Zeus smiled at her, causing the crinkles around his eyes to deepen. "Good girl. Remember, it does not matter what it takes. If it means wiping the mortals out in droves to claim the throne, do not hesitate.

"They are no more than insects. I permit your personal guards to attend you on this journey as well. Should the monsters drawn to the tower become too many, they will help."

Clotho stopped her jaw mid-drop, clamping her mouth shut, hoping Lord Zeus did not notice. She grimaced inwardly at the knowing smirk upon his face. Lyssa and Laren had been with her for as long as she could remember.

From the moment she was born, she was chosen for this sacred duty. As part of her training, as well as to ensure her safety, two of Athena's best were chosen to fight alongside her. Though they both lived on Olympus for centuries longer than her, they did not look older than young adults.

Zeus, not having missed Clotho's show of enthusiasm, showed off his brilliant white smile.

"Go now. Your things have already been packed and they are waiting for you by the gateway. Remember Clotho, it is our right to claim the tower. Do so by any means necessary."

His face suddenly clouded with a blatantly threatening aura. "Do not fail me."

Just as soon as it had appeared it was gone, replaced by a cheerful smile.

"LET US SEE OUR HERO OFF WITH A CHEER!" He roared at the onlookers.

Clotho stumbled away from the king of the gods, her mind reeling from the severity of his threat as she made her way towards the tunnel. She was still shaken when a warmth spread through the hallway, soothing away her frayed nerves.

"Be at peace, Clotho. Do not let my brother bully you into doing things his way."

She stared into the amber eyes of the goddess before her as the unease melted away, replaced by a renewed sense of resolve. She brushed a strand of her auburn hair back behind her ear before reaching out and placing a hand on Clotho's shoulder.

"Thank you, Lady Hestia." She bowed. Hestia had always been one of the kinder Olympians. She always looked out for Clotho during her training; tending to her wounds or giving her the courage to not give up on a particularly hard task.

"Have you come to see me off?"

Hestia smiled; her eyes filled with compassion.

"I have come to say farewell, yes. These years with you have been wonderful, and I am very proud of the woman you have become. Though I do not believe this will be the last time you and I speak, I think it likely that it will be quite some time before we see each other again. As such, I have come to you with gifts."

From behind her back, Hestia produced an ornate, golden spear. Ancient runes lit up along the shaft, casting a warm glow upon the room. A wickedly sharp blade protruded from the tip, perfect for piercing even the toughest armor.

The goddess placed the weapon firmly into Clotho's upturned palm, gently wrapped Clotho's fingers around the handle, and placed her hand warmly upon Clotho's closed grip.

"A weapon for you to use along your journey. While your spear is serviceable, I commissioned this one, especially from Hephaestus himself. You will find no godly weapon of finer quality. May it keep you safe from all who would oppose you on this journey."

Clotho was stunned. *"Lady Hestia I can't-"*

Hestia held up her hand, stopping the words before they could continue.

"Second, some advice. My brother would have you burn the world down around you so that he may traipse through the ashes unopposed. Though the Throne is important, do not lose sight of who you are to attain it. Zeus believes those lesser than himself," she curled her lip in disgust as she spoke. "Are nothing more than pawns to be sacrificed."

A small flame sprung to life on the end of her finger.

"But there is beauty in all life. From the smallest spark to the brightest flame. Everything has a role in this world. Do not forget that."

Clotho was touched by the passion in her words.

"Thank you, Lady Hestia. If I ever feel lost, your words will light my way."

Hestia smiled. "Go now Clotho. A grand adventure awaits."

With the goddess' words firmly implanted in her head, Clotho made her way to the gateway leading to the mortal realm.

"Clotho!" A woman with dark brown hair and pale gray-blue eyes bounded up to greet her. "It's about time you show up! Zeus had us waiting here since before Apollo even got the sun-chariot in the sky."

Clotho could not imagine how taxing Lord Apollo's job must have been. Being an Olympian was thought of as the absolute greatest honor that could be bestowed upon an immortal. Yet every morning, Apollo was forced to hitch his chariot to his fiery horses, who, from what Clotho had heard, had the tempers to match their manes.

Then for the next nine to sixteen hours, he guided them across the sky, keeping them just high enough to provide light and warmth to the lands below, yet far enough away to not burn the world to ashes. If she had to choose between that task, or claiming the Tower of Fate, she was happy doing the latter.

"Hello, Lyssa!" Clotho smiled in turn. "I am so happy Lord Zeus is letting you come with me."

"It was a shock to us as well," Laren said, dropping her stride next to Lyssa. She wore her long red hair in a high ponytail today, showing off her chocolate-colored eyes. "Throughout the entirety of your training, we were told we had to prepare you to survive without us, so when Zeus instructed us to accompany you, we were excited."

"Sorry for the late arrival," Clotho smiled. "Lord Zeus wanted to show me off to the masses one last time before sending me off. I trust the wait was not too excruciating?"

"It would have been worth waiting centuries if it meant we got to accompany you on your journey." Laren smiled.

Clotho's grin stretched ear to ear. As soon as she walked through the swirling green light of the gateway, she felt her life, her true purpose, would begin in earnest. She had fought the waves of anxiety all morning, but now that she was with her two best friends, she could only see the path ahead of her.

"Come on you two." She smiled back at the couple behind her. "Let's go claim a throne."

~~~

A manic tugging snapped Ashe out of the memory. She had only been weaving for a short time now, but she already felt at home. It was as though this was something she was always meant to do. At the Citadel she felt as if she was trailing behind Quinn and Levy; never quite their equal. Inside the tower though, she had purpose. This was *her* domain.

Some days were more exciting than others. There were times when it felt like she never stopped weaving. There were so many decisions to make and fates to cross. Even the humblest farmer had a story to tell.

Other times things were incredibly slow. It was on one such day she found herself exploring the higher reaches of the tower. Her first visit terrified her. Seeing Quinn's string entwined with Zeus', for instance, sent her into a panic. However, after a time that panic had worn off.

Ashe felt as though she had become two different people; one that split off from the other when she took the Tower. The part that was left behind was still very much in love with Quinn, but the part she inhabited now knew things could never be the same.

Still, it was bittersweet and cathartic to look into her past and reminisce about the time she had with him, even though the wounds felt fresh every time she sobered. She had a higher purpose now than romance. At least, that was what she told herself to numb the lingering pain.

The interior of the Tower was bathed in a pure, graceful, white hue that blanketed every inch of the walls, floor, and ceiling. The seamless, pristine surface of the tower emanated a tranquil ambiance, accentuated by the absence of any other color. Suspended in mid-air was a multitude of floating orbs, their soft glow illuminating the space around them.

Each orb pulsated with a gentle radiance, casting subtle shadows that danced along the walls. Delicate threads emerged from within the spheres, intricately weaving a web that spanned the entire length of the Tower. They created a mesmerizing tapestry of interwoven paths.

Making her way around the orbs, examining the powerful beings they represented, she saw a small grey cluster in the very corner of the room. As she floated closer, she noticed the cluster was a pocket of lacey yarn, filled with small translucent orbs.

As she followed the strings out from the cluster, she noticed they touched every single other entity within the tower. With a shock, she realized she was staring at the orbs of all the Weavers who came before her. Though most were dull, one still flickered with light in the center.

When she reached out and touched it, a bright flash overwhelmed her senses. Images flashed by so fast, that Ashe's head began to spin. It took all her concentration, but she managed to pull herself out of the vision. Though the images shot past her eyes at a sickening pace, there could be no mistaking the face she saw. This orb belonged to Clotho.

Cautious about triggering it once more, she floated back down to her throne and proceeded to spend the rest of the day figuring out how it worked. After hours of meticulous trial and error, she managed to slow the images down enough for her to understand what she was looking at.

The orb contained all of Clotho's memories. She spent the next few days attempting to dig into her predecessor's past, learning all she could. Clotho's parting words to her hadn't been forgotten.

Sometimes the world is going in a direction you cannot control, and you must choose the best of the worst in the hopes that from the ashes, new light will rise.

Clotho was willing to allow Chaos' ascent to the throne. If that was the best of the worst, Ashe needed to figure out what the worst was, lest humanity was doomed.

The frantic tugging came again. Ashe carefully placed the orb down on the cushion of the throne and floated to the string that was so urgently trying to get her attention.

This particular string was one of her favorites. It was bright purple with black, and gold woven into it, which sparkled in the uncanny light of the tower. It was only after she followed it to its source that she was hit by a wave of despair.

What she saw inside wrenched her heart. Even with the more recent and sordid parts of their history, Ashe could not help the fondness she still felt for what they once had. When she took control as Weaver, she became omniscient to all fates, so it was no surprise to her that he still lived.

Ashe hoped he would have seen the folly of his ways and started anew, now that the tower was lost to him. Instead, what she saw in the reflection of the orb made her eyes well with tears. This was not the friend she would have once trusted with her life.

With a deep breath, she began to frantically weave, tying all sorts of orbs to his in the hopes that he would somehow be brought out of the abyss he had fallen into. As she finished, she sat back, staring into the spectral eyes of her one-time friend.

"Please, Levy. Please do not do this.

CHAPTER 2

LEVY

Levy inhaled deeply, allowing the temperate air of Olympus to fill his lungs. He set his feet wide to steady his body, reaching out before him. With the patience of a warrior, he allowed his energy to slowly travel up through his arms, settling into each hand. As the mountainous boulder sailed toward him, he focused the energy into each knuckle, ready to…

BOULDER?

His eyes widened, barely diving out of the way in time as he felt the loose debris from the massive clump of earth pelt his chest.

"What are you doing, boy?" Ares called out, the ire in each word unmistakable. Ares' voice was deep and smooth, as one might expect of a god. Despite the lyrical tone, however, his sentences were often short and to the point, using the least number of words necessary to get his point across.

Though his face was handsome, he had scars crisscrossing from brow to chin; their paleness contrasting vividly against his bronzed skin and black, cropped hair. He was one of the few gods who didn't sport a beard, leaving his piercing yellow eyes the focus of his face.

"What am I doing?" Levy asked, incredulously. "What are you doing? That boulder could have killed me! In case you've forgotten

I'm not immortal like you."

Ares narrowed his eyes. "You may be mortal, but you have the essence of my traitorous aunt within you. I have been training you now for three years. If you are to continue in your role, it is time you stopped cowering and put that power to use."

Levy felt exasperated. It wasn't as if he hadn't tried. In the time since Zeus plucked him from the fall to his death, he had been on Olympus, training with Ares. While his body grew stronger, and his skills grew sharper, he was still barely able to access the power Hestia left within him.

Though Ares hadn't wanted to train him from the start; not even a god denied a direct request from Zeus. However, as time ticked by and Levy continued to struggle, Ares' attempts had grown more and more desperate. He figured Ares assumed that either something would click, or the training would kill him. Either way, he would be free of the mortal who didn't belong in Olympus.

"I told you," Levy said through gritted teeth. "When I reach for that power, it flees."

He ran his hand through his sweat-soaked hair, wishing he had cut it before beginning his training for the day. He gazed around the empty seats of the grand colosseum as unbidden memories of simpler times flashed before his eyes.

"It isn't like I'm not trying. It's as if Hestia is still in my head, disapproving of what I'm doing. I may have accessed her power before but I just can't seem to grasp it anymore."

Ares frowned. "That's part of your problem right there. Stop referring to it as 'Hestia's energy.' It is yours to harness now as you see fit. Do not allow it to dictate when you can access it. Wrap your mind around it and force it to the surface. Hestia is gone. As for your earlier accessing of it, what was it that triggered the power?"

Levy thought back to the two times before when he was able to harness the strength. "My life was in danger."

"Exactly," Ares replied. "Hence the boulder. Your problem is your cowardice. You are too afraid to grasp that power and face danger head-on. I saw what you did to Janus when you stole his essence. You could have cracked that boulder in half if you stood strong and willed it so.

"That is what you mortals don't get. You see your fragility and spend your lives trying to hide, rather than face danger head-on and overcome it. That is why, despite having the power of a god, you still lost to your friends. Until you learn to break that habit, you will always be weak."

Levy felt a cold rage creep up his spine. "I'm not weak. And I will never lose to Quinn again. Throw the boulder. I won't just crack it; I'll crush it into a thousand pieces."

Ares smiled triumphantly. "That is what I want to hear. Look alive, it is coming your way."

As Ares made his way back to the boulder, Levy took up his stance again, feeding his energy back into his hands. Ares' words stirred something within him. Mentioning his defeat at the hands of Ashe and Quinn had pricked at his biggest vulnerability.

This time, as the rage washed over him, he allowed it to consume him instead of beating it back down. He reached deep within himself, quieting his mind and locating the warm, flickering energy of Hestia.

No, not of Hestia. He reminded himself. *This is my energy; my strength.*

As he attempted to harness the power, he began to feel it pull away. With frustration, he reached out, wrapping his thoughts around it. It would not escape from him this time.

Just as he thought he had it contained, it slipped through a crack in his barrier. He imagined it giggling as it ran further from his reach, as if taunting his ineptitude.

"Ready or not kid," Ares bellowed.

Not ready, he thought, panicked. *Very not ready.*

He reached out again, pinning the energy in place. It would obey him. His life currently depended on it. The noise of rock scraping on earth informed Levy that he had only seconds before the five-ton boulder left him as nothing more than a smear across this arena's already bloody floor.

The look in Quinn's eyes, as he let Levy fall, flashed across his mind, further strengthening his resolve. As the energy made to escape, he pulled hard, managing to take a piece of it. He instantly felt strength begin to fill his body. Would it be enough? One way or another, he was about to find out.

Ares, using his godly might, hefted the boulder above his head as though it weighed no more than a baby.

"Here comes."

"Ares!" A cold voice cracked across the arena. Making her way across the grounds was a slender woman in an extravagant green toga. Her long, silver hair was held up in a loose bun by a golden peacock feather. A silver diadem was perched atop her head.

"Your Lord Father has called a meeting of the council. Dismiss your pet and come at once."

Levy bristled at the word pet, again thinking back to Quinn throwing the same taunt his way. He wasn't a fan of Hera. Despite sympathizing with her for having to put up with the lecherous Lord Zeus, it had turned her distant and sharp-tongued. Though her treatment of him caused his anger to flare, the scars along his back were a reminder to hold his tongue when in her presence.

"Mother," Ares' deep voice slid from his throat. "While I appreciate you bringing word to me, do remember that Levy here is an honored guest of Lord Zeus,' and should not be referred to in such a way."

Levy internally rolled his eyes. Though Ares didn't like him, none of the Olympians did for that matter, he hated his mother more. Hera was notoriously awful to her children, having gone so far as to throw one of her sons off Olympus simply for being ugly.

"I will speak to, of, and about a mortal however I please. Now hurry to the throne room. It is best not to keep your father waiting."

Ares let out a sigh. "That will be enough for today then boy. Go clean yourself up. You smell like a goat."

Without another look, he walked away. Hera shot him one last venomous glance and turned to follow.

It was not often Levy was free to roam the halls of Olympus. Most of his time was spent training or acting as a servant to the gods and goddesses. He had to earn his keep, as Zeus liked to say. They would make their move soon, he was assured over and over, but if Levy was to be a part of it, he had to be a good little mortal.

Though he enjoyed the strength he got from training with Ares, the gods still disgusted him. Seeing their lavish lifestyle only furthered that hatred. He needed them to get strong, and after that, he would be done with them.

He told himself that over and over, though after three years, the words had begun to ring hollow, even to his own ears.

Having washed up after being left on his own, he decided to spend his unexpected free time exploring the lower halls of Olympus. The realm was made up of an entire mountaintop floating in the sky.

The top was flattened out and a large city had been constructed upon its surface. In the middle of the city was a sprawling Temple. It was within it that the fourteen Olympians resided. Though, with Athena having burned out her energy, and Hestia splitting herself amongst himself, Quinn, and Ashe, that number was reduced to twelve.

The layout of Olympus was eerily similar to Stormhaven. Levy doubted that was a coincidence, though how the Masters had known to build it in such a way, he had no idea. It was one of the many mysteries he was determined to solve. Though the Masters were destroyed along with the Citadel in Athena's rage, he imagined there were answers to his many questions buried somewhere within.

He descended deeper into the bowels of the temple, listening for any sign of life. The further down he went, the mustier the air got, carrying the scent of mildew and waste.

Even immortals weren't perfect.

The walls shifted from polished marble to mossy green stone, lined with what he assumed were cell doors. The humidity intensified with every step, causing sweat to form along his brow. Having just washed away the grime from his earlier training, he decided he didn't want to go much further, but something in the back of one of the rooms caught his eye. He crept closer to the open door, letting his eyes adjust to the darkness.

"Ahhh my dear, do come closer. It has been so long since I last saw you and I would so love to chat."

Chained to the wall at the back of the cell was the most skeletal woman Levy had ever seen. Loose skin hung off her bones, deepening every wrinkle across her unclothed body. Stringy clumps of grey, matted hair hung limply from her head.

As she smiled at him, he noticed many of her teeth were

missing. With a shock, he realized it was the same woman he had seen beaten and bloodied in Zeus' realm the day he pulled Levy from the lava. Clotho, he had called her.

"Do not be alarmed my boy," she smiled. "Though I may look a mess, I assure you I will not bite." She let out a half-mad cackle as she pointed to her toothless mouth.

"I shouldn't be here," Levy said to her, slowly backing toward the door he entered from.

"No, you should not be. Yet here you are, so we may as well chat. It has been so long since I have talked with someone, let alone a hero of my own weaving."

That stopped Levy in his tracks.

"What do you mean a hero of your weaving?"

"Never mind that dear. Though I laid the groundwork, your future is no longer in my hands, and thus, the prophecy may be altered."

A chill ran down Levy's spine. He had heard of a prophecy repeatedly, both in Hestia's domain as well as from Janus, but this was the first time he heard his involvement spoken directly to him.

"What is…?"

"Don't bother asking," Clotho said with sudden clarity. "Even I, who wove it into existence, do not know the full extent of what it means. That is the way of prophecy. Those who seek to understand will only drive themselves mad."

As she issued that warning, her eyes again glossed over, leaving a toothless grin on her face. "Now then, how about we discuss you and what you plan to accomplish by slumming it with the Olympians."

Feeling the danger of such a topic, Levy felt it best he ended his talk with the delusional woman.

"I should be going," he said, making his way back toward the entrance of the cell.

"Of course, of course," Clotho grinned at him. "Things to do, people to kill. That is the way of this place. Do stop by again though. It is nice to have someone to talk to. Try not to jump at every shadow you encounter."

She cackled as though it was the funniest joke, spraying spittle across the room.

"Oh, and child?" She said, clarity back within her tone. "Even the most stubborn yarn can be worked with, given a little patience."

Levy narrowed his eyes. "I've made my choice. My path is clear to me, and no words will sway me from it."

Without another glance, Levy turned his back on the woman and made his way back toward the surface.

CHAPTER 3

MALLORY

The young drakon's tail passed millimeters from Mallory's face as she ducked beneath the scaly blow. Before she even had the chance to recover, a wooden sword came crashing down upon her. Using her momentum she tumbled back, catching herself on her hands, and kicking her feet into the air, completing a stunning back handspring.

However, before she could celebrate, the wooden sword was moving her way yet again. She let the strike pass by her with a quick spin before clamping down on her attacker's wrist and twisting their arm behind their back.

With a cry of pain, the attacker dropped the weapon. Mallory's victory was short-lived however, as the drakon's tail again took a swipe at her face, forcing her to release the arm and jump back, putting space between the two.

"Gods, Andra! You can give him orders now without even saying them aloud?"

Andra smiled with smug satisfaction, her opaque eyes glimmering with pride. In the time since the tower disappeared, the young lady had come into her own. After her friend Sen fell in battle to the legions of the dead, she and Nes took command of the Abyssillian people.

They attempted to lead them out of the Wastes and into better standing with humanity. Though it was no small matter, and it was slow moving, progress was made. For the first time in centuries, Abyssillians were welcomed, though hesitantly, to pass through most major settlements.

With hope for the future, they were scheduled to meet with a group of leaders later in the day to discuss opening trade.

"Horacio is smart," Andra replied, scratching the young drakon's chin. "He just has to read my emotions and he knows what to do."

The drakon nuzzled into Andra's neck, growling with delight. Though still shorter than most, she had grown in the last few years. Her shimmering hair now fell to her waist rather than her feet, and her face had become sharp and angular, matching the quick wit behind her eyes.

She wore a silver, cropped shirt, showing off the chiseled abs, developed with intense training. She was by far Mallory's favorite sparring partner thanks to her combination of speed and smarts.

"Quinn said your bloodline was strong, but communicating with monsters through only thoughts? That's next level."

Andra beamed at her. "I have a good sparring partner."

Mallory smiled back. Though Andra spoke more than she had in the past, she still didn't speak a lot. She preferred to keep things short and direct. It worked surprisingly well in contrast with her partner Nes, who sometimes didn't know when to shut up.

"That was a good session," Mallory said, tossing Andra a towel. "Let's stop there and get ready for our visitors. Something tells me if we meet them soaked in sweat, we won't be taken as seriously."

"We won't be taken seriously anyway." Andra rolled her eyes. "These old men may not call us monsters anymore, but they still see us as lesser. If they had their way we would be driven further from their lands, not invited into them. Doesn't it seem odd to you?" she asked.

"Doesn't what seem odd?"

"For three years we have been trying to establish trade with them, and for three years we have been at a standstill. They opened their gates to us, but only for means of travel and only out of a sense of obligation thanks to the role we played in the war.

"Yet now they not only reach out to us but offer to come to Petram, a land they have feared and despised for so long, in the hopes to establish trade after all? Something doesn't seem right about it. What do they really want?"

Mallory sighed. She thought the same thing but didn't want to rain on Nes' parade, since he was so excited when he received the missive. It made Mallory happy to know he had Andra with him to balance out his naïve hope. Nes was incredibly strong and very good to his people, but he still had a lot of room to grow.

"It seems odd, I'll give you that. It's best we keep on our toes. But maybe we have nothing to worry about and they just finally opened their eyes."

Andra looked unconvinced but nodded.

"I hope you're right Mallory, I truly do. Come, let's go get ready. They will arrive soon."

~~~

Mallory stood at the entrance to Petram, ready to meet the human leadership. Though she was human herself, she acted as an envoy between the people of Petram and the human settlements. She made a promise to Ashe before she'd left with Quinn to confront Levy, to unite the Abyssillians and humans, and she intended to keep it.

She wore a simple, black leather tunic and trousers: not threatening in the slightest, yet easy to move around in should trouble break out. Her long, brown hair was pinned into a bun to stop the dusty wind of the Wastes from blowing it into her face.

To her left stood Nes, the official leader of the Abyssillian people. He was dressed in a handsome black and gold doublet, symbolizing his status to the incoming visitors. His dirty blonde hair was also tied back in a bun, showing off the many scars that crisscrossed his face. Though his blue eyes were intense, there was an unmistakable twinkle of hope behind them as well.

Beside him, Andra was a beacon. She wore a form-fitting silver dress, which shimmered in the light with even the slightest movement. Her hair was back in a loose ponytail, showing off her sharp chin and strong neck. A slit ran up the side of the dress, revealing a black knife strapped to her thigh.

She had no problem letting the visitors know that while she hoped for advancement between their people, she was a force to be reckoned with if they tried anything. After all, her people were victimized for so long, it was only natural she be wary.

As the human envoy came ever closer, now more than mere specks on the horizon, Andra turned to Nes.

"Why do you think the leaders chose to speak to us now after all this time? We have always spoken to emissaries who carried us their word. Despite numerous attempts to speak directly with them, we were always turned away.

"Yet now they not only want to meet with us, but they are willing to travel the Wastes as well? Surely you don't expect good will to be their only motive."

Nes' eyes tightened at the corners.

"Andra, we have been over this time and time again. I agree it is odd, and I am not going into this blind to that fact. But how can I not be hopeful? For the first time, it is the humans who have reached out to us. What if they have been pressured by their people who see our plight?

"You know we have support amongst their settlements. For once we may be able to make real progress. As a leader, I have to hope this is real. I must do everything I can to provide for our people. This is a huge opportunity for us."

Andra gave him a look indicating she was unconvinced. He smiled and gave her a quick kiss on the cheek.

"Besides, I have you standing with me. I know if anything happens, you will be the first one to step in and deliver punishment to anybody who would try to hurt me or our people. You're our heart and spirit."

Andra smiled back at him, placated for the time being.

"No, it's fine guys," Mallory chimed in. "I mean, I'm standing right here, and have done a wonderful job of acting as emissary for your people, if I do say so myself. I mean honestly, I have put blood, sweat, and tears into this job. But it's fine, you keep having your moment. I'll just stand here awkwardly pretending not to hear you gush over each other."

Nes let out a hearty laugh, pulling Mallory into a one-armed hug.

"Now, now Mal. Don't think I'm not aware of how much you've done for us. We owe you a great debt of gratitude. You know you are always welcome here. As far as I'm concerned, you are as much Abyssillian as anybody else in the city."

Mallory sniffed, pretending to pick dirt from her nail.

"Well, as long as we are all aware of it."

The three friends shared a laugh as they watched the human envoy approach.

Twenty minutes later the group of humans reached the walls. The pack was led by armed guards who approached Nes and company with apprehension clear upon their faces.

"Welcome to Petram," Nes smiled, trying to ease their tension. "You and yours are most welcome here. If you will follow us, we will guide you to the palace where we will have our discussion."

"For the record," Mallory chimed in, loud enough for the leaders tucked away in their canopied carts to hear, "Palace is a term used loosely in this case. You'll find structures here to be much smaller than in your cities, due to lack of supplies and trade." She winked and nudged the closest guard with her elbow.

Andra chortled beside a flustered Nes. With a fluid turn, she looked over her shoulder to the guards.

"Come."

~~~

They settled around a large circular table set up in the middle of a sparsely decorated room. Around one section of the table, Mallory, Nes, and Andra sat, while across from them the three leaders stared back.

On the left sat an intense man, tall and thin with a wispy black beard and thinning hair. His eyes burned with poorly concealed malice as he looked at everything but Mallory and her friends. On the right was a small, rotund man with curly grey hair.

Small, round spectacles sat upon his rather bulbous nose. He fidgeted nervously; his beady eyes bouncing back and forth between

Nes and Andra before settling on Mallory.

The only one with any semblance of composure was the man in the middle. He sat straight in his chair; a warm smile spread across his rather handsome face. He had light brown hair that matched his eyes, and though lines formed along his brow, he still looked as though he were the youngest of the trio. All three men wore bright orange robes, with a brown sash thrown over their shoulders and tied around their waists.

"Greetings friends," the leader in the middle spoke. "My name is Master Cyrus. To my right is Master Darrik."

The man with wispy hair narrowed his eyes. "And beside me to my left is Master Enkar."

The little master gave out a squeak of a greeting.

"First of all," Cyrus continued, "Allow me to thank you for the part your people played in saving us from the undead. Without you, we likely wouldn't be here to have this discussion."

"You're welcome," Andra began, cutting Nes off before he could respond. "However, while we're on the subject, where were you while that war waged on? It was my understanding that all the Masters of the Citadel perished when Stormhaven fell. Imagine my surprise to see three of you sitting in front of us now, leading the humans no less."

Nes cleared his throat, shooting an annoyed look at Andra.

"My apologies Master Cyrus. What Andra means is that we are grateful for this opportunity to finally meet and speak with you in the hopes of opening new possibilities between our people. Perhaps it would benefit us all to clear things up before we continue. This is a rather shocking development."

"Oh, come on Nes. Our people died in that fight. Sen died in that fight. And now…."

Nes cut her off with another look.

Master Cyrus raised his hands in a placating gesture.

"I assure you; no offense is taken. I can completely understand where Ms. Andra is coming from. Allow me to offer my most sincere condolences for the loss of your people. The fact is, when Stormhaven fell, all of our resources fell with it.

"Most of the Masters didn't escape Athena's wrath, and those of us who survived were scattered. We were in no position to offer any assistance like we were from the Citadel, let alone march to the front lines and fight.

"It was only thanks to your people, and the war ending that we were able to recuperate and regain what we lost. In doing so took time. That is why we only spoke with you through emissaries up until this point. Currently, we are the last three Masters we know to be alive, so it has taken a considerable amount of time to recover."

Nes nodded. "I am sorry for your loss as well. From what we have been told, the Citadel put decades into this war. I can only imagine how gut-wrenching it must have been when one of your own turned on you and made all your time and effort for naught."

"I thank you for your kind words, young man. It is indeed a shame that young Levy made the decision he did. We had such high hopes for him. However, not all was for naught. Ashelia did exactly as we had hoped and claimed the tower, ushering in a chance for a lasting peace for humanity."

"And Quinn?" Mallory spoke up for the first time. She wasn't a huge fan of the three Masters before her.

The entire time Nes and Cyrus had been speaking, the other two Masters shifted in their seats, as though extremely uncomfortable to be present. At the mention of Quinn's name, the man named Darrik lifted his lip in an ugly sneer. Enkar sniffed rather haughtily, pretending to clean his glasses for the hundredth time.

Cyrus' tone became slightly brittle, as if what he was saying left an unpleasant taste in his mouth.

"Of course. Young Quinn did very well in helping Ashelia take the throne."

"As was his duty," Master Enkar chimed in.

Mallory was immediately on guard, not liking the way the three men reacted to her friend's name.

"Is Quinn here in the Wastes?" Darrik asked, eyes somehow narrowed even further.

"Not at the moment, no," Mallory replied. "He is currently away, training."

"I see," Darrik replied, sounding slightly relieved.

Quinn came back to Petram long enough to share the news of what happened with Levy and the tower before heading out with a man named Talius. Though he wanted his whereabouts to remain unknown, he shared they would be staying with Mallory if he was needed. He mentioned something about the potential for further trouble on the horizon and he needed to be stronger for it, though Mallory wondered if that was true, or if he was just trying to find a way back to Ashe.

He was heartbroken when telling her about how he had to leave her, and Mallory could sense he wasn't about to give up on seeing her again. His loyalty to Ashe made Mallory smile.

"Now then," Cyrus said, breaking Mallory from her thoughts. "Back to the business at hand. The last few decades have been incredibly hard on the Abyssillian people, and though I hate to admit it, we Masters have not exactly been helpful in that matter.

"I hope you understand we were already stretched very thin with the war for the tower and did not have the resources to send aid to your people as well."

Andra began to speak but Cyrus held up his hand.

"However, we also failed your people in preaching peace to humanity. We allowed hatred for you and yours to fester while turning a blind eye to your plight. For that, I apologize."

Nes cleared his throat.

"I thank you for your kind words, however, what is in the past can stay there. It is the future I wish to discuss today. The fact of the matter is, if things continue as they are now, my people will starve.

"Food is getting harder and harder to come by out here in the Wastes, and while we are thankful your settlements have opened their gates to us for travel, most people still refuse to trade with us.

"If this continues much longer, I fear for our survival. I say this as a plea, not as a threat, but with severe hunger comes desperation. And if my people become desperate, I cannot guarantee I will be able to stop them from poaching your lands. I fear conflict on the horizon should that come to pass."

Master Darrik raised his head at Nes' words.

"I'd like to see them try."

"Darrik!" Cyrus barked. "Put your pettiness aside. We came here for discussion, not for idle threats and posturing."

Andra locked eyes with the master. Nes reached for her hand under the table, holding it in his own and calming her.

"Again, I do not say that as a threat," Nes said, trying to ease the tension. "Only as a man who wishes to see the suffering of his people end. You have the resources that we do not. We do not ask for charity, only for the chance to thrive.

"We have an abundance of rare goods to trade for food and water. Andra can speak with and tame monsters. We have hides, weapons, medicines, etc. that your people do not have access to. Both of our people can benefit."

Master Enkar's eyes lit up at the mention of rare monster parts.

"I wish it were as easy as that," Cyrus replied. "However, while things have improved, there is still a deep prejudice for your people rooted in our settlements. It is not as simple as me arranging with you. I cannot force traders to trade."

"Not all of them need to," Mallory responded. "You can't tell me that if you announced opening trade with us, and told your traders of the goods the Abyssillians have to offer, none would take up the opportunity. Some trade is better than no trade for our people."

"I assure you, while there would likely be some takers, you would not have enough to survive."

"Then why bother making the trip out here?" Nes asked, his voice beginning to waver. "Did you come simply to tell us it was impossible? Surely not."

This time it was Andra's turn to calm Nes. She stroked his hand, squeezing gently.

"Of course not," Cyrus replied. "I came here to offer you an opportunity."

Andra narrowed her eyes.

"We are listening."

"What if I told you the Wastes were not always a desolate land, but instead a land lush with greenery and wildlife?"

"I'd ask how stupid do we look?" Andra responded.

"I assure you I am not trying to pull the wool over your eyes." Cyrus continued. "Our time at the Citadel was not always spent on the war effort. We each had other duties as well; other specialties, so to speak. Do you know how Levy was able to summon an army of the dead?"

Mallory didn't like where this was heading.

"He stole the Orb of Hades from your vaults."

"Exactly," Cyrus said. "My specialty within the Citadel was ancient artifacts. Godly artifacts to be exact. I was responsible for their containment. I spent years researching myths and tracking down artifacts; locking their powers within our vaults and weakening the gods, while at the same time strengthening our realm from them."

"So, you're saying you know of a godly artifact that can make the Wastes come back to life?" Nes asked.

"Nes," Mallory warned. "Those artifacts were locked away for a reason. I know you are desperate for your people to flourish, but there are other ways of making that happen."

"Just so we understand each other, I am not saying I can guarantee what I said is completely factual," Cyrus said, ignoring Mallory and staring straight into Nes' eyes. "I simply know of myths. I have never actually found this specific item.

"However, there is no mention of the Wastes in the ancient stories until more recent times. Surely a land like this would bear mention. I believe there is an artifact locked away here, sapping the land of its life. That is why we have come to you today.

"Allow us to find it together. We can take the item and lock it away in our vaults. In the process, life can return to the Wastes and your people can get the sustenance they so desperately need. As a bonus, you working with us, and giving us the orb as an act of good faith will further your cause with our people.

"With your land flourishing, and our people seeing you as a continuous ally, more talks can open about our people's unity. That is why we have personally traveled to you. We offer help, as well as friendship."

Mallory and Andra exchanged a glance. This all seemed too good to be true, and the speed at which this information was dumped upon them, as well as her own experiences with godly artifacts, raised red flags in Mallory's mind.

"Agreed," Nes said.

Both Mallory and Andra began to object.

"No." Nes cut them off. "I understand your reservations, but for all we know this artifact doesn't even exist. However, if it does, then this cannot only help our people but also build a bridge of future friendship with theirs. Come with me Masters," Nes said beckoning them toward a back room.

"Inside I have maps of the Wastes marked with major landmarks. We can discuss potential spots where this artifact may reside and come up with a plan. Andra, I would like you there as well. I know you will need the most convincing, and I think if you see this with your own eyes it will help."

Nes and the Masters stood up from the table and proceeded to make their way to the map room. Andra got up from the table as well, anxiety and uncertainty plain on her face.

"Andra," Mallory said. "I don't like this. Though Cyrus seems friendly, we have both seen what a godly artifact is capable of."

"I know," Andra replied, biting her lip. "For now, I'll play along with it. Surely, if such an artifact does exist, it is going to take time to find. Otherwise, it would have already been discovered. If it does exist, I don't trust it in their hands. In the meantime, I would like you to do me a favor."

"Of course. What is it?" Mallory asked.

"We need Quinn."

Mallory smiled. "Understood."

CHAPTER 4

QUINN

Quinn, I love you.

The last words Ashe spoke to him played over and over in his head day after day. For years now he'd heard them, as if whispered directly in his ear, taunting him. At first, it was a sweet memory, something Quinn held close to his heart. Yet after a while they began to take a sinister turn, changing from the warm loving voice of Ashe to the cold and mocking tone of Chaos.

That is right, little hero. You may have lost the mask, but you still turned your body over to me. We are one, and with the girl locked inside that tower, nobody else can stop me. It is only a matter of time before I walk this earth again.

A familiar, cold dread washed over Quinn's body. Despite training every day to control it, he knew Chaos was right. Despite the mask having shattered inside the volcano thanks to Ashe's fire, Chaos hadn't left him. The pull of that other realm was stronger than ever within him, and he could feel Chaos' consciousness becoming stronger every day.

"Focus, Quinn!" A gruff voice pierced his rumination. He opened his eyes to find the weathered face of Talius mere inches from his own. The man's head was bald as the day they had met. His long brown beard was speckled with grey and tangled in such a way it reminded him of a musty, straw broom. His brown eyes tense, but not unkind.

"I am focusing," Quinn said, tucking a strand of hair behind his ear. He'd grown it long in an attempt to hide the burns left on the side of his face where Ashe's fire struck the mask.

He didn't care how it looked, but anytime he went into town to buy supplies for Talius, people couldn't seem to look away. He'd gone his entire life being stared at by people thanks to his Abyssillian blood, and he was tired of it.

"You were thinking about Ashe again. I could see it in your face."

Quinn threw his hands up.

"Of course, I was thinking about Ashe. How can I not when I have this voice whispering in my ear all the time?"

"That is why we're doing this, Quinn. So you can learn to control it. I know it seems like a curse, but Chaos gifted you with immense power. If you learn to harness it then you can stand toe to toe with an immortal. Our world needs that if we are to survive what's coming."

He and Quinn held this discussion a thousand times, and every time it left Quinn feeling more helpless. According to Talius, Zeus was planning a mass invasion of their realm. Though Ashe and Quinn stopped his initial attempt by claiming the tower for the first time in history, Talius seemed convinced there would be more conflict to come.

"That power will be pointless if I'm not in control of it," Quinn said, feeling déjà vu. "Every day its whispering gets louder and the pull of that realm gets stronger. Meanwhile, I feel like I haven't gone forward at all."

Talius reached his hand out, laying it upon Quinn's shoulder in a fatherly gesture. Quinn hated to admit it but it felt nice. He hadn't grown up knowing any kind of parental love. The closest thing he had was the other Masters and it was no secret most of them had hated him.

"I know it is scary, Quinn. I do not envy the stress and weight this responsibility puts upon you, but you must learn to control it. The key is steadying your mind, and controlling the fear that rises within you.

"Chaos thrives on the tumultuous emotions he elicits. If you cannot hamper that fear, he will consume you. Remember, you are in control, not him. Leave your fears in the past. He lost his chance thanks to Ashelia, and now his power is yours. You need only the confidence to take it."

Quinn nodded. A steely resolve surfaced where before there had been fear. He didn't want to disappoint Talius. Since meeting him, he'd been nothing but kind to Quinn, training him better than any of the Masters before him.

Not only that, but he felt respected by the older master. Talius didn't look at him as a monster or as a boy. He looked at him as an ally and placed his hope in him. With a deep breath, he closed his eyes, reaching out to the dark, swirling energy in his mind.

And the prey comes willingly back, pushed to his end by the feeling of acceptance he so longingly desired. The toothy grin of Chaos taunted him.

As was normal whenever Chaos spoke to him, a fresh wave of fear crashed into him. It was all Quinn could do to keep his thoughts from scattering. Despite Talius' words, he felt himself slipping away, unable to keep his emotions in check.

"Focus," Talius spoke calmly in his ear. Quinn felt his mentor's hand on his back, grounding him. "You are in control, Quinn."

Quinn breathed deeply, centering himself and shoving the fear aside.

What will you do without the girl here to save you? Chaos taunted him again. Some hero you are, giving yourself to me to save the one you loved. You didn't even think about the consequences; what I would have done to your realm had she not been there to stop me.

That taunt hit a sore spot within him. All his life he'd been praised for his mind. Yet time and time again, when it came to Ashe, he'd acted purely on instinct. He used to taunt Levy with that as children when they'd spar, yet when the stakes were high, he was no better.

That's right, Chaos chuckled. You could have stopped Levy before he ever unleashed Athena, but you were too worried about your girlfriend. Face it boy, your realm is better off without you.

Look how your people thrive without you. For the first time in centuries, they are walking within the walls of the human towns. They follow that boy you left them unquestioningly, yet it took the words of a child to get them to march for you when you asked them to. What have you accomplished without the help of another?

Quinn tried to steady his shaking breath. Every word Chaos spoke hit true. Without Ashe, Chaos would have consumed him. Without Sen, his people would not have marched with him. And without Nes, his people would likely still be banished to the Wastes.

Look at you, wallowing in self-pity. I barely scratched the surface of your failures and already you are filled with doubt. Fighting me is senseless. You think only of that girl, yet if she could see you now, how little she would think of you.

Quinn let out a snort of laughter. The pressure of Chaos let up suddenly, leaving in its place a vague sense of confusion. Chaos slipped up with that last comment. Quinn thought about Ashe and what she would say if she could see him now.

Back when they were kids, the Masters all but convinced Quinn he was a monster. He'd overheard them time and time again talking in hushed tones behind his back. When he would fail, they would punish him severely, yet when he succeeded, he was told not to celebrate as he did exactly as he was supposed to do, and anything less was worthless to them.

As a result, he became glum and self-sabotaging. One day, after a particularly rough beating by Master Darrik, Quinn stormed out of the arena. He knew it would lead to another beating but he didn't care. He'd had enough of that treatment. Ashe ran after him, stopping him and turning him to face her. Not wanting her to see him cry, he kept his eyes to the ground.

"Where do you think you're going?" she asked him, frowning.

"Away." He replied, stubbornly refusing to meet her gaze.

"Don't be silly," she chided. *"I know you aren't treated fairly, but this will only lead to more trouble for you. We can figure out how to stop this another way. I'll go to the other Masters or something. But don't sabotage yourself like this."*

"What's the point?" He complained, feeling the unwanted pressure of tears building behind his eyes. *"Nothing I do will ever be good enough. I could save one of the Masters from falling off the*

wall and all I'd get is a cuff to the ear and a 'you didn't catch me comfortably enough.'

"No matter what, I'm a monster and I always will be thanks to what I am." *Warm tears began falling partway through his words. He felt soft fingers under his chin, lifting his head so that his eyes met her own.*

"Stop that," *she commanded, stern but kind.* "You are no more a monster for what runs in your veins than the Masters are human for what runs within theirs. Actions and intent are what make you who you are, and by those standards, you are less monster than anybody else here.

"Stop feeding the self-pity. When I first came here, abandoned by my parents, it was you who made me feel welcome. When Levy was intent on doing things alone, it was you who convinced him to be a friend.

"Stop caring what the Masters think of you. Stop caring what anybody else thinks of you. You know in your heart who you are and what you are, and your words and actions prove it every single day.

"When you are down, I'll be here to pick you up, as you are with me. But don't you ever let anybody else make you feel lesser." *She wrapped him in a hug, lifting him from the depths he'd fallen into.*

Quinn smiled internally at Chaos, showing his teeth for the first time.

"If Ashe were here, she would tell me to stop sniveling and start acting." *He pushed back at Chaos, making his presence step back for the first time.*

"She'd tell me to stop being self-deprecating and to start being who she knows me to be."

He pushed out with his mind again, forcing Chaos back further.

"And, she'd tell me to boot your cold, lifeless presence out of my head, or she'd kick my ass."

He smiled harder, straining against the might of the Primordial. He could feel the sweat begin to form on his brow as he pushed harder until eventually he reached his limit.

Looks like you aren't completely worthless after all. The strain within Chaos' voice was unmistakable, though Quinn knew pushing him out completely wouldn't be so easy.

Just as Quinn was about to lash out at him again, he heard Talius' voice reverberate in the darkness around him.

"That's enough Quinn."

He opened his eyes, gasping for air he hadn't realized he needed.

"I can see by the look on your face that you made some progress. That's good. But don't push yourself too hard. You stopped breathing for over two minutes and your face was scarlet. We can go back to this another time. For now, we have company."

Quinn looked over to the woman standing next to him, still trying to catch his breath.

"I know I usually leave men speechless," she said, swishing her long brown hair over her shoulder and batting her eyelashes. "But breathless? My goodness, you always know how to flatter me."

He smiled, getting back to his feet.

"Mallory!" He walked over and pulled her into a hug. "It's great to see you."

"You're sweaty," she said, pushing him out to arm's length. "I'm not saying another word until you bathe, stinky."

Talius chuckled, beckoning to the cottage in the distance. "Come, we can have tea while he cleans up."

~~~

"You're sure he said his name was Cyrus?" Talius asked, hands steepled in front of him on the table. His brow was crinkled, showing the deep worry lines etched into his forehead.

"I am," Mallory replied. "He wore the Master's robes, the same as the other two who were with him. Derk and Inky or something like that."

"Darrik and Enkar? Figures that the only Masters to survive Athena's wrath were the two who hated me the most." Quinn sipped his tea, smoldering. "Who is Master Cyrus though?" he asked Talius. "I don't remember ever hearing of him at the Citadel."

Talius blew air out of his nose.

"Cyrus was before your time." He answered with a far-off look in his eye. "He and I worked closely with one another to hunt down and lock away the immortal's symbols of power so that they were unable to reenter our realm."

"I take it things didn't end well between you?" Mallory asked. "You have this 'I thought he was dead but finding out he is alive makes me angry' look about you."

"It's complicated," Talius said. "I did think he was dead, but finding out he still lives scares me more than angers me. He was ambitious at the best of times. But his lust for power went beyond merely locking the gods from our realm. He wanted to become one."

"Gee," Mallory deadpanned. "Whoever did we know like that?"

"Levy's lust for power was certainly comparable. Eventually, our differences in opinions led to an inevitable split, and I exiled him from the Citadel."

Quinn scrunched his brows. "What part of that made you think he was dead?"

Talius' eyes went distant again. "It was just a long time ago. I have not heard anything since. It does not matter though. If he believes there is some item of power in the Wastes, I would not be surprised at all to find out he was correct. Locating those items is his specialty.

"Quinn, I am sorry to put your training on hold, but I think it necessary we head to Petram and confront him. He may not be an enemy, but I do not feel comfortable letting this item fall into his hands, at least without talking with him first."

"Fine by me," Quinn shrugged. He would not mind seeing Nes and Andra again. It had been a while and from what he heard, they had both grown quite a bit.

"Awwwwww yeah!" Mallory pumped her fist into the air. "Family reunion, let's go!"

CHAPTER 5

ASHE

The mortal realm was more spirited than anything Clotho would have imagined. Sure, compared to Olympus it was dull and drab. It was ridiculously loud and every street carried the smell of waste. But in her time on Olympus, the mortal realm had always been talked about as though it were merely a mound of dirt with little insects scurrying about it.

Yet here she stood, in the middle of a bustling market. Hawkers shouted their deals over throngs of moving bodies, all dressed in a vibrant array of colors. The buildings were meticulously carved from giant slabs of stone, resembling the architecture of Olympus. These were no mere insects. These were cognizant, prospering people.

"Are all settlements like this?" Clotho asked her guards while doing her best to locate where that strong smell of spiced meat was coming from.

"Not in the slightest," replied a bored-sounding Lyssa.

"We are currently in a major city right now," added Laren. "Though others like this exist in this realm, they are few and far between. Most of the towns you come across will be small with

minimal wealth and delicate structure."

"Why don't they all build their homes like this?" she asked. "Surely they see the benefit in bustling trade and diverse culture."

"The humans aren't advanced enough," Lyssa replied, matter-of-factly. "They lack the means to procure enough wealth and resources to live like this everywhere. You'll see as we travel that most are ignorant of a more lavish lifestyle.

"They will grow just enough food to feed their families and hunker down in small, wooden huts when the sun sets. It's their way of life. That's why they cannot claim the throne's power. We are doing them a courtesy if you think about it."

Clotho wasn't so sure of that. She knew the way immortals thought about humans. They were considered too simple to grasp the elevated way of life the Olympians enjoyed; too ignorant of the powers of the world around them.

However, as Clotho stared at the bustling people around her, she wondered if they were truly too limited, or if they just hadn't been given the time and the knowledge to prosper and grow.

"I know that look." Laren caught her eye, pulling her from her thoughts. "Immortals have been punished for that look. Whatever thoughts you are having, keep them to yourself. Lord Zeus would not take kindly to them."

"You're as wise as you are beautiful, dear." Lyssa bumped her shoulder with Laren's. "We certainly don't want to anger the ol' sparkler in the sky. Now let's figure out where the damn tower is and start heading to it. The sooner we complete this mission, the sooner I can get out of this gods-forsaken realm."

"Do you mean that last part literally, or…?" Clotho joked.

A loud crash echoed across the square.

"THIEF!" an older vendor cried out, pointing to a small bundle of cloth sprinting down an alleyway.

"Come on!" Clotho said, pulling the spear from the straps on her back and yanking her guards toward where the figure retreated.

"Why are we getting involved in mortal affairs, again?" Lyssa asked, reluctantly jogging behind. "This has nothing to do with our mission."

"Because," Clotho replied through her grin. "If I am going to be locked in a musty old tower for the next thousand years, I'm going

to enjoy the freedom I have left."

"And skewering a mortal thief sounds like fun?" asked Laren.

"See! She gets it!" Clotho sang.

"Whatever, let's just get this over with and get on with our actual purpose." Lyssa rolled her eyes as the three companions plunged into the darkness of the alleyway.

It didn't take them long to catch up to the mound of cloth that had somehow sprouted legs. Whoever was hiding under the olive-green patchwork of a cloak didn't have a lot of stamina. The legs that stuck out of the oversized garment were so thin, that Clotho wondered if there was any meat between the skin and bone.

"Alright," Lyssa said, not even remotely winded. "That's far enough. Give us back what you stole from the old crone and you get to keep your life."

"Seems like a pretty fair trade to me," Laren added. "Be thankful, you caught her on a merciful day."

The mysterious figure pressed his back against the wall, legs shaking violently.

"Take it easy you two," Clotho said, putting herself between the thief and her overzealous companions. "He's terrified."

From beneath the hood, two wide eyes stared back at her. She raised her now empty hands out in a placating gesture.

"Do not be frightened. We will not harm you. If I am being honest, we do not need to take back what you stole. I would rather we do this peacefully. Is there any way I can convince you to return what you took?"

The figure slowly raised his hands to the hood, gently lowering it. To Clotho's surprise, it was only a child, no older than thirteen, staring back at her. His shoulder-length brown hair was greasy and unkempt.

"My name is Clotho," she said, trying to be as soothing as possible. "These are my companions, Lyssa and Laren. Despite how prickly they look-"

"OI!" Lyssa sniffed.

"I assure you they won't harm you as long as you agree to give us back what you took from the old lady at the market."

"I-I can't," The boy mumbled, trying desperately, and failing, to pull his saucer-like eyes away from hers.

"Why can't you?" Clotho asked.

"I was...was ordered to take it. I'll get beat again if I don't bring it back with me. And I won't get my rations."

"You get beaten and refused food?" Clotho asked, aghast.

"We all have to bring something to trade for food and clothes." The boy replied. "If we don't bring any value, we don't have any value."

The boy's eyes dropped. Judging by his absurdly lean frame and the bruises along his jaw, she doubted he brought in much of value often. She looked over her shoulder at her guard.

"Oh, no!" Lyssa said. "You are not bringing home a stray mortal."

"I agree," Laren added. "This little aside has already lost us valuable time. An untrained urchin will only slow us further."

Clotho simply stared at them; her eyebrows scrunched together.

"Oh gods," Lyssa looked to Laren. "She's bringing a stray home."

Laren sighed. "It is her quest. She gets the final say."

"I knew you'd see it my way," She smiled back at them.

"Fine, but you are training it and are responsible for feeding it." Lyssa shot back. "And for Zeus' sake, bathe it. I could smell it from the end of the alley."

Clotho turned back to the boy, proud of herself for standing her ground.

"Here's the deal kid," she said, formulating a plot in her mind. "You hand over what you stole so we can return it to its owner. In return, we will take you with us on our journey. We will make sure you have food and clothes that fit you, as well as training to properly defend yourself.

"I will not lie, what we are doing is very dangerous. You will probably die before we can turn you into a proper fighter, but I assure you that it's a better deal than staying here and slowly starving to death. What do you say?"

"Keep in mind," Laren added from the background, "That should you refuse this extremely over-the-top, ridiculous, nonsensical...."

"Get to the point," Clotho snapped."

"Offer from our dear Clotho, the alternative is we stick you with

our spears and take it from you anyway."

The young boy's eyes widened again. Slowly he reached his hand within his cloak. Clotho tensed. Though she didn't fear the kid, centuries of training and battle instinct wouldn't allow her to be caught off guard. He produced a small pouch of coins and held them out to her.

"Goodness," Laren sighed. "All of this over a small sack of silver."

Clotho grabbed the pouch and stood, reaching her hand out to the boy.

"What is your name?" she asked.

"I don't have one." The boy replied, meekly.

Clotho raised an eyebrow. Mortals were so strange.

"I guess I will just have to give you one then. Let us see, from now on, we'll call you Talius. Welcome to the team, kid." She smiled. "Training starts as soon as we get you some shoes, a hot meal, and an even hotter bath."

~~~

Ashe recoiled from the orb as if she had been slapped. It was not uncommon for people to share names. Some names were much more common than others. However, she had been dealing with gods and powers and the forces that be, long enough to realize when something important was staring her in the face.

Was it possible that this Talius from over a thousand years ago was somehow related to the man she had woven together with Quinn? Alarm was ringing throughout her mind. The only way to know more was to keep experiencing Clotho's weavings, and yet with this revelation, a sinister feeling had begun to creep into the atmosphere of the tower.

Had the lights dimmed as well, or was that simply her imagination? She sat back in her chair with a sigh. Something was happening, but it was just out of reach from her. The only way forward was to keep at it. So, with a few calming breaths, Ashe lifted the orb once again.

CHAPTER 6

LEVY

"Remind me again why we're working with a mortal?" Levy asked Ares as he strapped his armor on.

"Because when opportunity comes knocking, you answer the door," Ares replied in his typical dulcet tone. "Thanks to your pillaging of Hades' orb, a small amount of godly energy has reentered the mortal realm, weakening the barrier enough for the two of us to slip back through."

They were in a small armory off to the side of what the Olympians referred to as the 'Gate Room.' It was a large room carved out of marble holding a massive obsidian gateway that, when powered with godly essence, let them step through to the mortal realm.

Though for centuries it had been dormant thanks to the Masters' meddling, it swirled once again, though meekly, with a pale green light.

Levy finished strapping his shiny new breastplate on, gold to match Ares and began to work on the wrist plates. He did not care much for full plate armor like Ares did, instead opting for pieces that covered only the vital organs for ease of mobility.

Ares looked over, unimpressed. "You are mortal, yet you leave the majority of your body open for attack. Do you have a death wish or are you just stupid?"

Levy ignored the jab, finishing up and reaching for his sword belt.

"No," Ares said, grabbing his arm.

"Sorry?" Levy asked incredulously. "You just asked if I was stupid for not covering my body head to toe in armor, yet you want me to fight without a weapon?"

"That sword is dull and unimpressive. And it is a sword you lost a battle with once already. I will not have you using it in my presence. I am a god, and if you are with me, you will look the part as well." Ares walked over to a long display near the opposite wall of the armory.

Levy imagined the look of rage and contempt Janus would have had on his face at hearing the sword he had gifted him called dull and unimpressive. It made him smile.

From the case, Ares produced a spear forged from pure, radiant gold. It was a weapon that embodied the power of the gods themselves. Every inch of the magnificent spear gleamed with an ethereal glow, reflecting the celestial light in a mesmerizing display.

Emblazoned along the length of the spear's shaft were intricate engravings that told tales of the gods and their deeds. Ares placed the spear in Levy's hands.

It was lightweight, yet incredibly strong. Its perfectly balanced design would allow for swift and precise movement, granting Levy unrivaled agility in battle.

"You have been trained in every manner of weapon, yes?" Ares asked him.

Levy snapped out of his stupor. "Yes, though sword is my preferred weapon, I am more than capable of wielding a spear."

"Good, then you should have no trouble using this. It is a spear forged by Hephaestus himself. May it bring you greater fortune than its previous bearer. At the very least it should keep you from weighing me down."

"What happened to its previous owner?" Levy asked, only half listening as he continued to gaze at the spear. It was easily the greatest weapon he had ever held.

"It does not matter what happened to her. Do not disappoint and the same will not happen to you. Now, let us go. The power in that gateway is shaky and we need to cross over before it disappears."

Loathe as he was to break his gaze from the spear, Levy strapped it to his back and walked out of the armory with Ares.

"You still haven't told me what we're doing in the mortal realm," Levy said.

"And you do not need to know. Know your place, boy. You are not my companion, you are a weapon for me to point where my father directs me. Since he has leashed you to me, I have no choice but to take you with me.

"When we cross over, we will march to where I have been told to go. You will fight when I tell you to fight, and you will continue to work at grasping your power when we are not. Now shut your mouth and follow."

A fresh wave of anger washed through Levy. It wasn't as though he thought of himself as equal in power to the gods. He was well aware of his shortcomings and that he was at their mercy. But he was tired of being treated like dirt.

"Just because I'm mortal does not mean I'll keep cowering every time you disrespect me," Levy said through clenched teeth, unable to stop the words. "You may be stronger than me, but Zeus saved me for a reason. He has a use for me, and I will not continue to be talked down to and kicked around."

Before he realized what was happening, Ares had his arm pushed underneath his chin and against his throat. His body slammed back against the wall and no air could enter his lungs. The god's face was beside his own, his lips inches from Levy's head so that with each word, Ares' warm breath tickled Levy's ear.

"You will never speak to me that way again, or there will be no saving you a second time. My lord father may punish me, but I assure you it will be nothing compared to what you will endure. You are not special. You are a mortal dog who has been graced to walk our hallowed halls. Do I make myself clear?"

The pressure lifted from Levy's throat, allowing him to suck in air. He forced himself to meet the angry god's eyes. He felt an equal amount of anger and shame but knew it would be fruitless to act on either. Instead, filled to the brim with malice he simply said, "Understood."

Ares smiled a knowing smile. "Good. Now come."

Levy took a deep breath, swallowing his emotions. This was a limited-time arrangement. Soon he would ascend past even the Olympians. He simply needed to bide his time and wait for the opportunity. It would not do to get himself killed before that happened. He cracked his neck, rolled his shoulders pushing the rest of the tension from them, and followed Ares through the meekly glowing gateway.

As he stepped into the mortal realm for the first time since his "death", he was hit with a wave of nostalgia. He spent the last few years walking intricately carved stone and marble. Stepping on packed earth again for the first time in so long sent energy coursing through his body. Compared to here, Olympus felt cold and dead.

He filled his lungs with the warm air and took stock of their surroundings. They stood on the edge of a forest, the earthy scent of soil and mildew filled Levy's nose. Behind them, the forest became darker and the trees thicker and tangled.

In contrast, ahead of them, there was no life to be seen. It was as if a line had been drawn in the ground, and nothing past it was capable of surviving. Past that line was dry, dusty earth and cracked planes as far as the eye could see.

The sky was muddy and dark, casting a dull grey upon the world, though no rain fell. Though he had never been here himself, Levy realized they were standing at the border of the Wastes.

Thoughts of Quinn suddenly filled his head. This is where his former friend had originally been from. Somewhere out in this lifeless expanse of land, Quinn's people somehow scraped out a living.

He heard stories of how dead it was here, but that couldn't have prepared him for the impact of seeing it in person. For a split second, he felt pity and understanding. Pity for his friend for how he must have felt knowing his people suffered here.

He understood the guilt that must have wracked him, knowing he lived a comfortable life in the Citadel while his people starved. He became aware of Hestia's essence flickering to life inside of him, as if in response to his feelings.

"Don't," Ares said, pulling Levy out of his thoughts, and causing the essence to slip away again.

"I know that look." Ares stared Levy in the eyes. "Pity and compassion are for the weak. These people are a scourge. If they want to escape this place, they could simply take what they need to survive. Yet they do not. Be a warrior, not a sympathizer, or you are no better."

Ares was right, Levy thought. They had no reason to subject themselves to this life. If they were too weak to escape it, then they deserved it. The fact that he had felt some connection to Quinn again irked him as well.

It had been some time since he had truly allowed himself to dwell on his past companions, and he felt ashamed that the first time he did, he had allowed weakness to enter him. He looked back at the horizon, wondering if Quinn was out there right now and if he ever thought about Levy. Probably not. As far as he knew Levy was dead.

"Come," Ares said, walking further into the Wastes.

Levy was left with no choice but to follow. He was starting to suspect what they had come here to do and he felt excitement begin to build. If it was what he thought, it would likely mean coming face to face with his old friend again, and the thought of Quinn's eyes widening at seeing Levy alive tickled him.

Look out, old friend. The past is coming to get you.

CHAPTER 7

OLD BARTIMAEUS

The years since the war for the tower ended had been kind to Bartimaeus. He was well prepared to die in battle, doing something he was proud of in defending humanity from the beasts that would see them all dead.

When the girl from the Citadel showed up, claiming to be a demigod and asking to fight in the war, Bart laughed and shooed her away. When she refused to go, he begrudgingly allowed her to join the fight, though he did his best to keep her at the edges of the true combat.

After all, she was a young, pretty thing. War was no place for her. And then, one fateful night, a large group of monsters caught the company unaware and descended upon them. Bart fought well despite his age, but it seemed futile. He had gotten complacent and led the army into a slaughter.

Yet when all seemed lost, that same girl showed up and lit the world ablaze. Monsters burned to ashes in seconds and the night sky was bright as day. The girl, Ashelia, turned the impossible into possible and saved them from certain doom.

Bart was among the first to recommend she be elevated to

command. Lend was not far behind, which shocked Bart. They hadn't seen eye to eye, the young and impetuous whippersnapper that he was.

Yet even he could see the power the young girl possessed and the hope she freshly instilled. Under her command, they marched closer to the tower than they ever managed before.

Then the night of the dead came and all seemed lost again, before another youth possessing powers unheard of within mortals came to the rescue. Bart knew then the world was changing and he was out of touch.

When the orders from these two, who seemed to know each other well, came for the army to disband, a wave of sorrow went through old Bart. He was well aware he was no longer capable of standing up to the enemy, yet he didn't know what to do if there wasn't a war to fight.

It was with immense joy that Commander Ashelia asked the army to spread the word of how the Abyssalians came to their aid in the hopes of bridging the gap between the people, he proudly took up the cause. He recruited young Lend to his side, knowing the boy would be eager as well to have a goal to achieve.

Yet despite how hard they tried, progress was slow, and at points impossible. Though the people in each town and village they came across seemed receptive to the idea, they were stonewalled by leadership at every turn. It was as if some unseen force worked against their efforts and it frustrated Bartimaeus to no end.

It was after the twentieth village they visited that Lend came up with a brilliant plan. It was clear they were making no real progress. The two peoples became far too detached from one another, and human leadership shut them out at every turn.

If things were going to change, The Abyssillian people needed to be reintroduced to everyday society. They changed course, deciding instead to give them a home outside of the Wastes for the first time in known history, and they knew just the place.

However, as time went on, Bart felt again that he did not belong in those efforts. Lend had them well under control, and Bartimaeus missed the thrill of battle. He missed living off the land as they did when they marched on the tower.

So, it was with full faith in his companion to finish what they started that he left, making his way back out to the wilderness to retrain his body and live the rest of his days as he liked. He was surprised to no end when two men wearing obscenely bright armor popped out of thin air in his backyard.

He recognized one of them to a point that made his blood boil like it did in the old days. He called out to the young man he lived with to fetch him his armor and sword. He explained to the youth while strapping in, that he had an old score to settle.

He wrote a letter on a piece of paper and gave the lad clear instructions on how to get to a place called Petram out in the middle of the Wastes. He told him to hand the letter to a man who he described as "The spookiest motherfucker in the group."

He felt bad that he couldn't remember the young man's name who rallied the Abyssillians and came to their aid, but he would never forget the aura he gave off. He smiled, knowing this was his chance to repay the debt he was given that night.

Once the lad ran off on the errand, following his instructions to go wide around the two men staring out at the desolate landscape, he wrote another letter. He attached it to the leg of the messenger bird he used to keep in contact with the few men and women he still knew.

After feeding the bird some seed for the journey, he tossed it out the window and watched as it flew off toward where he knew Lend was hard at work. He took one last look at his little cottage, appreciating the life he made for himself here, and wrapped his hand around the hilt of his broadsword, carrying the blade with him as he walked out the door.

CHAPTER 8

QUINN

The cobbled walls of Petram were grander than they had ever been before. Quinn looked up at them, smiling in awe at what his friends had accomplished in the three short years he had been gone. He could hear a surprising amount of noise coming out from the streets of the town; a stark contrast to the grave silence he'd been met with when he first came back from the Citadel.

Scents of spices drifted out to him that he knew were not native to these lands as well, further showing that progress was made. He felt pride well up within him for his former pupils.

"This is the most alive I have ever seen this place," Talius murmured from beside him.

"You've been here before?" Quinn asked, surprised.

"I've been to many places in my time," Talius said, skirting the question.

"Nes and Andra have been hard at work since you've been gone." Mallory cut in, stopping Quinn from pressing further. "They're going to be so excited to see you again!"

She beamed up at Quinn, brushing a strand of her brown hair from her face and tucking it behind her ear. "They talk about you all the time, you know."

Quinn gave her a sad grin. He felt bad having dumped such a huge responsibility on the two. They had been up to the challenge, but it was a lot to ask of them.

"They needed something to focus on after what happened," Mallory said to him as if reading his thoughts. "This was good for them, Quinn. Don't feel guilty."

"Shall we?" Talius asked, entering the city through the gates.

Quinn made to follow before feeling a slight tug on his arm.

"One thing," Mallory said quietly so only they could hear. "Nes is probably going to feel a little insecure having you back. You were in charge not too long ago, you know? Just keep that in mind."

Quinn smiled down at her. She had grown close to Nes and Andra, he could tell. He was happy she was looking to protect their feelings.

"Of course. I wouldn't dream of stepping on his toes."

They made their way through the streets heading in the direction of the largest building in the back of the town. Mallory called it the palace, though it looked more like a dome to Quinn. The streets of Petram were paved with simple stones and were not quite as winding and mazelike as the roads within Stormhaven had been, but they still had to take a few twists and turns to reach the palace.

As they walked, Abyssillians stopped and whispered, pointing to the group. Children ran up and tugged at Mallory's clothing or gave her high fives. Quinn was no stranger to the people here, and Mallory had made herself well-liked in the time she had been living here.

There were many new buildings compared to the last time he had been here. With the small bit of wealth they brought in from tensions slowly easing, resources became more readily available.

People didn't have to huddle multiple families in a house anymore. Most of the buildings were carved from stone or packed earth from the Wastes, however, so the town was still fairly monochromatic. Quinn hoped as things continued to improve, a little bit of vibrancy may find its way here as well to add a little color to their lives.

As they made it to the inner gates of the palace, guards stopped them before seeing Quinn and Mallory and eagerly permitted them access. Inside was a bit dim. Though there were windows carved into the sides of the walls, not a lot of light was able to find its way inside thanks to the perpetually overcast skies of the Wastes.

There were torches lit along the mostly bare walls to help, but with resources limited, they were few and far between. Mallory pointed them to a set of double doors ahead, and as Quinn drew near, he heard a voice he thought, until recently, he would never have to hear again.

"I apologize for the lack of comfort," Nes was responding; politeness emphasized in his strained voice. "If we were able to trade for more resources with your people, the beds would have far more feathers in them and much less hide and stone."

"Yes well, that's why we are here is it not?" the squeaky-voiced master responded. "The sooner we find the artifact, the sooner you will have your resources and I can be back home in my bed."

Quinn couldn't help the contempt he felt inside at the snide little man.

"What's the matter, Enkar?" Quinn said, walking through the door and inserting himself into the conversation. "Can't handle life away from your cushy Citadel?"

The rotund master squeaked at the perceived insult and leaped to his feet, knocking his glasses from the perch of his nose, and turning his flushed face to the new voice.

"How dare...." He cut off when he saw Quinn. "YOU! That's Master Enkar to you, you sniveling little...."

"Peace, Enkar," a smooth voice said from behind him. He was a taller man, though slender, and his light brown hair matched his eyes. He had stubble beginning to form on his cheeks, indicating he had been here for some time. "I am quite certain you are giving him the rise he wanted. Quinn, I presume?"

Quinn noticed that the man wore the orange robes of a master, though he had never seen the man in his time at the Citadel.

"QUINN!" Andra exclaimed as she ran past the fuming Enkar and wrapped her arms around him. He was taken aback by the woman who stood before him. When he'd left, Andra had been about half a foot shorter and still mumbled to the ground when she spoke.

The woman in her place now had strong, angular features and confidence behind her eyes that spoke to who ran things around here. The pride Quinn already felt doubled and he fought to hold back a tear.

"Hello, Andra," he said, hugging her back.

He walked over and clasped Nes' forearm. He had grown as well, now standing equal in height with Quinn. The man had a smile on his face, though Quinn noticed he puffed his chest out a bit. Mallory's words came back to him and he smiled a placating smile at the youth to show difference.

"It's great to see you, Quinn," Nes said, squeezing his arm back.

"You as well, Nes. I love what you guys have accomplished here."

Nes beamed at him, pride clear as day in his eyes.

Quinn turned back to the master who had spoken to him, an eyebrow raised on the man's face. He was likely not used to being ignored as he had been.

"You must be Cyrus, I presume. It's a pleasure to make your acquaintance."

"That's Master Cyrus to you," Darrik said entering the room with Talius and Mallory.

Despite all the changes in the world since he'd last seen the man, Darrik looked the same. He still had thinning hair and a wispy beard that looked like it had been hastily pasted to his chin. His face was gaunt and eyes shallow as if he were one of Levy's walking corpses. Quinn despised this man more than anyone else in the room.

"There are no Masters anymore Darrik," Quinn responded coldly. "The Citadel has fallen and the Tower has been claimed."

Of course, the only two Masters to survive the collapse of the Citadel were the two that hated Quinn the most. Enkar and Darrik had been responsible for the worst of his punishments and beatings growing up.

They did nothing to hide their contempt for what he was, and Quinn held no fond memories for either of them. He was surprised they had made the journey out here.

"Come now, Quinn," Talius said, walking up to the group. "Put your grievances aside. There are much more important matters at hand."

"Of course, Master Talius," Quinn responded, shooting a look at a bristling Darrik as he referred to the man as Master. He wasn't thrilled to be speaking to the two Masters again, but he respected Talius enough to feel a bit of shame at his pettiness.

"As I live and breathe," Cyrus said, his voice never wavering from the calm, smoothness. "I thought you were dead, old friend. It is wonderful to see you again."

He walked over and, to Quinn's surprise, embraced Talius in a hug.

Talius, for his part, seemed more reserved to give Cyrus the title of friend but kept his politeness.

"Yes, it has been far too long," he responded.

Nes, not wanting to lose control of the room, cleared his throat and said, "Perhaps now that the entire group is here, we should sit down and discuss our next course of action?"

A handful of minutes later they were all seated around a large circular table. A map of the Wastes was laid out upon it, a couple of sites already marked with a red X making Quinn think of the stories of old treasure maps he had known as a child.

"Just so I have this straight," Talius said, clearing his throat. "You believe a godly artifact is buried somewhere in the Wastes that is powerful enough to sap the life out of the very land?"

"I do," Cyrus responded, staring at the Master as if trying to gauge his response. "Think about it, Talius. In all the old texts there is never a place referred to as the Wastes, or even a place described as utterly devoid of life.

"That must mean it was formed at some point within the time between this most recent occurrence of the tower, and the time when the tower appeared before it."

He spoke quickly now, his voice betraying the cool emotionless features of his face.

"The only major event I can think of that happened in that time was the Masters locking away divine artifacts. That was a process that took many, many years to accomplish, and a handful of Masters over that time to do so.

"It is no secret as their powers waned, the gods became desperate and we lost many of us to their attempts at stopping us. It would be so easy for one of them to have been placed here, and have that master perish before recording that knowledge."

Talius looked contemplative, twirling his fingers through his beard as he listened to Cyrus' words.

"I cannot say you are wholly incorrect. There is much knowledge we have lost from that time. And it would surely be viable that an artifact strong enough could have such an effect on the land." His eyes were distant as if attempting to put together the pieces of a puzzle in his head.

"Say that this artifact is what's affecting the Wastes." Quinn cut in, unable to keep the suspicion from his voice. "What would your price be for giving us that information and helping us find it? I assume you would want the artifact, the trade being that out home would come alive again. What use do you have for such an item?"

"The last time an item was taken from its seal," Andra cut in, "Master Talius said it weakened the barrier protecting us from the gods."

Quinn was thankful Andra seemed to be suspicious of the Masters as well. She balanced the youthful excitement Nes clearly showed.

Talius turned to her with an eyebrow raised.

"Sorry," she said, not backing down. "I overheard you and Quinn talking one night."

Quinn was amazed at what he was witnessing. The old Andra would never have admitted that let alone held eye contact. She had grown into a wonderful leader.

"That's true," Cyrus admitted, turning his hands up. "To both of you. To answer your questions in the order received, yes we would want the artifact and yes the trade would be that life would come back to your land.

"As for why we want it, it is because it's our history. Though the main purpose of the Citadel indeed was to train you and your friends to seize the Tower, there is a deep history entwined within our organization.

"We Masters were the keepers of said history, and we do not want it to be lost to time, but instead to preserve it for generations to come. As for your concerns about the barrier, Miss Andra, we do not plan on breaking the seal. I have a long history of dealing with these artifacts, as Master Talius can attest, and I am confident I can safely move it, should we find it, without any more damage being done."

Quinn looked over at Nes, who had been quiet for most of the discussion.

"And is this something you would agree to should the artifact be successfully located?" he asked his friend, who was still staring intently at the map on the table.

Nes nodded, without so much as looking up.

"If it were to bring life back to our home, I would gladly trade it to them. I understand the concerns. I certainly don't wish for the barrier to weaken and allow the gods to come mucking about in our lives again; but without this plan, what else do we have? Our people cannot continue life like this. It isn't sustainable."

He looked up finally, making eye contact with everyone before settling on Quinn. Again, Quinn felt a slight insecurity as they stared at one another. He needed to be reassured that he wasn't being second-guessed. Quinn nodded to him.

"If you're sure this is what you want, then I have no qualms with it. You have our support, not that you need it," he threw in to appease Nes' insecurities, "And our support wherever we may give it."

Nes smiled at his friend, thankful for the confirmation.

"Very well then. Let's stop for today now that we have that out of the way and meet again tomorrow to come up with a plan. Master Talius, if you wouldn't mind hanging around for a second, I would love to get your input on locations of interest within the Wastes you believe could house an artifact of this magnitude."

Quinn smiled as the room emptied. He watched Nes and Talius huddle over the map for a few moments, muttering and pointing to a few different locations, before circling a mound of stones Talius was certain at one point was a temple. With that concluded, Talius left the room, nodding once to Quinn.

When they were the last two within the room, Nes sat back down in his chair. He leaned back and let out a long sigh.

"Is it hard, leading everyone?" Quinn asked, looking at the young man before him.

"You tell me," Nes replied with a tired smirk.

"It is." Quinn thought back to his brief experiences trying to gather the people in the square to listen to him and lend him their support. "I wouldn't have been successful without you guys."

"Nah, you would have found a way," Nes said, peeking out from behind his fingers as he massaged his forehead.

"I don't know that I would have," Quinn replied, contemplating. "I never really led at the Citadel. That was Levy's role. I didn't lead the army fighting for the Tower. That was Ashe. The one brief time I led anything was trying to bring our people into the conflict, and I would not have succeeded at that without you and your brother saying the quiet part out loud."

There was an extended silence before Nes said, "I miss him."

Quinn thought about Sen, the young man with overly large ears who had helped rally his people to come to the aid of humanity. He died in the fight but succeeded in starting the process of uniting the Abyssillians and the humans.

"I'm proud of you Nes," Quinn said to his friend. "You and Andra both. What you guys have succeeded in here is nothing short of incredible. I am here to support you, I promise. I have faith in you and your vision."

Nes looked up at Quinn then, reading his face for any sign of mockery. He knew better than that, but Quinn knew what it was like to second guess your every decision. After a moment he looked relieved.

"Thank you, Quinn. That means more than you know."

Quinn got up from his chair and clasped Nes on his forearm again, helping him up from his own. With renewed vigor, Nes clapped him on the back and said, "Come on, let's go get some food. I'll give you a tour of all the changes in Petram since you've been gone!"

~~~

It was well after sundown by the time Quinn returned to his quarters within the palace. As with all of the rooms within the structure, his walls were fairly unadorned, save the few torches which cast a dull flickering light. Andra set him up well, however, giving him a room with an open skylight so he could look up at the stars.

"I love this room," she said as she showed him to it. "Sometimes I come in here at night and just sit, looking up at the sky and imagining the stars are shining down on me. It gives me hope that even in a place as barren as the Wastes, you can still find beauty."

Staring up at the hazy sky now, those words resonated with Quinn.

You stare at the night, admiring. Meanwhile, Ashe is locked away in a tower, and Levy is burnt to a crisp in lava by your hand. What right do you have to enjoy this?

"Shut up," Quinn said, pushing the rasp of Chaos from his mind. "Ashe is where she is meant to be, and Levy did that to himself."

You do not believe that. Quinn could hear the joy in Chaos' voice. *You toss and you turn when you try to sleep. You scream his name and reach out your hand. You shed tears as you are wracked with the guilt that you could have saved him from that fall.*

"I couldn't have," Quinn said, squeezing his eyes tight as if it would shut off the Primordial's voice.

You let go. The voice reminded him. *You were angry. He stabbed Ashe. She was going to die. You did what anyone would do in their grief and anger. You killed him.*

"Shut UP!" Quinn said again, covering his ears despite knowing it would offer him no respite. He felt the cold tendrils of power from the Realm of Night begin to swirl around him. "He would have killed me too."

Of course, he would have. Chaos cooed. *You did what you had to. Does it help to hear me say that?*

Quinn knew he had to find a way to stop this internal dialogue before the Realm of Night consumed him. He had worked tirelessly with Master Talius since the events of the Tower, both to control the Realm of Night from consuming him and also to harness it, though he knew that harnessing it would not be a problem.

Loathe as he was to admit it, it was a part of him. He felt it always, pulling at his essence. However, controlling it was something else entirely. Chaos picked at his frayed nerves constantly. He knew he was one slip-up away from being consumed.

You have all of this power at your fingertips. You could use it to take vengeance upon those who twisted Levy against you. You need to simply grasp it. Allow me to help you, as I once did before.

"No more," Quinn said, feeling his grasp over the power slipping. "Please. I am too weak to control it. I don't want to lose myself again. Just leave me be!"

It was no good. Chaos picked repeatedly at the scab that was Quinn's everlasting guilt and self-loathing over all his decisions up to this point until it was once again bleeding. He wasn't sure he would be able to hold it back this time.

Good. Chaos whispered hungrily in his ear. *Let it go. Let it all fade to nothingness.*

A knock came from the other side of the door, loud enough to reverberate around the stone walls of the room. Chaos's awareness snapped to it at once, allowing Quinn to take advantage of the reprieve and slam his mental defenses down once again, shutting the Realm of Night away temporarily.

"Quinn?" Talius' voice could be heard from the other side. "May I come in?"

He took a few deep breaths, wiping his eyes and collecting himself as Talius had taught him to do when he started feeling overwhelmed.

"Enter," he called with a confidence he did not feel.

The heavy door opened with a creak and Talius shuffled into the room, closing it behind him. He wore his orange robes as per usual, though a purple, silk nightcap now adorned his head. Quinn raised an eyebrow at it.

Talius noticed him looking and said, "When you have lived as long as I have, you learn not to pass up on any comforts life has to offer."

Quinn thought that statement was odd, considering the man didn't look older than fifty, but he simply shrugged it away. He was too exhausted to worry about anything more.

"Are you ok?" Talius asked. "I felt a sinister presence."

"I'm...." Quinn was about to lie and say he was fine but then thought better of it. Ashe had always hated when he did that.

"You are NOT fine, Quinn." She would always say, glaring up at him. Her lower lip would always pout out a little. "Stop burying your worries because you don't want to burden me. I care about you and I want to help. I wish you could just be open and be as kind to yourself as you are to other people."

He smiled at the thought of her scolding him now. He missed her dearly.

"No, I'm not." He finally said, looking up at Talius. "He spoke to me again. He's getting better at drawing the power out of me and it is getting harder for me to hold him back."

Talius scrunched his eyebrows together, deep in thought.

"That is certainly worrisome. There is trouble on the horizon I fear, and having control over your powers would be a great help to solving them.

"Yet, we cannot lose you to Chaos. Perhaps it is best we put a pin in your training for now until this business with the artifact has been solved. There are herbs I can try to get my hands on that may subdue them for the time being."

Quinn hated the idea he may be useless for the fight ahead. Perhaps useless wasn't the right term, as he could still beat most people in normal hand-to-hand combat, but that wouldn't help anyone if they encountered anything godly.

Considering the artifact they searched for was just that, the odds of encountering 'godly' were great. Yet, at the same time if it kept the scratchy voice of Chaos out of his head for a time, he wasn't sure he was against it.

"You haven't led me astray yet," he said to the Master. "If you think it best, then I will agree."

Talius nodded and walked towards the door.

"Very well," he said, reaching for the handle. "I will investigate it first thing in the morning. It may take some time, however, as I will likely have to put out an order for the herbs I need to come from beyond the Wastes.

"I doubt they have any of the necessary ingredients here. In the meantime, do your best to keep control. A very dangerous presence appeared suddenly this morning, and it wouldn't do to have to worry about two of them."

"A dangerous presence?" Quinn asked, surprised he couldn't feel it himself. After all, sensing was a specialty of his.

"Someone very strong, and filled with malice." Talius stroked his beard, eyes distant as he tracked the power. "And I fear it is heading this way."

"We should warn Nes and Andra!" Quinn said, jumping to his feet.

"At ease, child. I have already done so." Talius raised his hands in a placating gesture. "It is still a ways off, and moving somewhat slowly. They do not appear to be in any hurry to arrive. I will continue tracking it to see if they alter course at all.

"Perhaps we will get lucky and be off on our mission before it arrives, or better yet, it will turn and miss us entirely. Either way, fretting about it now will do you no good. Get some sleep. We will discuss it with everyone in the morning."

With that grim news, Talius left him. Knowing it was futile, Quinn snuffed the torches on the wall and climbed into his bed, trying hard to catch what little sleep he could.

CHAPTER 9

ASHE

"On your left!" Lyssa shouted as Talius ducked the spear which sailed over his head.

"Your other left!" Laren joined in, ripping a slice through the young man's shirt as he twisted away from her blade.

"Easy on the clothes!" Clotho yelled from the sidelines as she watched her companions spar. "I just bought him that yesterday!"

"It's not like it matters," Lyssa called back, retrieving her spear from where it stuck in the soft earth. "The kid is growing an inch every day it seems. It won't be long before he needs a new one."

That was true, Clotho thought. Talius had been with them for two years now in their journey to find the Tower. It moved around too damn much for them to be able to just go straight to it. They had to track it based on sightings and make estimations on where it may show up next from the power it gave off. This mission was a pain.

During that time, the scrawny, scraggly kid grew into a muscular teenager, in part because of the grueling combat training her guardians were putting him through. They figured that so long as he was going to travel with them and needed to eat and be clothed, he may as well learn to fight so he could earn his keep.

Talius, for his part, eagerly took to it. Long after their sparring sessions he stayed, practicing his form with his staff. He preferred to fight with a long, oaken rod, each end tipped with weighted metal. At first Lyssa and Laren had scoffed at it, as they believed one chop with a blade would break it in two. When they teased Talius about it, the boy simply shrugged and said, "Then I'll have two staves."

Clotho found it particularly humorous. They were swiftly shown the error of their way, however, when the staff found its first solid contact.

As time passed, the young boy continued to come out of his shell, sometimes staying up past his appointed watch to sit with Clotho and ask her questions about Olympus and why she sought the Tower. She in turn asked him about the mortal realm and the things he liked about it.

She knew he had come from a horrible situation. That was one of the things that convinced her to take him along with them. She was surprised at the compassion she felt for the boy when they'd first cornered him in the market alleyway.

However, the more she spoke with him the more she found herself thirsting for more knowledge of these people and their ways. Olympus prided itself on their gleaming palaces and surplus of riches and status, yet compared to this place they all looked down on so much, it was stale and dull. Sure, the mortal realm was dirty, and most of the settlements smelled like waste, but the people here were lively and spirited.

She realized she wanted to spend more time here, learning the mortals' cultures and customs. They interested her to no end, much to the chagrin of her guardians.

"It's not that we think less of you for it," Laren said to her one day. "You have always had a curiosity in you and honestly Lyssa and I respect you for it. But having an interest in these mortals is dangerous. Lord Zeus would not look kindly upon you for that. He gave you your mission and anything that slows you or distracts you from that will anger him. He chose you for a reason and he expects results."

"Zeus is not someone you want to cross, little one," Lyssa said, eyes focused on the thunder clouds in the distance.

Maybe it was because she was young, as far as immortals went anyways, but she didn't like the fear that her guardians had when thinking about Zeus and his authority. How could anyone be happy living under someone who got angry for their interests?

Just because he thought less of the mortals should not mean they all had to. If they were truly just insects to him, what fear should he have of some of his people taking an interest? She kept such thoughts to herself, however. She was young and impetuous, but she was not stupid. Still, she hoped it would take a little longer to track down the Tower. She was enjoying her time here and didn't want it to come to an end too quickly.

"That's enough for today," Laren said, calling a halt to the sparring. Clotho looked up, realizing she was lost in her thoughts again as Lyssa and Laren came over to her. Talius did what he normally did when they called a stop for the day and continued his stances, twirling his staff in the air and striking make-believe enemies.

"I'll give him one thing," Lyssa said, wiping the sweat from her forehead on her shirt. "He definitely works hard."

Laren grunted her agreement. "He's a fast learner too, especially for a mortal."

"Have you trained mortals often?" Clotho asked.

Laren rolled her eyes. "Obviously not. But they are supposed to be slow-witted, aren't they?"

"That one sure isn't" Lyssa confirmed. "Anyway, what do you want us to hunt tonight for dinner? These woods are filled with all manner of rabbits and birds."

"Rabbit sounds nice," Clotho replied, mesmerized by the tip of Talius' staff catching the waning sunlight as it twirled through the air.

A couple hours later they were sitting in a circle around the fire, each gnawing on a small hare. Laren and Lyssa were murmuring to themselves about where they would head tomorrow and where the pull of the Tower felt strongest.

Talius ate silently, staring into the flickering flames. Clotho had finished early and went to set up her place for the first watch. Her guardians always made her take the first watch as it was when the night was safest. Though Clotho was plenty capable of defending herself against the wildlife or any random monster that wandered too close to their camp, they insisted upon it.

She had taken to drawing her surroundings with some charcoal on a pad of papyrus she had picked up in one of the nearby towns. Each new campsite brought a new variety of flowers or trees. New animals and bugs.

This world fascinated her. Lately, Talius had also taken to sitting with her as she sketched. He would tell her the names of the plant life and wildlife. She was shocked at how well-versed he was considering his upbringing.

He explained that one of the older women he lived with had knowledge in that field and would tell them all stories about the world around them. It was one of his few comforts.

In return for his knowledge, she began telling him of Olympus and the immortals. Humanity always worshipped the gods in ancient times. They were believed to be the life-givers, fire-bringers, and food-sharers. Mortals would sacrifice to them and worship them, and in return, the gods' power would grow with their influence.

However, as the gods became more and more powerful, the mutual relationship was strained. Eventually, mortals were looked down on for their weakness while the Olympians continued to hoard their power and riches. What was once a healthy relationship turned sour, and the mortals began to live in fear and squalor.

Clotho sketched a particularly pretty flower that night, one with bright orange petals and a yellow and brown pattern inside that looked like an eye—Talius called it a tiger's eye. He asked her a question she was dreading.

"What happens when you take the Tower?"

She continued to sketch, though now she found herself much less focused.

"When you take the Tower, what happens to me? What happens to my realm? I listened as you talked. I know Zeus doesn't like my people. You're doing this mission for him, right? I appreciate all that you have done for me, don't think I don't. But when you take the Tower, what then?"

Clotho put her charcoal and papyrus down and pulled her knees to her chest.

"When I take the Tower, I will be in charge of making sure the

world continues to run as Zeus would have it run."

"And what does that mean? How does Zeus want you to have it run?" He turned to her, looking directly into her eyes.

"It means the same thing that it does currently. It keeps the balance of power in Olympus." She looked away.

"Is that what you want?" he asked her.

"It doesn't matter what I want." She responded, still staring at the dirt.

"Why not? You have said yourself you are fascinated by this realm; by its people. Why can't you make it so that that doesn't just continue, but instead flourishes?"

"Because Zeus...."

"Who cares about Zeus?" Talius interrupted.

Clotho exploded up off the ground, covering Talius' mouth with her hand and looking over at where Laren and Lyssa slept. They still seemed to be out cold.

"Quiet," Clotho hissed. "You don't know the magnitude of what you just said."

Though Talius looked slightly abashed, he did not back down, though he did thankfully lower his voice.

"The way I see it, you are going to be in charge. You can do what you want and he can't do anything about it. You may even be able to placate him by allowing for some things to stay as they are while advancing others.

"I'm not saying you should throw it all in his face. I'm just saying, that you care about my people and my realm. It doesn't seem like the other immortals do. Why not help us? What will that hurt?"

The way he looked at her when he said this, eyes wide and impassioned, broke her heart. He was right. She did care about his people and his realm. She didn't want to leave it, locked away in a tower weaving fate for 1,000 years.

She accepted it was her duty to do so, and she would do it. But did that mean she also had to follow the orders of a god who cared nothing for these people whom she discovered such a fondness for?

She placed a hand on his shoulder and said, "I cannot promise you that I will go against him. You are ignorant of his power and what he can do should he decide to do so. But I promise you that I will think about what you said. Your people are not the mindless worms the immortals think you to be and I think there is benefit to allowing you that free will."

He smiled and warmed her heart. It was rare he showed any emotion, and when he did it wasn't but for a moment. Yet here he sat, beaming at her for being willing to simply listen to his thoughts and promise to think about not shattering his people's existence.

No, these people were not at all the dull folk the Olympians proclaimed them to be. Were the roles reversed, and his people held the throne, would they treat the Olympians the way they were treated? Would they deserve it? That was a thought she would have to think about.

"Your watch has ended Clotho," He said, pointing to the moon now high in the sky. "Get some rest. I'll wake you in the morning."

She nodded to him and picked up her drawing utensils, making her way toward her sleeping area.

"Thank you." She heard him whisper to her back. "Thank you for hearing me out."

She fell asleep that night, and dreamt of the future she would weave, should she have the choice.

~~~

Ashe pulled out of the memory, sensing it was near its completion. She was invested in Clotho's story and wanted to finish it soon, but the effort it took to peer into the orb and see its contents in such a detailed manner took so much energy out of her. She was sure Clotho left thoughts for her to find for a reason. Between the boy named Talius, and the references to what she felt was happening in the present, she did not imagine it was a coincidence she discovered these memories.

Though as always happened when she tried to watch, something else pulled her from the orb's contents. The strings around her were all frantically vibrating. That wasn't necessarily odd, the strings tended to do that occasionally.

What set her internal alarm off was the number of decayed strings that came unattached from their orbs. No matter the color of the string, they all let off a small glow indicating the essence of the Weaver which tied them to their fates. From time to time, strings would detach themselves or naturally decay.

At times Ashe forced them to as well, because people could not live forever. She reflected upon how her old self would have found that callous and cold, but she ascended from those mortal feelings when she took up this power and understood it was simply part of the job. She did find herself wondering if Quinn would think her cold for it though. Try as she might, not all mortal feelings could leave her.

However, as she looked around at the orbs in her immediate vicinity, she noticed large swathes of thread turning grey and disintegrating. The orbs they were attached to started to dull and crack as well. Looking up she noticed more thread hanging limply. She did not like the implication.

As she floated up the Tower, she did her best to reattach as many as she could. Some took to her touch and mended, though most immediately fell apart again.

One orb even shattered at her touch. She looked down at the blood that oozed from her finger. She found that odd. Though she was immortal now, she still bled mortal blood instead of ichor. Deciding to shelve that thought until a later time, she sucked on her finger and continued to the top of the Tower.

She still hated coming up here, the power from these orbs left her feeling cold, but whatever was happening originated from this section of the Tower. It was then she noticed Zeus' orb glowing bright blue. Electricity arced along the strings, zapping orbs as they passed and disintegrating others.

Curiouser still was the smaller silver orb next to it. Though once sparkling and serene, it now had gone dull. A large crack formed vertically along its surface and it floated incrementally forward, seemingly on a collision course with Zeus'.

The light within the Tower flickered and the very structure shook for just a moment before everything stood still. To Ashe's surprise, the strings that once hung limply or fallen apart returned to their normal state. The orb that had shattered returned to its rightful place and the wound on her finger was completely gone. The silver orb was back to sparkling and was no longer heading in the direction of Zeus'.

Ashe floated in place, shocked at what she just witnessed.

Though she had not been within the Tower long, she had never felt anything quite like that. A feeling of absolute dread washed over her as she began to understand what was going to happen.

Over my dead body, she thought, racing to each corner of the Tower. She focused her energies and began to furiously weave, attaching her thread to the very building itself.

After each cluster of yarn she wove, she wrapped them around her arms. When her arms were covered, she moved to her hands, and eventually her fingers until every bit of them were covered in string. With a thought she snapped them out of existence, knowing they were there if she needed them.

With that done she floated back down to her throne and took a deep breath, picking Clotho's orb back up.

She did not fear what she believed was to happen. Instead, she steeled her resolve and hurried to finish watching what Clotho wanted her to know.

Come and get me then.

CHAPTER 10

LEVY

Levy spat what little moisture remained from his mouth. The air in the Wastes was acrid, and dust from the barren earth kept swirling up into his mouth. He desperately wanted to take a swig of the water he held in the small, leather canteen at his hip but decided against it as it was running fairly low.

He wasn't sure how much longer it would take to get to their destination and Ares wasn't exactly welcoming to any questions he asked. He was starting to dislike spending time with the god.

If he ever spoke without being spoken to, he was met with disdain and insult. If Ares initiated any kind of conversation, it usually ended in a small bout of verbal sparring followed by a cheap threat reminding him to know his place. He was beginning to wonder why the gods were ever revered in the first place—the headstrong, egotistical bastards that they were.

Remind you of anybody? He pictured the essence of Hestia mocking him from within his head. The more he worked with trying to harness that power to its fullest, the more it had begun to change.

At first, it stayed on the edges of his consciousness, flitting about, just out of reach. However, the more attention he showed it, dragging it to the forefront of his mind, the more it evolved, almost as though it were developing a personality of its own.

He was beginning to wonder if it truly was alive, or if his consciousness was just finding new ways to torment him.

"We're being followed," Ares stated, nonchalantly. Levy looked around, not noticing anything out of the ordinary. "Behind us, about 300 yards. Can't you sense these things?" he asked, lip curling.

"That was never my specialty." He said, monotone. He refused to rise to Ares' bait.

Sure enough, as he looked in the direction Ares indicated, he saw the glint of light off a set of armor.

"We've been walking for a day straight with no sign of civilization," Levy said, unsure if he was bewildered or impressed that the man had kept pace with them. Perhaps both. "Where could he have possibly come from?"

"He's been with us since we set off," Ares replied. "Rather impressive honestly, for a mortal."

"What should we do?" Levy asked, annoyed at the respect Ares showed the stranger.

Ares smirked, picking up on the irritation within his voice. "Seems to me like this would be a good time for you to test out that new spear of yours."

"You want me to kill him?" Levy asked, surprised.

"Why not?" Ares responded, coolly. "We cannot have him follow us to our destination, and he has some sort of business with us. Consider it a training exercise."

"What if he is just a traveler who happened to be going in the same direction as us?"

"Then fate was not kind to him, and he chose a bad day to travel."

His smile was wolfish. Ares enjoyed using words to remind Levy of Ashe and Quinn. He got a sick pleasure out of seeing him flinch, or his eyes narrow. If Levy reacted too harshly, the god would call him soft and laugh his arrogant, self-assured laugh.

Doing his best to keep his face still, Levy undid the spear from his back, twirling it once in the air to get a feel for its weight before bringing it to stand at his side.

"Very well," Levy sighed. It wasn't like killing was new to him.

Around five minutes of waiting was all it took for the armored pursuer to reach their location; huffing and puffing under the weight of his mail.

"It's hotter than a drakon's ballsack out here," he said between breaths in way of greeting.

"Are those typically rather hot?" Ares asked, an eyebrow cocked in bemusement.

"Of course they are, son," the man replied. "They live in volcanoes. Everything is hot in a volcano."

The man was older than Levy thought he'd be, considering the length of the walk and the pace at which he'd have to have traveled to keep up with them. His bald head gleamed brighter than perhaps even his armor.

He wore his beard long and grey; covering what Levy could only assume, based on his heavily creased forehead and sunken eyes, was a very wrinkled face. Something seemed familiar about the man, but he couldn't place what.

His armor was rather plain and unimpressive, much like the old man himself. Simple chainmail fell to his knees, covering most of his body. He wore a typical, silver breastplate over his chest, as well as standard-issue vambraces and gauntlets.

Everything about the man screamed veteran. Even the broadsword he carried, unsheathed Levy noticed, was unadorned with any special marking or jewel.

"What do you want, old timer?" Levy asked, testing to see if the lack of respect would trigger any anger in the grizzled warrior.

"HA!" the man bellowed. "I've had soldiers greener than a seasick Medusa throw better jabs at me, boy."

Heat crept up the nape of Levy's neck at the taunt.

"You get riled far too easily," the man said as if sensing the tension in Levy's back. His tone changed in an instant to something far more serious.

"I constantly tell him that," Ares said from off to the side, shrugging as if to say 'What can you do.'

"Shut up, both of you," Levy growled, raising the tip of his spear so it was even with the man's chest. He noticed Ares shot him a warning glare from the corner of his eye but chose not to acknowledge it. "If you have something to say, say it before I plunge this through your heart."

The warrior narrowed his eyes, seemingly unphased by the threat.

"Aye, I have something to say. My name is Bartimaeus Crowe, former commander of the Last Regiment, sworn to march for the Citadel in the fight for the Tower. The very same army whose cause you were sworn to before you turned your back on your ideals and unleashed a horde of the dead upon us."

Levy's eyes widened in surprise. No wonder the old man looked familiar. He was a survivor of the night Levy nearly decimated what was left of the Citadel's influence over the land.

"Bartimaeus, was it? Funny, I don't seem to recall you." He fibbed. "Some commander you must have been." This time the warrior bristled at his jab, much to Levy's satisfaction.

"Aye, I failed in my time as commander, that is true. Were it not for Ashelia and the boy in the mask, we would likely have been overrun and destroyed. I lost a lot of good men and women that night. I've come to repay that debt."

Levy flashed his teeth, adrenaline pumping through his veins after hearing of the deeds of his former friends once again.

"Well then, what are you waiting for?" he half whispered. "Come repay them."

Bartimaeus let loose a wild bellow, raising his blade faster than a man his age should have been able to, and let loose a swing meant to cut Levy's head off in one go. Levy was ready for it though, expecting his little jab to push the man into action.

He pulled his head back, feeling the breeze as the tip of the broadsword sailed just past his throat. Using the momentum, he dropped his shoulder and spun, gripping the shaft of his spear with both hands and stabbing out with the intent to plunge the point straight through the old warrior's ribs.

Again, the old man surprised him, sparsely bucking his hips out to the side so the spear hit nothing but air. He brought his blade down quickly, following his movement, hoping to catch Levy at the end of his thrust, but Levy had the benefit of youth on his side. He swiftly pulled back, watching as the sword missed its target and slammed, tip first into the ashen dirt of the Wastes.

Before Bartimaeus could recover, Levy grabbed hold of some

of Hestia's essence and punched, making solid contact with the old man's jaw. His head reeled back, blood cascading from his now split lip. It fell rapidly to the ground, greedily consumed by the parched earth. Before he could recover, Levy struck out again with his other hand, rocking the man once more.

To his astonishment, instead of dropping to the ground, Bartimaeus smiled a bloody smile and slammed his head forward, smashing it into the bridge of Levy's nose with a loud crunch. He felt the warmth as blood gushed down his face from the impact, dripping from his chin.

"Doesn't feel so great, does it?" he laughed, seeing the pained expression on Levy's face.

Levy snarled, flinging up the tip of his spear and just barely catching Bartimaeus on the chin as the old man ducked back. Back and forth metal on metal clashed, ringing out amongst the empty landscape. Levy hated to admit it but his opponent was skilled.

It was no wonder the army was able to survive as long as it did in its conquest of the Tower. He held a begrudging respect for the warrior he was now trying to kill.

"Give it up boy!" Bartimaeus yelled, blood and spittle spraying from his mouth. "I've a lifetime of experience behind this blade. You'd be dead had you not hidden yourself behind your undead."

"I have defeated a god!" Levy yelled back over the crash of the weapons, an image of a broken Janus in his silver room flashing in his mind. "You are nothing to me!"

With each swing, Levy harnessed more and more of Hestia's essence. Normally when he tried to grasp it, it wriggled free, fleeing just out of reach. Now he didn't give it the option. He mentally snatched at it, quicker than it could react, and ripped off chunks with each swing.

The power behind each strike was beginning to weigh on the old man's arms. Each block came slower and slower, each step back shakier and shakier, until on one such swing the broadsword flew from Bartimaeus' hands, landing in the dirt a few yards away with a thud.

Bartimaeus dropped to a knee, gasping for air in the sweltering heat. Sweat poured from his head, mixing with his blood-caked lips. Levy saw him glance over to his blade and knew he had to act before the man made a desperate lunge for it.

Just as Bartimaeus began to move, Levy drove the tip of his spear through the back of the warrior's leg and into the very earth, pinning him in place. Bartimaeus gritted his teeth and grunted, but to Levy's surprise did not bellow out in pain.

"Well done," Ares said, walking up to Levy. "He fights well for a mortal. An old one at that."

Bartimaeus looked up at them, a mixture of anger and resignation in his eyes. "Be on with it then," he grumbled.

"You came out here expecting to die," Ares said. It was not a question. "What fools you mortals are; throwing your lives away for your pride." He looked the man up and down with disdain.

Levy walked over to Bartimaeus' blade, picked it up from the dirt, and strolled back over to the old man. "Killed by your own blade, how poetic."

"No," Ares said.

"What do you mean no?" Levy asked. "You told me to kill him. My spear is currently holding him in place. Unless you want to loan me your weapon, this will have to suffice."

"No," the god said again. "I want you to use your power."

"Come again?" Levy asked, unsure of what he meant.

"This is good practice. Take control of the essence inside of you and harness it to increase your strength."

"And do what exactly?" Levy asked, unsure of what he was being asked to do.

Ares smiled, sinister and toothy. "Strengthen yourself, and then crush his head like a grape."

Bartimaeus' eyes widened.

Levy paled. He did his fair share of killing and wasn't squeamish about it. That was part of war after all, and the Masters made sure growing up when the time came it wouldn't be a problem, but that was with a weapon and in combat. Crushing an opponent's head after he was already defeated seemed unnecessarily brutal. Bartimaeus, for his part, stayed completely silent.

"With all due respect, Lord Ares," Levy said carefully, not wanting to anger the god again, "I feel pretty good about my control over that power. I wouldn't want to tire myself out before we reach our target."

"Weak." Ares spat.

Faster than Levy could react the god struck his hand out, contacting the old warrior's skull and splattering it across the ground. A crimson mist hung in the air where his head had once been. The now headless body slumped forward watering the desolate land. Levy looked up wide-eyed and rooted to the spot.

"That is your last grace," Ares said, quiet yet controlled. "You had better eliminate that mortal weakness before we get to Petram. Failure to act as I say from now on will end for you as it just did for him. Do you understand, boy?"

Levy swallowed, forcing the bile back down. He was disgusted by what he just witnessed. He knew he was out of his league amongst the gods, but that hadn't stopped his ambitions. He was able to temper that fear by focusing on his training and planning for the future.

Yet as he watched the blood soak the earth in front of him, and he looked back into the golden eyes of Ares, for the first time since he was pulled from the lava, he felt the true weight of the decisions that brought him to this point. And he was afraid.

"Yes sir," he said quietly. Because what else was there to say?

"Good. Then let us be on."

Without a second glance, the god turned back and continued on the path toward the center of the Wastes. Levy took one last look at the headless body before strapping his spear on his back once again and wordlessly set off after him.

CHAPTER 11

QUINN

The cavern was lit with an auburn glow, the brown of the stone mixing with the orange lava that bubbled some fifty feet below. Quinn stared down, transfixed at the sight before him, unable to look away from the horror he inflicted.

He could still feel the sting of sweat as it dripped down his face, contacting his numerous open wounds. He stared into the wide eye of Levy as he sunk into the magma. Half of his face had already been consumed by the molten rock. An arm was extended in the air, fingers splayed out as if asking Quinn to take his hand.

"You could have saved me." Levy's voice drifted from every inch of the room as if seeping from the very stone itself. "Instead, you let me fall. You murdered me, Quinn. Some hero you are."

As always when he revisited this place in his dreams, Quinn could not speak. He could not move; could not even breathe. He was simply stuck in place, transfixed upon the burning face of his friend, as though he had been turned to stone.

He wanted badly to call out, to deny the accusation. Yet, he knew even if he could speak, denying them would be a lie. Whether letting go of Levy and letting him fall had been necessary or not, part of him still wondered if he could have succeeded in subduing him instead. No number of excuses or justifications made the gut-wrenching guilt that boiled within him any easier to manage.

Suddenly the voice cut off. The cavern fell deadly silent around him, and the flickering light froze. This had never happened before. Down in the lava, Levy's eye widened. His pupil, normally hazy and unfocused, snapped up to Quinn's, making direct eye contact.

The unburned half of his face smiled, sending a shiver down Quinn's spine. To his horror, Levy began climbing out of the lava, as though it had become solid ground. As if that wasn't terrifying enough, as Levy pulled his face from the molten rock, Quinn could see that everywhere the lava touched was burned away, leaving just a skeleton behind.

Levy stood on top of the lava now, peering up at him, half smile, half skull. A skeletal arm pointed up at him, his head tilted to the side like Quinn used to do when he wore the mask to off-put his opponents.

"You killed me, Quinn." The skeletal visage of his friend spoke up at him. His voice was somehow both sharp and hollow at the same time. "And now I will return the favor."

"He's coming, little hero." The voice of Chaos now spoke from all around the cavern. Here in his dreams, the voice was always solid and clear. "And there is naught you can do to stop him. Your world is about to burn."

Chaos cackled as if he had told the funniest joke, the sinister crowing amplified and reverberated from the stone until it overloaded Quinn's senses.

Quinn awoke with a start, crying out and reaching forward toward a hand he knew was not there. He was soaked in cold sweat, his undershirt plastered to his chest. He took a few deep breaths, centering himself against the mental onslaught of the nightmare.

There was a quick tap at the door, and Mallory slipped into the room before he could answer, shutting the door silently behind her. A pale, grey light filtered in from the skylight above, alerting Quinn to the fact that the early morning had come.

Mallory set a cup of water down beside him, gesturing for him to take a drink. He gulped it down greedily, unaware of just how thirsty he had been.

"Thanks" he rasped, setting the cup back down on the side table.

"This is the third morning in a row you've awakened screaming," she said gently, sitting at the end of the bed.

"You've heard that, have you?" Quinn replied, staring down at his open palm. He still pictured Levy's outstretched hand.

"I share a wall with you." She pitched a thumb toward the far wall of the room. "Though honestly, I'd be shocked if the whole palace hasn't heard it."

There was no accusation or malice behind the words. Just gentle concern. "Talius told me a little of what is happening as far as your powers are concerned. He asked if I knew of anywhere he could get hold of some Grey Lace to help blunt your essence for a bit. I was suspicious when he asked for that so I made him explain before I told him anymore."

"I'm sorry I've woken you," Quinn replied, embarrassed.

"I've lived with an army in active combat for years. Yelling is part of it. You learn to sleep under any conditions," she said, nonplussed. "Quinn, soldier's heart is normal. You've been through more than almost anybody. I'd be worried if you didn't have nightmares or anxieties."

She placed her hand on his shoulder, pulling his eyes to hers. "But what does worry me is you bottle it up, refusing to let those of us who care about you help. You've been through difficult times, Quinn. It's no wonder your power is eating you up. Anything under that amount of pressure is going to eventually explode. Let us help you, please."

For a second, as he looked into her eyes, he saw Ashe sitting before him. How many times had they had this exact conversation? He thought the memory would bring a spike of pain to his heart, but instead, a wave of comfort washed over him. She would have been happy to know Mallory took up her mantle in this regard, and he chuckled at the thought. On instinct, he pulled her into a hug, allowing his stress to wash away.

"Thank you," he said into her shoulder.

She patted him on the back, allowing him a few moments before saying, "You are really sweaty."

He sat back up and they shared a laugh. He spent the next hour telling her of everything that had been pulling him down. How he struggled with his powers, still hearing Chaos in his head. He told her of his nightmares and his guilt over how things had ended with Levy and ended his tirade with how much he missed Ashe.

"I miss her too," Mallory said with a faraway look. "She was the sister I always wanted growing up. I wouldn't be where I am today without her."

"How do you handle it?" Quinn asked, holding a scrunched-up ball of his soaked shirt over his heart. "When I think about her, I feel as though there is a piece of me missing, and no matter how hard I try to be happy for where she is now, and the good I know she is doing, I want nothing more than for her to be with me again. I know it's wrong, but I want to be selfish about this."

Mallory smiled a genuine, heart-warming smile at his words.

"There are so many things in this world that I don't know," she said, holding his hand in her own. "But one thing I am certain of, Quinn, is that she is incredibly lucky to have you in her life. Don't lose hope. I don't believe for even a second that she is gone from our lives for good."

He smiled, letting the warmth of her words fill the hole in his heart.

"Thank you, Mallory, truly. I appreciate you more than you know."

"Now then," She said, swinging her legs off his bed and walking towards the door. "Get in the bath and clean the sweat off yourself. We're meeting soon to decide our plan moving forward, and you don't want to show up smelling like a zoo."

She walked out of the room grumbling about why she couldn't meet a man so devoted to her and how life wasn't fair.

Quinn smiled to himself, allowing her words about Ashe to raise his spirits, before getting up himself and heading towards the stone basin in the corner of the room.

~~~

Sometime later, Quinn entered the same room they had met in before. Similar to last time, all members of the party were huddled around the large, circular table, pointing at the map and muttering amongst themselves. As Quinn walked over to Talius, he noticed how despite their alliance, both groups seemed to be quietly discussing plans within their little cliques.

Darrik looked up and squinted at Quinn, notching his lip in a half sneer, before ducking his head back into their huddle. Nes, Andra, and Mallory seemed more focused on where Petram stood on the map than the ruins they had decided likely held what they were seeking.

It was clear the news of a powerful presence heading toward the town didn't sit well with them. Nes glanced up and nodded in his direction, before continuing what seemed to be a heated discussion with Andra. Talius, for his part, stood off to the side, taking in both parties, though his eyes continued to drift over to Cyrus.

"You were screaming again last night," Talius said as Quinn stood beside him.

"It's been addressed," Quinn replied, wanting to cut it off there. He felt the sharp gaze of the Master upon him. Thankfully he seemed to take him at his word.

"If you're sure," he said, looking back over at Cyrus.

"What's happening?" Quinn asked, hoping to change the subject.

"There is a bit of a disagreement. The news of our visitors seems to have set everyone on edge, though that is hardly a surprise. The Masters, and surprisingly Nes, wish to leave immediately in the hopes of procuring the artifact.

"Young Andra and Mallory wish to wait until the visitors are no longer in play before leaving. They fear for the safety of their people should they not be here to meet this potential threat."

Quinn didn't blame them for being nervous. Petram had come so far in such a short amount of time, and the thought of all of that being for naught set him on edge as well. Yet, at the same time, he could understand the desperation Nes felt at procuring the artifact and returning life to the land once more.

"What do you think the right course of action is?" he asked Talius.

Talius was about to respond when a sharp, "QUINN!" silenced the room. Andra was standing there, hands on her hips and eyebrows scrunched together.

"Come tell Nes that giving up Petram to a potential enemy for the sake of an artifact is the most boneheaded decision a leader could make."

"Andra," Nes said, clearly hurt. "I'm not advocating for giving up Petram. I'm simply saying we don't even know these people are even intending to arrive here. And if they are coming here, it is likely not the people that live here they are after."

He looked at Quinn, silently pleading. "I'm simply suggesting if we were to leave here for the artifact before they arrive, then not only will we have a head start on it, but they are more than likely to walk right through after us and leave the town alone."

Quinn had to admit that it made sense. Then another thought struck him.

"What are the odds these people, whoever they might be, are here for the same artifact you are?" he asked, looking into the eyes of the lead Master.

Cyrus, for his part, seemed genuinely puzzled.

"I can say, truly, that I have no idea who this presence belongs to, nor that I knew of anybody else aware of our artifact. Though I would not put it out of the question that they may have their sights set on it, it seems more likely to me that they hunt something, or someone, else."

"If that is the case," Nes cut back in staring at a flushed Andra, "Then that is all the more reason to leave the town now and draw them away from it."

Andra was having none of it.

"There is no guarantee of what they are after!" Andra protested. "You would have us abandon our home under nothing more than an assumption. What if it is the town they are truly after? Then you would have us run as our people burn? You're smarter than this Nes.

"I know you want the artifact, and I know you want the future it promises to bring, but you are a leader. You need to think of our people's current needs first before you try and fix the future."

A small, black drakon scampered up her back and sat on her shoulder, ears tucked back as if sensing Andra's anger.

"Easy, Horacio," she said, patting the drakon on the head and collecting herself. "Please Nes, don't risk our people for this quest. I know you have the best intentions, but this plan is too risky to commit fully to."

Quinn pondered the situation carefully. There was merit to both ideals, though he tended to agree more with Andra. Leaving the town defenseless in the hopes that whoever was emitting such a powerful essence left it alone as well, electing instead to follow them, seemed far riskier than he liked.

It was a plan that allowed no error in judgment, lest the consequences be dire. There was no coming back from the consequences should they assume wrong. At the same time, if it was truly the artifact, or potentially even him these people were after, a fight within the city could have been avoided if they left.

Before he was able to say any of these thoughts out loud, the doors to the conference room burst open. Guards escorted a young man, pale and panting, to Nes. The boy reached out with shaky hands, delivering a rolled-up letter to the leader.

"What's this?" he asked, taking the missive from the boy.

"I know you!" Mallory said looking at the youth's face. "You're Bart's squire. Leander, right?"

"Aye," the boy said between gasps for air. "I ran straight here to deliver his letter. Two men in shining golden armor appeared out of nowhere on the border of the Wastes a couple of days ago. He wrote this and commanded me to deliver it as quickly as possible, skirting around them."

"Where is Bart?" Mallory asked, worry creeping into her voice.

"He put on his armor and went to confront them." the boy said, grimly.

Nes sucked in air through his teeth as he read the letter. He lifted his eyes, solemnly, to Quinn, before offering it to him.

"You're going to want to read this."

To those in charge of Petram,

It is with great sorrow I write to inform you that enemies stalk your home. Just moments ago, two men wearing armor I can only describe as regal, appeared from thin air in my backyard at the border of the Wastes. One man gave off a presence the likes of which I have never felt before.

I fear that, despite my many years of service within the army, I have never met an opponent who shook me to my core as this man has. The other is someone familiar to me, and I imagine even more familiar to one of you.

The last time I saw him, he was unleashing an army of the dead upon my troops. I send this in the hopes it reaches you in time, so that you may prepare however you see fit. I will do my best to slow them down, though I fear it will cost me my life.

I am thankful for the life I have lived, and hope that with this act, I can succeed in my final mission; seeing our people united. Long live Humanity. Long live the Abyssillians. Fuck the gods.

~Bartimaeus Crowe.

Quinn reeled back as though he had been slapped, the parchment falling from his hands. He could feel the blood drain from his face as he looked over to Mallory with wide eyes. Talius reached down and picked the parchment up from the ground, skimming it.

"It is as I feared," he said, far calmer than Quinn could have been. "There are enemies at our doorstep. We must act swiftly, one way or another, to prevent devastation."

He proceeded to relay the information to everyone else, passing the letter around as well for good measure.

"That settles it, we cannot leave our people undefended," Andra said again. "We played a part in foiling that man's attack. He will not be forgiving. He turned against his people, think what he will do to us."

"We can't just wait for him to get here," Nes replied, brow furrowed. "If we do that, we not only run the risk of putting our people in danger but also that we will fail and never reach the artifact."

"I would advise against meeting these two at all," Cyrus' smooth voice cut in. He and Talius had shared a look previously and now shared it again. "This is no mere enemy we face."

"What do you know?" Quinn asked, still reeling at the apparent news that Levy had somehow lived.

"It is highly likely the presence we feel is that of a god," Talius said, matter-of-factly. Again, Quinn got the feeling Talius had experienced far more in life than he let on.

"A strong one at that," Cyrus confirmed. "I do fear that if we go out to meet this threat, we severely risk our chances at ever making it to the artifact in one piece."

"I don't understand," Mallory cut in. "I thought the barrier was still in place. How did a god make it into our realm?"

"When Levy removed the Orb of Hades from its seal, it weakened the barrier significantly," Talius replied with his far-off look. "Though it still stands, I do not doubt that it was weakened enough for a single god to have access."

"Doesn't that mean we should not risk weakening it further by finding this other artifact?" she asked Cyrus. "I know you believe you can remove it without breaking the seal, but if you aren't sure you can, then wouldn't it be best to not try it at all?"

"We need to claim the item!" Enkar squeaked from where he sat. Up to this point, the little Master had been abnormally quiet.

Yet, at the thought of potentially losing the artifact he and the other Masters appeared so desperate to get their hands on, he chose this moment to jump in.

"Both of us need that," he amended quickly. "We must not allow the gods to bully us."

"I concur," Cyrus said with far more tact. "If we give up on this mission before we have even started, it shows the gods we still fear them. It shows weakness."

Andra looked as though she were going to explode.

"Our people come first," she said, quietly. Dangerously. "So long as they are in the way of danger, we cannot run off on what could be no more than a fairy tale." She looked over at Nes who appeared to be deep in thought. It was no secret that he desperately wished to find the artifact as well.

Quinn sighed, knowing full well what would have to happen. He knew a clash with this god was coming, whether he liked it or not. If he ran and the people of Petram paid the price, he would never be able to live with himself. He would also not allow damage to come through infighting.

"We split up," he said with confidence born only from resignation.

"Are you sure?" Talius asked. "It will mean confronting your past before you are ready."

Quinn nodded, dreading what he knew was to come.

"Elaborate," Cyrus said with far more intrigue than Quinn liked.

"Nes and Andra can go with the Masters after the artifact. We believe we have it narrowed down to the area it can be found in and so it should be a fairly direct trip. If it is indeed there, and you succeed in your mission, life can be returned to this land at no great sacrifice to its people." Quinn shifted his eyes over to Nes who gave him a quick nod of thanks.

"Mallory can take the people of Petram and evacuate to the north, as we did when we marched on the Tower. Once at the border, steering far clear of Levy and the god he walks with, they can make for your territory," he said nodding to Cyrus. "If you write them a letter granting them shelter, there should be no quarrel."

Cyrus appeared to contemplate this before nodding his head in agreement.

"If it will allow us to continue on this mission, I can see it done."

Now for the part of his plan, he dreaded most.

"Talius and I will stay behind in the empty city and meet them head-on. If nothing else, we should be able to hopefully delay them long enough for our people to escape danger and for you to put enough distance between yourselves that you can find the artifact."

"No," Andra said, looking at Quinn.

"Andra…." Quinn began but she held her hand up.

"Mallory cannot lead our people from the Wastes. They have grown to trust her inside our walls, but for a mission that involves uprooting them and leading them into what was once enemy territory, they will not trust an outsider with this.

"If we are going to do this, they will need an Abyssillian to lead them. Horacio and I will go. Mallory can go with Nes and ensure that his mission is a success." As she finished speaking, she shot a glance at the Masters, showing her distrust.

Nes for his part was beaming. He was thrilled to have found a solution that allowed for his goal to still be met while also keeping the people of Petram safe.

"It is decided then," he said. "Get your things ready and meet me at the western gate within the hour. The sooner we leave, the more distance we put between us." Nes stood up from the table, leading the Masters out of the room.

Andra stared at him, sadness written on her face, before getting up and leaving to make her preparations. The people of Petram would not like this, and removing them from the city swiftly would take a lot of effort. As Mallory began to follow, Quinn reached out and pulled her over to the side.

"Watch him, please," he said, thinking of Nes. "He is so eager to see life returned to the land, I fear he has blinded himself to the threat that stalks him from the shadows."

Mallory nodded and said, "Don't worry about us. I mistrust the Masters as much as you do. I will do my best to keep his eyes open."

Quinn thanked her and began to walk away but she turned him back to her.

"We aren't finished."

She had an intensity about her that he hadn't ever seen before.

"Don't be reckless."

"I won't," he answered automatically.

"I mean it, Quinn," she said, unconvinced. "Never mind the fact you are about to come face to face with a god, you are going to see Levy again. Don't act like that isn't scaring you. It's okay to feel guilty about what happened, though I don't think you should.

"Don't let that distract you when you see him again. I refuse to have to tell Ashe about your death when she returns." Tears began to form in the corners of her eyes as she finished. Quinn smiled, truly thankful for her friendship.

"I promise," he said. "I will not let myself be killed by my doubts."

She looked back at him unconvinced but left it at that.

"Be safe," he said, heading after Nes.

He watched her go, knowing in his heart that if they both survived the coming trials, neither of them would be the same.

CHAPTER 12

ANDRA

The Abyssillian people were hard at work, preparing to leave everything in their meager lives behind. The call went up soon after the counsel dispersed and Andra saw to it that every citizen was accounted for.

Despite the myriad of protests she received, none could argue once it was clear just what was coming for their city. She hoped to be on the road by dawn tomorrow and far from the threat that came for her city.

She sat on the roof of the domed palace, watching the commotion under the haze of grey that made up the sky of the Wastes. Tears fell from her eyes, leaving clean streaks amongst the dust on her cheeks. Horacio was curled around her neck, rumbling in an attempt to cheer her up.

"May I join you?" Nes asked, squatting down beside her.

"Shouldn't you be on your way to find your treasure?" Andra asked, making no attempt to hide the fact she was crying.

"I delayed it for an hour," he said, wrapping an arm around her. "It didn't feel right to leave without saying goodbye."

At his words, another sob escaped unbidden from her lips.

"I don't like that word," she said, still not meeting his eye. She knew if she did, the tears would fully come again.

"What word?" Nes asked though he sounded a little choked up as well.

"Goodbye," she repeated in a whisper. "It is too final. We said goodbye to Sen. I don't want to say goodbye to you."

Now she looked at him, allowing the water to fall from her eyes again.

"This mission of yours, I don't like it. I can't help but feel like it's a trap. Mallory feels as though it is a trap. Quinn feels as though it is a trap. He grew up with these people Nes. If his instincts are screaming at him, we should listen."

He looked down, refusing to meet her eyes again.

"I know. I'm not blind to the risks involved." He sounded defensive. "I'm not going into this thinking the Masters are our friends. I can hear the lust in their voices when they speak of the artifact." Now he did look at her, filled with a mixture of determination and stubbornness.

"But I am strong. And Mallory will be with us as well. If they try to pull anything, we will smack them down."

"I know you are," Andra said, frustrated he was so set on this course. "But it worries me you were willing to leave our home undefended to run off on this quest.

"It makes it seem as though you aren't thinking about anything outside of what could be. We don't even know that this artifact exists. I don't want to lose you Nes. I can't lose you."

"You won't," he smiled at her, lifting her chin, and pressing his lips to hers. "I promise."

He stood up, making his way back towards the stairs leading to the ground. "Be safe and lead them well." He shot her a smile, His white teeth contrasting his bronzed skin. "When you return, this land will be lush and full of bounty."

She sat on the roof long after he had gone until the moon was high in the sky; her knees tucked up to her chest. Horacio glowed with fire in his belly, acting as a furnace to keep her warm under the chilly night air.

Tomorrow, she would lead the entirety of her people from the Wastes for the first time in known history. She shuttered, feeling as though they would never return.

CHAPTER 13

LEND

The sound of hammering steel rang throughout the city. Fresh lumber was stacked neatly to the side of buildings, giving off a crisp, pungent smell. Lend took a deep breath in, holding the aroma in his nose before releasing it.

He loved the smell of freshly chopped wood. It reminded him of civilization, a luxury he was happy to have back in his life. With the Tower claimed by the good guys, he set off with Bartimaeus on a mission to bring people together; a truly noble cause, he felt. He had not always felt that way, however.

Growing up in a large town near the Wastes meant the lands around his home his people relied on for trade were often poached. This led to a deep distrust of the Abyssillians, which had been ingrained within him from an early age. It was a distrust that stayed with him through most of his early life.

That changed the night the dead attacked. He was sharp of mind and was no fool when it came to military tactics. It was because of his tactical mind he climbed the ranks in the first place. So, it was easy for him to see that had the Abyssillian people not come to their aid, they would have been wiped out, without question. Even still, he was hesitant to change his ways.

REALM WALKER

The Abyssillian leader, the young man in the skeletal mask, chilled him. It was as if he cast a shadow twice as long as his body should have allowed. Yet Commander Ashelia had trusted him without question, and so Lend had worked hard to swallow his prejudices and accept that his closed-minded way of thinking may have been wrong.

Once he managed to do so, a whole new world of purpose and pride opened to him. He and Bart saw to it a larger selection of goods began making their way out to the Wastes. Despite the leaders of human villages and outposts shutting them down, the general populace heard the stories of the brave people of the Wastes coming to their aid in a time of great need.

They began opening their hearts to their plights. When Bart got sick of being stonewalled by those with the power to enact change, Lend came up with the brilliant plan he found himself currently hard at work on. If they could not bring goods to the Abyssillians, then they would have to bring the Abyssillians to the goods. None of humanity's leaders were willing to open their gates to an entire civilization, however.

Lucky for him, he knew a good plot of land with the right amount of fixing up would be perfect. With the promise of pay and shelter, as well as the chance to repay the Abyssillians for their help, finding bodies to put his plan into action had been easy as well.

Partway through seeing their plan come to fruition, Bartimaeus had become restless. He trusted Lend to finish what they started, and left to go live the rest of his days in a manner he felt was more fit.

Knowing him, that was probably drinking mead and swinging his sword at tree stumps. The old man was a warrior through and through. For a while Bart kept in touch, sending letters with birds so he could be kept up on progress, but over the last year, they had become less and less frequent. He hoped the old codger hadn't kicked the bucket. He made a mental note to go and visit once work here was done.

As if willing his thoughts into being, a loud trill brought his attention to the skies. He looked up to see a winged shadow descending upon him. He reached out his arm, giving the old, grey hawk a place to perch.

He knew hawks were quite intelligent, but it still amazed him that Bartimaeus had managed to teach the creature how to find Lend specifically, considering he had never seen the bird before the first ever letter arrived.

With deft fingers, he untied a scrap of parchment from the bird's leg, lifting his arm back into the air so it could once again take flight. Likely it would snack on bugs or mice in the forest to the east before returning home.

He unrolled the parchment and read the few hastily scribbled words. *Trouble in Wastes. Goodbye, friend.*

The first words were a call to action. The only thing in the Wastes was Petram, the home of the Abyssillians. If there was trouble there, it meant they would likely be on the move. Their schedule would have to be hastily advanced. They weren't fully ready for long-term living just yet, but the buildings were good enough to shelter in for the time being.

The second sentence hit Lend harder than he cared to admit. In their time together leading the army towards the Tower, they sparred repeatedly, both verbally and physically. What started as dislike, however, had turned to respect as time went on. After the war, that respect turned into friendship.

If the old warrior was saying goodbye, it meant he wouldn't be around to see this plan of theirs to its completion. He bowed his head and did a quick salute to the man, his fist pressed to his heart, before turning swiftly and marching toward his command post.

He needed to figure out the best way to approach this. He doubted the Abyssillian people would be welcomed into their lands with open arms. The leadership still opposed such actions. It would be best to try and meet them at the border, to guide them here. That was easier said than done though.

The border of the Wastes was vast and there were many places they could cross. Bartimaeus left no description of the troubles they were facing, the scrap of paper the bird carried was far too small for such detail, so he was left trying to use logic to decide where best to go.

In the end, he sent out three scouts to cover three different zones of the border, while deciding to head to the northern zone himself. He wanted to be the one to meet the Abyssillians, as a somewhat recognizable face would do more to calm their likely frayed nerves than a stranger's would.

He had to do his best to cover as much land as possible. He sent the others to key towns along the borders, hoping to intercept the party as it tried to cross over. There were no major towns to the north, but it was a path they had walked before when marching toward the Tower. If they needed to flee into an unknown land, he felt it likely they would at least travel a road they had walked in the past.

With haste he set off, leaving instructions for his second-in-command to work as fast as they could while keeping the craftsmanship to an acceptable level. Should all go well, the Abyssillians would be home before they knew it.

CHAPTER 14

QUINN

Talius and Quinn stood at the main entrance to Petram, waiting for their guests to arrive. The black leather jerkin he adorned hung just past his knees, the ends flapping in the abnormally strong winds. It was as if the weather knew of the conflict to come, and had amped itself up in anticipation. His sword was strapped to his back, the pommel sticking up over his right shoulder.

After the war for the Tower, the smiths in Petram fashioned him a new blade as a thank-you for moving them to action. It was an act that triggered the beginning of the new treasures as they found their way out to them. Though he felt the resources used in it were far too rich to waste on him, they insisted on creating the most beautiful weapon he had ever held.

The blade was straight and narrow, sharp on only one side, and made from Damascus steel, inlaid with crushed obsidian, giving it an intricate black pattern. The sharpened edge drew blood with no effort, yet sturdy and able to withstand blow after blow without dulling.

The hilt was made from the same steel and wrapped tightly with black drakon hide. Bands of silver crisscrossed along it, a stark contrast to the blade itself. It was tipped with a simple silver pommel, form-fitted to the hilt.

The sky was grey as usual, lighting the world around him in muted color. He was so used to fighting with a mask perched on his face, it felt strange now to feel the breeze against his cheek. He rolled his neck for the thousandth time, trying to work out his nerves.

"Remember," Talius said, voice solid and unwavering. "Only use the power you know you can. Leave the god to me. If we get separated and you find yourself overwhelmed, call out to me." He stood straight, shoulders back and eyes narrowed into the distance.

He still wore his burnt orange Master robes, apparently feeling as though armor to fight a god was unnecessary. He held an old oak staff in his hands, the ends tipped with what looked like weighted brass. As far as weapons went, his appeared to have seen better days; but Quinn knew how deadly he could be with it.

Quinn nodded; eyes locked on the presence he was finally able to feel in the near distance. He hated feeling so weak. He grew far too used to relying on the power of Chaos in his fights, and now that he was limited in its use, it felt as though a limb had been chopped off.

He was still able to channel some of it, enough to enhance his speed and strength, and to cushion some of the hits he took. However, he doubted it was enough to keep him in a fight for long against a god. He hoped that however Levy managed to avoid the Underworld, it stripped him of some of his strength as well. Considering he was walking with a god, Quinn highly doubted it.

As for Talius, Quinn had no idea how he expected to keep pace. The man was pushing sixty at least, and though he was a very good teacher with a lot of knowledge, he doubted that translated to fighting prowess the likes to match a deity.

Talius was always closed off when Quinn tried to bring up his past. In the time he'd known him, he'd only managed to get the man to spill small details. He had known Hestia on a personal enough basis to have called her friend.

That was interesting. Yet, when pushed to elaborate further, the man clammed up, changing the subject back to Quinn and his training. Normally that would raise plenty of red flags within him, but Quinn was desperate for his tutelage following their conversation of the storm that was to come.

So far, the man was nothing but good to him, seemingly caring about his struggles and awakening his potential. Quinn felt bad that after three years he hadn't improved as much as he'd hoped.

"They're coming." Talius cut into his self-deprecating thoughts. That had become a habit in the last three years as well. Even more so than it had already been. He could sense Chaos laughing deep in the back of his mind. He shook his head, clearing his thoughts and focusing on the power that was cresting the horizon.

Two figures sauntered into view, their armor extravagant in the lifeless world around them. The man on the left was tall and toned, his bronze skin offset with pale scars. His hair was black and cropped short, a style found common amongst any army.

"Ares," Talius grumbled, apprehension evident in his voice for the first time. "That's rotten luck."

"You've met him before?" Quinn asked, shocked that Talius was able to identify him on sight.

"We've met," Talius said, his words clipped with no explanation following.

Quinn wanted to push more, but stopped when he looked at the person walking at Ares' side. Up to this point, he was hoping Bartimaeus was mistaken and he had simply seen someone who looked similar to Levy. Perhaps even another god.

As silly as it sounded, Quinn would have preferred that. Alas, the man walking next to the god was without a doubt, Levy. Quinn's heart hammered in his chest, his breathing becoming short and fast.

The last time he'd seen Levy, he was falling, wide-eyed towards the lava below. Now he stood before him again, looking healthier than Quinn had ever seen him. His muscles were larger and more defined, and his brown eyes filled with life.

"Easy." Talius steadied him, sensing his breathing falling out of sync. "This is a fight you have fought many times before. Shut your emotions away until after it is done."

Quinn shut his eyes for a moment, taking a deep breath and centering himself. It would do no good to lose control now. When he opened them again, the two were much closer. Ares looked as though he were angry at what awaited them. Levy wore a sneer, staring straight at Quinn.

They stopped five yards away, glaring at the empty city behind them.

"What's the matter, Quinn?" Levy called out, breaking the silence first. "You look like you've seen a ghost."

His glare was intense, burning holes into Quinn. Before he could respond, Ares shot Levy a look, wiping the smile from the youth's face.

"Still doing the bidding of the gods?" Quinn asked. "Some things never change." Leave it to Levy to rile him up, despite the anxiety that was shooting through him like lightning.

Levy started at the comment but Ares spoke before Levy could respond.

"You were alerted to our coming." His voice was deep and melodic. Quinn found it oddly soothing, despite the undertone of danger within it. "The old man?"

Talius took a step forward.

"Petram is emptied, Ares. There is nothing here for you. Go back to Olympus where you belong."

Ares' eye twitched, clearly perturbed at the Master's tone.

"On the contrary, Talius, both of our targets stand before us. How kind it was of you to deliver yourselves."

Well, that answers one question, Quinn thought. He wasn't fully surprised to be considered a target after his involvement in Zeus' plans for the Tower, but he was curious as to what they would want with Talius. The mystery surrounding the Master continued to deepen.

The god looked over at Quinn for the first time. He regarded him with disinterest, as though he were a fly buzzing around his head.

"You get one chance to surrender without conflict. I can end your life in an instant and you will feel no pain. My father can be forgiving should you let him." He looked back to Talius, regarding him with a cool anger. "You, however, are to be brought in front of Lord Zeus to answer for your crimes against Olympus."

"I decline," Talius rumbled, brandishing his staff, in front of him and saying nothing further.

"It wasn't an invitation," Ares hissed, pulling his blade from its sheath.

The god of war's blade was abhorrent, yet strangely beautiful.

The steel was somehow dyed a deep crimson, resembling fresh blood. The guard was black as night and fashioned after a boar's head. The grip was wrapped in black leather to match. A ruby skull glinted in the pommel.

The god ducked into a ready stance blade held wide at his side. Without warning he lunged, faster than Quinn could track. Ignoring Talius, he swung wide for Quinn, attempting to sever him in two in a mere instant.

From his left, Talius' staff arced down, knocking the blade low and trapping it against the dirt. Talius spun, catching Quinn with his foot, and kicked with inhuman strength, sending him flying back through the gateway and into the empty town.

"After him!" Ares cried out, turning his attention back to Talius.

Quinn looked up, having used what power he could to shield himself from the impact he took. Levy was charging through the gateway, his spear held high, grinning a murderous smile.

He got shakily to his feet and turned, running deeper into the empty streets, away from the god who had just tried to end his life.

CHAPTER 15

LEVY

Finally, after three years of intense training, Levy came face to face again with Quinn. To his utter amazement, he looked scared. Quinn was many things, but being scared of battle was not one of them.

Yet as he raised his eyes to his friend, anxiety and, was that guilt? It was! Fear and guilt were written all over his face. And then he almost lost his revenge in an instant. Ares tried to strike before anyone knew what was happening.

Had it not been for the old man in the Master's robes Levy had never seen before, Quinn would have been cut in half as if he were nothing more than a sack of meat. Even more surprising, the man then proceeded to punt Quinn back into the city as if he weighed nothing.

"After him!" Ares yelled, now locked in combat with the staff-wielding master.

He didn't need to be told twice. He had been waiting, salivating even, for this chance to exact his revenge. Quinn, of all people, had beaten him in the volcano. He'd dropped him into lava as if he were nothing. Quinn claimed the Tower, though it was Ashe who sat in it now. He was tired of losing to Quinn.

He charged in through the gates of the city, spear raised high above his head, looking to end the fight in an instant. To his surprise, Quinn was already back on his feet. The mask was destroyed by Ashe after Chaos took control of his body, yet somehow, he managed to cushion a blow that should have at the very least, knocked all the wind from his lungs. He saw Levy coming and responded in the most un-Quinn-like way possible.

"Are you RUNNING?!" Levy roared in disbelief. Who was this coward before him, and what had he done with the warrior he'd once called friend?

Levy sprinted after him, pushing essence into his legs to strengthen each step. As he gained on him, he pulled his spear back, aiming the tip right between Quinn's shoulder blades.

"Not so fast now, are you?" Levy taunted, launching the weapon with all his might.

Just before the spear made an impact, a small crackle of black energy shot out of Quinn's feet, catapulting him onto the side of the nearest building. Another crackle exploded from the foot on the building, and Quinn gracefully twisted his body over the top of the spear, allowing it to pass mere centimeters underneath him. He landed in a soft crouch, his hand on the hilt of his blade, eyes locked on Levy now.

"You were saying?" he smiled.

Levy couldn't help smiling back at the jab. This was the warrior he knew growing up. No fear in his eyes, adrenaline coursing through his body, adding barbs to every taunt.

Quinn pulled his blade and ran at Levy, now realizing he was weaponless. As the warrior closed in on him, Levy pumped strength into his legs and jumped, hurdling over the attack and landing at a run. He crouched and pulled his spear back into his hands, turning just in time to block a vicious vertical strike from splitting him in two.

Quinn stayed on the attack, relentlessly raining blow after blow down on the shaft of Levy's spear. Levy continued to parry the blows away, waiting for a chance to strike. Fortunately, though he still could not entirely control it, Levy managed the ability to pull chunks of Hestia's essence into his arms, keeping them from becoming tired at the impact.

As Quinn became more and more winded, Levy took the chance to strike, slapping Quinn's blade away and jabbing out with the butt of the spear. Quinn tried to pull away from the attack but was too slow, catching the tip of it on his lower jaw.

He staggered back, trying to shake off the daze from the strike. Levy, not wanting to lose his advantage, pressed forward slicing multiple cuts toward Quinn's unguarded body. His friend was sluggish, still reeling from the hit he took to his jaw; a bruise already beginning to form.

Though he dodged most of the strikes, deflecting a few others, more still struck home, opening mostly shallow gashes along his arms and chest. Blood began to seep from the wounds, staining the leather an even deeper black.

"What's the matter, Quinn? Don't have a Primordial to save you this time?" Levy laughed, kicking his boot into his chest, and sending him sprawling backward. "No damsel in distress to spur your strength?"

Quinn got back up on a knee, gritting his teeth against the pain.

"Thought it was only fair," he panted. "To give you a chance this time."

Levy smirked. "Scoreboard Quinn. I beat you at the fortress, remember?"

"I dropped you in lava," he replied, wincing at the words as they left his lips.

Levy raised his arms, shrugging. "Did you though?"

Quinn got back to his feet, sword held out in front of him.

"You talk too much," He crouched, ready for the next onslaught. "If you keep letting me catch my breath, you'll be one and two."

Levy raised his spear, looking to finish the fight on the next pass. To his shock, black energy erupted from Quinn, propelling him forward faster than he expected. His sword slipped inside Levy's guard, opening a cut just beneath his eye. Levy spun around but Quinn was faster still, throwing another stab towards his chest. With all the power he could muster, he launched himself backward, tumbling as he hit the ground before regaining his feet.

"Careful now," Quinn said, his voice slightly doubled. "You

tumble too hard while holding that spear and you're likely to stick yourself."

"Oh?" Levy asked, hiding the fear at the change in Quinn's voice. The last time he heard that voice, he watched Janus get ripped into a million pieces. "Is our Primordial friend going to come out and play after all?"

Quinn froze his advance, eyes widening. Levy took the hesitation as a chance to strike, lunging forward and punching the blade of his spear straight at Quinn's chest.

CHAPTER 16

QUINN

Not like this, Quinn thought, doing everything in his power to dampen the amount of energy pouring out of him. He hadn't even noticed how much of Chaos' energy he was using until Levy mentioned the double voice.

Now he couldn't stop it from pouring out of him. Fear rose within as he realized he'd left himself open to a strike by Levy. The tip of his golden spear was hurtling toward his chest, and he was out of position to stop it.

Without prompting it, black energy flooded from every pore, creating a cloak around him, and stopping the spear inches from hitting home. Tendrils whipped back and forth as if blown by the wind, reaching out at anything within the vicinity.

Stop, Quinn commanded internally, doing everything he could to pull the energy back inside himself.

What was it the girl said to you again? Bottle something inside for long enough and it is bound to explode? The voice of Chaos mocked gleefully inside his head.

The mass of energy locked onto Levy, whipping forward as the tendrils attempted to grab him. There was a look of panic on his face as he slashed away anything that came close to him.

"Get back," Quinn called out to him, trying desperately to regain control.

Levy looked up at him, bewildered.

Quinn supposed it must seem odd, locked in a fight to the death only to have the opponent advise them to do something that would prevent them from dying.

The tendrils had minds of their own, slamming hard into everything around them. Within seconds, the surrounding buildings were turned into debris. Levy was a blur of gold, doing everything he could to keep the power at bay.

Quinn felt lost. He had lost control entirely. Talius warned him if he felt it slipping, to call out for him, but he hadn't even noticed until it was too late. He tried every technique he was taught to rein the energy in and bring it back under control.

Deep breaths, centering himself, focusing on a single point in front of him. Nothing worked. The entire time the voice of Chaos was cackling in the back of his head.

It will not be long now, little hero. Your body will belong to me again soon enough.

Quinn was desperate. He did not want to be a burden upon this world. He fought so hard to protect it, losing everything in the process, only to become the very thing he tried to protect it from. He could not, would not, allow this to take control. He would sooner die.

With all the will he had left, he reached out, imagining himself snaring Chaos, bit by bit, and reeling him back inside. It felt as though he were Atlas holding up the weight of the world, but little by little he managed to take back control. He knew it wouldn't last long, but he didn't need it to. With the last of his strength, he raised his head and yelled, "LEVY!"

CHAPTER 17

LEVY

He was fighting a nightmare come to life. The shadowy tendrils snaked all around him, attempting to find an opening. It took everything Levy had to keep up, slashing them away as they got close. He knew if even one managed to grab hold of him, it was over.

The problem was that he was starting to get tired. Quinn seemed to have an infinite amount of these things, whereas Levy's energy was limited. Even in the wake of all his training, Quinn still managed to outclass him. Though at this point Levy wasn't sure if he was even fighting Quinn.

He had barely spoken since the energy first came bursting forth, instead looking as though he were fighting his own internal battle. At one point Quinn even shouted for him to get back, as though he hadn't been trying to kill him moments before.

"LEVY!" Quinn shouted, pleading. The tendrils recoiled a few inches, allowing Levy a moment of respite. He caught his breath and watched Quinn suspiciously as Quinn stood still, arms out wide as if he were inviting him in for a hug.

"Levy please!" he shouted again.

"Do you take me for an idiot?" Levy shouted back, staring at the tendrils frozen in the air. He imagined himself taking the bait, only to be skewered from a hundred different angles as he took a step.

"I can't hold it back much longer," his friend implored, dropping in and out of his double voice. "Please," he was crying actual tears. "I don't want to be a monster, Levy."

Levy was frozen by a wave of nostalgia. An image from not so long ago drifted back to him. He and Quinn sat on the roof of the Citadel after Levy had exposed the mask to the Masters.

You aren't a monster, Levy said to his friend. He just learned of how Quinn acquired the mask. This may be the Fates at work, but I assure you one thing, you are not a monster.

After all that happened between them, Levy still remembered that conversation as clear as day. He looked back at the mass of black, swirling energy engulfing Quinn now, and decided he couldn't let it continue. Despite all that had come between them, the rage and bitterness that he felt towards Quinn, he did not want to see things end like this.

He stood up, gripping his spear hard so that his knuckles turned white. Slowly he advanced, somehow knowing he had time. He stopped in front of his friend, holding his gaze for a moment. Surprisingly, Quinn found some peace and was looking up at him now with gratitude.

"You're not a monster," Levy said, surprised to find he meant it with every fiber of his being. Then, without hesitation, he lifted his spear, ramming it directly through Quinn's heart.

Quinn slumped forward; his limp body held up by the weapon's shaft. The black cloak that swirled around him retreated within.

"Goodbye, my friend."

As he began to pull his spear from Quinn, the body began to shake. At first, it was a low vibration, but it swiftly increased in magnitude until Levy felt his entire arm shaking. Energy burst forth from the puncture, engulfing Quinn in black flame.

A raspy voice filled the air, howling with glee as the flame intensified. Levy tried to shake the body from the end of his spear, fearing it would begin to spread up the shaft. Then, as quickly as it started, it stopped, leaving nothing behind, not even a body. All that remained in the abandoned city was the crumbling wreckage of their fight and a very out-of-place silence.

CHAPTER 18

MALLORY

Mallory tried to ignore the sweat trickling between her shoulder blades. For a land that never saw sunlight, it was ridiculously hot in the Wastes. At least the flat and arid landscape made travel easy. The parched, cracked planes provided little in the way of sight-seeing during their journey, but she preferred it to speaking with the Masters.

Darrik tried to make small talk with her early on, but she was still rather cross with him for his mistreatment of Quinn. He had gotten the message after the third time she "accidentally" stepped on his heel, causing him to stumble on the chalky earth.

As for Enkar, he could barely keep himself upright, let alone make any meaningful conversation. The small, rotund Master had to walk twice as fast to keep up with the rest of the party, and the amount of sweat that poured from his head would have provided the Wastes enough water to finally grow some plant life.

"I still don't understand why we couldn't ride any of your tamed drakons," he whined in his typical nasally voice. His face was stained red, though whether it was from the sun or the exertion, Mallory didn't know.

"Be thankful we didn't," she said, cheerfully. "It would have likely mistaken you for a tomato and gobbled you up."

Nes shot her a pleading look which screamed *behave*, but to her surprise, Cyrus let out a throaty chuckle.

"You are looking rather scarlet my friend." He added, throwing a brief wink in her direction.

Mallory was still unsure what to make of Cyrus. On one hand, she didn't trust him as far as she could throw him. If he just acted like Darrik and Enkar, she would feel so much better about her mistrust of him.

Yet, on the other hand, he was incredibly down to earth and, loathe as she was to admit it, rather likable. He never raised his voice, speaking rather gently even. He treated Nes as well as he did the Masters, despite his Abyssillian heritage—something neither of the other Masters even tried to hide their disdain. And he made for excellent conversation during the long trek to the ruins. He even treated Quinn with respect over the brief days they spent together.

Quinn. She was still worried sick for her friend. He just had not been the same person since arriving back in Petram. He still had the same gentle voice, and his kindness towards others hadn't changed, but his self-confidence was in tatters.

She tried her best to give him space the first couple of nights she woke to his screaming, but eventually, she just couldn't stand it anymore. Her heart ached for him knowing how he was suffering. She loved him in a purely platonic sense.

When she first met him, she could see right through the cool and aloof persona he tried to wear. He attempted to be serious, yet as soon as he spoke to Nes and Andra, that shell disintegrated and his pride and warmth shone through.

The pure love and adoration in his eyes the first time she saw him look at Ashe just confirmed what she already thought of him. He was just a genuinely good guy. Now he was a shell of that. His eyes held paranoia and fear. He jumped at the shadows he once commanded and walked hunched over as if at any moment something might strike him.

At first, she was concerned Talius was mistreating him, but she quickly dismissed that hypothesis when she realized the only time she saw glimpses of his former self was when they talked quietly in the corners.

"He's going to be fine," Nes said from beside her. She hadn't even noticed him drop back from his conversation with the Masters.

"Is it that obvious?" she asked, internally scolding herself for dropping her guard.

"You've looked back towards Petram about a million times since we left, always with the same worried look on your face. If you're not careful, those worry lines are going to stick you know."

He said it with humor, though quickly dropped his smile when she didn't share it. "Relax, Mallory. This is Quinn we're talking about. No matter what's been happening with him, he is the strongest warrior I know. We both know he is not going to die before he sees Ashe again."

Mallory released the breath she hadn't realized she was holding.

"Well, it's not like there's anything I can do about it now." She surrendered, trying to push the worry from her mind.

"Exactly!" Nes exclaimed, smiling as though he'd successfully cheered her up.

"What do you think we're going to find when we make it to these ruins?" she asked, trying to change the subject.

"Hopefully our people's saving grace," Nes responded, cheerfully. "Imagine the look on their faces when they come home and everything is green!"

"I hope that happens," Mallory replied, not wishing to trample on the young man's dreams.

The truth was she had major doubts about this mission. There were so many unanswered questions they didn't have time to sort out before being hurried out the door. The timing of the god's visit to Petram was also suspicious to her.

The Masters hoped to be on their way well before now, but Andra continuously held them up, asking a stream of never-ending questions about the artifact and what the Masters intended for it. Every time Cyrus pushed to be on their way, Andra delayed further.

Quinn and Talius showing up was also likely an unwelcome surprise. They had to be brought into the plan and have their questions answered. Enkar especially grew impatient, though Mallory was unsure how much of that was because of the delay compared to the presence of Quinn.

It was likely paranoia, but she couldn't shake the feeling as though the god pushing them out the door was more than mere coincidence. Yet more than anything, one question still burned in the back of her mind. It was something she deeply regretted not thinking to ask before they had set out.

"Nes," she lowered her voice so only he could hear her. "Why do you think the Masters came to us in the first place?"

Nes furrowed his brow, tilting his head in thought.

"What do you mean?" he asked. "They wanted to find the artifact."

"Yes, but why come to you and Andra about that? The Abyssillians live out here in the Wastes, but it's not as though you own the land in the same way a kingdom owns theirs. You don't have multiple civilizations spread throughout it."

He squinted at her, still not following along.

Thank the gods he has Andra, she thought, silently admonishing herself for her choice of verbiage. That would be a vernacular habit she would have to work on breaking. She tried again, spelling it out for him as directly as she could.

"If they wanted an artifact out here, and you do not own the Wastes, why did they feel the need to come and meet with us instead of just going and looking on their own?"

Nes' eyes widened in understanding.

"Oh! Probably because they didn't know where in the Wastes to look. We may not own the land, but we know it."

"Yes, but they have maps as well, do they not?" She countered. "They could have circled landmarks on their maps and checked them one at a time. Or, for the sake of argument let's say they couldn't and they needed your maps and your expertise. Once it was decided where to look, what stopped them from going out and getting it when we were not paying attention?"

He let out an exasperated sigh.

"Fair trade, obviously. They are opening a dialogue between our people. Honestly, you and Andra need to let this whole suspicion thing go. They have been nothing but kind to us, and you both treat them like the enemy. Amazingly, they haven't cut ties already."

Mallory rubbed her temples, trying to relieve the headache she felt swiftly approaching.

"That furthers my point!" she proclaimed. "If we are treating them so poorly, why stick around once they have the information they seek? Also, I won't deny Cyrus has been kind, but you can't tell me Darrik and Enkar have. Enkar complains non-stop about the living conditions in the palace, and Darrik looks like he wants to murder Quinn every time they are in the same room together."

They walked another few minutes in silence, Nes deep in thought. The Masters were a good twenty yards ahead of them, heads huddled together as they walked, lost in a conversation of their own.

Or scheming, Mallory thought.

The more she spoke her questions out loud, the less trust she found she truly had for them.

After another half mile or so of silence, Nes sighed. Nobody could say Nes was the brightest person in the room. He was strong on the battlefield and had a natural charisma about him that made people listen when he spoke. Critical thinking, however, was not his strong suit.

"I don't know what to tell you, Mallory," he finally said, looking at the Masters as he spoke. "You're probably right. I am probably too naïve in this, and too trusting for my own good. If you'd like, I can raise your concerns with them when we stop for the night, though I feel as though if they do mean us some kind of harm, that may put us in a sticky situation before we're ready."

"Are we ever ready for a trap to be sprung?" She replied. "Seems like a pretty awful trap if so."

He gave that a half-hearted grin.

"If your people were suffering, wouldn't you do anything you could to solve it?" He said, looking at her with pleading eyes.

She realized with a start he needed her to say yes. This entire time he was wearing a mask of absolute confidence. She thought him naïve, yet she realized now he was simply desperate. He loved his people dearly and was willing to sacrifice everything for a chance to fix their problems. The realization sent a small tremor through her.

"I'm sorry, Nes," She said. "This whole time we have doubted your every decision, thinking you were being too short-sighted when you have been carrying the weight of the entire city on your shoulders."

He must have been thankful to have gotten some validation, because his power was leaking out a bit, slightly shaking the earth. Actually, he was shaking the earth quite a bit.

"Nes? You're quaking." She pointed down to the loose rocks, dancing around the cracks in the plane.

"I'm what?" he asked, realizing the tremors for the first time. "That isn't me."

"What do you mean it's not...DOWN!" She roared to the Masters, grabbing Nes' arm and pulling him to the dirt.

The ground split apart propelling rocks and dirt high into the sky. If the grey haze of the Wastes hadn't already blocked out the sun, the maelstrom of debris certainly would have. Shards of earth and rubble were flung through the air, creating a very dangerous hazard. A tempest of dust and gravel blanketed the travelers.

The behemoth that burst forth was a sight as awe-inspiring as it was terrifying.

"Skorpios!" Cyrus bellowed as if Mallory wasn't already staring at the beast.

The giant scorpion monster stood at a height of at least twelve feet and stretched a staggering twenty feet from pincer to tail. Its body was covered in a thick, glistening exoskeleton which gave off a dark, metallic hue.

A massive, chitinous head was adorned with a pair of menacing black eyes that constantly scanned its surroundings, alerted to the movement of its prey. Razor-sharp, serrated mandibles capable of crushing bone and tearing flesh lined each side of its face, next to two large, venomous fangs.

Perhaps the most terrifying aspect of all was the tail. It was elongated and segmented, already raised in an offensive posture. A bulbous stinger protruded from the end of it, dripping with a potent, green venom.

"Get back!" Nes yelled to the Masters, pulling his axe from the strap on his back.

Mallory unsheathed her sword, dropping into a defensive stance. She fought many different types of monsters in her days, though most of the time Ashe at her side, ready to burn them to a crisp.

Cyrus and Darrik sprinted back towards the warriors, though

Enkar's stubby legs couldn't carry him quite as fast. The monster reared its tail back, poised to strike at the lagging prey.

"RUN!" Cyrus called back to him, not stopping for even a second to help.

Nes and Mallory charged forward, attempting to draw the scorpion's attention. It spared them no thought, instead crouching low to the ground. Its beady eyes were locked on the little Master.

With a sudden burst of speed, the giant scorpion lunged forward, covering the distance between itself and Enkar in an instant. Its tail, tipped with the vicious stinger, arced through the air like a deadly projectile. The enormous barb glimmered in the dim light, poised to pierce flesh and bone.

A triumphant hiss filled the air as the tail found its mark. Enkar was impaled by the massive stinger, piercing through his torso with brutal force. His wail was soon replaced with a choked gurgling as the Master's saliva began to foam from the venom. With smooth motion, the Skorpios pulled its tail back, raising the punctured body into the air.

Mallory watched in horror as one swift flick was all it took to dislodge the body from the stinger. For a moment it seemed as though Enkar was suspended in mid-air, before his corpse came crashing down into the eager monster's open maw.

Cyrus sprinted past Mallory and Nes, pulling up a few meters away. Darrik, for his part, stopped beside them, turning to face the beast with sword drawn. Though she wasn't a fan of the man, she certainly could not call him a coward.

"Don't you have a weapon?" Mallory asked Cyrus, who now crouched low to the ground as if trying to blend in with the upturned earth.

"I am a scholar," he replied, surprisingly nonchalant given the situation.

"Then throw some books at it," Mallory grumbled, turning back to face the armored scorpion.

"Any plans, guys?" Nes asked with a slight waver in his voice. "Because something tells me it wants seconds."

Sure enough, the Skorpios had finished chewing and turned its sights back on the party before it. Its excited chittering pulsated from its mouth as it started scuttling closer, kicking up little clouds of dust with each step its eight legs took.

"We need to cut off the tail. Its pincers are dangerous but that stinger is deadly," Darrik said, positioning himself in front of the oncoming monster. "Your axe would be best for the job. If you can get enough raw power behind your swing, it shouldn't take too many chops to detach, provided you have an opening. The girl and I will distract it."

"The girl has a name," Mallory grumbled, sidling up next to the Master.

"And if the girl wants to keep her name, she will help me distract the scorpion long enough for Nes to do his part," he growled back.

"Prick," she mumbled to herself.

She hated to admit it but she was impressed at how calm Darrik was in the face of not only his impending death but the death of his friend. It would have been easy to lose one's bearings under such a threat, but he stood with confidence and perhaps even a little pride as he faced the oncoming threat. Perhaps the Masters weren't all smoke after all.

"Get ready," Darrik shouted, waving his arms to draw the scorpion's attention. "Once it comes for us, try to get behind it without being seen," he ordered Nes. "Be fast or we're all done."

Nes began sliding to the side of the monster as it came within range, careful not to move too suddenly and pull its attention.

"Let me parry the stinger," Mallory offered. "You focus on keeping its attention."

Darrik grunted in acknowledgement, before bellowing a challenge and charging forward, sword at the ready.

Mallory's fight was almost over before it even began. The stinger came swiftly and it took everything she had to react in time. With a cry of her own, she dove in front of Darrik, pulling her head to the side so the venomous tip slid just past her face.

The noxious fumes of the venom were strong enough alone to nearly paralyze her. She set her feet and with both hands gripping the hilt of her sword, she twisted her upper body, slamming the metal into the armored tail. A shockwave ran up her arms, nearly causing her to drop the blade, but she succeeded in forcing the tail out of Darrik's path.

Then it was Darrik swooping in, deflecting a pincer as the scorpion tried to take advantage of her recovery. They continued this way, switching in and out and parrying every strike the monster threw at them, almost as if it were a dance. Despite never having fought together, the duo moved seamlessly, never missing a step.

Until they did.

After Mallory deflected the stinger for what felt like the hundredth time, Darrik swooped in to take the next blow. Only this time the Skorpios learned from past attempts, and struck with both pincers at once, attempting to crush the old Master between them.

Seeing what was to come, Mallory exploded forward, trying to intercept the second claw. It struck with a viciousness unlike any of the other strikes, slamming into their blades and pushing them into one another.

Mallory felt the air forcefully expel from her lungs as they collided, sending their weapons scattering from their hands in different directions. The Skorpios hissed in victory, seeing its prey defenseless. She watched in abject terror, unable to move, smashed as she was between Darrik and a pincer. The barbed tail raised in the air, poised to strike, and she knew without doubt that her end had come at last.

CHAPTER 19

NES

A piercing screech rippled across the battlefield, shaking Nes to his very core. He managed to sneak around to the side of the Skorpios without being noticed thanks to the two-pronged attack from Mallory and Darrik, however, he realized rather quickly that he'd need a new plan now that he was here.

He was meant to chop the tail off while the monster was distracted, but he couldn't do that if it wouldn't sit still. The chitinous behemoth just would not stop moving. Its steps were quick and powerful, scuttling a handful of feet away from Nes with every minor turn of its body.

Even if it stood completely still, it was relying far too heavily on stabbing at his friends with the venomous tip. Every time he swung his axe, the scorpion would twitch away and he'd miss his mark. He felt as though he were playing with a high-stakes piñata and it was driving him mad.

"Can you guys try and hold it still?" he yelled back at his compatriots. He knew it was stupid to risk grabbing the monster's attention, but they wouldn't last much longer if he didn't get results.

When he heard no response, he turned to face them. He assumed they hadn't heard him over the creature's loud clicks and squeals, but the color soon drained from his face as he realized the truth.

Mallory and Darrik were sandwiched together between the creature's claws and unconscious. It was likely the force at which they were brought together knocked them out. The scorpion's tail was raised high, ready to deliver the final blow. Nes knew he had to act fast if he wanted to save them.

He channeled his energy throughout his body, doing his best to disperse it evenly as Quinn had taught him that handful of years ago. It had been a while since he last used his Abyssillian gift, though the knowledge of how to was still present.

He tried not to rely on it often, as the immense pain he felt as it tore through him was enough to caution him away from overuse. His body was crisscrossed with scars for a reason. As the thrumming energy reached a crescendo within him, he focused on the ground beneath the monster's feet.

With a thunderous cry, he released his hold on it, pushing the energy forcefully from within. He felt his scars tear open again as warm blood trickled down his arms and legs. He cried out now in pain, feeling as though his body was shredding.

Though the pain was enough to make him want to blackout, the plan worked. The monster began to lose balance on the quaking earth, skittering back and forth to try and keep from falling. Nes lunged toward his allies, collecting them within his arms and dragging them back towards where Cyrus was hunkered down, watching the fight with keen interest.

"What now?" Cyrus asked as the quaking began to subside.

Nes turned back to his foe, a grim determination on his face.

"Now you see why I am the leader of my people."

He tightened his grip on the shaft of his axe. It was slick with the blood that ran from his arm. He would have to finish this quickly; the lethargy from his blood loss had already begun to seep in.

He walked back toward his foe, determined to finish it off. The day's light was dying now, casting a shadow over the desolate wasteland. He knew he was in for a tough fight, but the familiar weight of his battle-axe was a reassuring presence in his hand. The wind whipped through his hair, carrying with it the monster's acrid stench.

The Skorpios loomed before him, its carapace glistening under the fading light. Large pincers clacked together menacingly, its stinger swaying back and forth, ready to strike. Nes braced himself, his heart pounding with anticipation, and a touch of fear.

With a raucous screech, the scorpion lunged forward, its massive pincers aiming to smash him. He swiftly sidestepped, narrowly avoiding a crushing blow. The ground shook as the scorpion's claws crashed into the rocky terrain, sending up a cloud of dust. Nes seized the opportunity and swung his axe in a vicious vertical strike, aiming for the monster's more vulnerable underbelly.

The Skorpios was quick to retaliate, its stinger arcing through the air as it tried to push him back. Nes rolled to the side, feeling the brush of air as the poisonous barb grazed his shoulder. Ignoring the searing pain, he sprang back to his feet, determination burning in his eyes. He knew he had to press on, or everyone would die.

As the battle raged on, Nes noticed a weakness in the scorpion's movements. Each time it struck, the earth trembled beneath its weight. An idea began to form in Nes' mind; a daring plan that might just give him the upper hand if he timed it perfectly.

Nes lunged forward, closing the distance between himself and the scorpion. With a grunt of pain, he pushed more power from within, ignoring the fresh spray of blood. The ground quaked beneath their feet, rattling the scorpion's already unstable balance. Seeing its momentary weakness, Nes swung his axe with all his might, aiming for the creature's tail.

The edge connected with a resounding thud, and a spray of golden ichor erupted from the scorpion's severed appendage. The monster shrieked in agony, its scaly armor quivering. Nes felt a spike of pride that he managed to sever the scorpion's most lethal weapon, but he knew the battle was far from over.

The Skorpios, driven by pain and fury, launched a relentless counter-assault. Its pincers snapped at Nes; the sheer force behind each strike was enough to crush boulders. Nes dodged and weaved, his agility and reflexes pushed to their limits in his battered and bloody state. He knew he couldn't afford even a minor mistake.

With every swing of his axe, Nes carved deep gashes into the scorpion's armor. Darrik was right about his weapon being the best for damaging the thick carapace. The monster's ichor stained the ground, mixing with the dust and turning it into a muddy sludge.

Nes fought on, trying not to slip on the goopy earth. His muscles were burning, but his mind was focused solely on the task at hand.

Though he was making good progress on the scorpion's armor, Nes knew he had to give it one final push if he were going to fell the beast. He reached deep within himself, grasping his remaining energy, and pushed, causing the ground to rumble beneath them once again.

The Wastes split open, a deep fissure snaking its way toward the Skorpios. Nes took advantage of the distraction, lunging forward and landing a devastating blow on the creature's exposed flank. The scorpion wailed, its cries warbling through the air.

With a final surge of energy, Nes pressed his advantage, delivering a series of lightning-fast strikes, each blow precise and calculated. Piece by piece the scorpion's armor crumbled, revealing the vulnerable flesh underneath. Victory was within his grasp.

Summoning every ounce of strength left within him, Nes raised the axe high above his head. The Skorpios, sensing its impending demise, made one last desperate attempt to strike. It was still shockingly fast, despite the onslaught it received, but Nes was faster. With a primal roar, he brought the axe down with all his might, fatally cleaving the monster.

Silence descended upon the battlefield as the scorpion's lifeless body slumped to the ground. Nes lay on his back, his chest heaving, covered as much in his blood as he was the monster's viscera. He felt the burn of the monster's venom as it crept through his veins. He knew he had overused his gifts, every part of him screamed from the exertion. The battle was won, but the cost was great.

A blurry Cyrus appeared before him, looking down at him with worry etched along the lines of his face. He thought for just a moment he caught something else in the Master's eyes as well- a hungry glint. But exhaustion washed over him like a tidal wave, the weight of which forced his eyes closed until he was surrounded by only darkness.

~~~

Mallory's worried face came into view as he opened his eyes.

An off-white bandage was wrapped around her forehead, trapping a few strands of her chocolate brown hair against her face. He lay on a rough cot; a soft, orange light flickering along the walls of a canvas tent. Outside of a dull, throbbing ache, Nes' body felt surprisingly numb. He tried to sit up, but Mallory reached out and gently pushed him back down.

"Don't move just yet," she said, soothingly. "You'll rip your stitches."

Nes looked down at himself, noticing the patchwork that made up his body for the first time.

"I thought I was a goner," He said, matter-of-factly. "Between the blood loss and the venom, I didn't think I was going to wake up."

"And you wouldn't have," Cyrus' voice drifted in from somewhere nearby, "If I didn't have a lifetime medical practice as well as the materials to create an anti-venom." He walked into view.

"How did you know what to use for ingredients?" Nes asked, amazed at how quickly the Master must have had to work.

"As I said, I am a scholar." He gave Mallory a self-satisfied grin. "All anti-venoms require similar base ingredients. Having a sample of the venom on hand was also a benefit."

"Did you stitch me up as well?" He asked.

"That was me," Mallory answered, sticking her tongue out at Cyrus. "Years spent in the army require you to learn how."

"How's Darrik?" Nes realized the master was nowhere in the tent.

"He will survive," Cyrus replied, calmly. "His pride is hurt far more than he is."

"Where is he?" Mallory asked, as if she too just remembered he was gone.

"Making a gravestone in memory of Enkar I would imagine. The two were good friends. No doubt his loss will sting quite a bit."

The Master shifted his cool, brown eyes back to Nes.

"How soon until he will be strong enough to travel?"

"Surely you can't be serious." Mallory stood up, whirling around on him.

"I am quite serious," he replied. "We are near our target destination. I do not find it a mere coincidence that a Skorpios of that size was randomly here. They normally hunt the borders where they can find food."

"You think it was some sort of guardian?" Nes propped himself up onto his elbows, wincing at the pressure from the stitches.

"I think precisely that." He shrugged. "And now it is disposed of."

"Even if that were true, Nes is in no shape to press forward. It will be hard enough for him to walk, let alone fight again should we need to." Mallory had her arms crossed, squinting up at the Master.

One of the things Nes respected most about her was how fiercely protective she was of the people she cared for.

"It's fine, Mal," Nes said, swinging his legs over the side of the cot. He bit back a grunt as pain flared throughout his body. If what Cyrus said were true, they were incredibly close to their goal.

He would not let his condition stop them from reaching it. "If we run into another fight, you and Darrik can handle it. Though, I agree with what Cyrus said. I think we are out of the woods now."

"If you think we were ever in the woods, then you need to lie back down." Her words were laced with sarcasm. Mallory looked cross with him. No doubt she knew she was fighting a losing battle.

He gave her his best reassuring smile. The fact of the matter was, if she pushed hard enough to delay, or even turn back, he was in no physical position to stop her. He had to convince her that moving forward was the right thing to do.

"Honest Mal, I'll be ok. We are only a mile or so from our destination. We're so close."

She sighed, sitting down on the edge of his cot with a look of resignation.

"Fine," she didn't look happy about it. "If you're so intent on killing yourself then we can keep going." She looked back at Cyrus. "But we are waiting for morning. At least allow him the night to rest."

Cyrus nodded, satisfied with the compromise.

"Then I will bid you both a good night."

The Master made his way over to the entrance flap of the tent, lifting it and allowing the cool night air to filter through. Nes shivered in delight as it ran over him, cooling his heated body.

Once the Master was gone, he looked back to Mallory, who was staring at the floor. Her brows were drawn in worry as she chewed on her lower lip. He felt bad for pushing her to go along with this.

Logically, he knew it was stupid to push himself in his condition. He wondered if he would still be fighting as hard to continue if the roles were reversed. It was easy to make that decision when it was his own body on the line.

"I promise I will be careful, Mal." He patted her on the shoulder, trying to be reassuring. "If another fight breaks out, I'll hang back with Cyrus. But you said yourself when Levy stole the Orb of Hades from the northern vault, it was only Cerberus guarding the artifact.

"I think it's fair to assume there would be similar defenses here. Anything more and it would probably have attracted attention to it long before we ever came traipsing about."

Mallory nodded. She was not convinced but appeared resigned to the fact she had lost this fight. She stood up from the cot and walked over to the far side of the tent, rummaging through a bag before choosing a glass bottle with a tan, cork stopper in it.

Returning to him, she sat so that his back was to her. The cork was removed with a *pop* and a light, amber substance poured out onto her hands. It smelled of cedar and fire—a strange but not unwelcome combination.

"What's that?" He asked, uncomfortable with the glimmer in her eye.

She smirked at him, raising her hand to her nose and inhaling.

"If you insist on moving forward with your injuries, you need to be able to walk, as well as keep yourself safe from infection." She reached forward, no longer trying to hide the satisfaction she felt.

"Mal," Nes' voice shook. "What is that?"

"Antiseptic, as well as a numbing agent," she replied, overly sweet. "And yes, it will sting."

Nes gulped, turning so she could apply the liquid to his skin. It burned like fire as it encountered his many wounds. A wave of icy chill followed, numbing the stabbing pains he felt anytime he moved, and soothing his aching muscles.

It was as if a tug-of-war was being fought between the two sensations, neither gaining an inch of ground. It was with immense relief that he eventually nodded off.

When they awoke the next morning, he genuinely felt better. He was still sore and tender, each twist and turn of his body sent little ripples of pain throughout him, but he was able to keep from lagging far behind the group. They ate a simple breakfast of dried meats, washed down by a couple of swigs of cold, mint tea Cyrus brought along, before packing up their camp and continuing forward under the typical grey gloom of the Wastes.

Not long after they set off, Darrik came running back from scouting ahead, excitement dripping into every word.

"Ruins ahead!" He waved, pointing at a smudge on the horizon.

Nes smiled, trying his best to increase his pace without overdoing it. The future of his people lay in the near distance. He was almost there. He imagined Petram, sitting amongst a lush, green world of plants and trees.

The thought was so foreign and exciting, that it made him shiver with anticipation. His people would finally be able to thrive, as they deserved to do for so long. Just a few hundred more steps until he reached his goal. He looked at Mallory and smiled.

Just a little further for a brighter tomorrow. Success was within his reach.

CHAPTER 20

TALIUS

Dust from the cracked planes whipped through the wind, swirling between Talius and Ares as if trapped within their tumultuous auras. Quinn and Levy disappeared deep into the streets of Petram, reverberations from their weapons colliding echoed amongst the earthen structures of the city before spilling back out from the gates.

Under less dire circumstances, and between different combatants, it would have been music to Talius' ears. He spent his younger years lusting for battle, as most young men in his day did, though he had the benefit of being trained by two of the best warriors he had ever known.

However, his time for true battle had long since passed. As he looked at the angry god before him, he wondered if everything he had worked to achieve was about to come crashing down in front of him.

Ares wore an ugly sneer on his otherwise handsome face. His crimson sword was held in front of him, scarlet energy crackling up and down the blade like lightning, as if Zeus himself had blessed it before this battle. Considering they had come here partially for

Talius, that was rather likely.

Talius stood tall, his grip firm around the ancient staff he had fashioned so many years ago. At the time it had been nothing more than a reinforced stick of oak, diligently carved and weighted with brass on each end for an extra punch.

Now it pulsed with essence from the immortals, unbreakable through simple means alone, at least by another's hand. Though Ares was incredibly strong in hand-to-hand combat, Talius was a skilled warrior in his own right.

The battlefield snapped with their energies as Talius locked eyes with the imposing figure of Ares. The god's chiseled physique radiated raw power, his golden armor glimmering from the energy his blade output.

Ares sneered, his voice dripping with the arrogance typical of an Olympian. "Stand down, Talius. Try as you might, you are not one of us."

Talius continued looking into the god's eyes, saying nothing. It was not that he was scared, or intimidated. He simply knew not responding would infuriate the god more than anything else he could say. An angry enemy was an easier enemy to kill—a lesson he had tried to get the Masters at the Citadel to instill in Levy as he grew. Sure enough, he could see the vein in Ares' forehead bulging.

"Nothing to say, thief?" Ares spat, knuckles whitening on his blade's hilt.

"I am no thief," Talius replied, keeping his voice calm.

"You took immortality that did not belong to you," Ares barked, losing all sense of composure. "What does that make you?"

"Immortal," Talius replied evenly.

"You may be immortal, but it does not make you one of us." The Olympian repeated as though trying to drive the point home.

"And the world is better for it," Talius shrugged. He had never wanted the burden of immortality. It was simply thrust upon him.

The dust picked up around them, surging into the city in violent gusts. From within Petram, a loud, inhuman roar ripped apart the peaceful quiet. Cold, sinister power leaked out from the main gate, running its chilling fingers down Talius' spine.

Talius realized what was happening. The fight between Levy and Quinn must have increased in intensity and Chaos was ripping free from the boy having lost control. Talius turned to run towards it, readying himself to try and contain the power before it was too late.

Three steps into his run, Ares materialized before him, punching out with Olympian-level strength. It was all Talius could do to raise his staff and block the strike, though the impact still sent him sailing fifty yards back.

"Ah, ah, ah," Ares cooed.

From this distance, all Talius could see of the god through the dust storm was his crackling, red blade. "Let the kiddies play, Talius. We still have a score to settle, you and I."

"Don't be a fool, Ares!" Talius bellowed. "If a Primordial breaks free into this realm, we're both dead."

"Then I'd better kill you quickly so I can stop that." He laughed, swishing the blade through the air.

"I thought Zeus wanted me alive to 'answer for my crimes'." Talius countered, getting back to his feet.

"I am sure he will understand." The voice from the dust called back.

"Yes, Zeus has always been the understanding type," Talius said, deadpan.

Without warning, Ares charged forward, his sword raised high in the dusty haze. Talius swiftly raised his staff, its wood glowing with a radiant energy. He intercepted the blow with a resounding crash, sending shockwaves of energy through the air. Sparks erupted where the two forces collided, their combined strength battling for dominance.

Talius pushed against the god's relentless assault, channeling his ancient energy into the staff. With every strike, he felt the power surging through his veins, empowering his every move. Once enough energy was built up within it, he released it in a wave of power which pushed Ares back, briefly breaking the god's offensive.

However, Ares was not so easily deterred. He gathered his strength and unleashed a furious barrage of strikes upon Talius, his blows striking with the force of a thunderbolt. Talius truly wondered if Zeus was somehow backing Ares, despite the barrier, weakened as it was, still intact. The ground rumbled beneath their feet each time their weapons met as their clash intensified.

Talius stood strong against the onslaught. He always had a fondness for his students, despite some of the strings he pulled for the sake of the realm. But in the last few years, while working with Quinn, he truly began to care for the boy. He could not let him fall into the hands of Chaos, no matter what it may take to stop that from happening.

With unwavering determination, Talius countered Ares' strike, spinning his staff with remarkable speed and precision. Each swing sent shockwaves of energy cascading toward the god, pushing him back step by step. Ares roared in frustration, his confidence waning as he realized Talius possessed a power he had not anticipated.

Talius seized the moment and focused all his energy into one final strike. He channeled the full force of the staff, unleashing a devastating blast of energy that sent Ares hurtling backward into the outer wall of the city. Cracks spread up the stone wall, raining debris that dented and *pinged* off the Olympian's otherwise pristine armor.

With heavy breaths, Talius hobbled over to where the god lay, leaning on his staff to hold him up. He hadn't meant to expend quite so much energy, but when dealing with a god, it didn't hurt to be thorough. Ares struggled to stand, his proud demeanor shattered. He looked up at Talius, a mix of fury and shame in his eyes.

"To think a mongrel such as yourself would bring me to this state," he growled, his deep voice seething with rage.

Talius raised his staff, the weighted tip pointed directly between the god's eyes. Another thing you did not do with a god, if given the chance, was leave them alive. He had learned that the hard way with Athena.

The device which used her essence to power the walls of the Citadel would have worked just as well if she were dead, as it did alive. He allowed his pride, once he had bested her thanks to the help of Hestia, as well as his hatred for the Olympians to cloud his judgment. Because of that, the Citadel had fallen to ruins when she was set free from her bindings.

"NO!" Ares screamed. "I WILL NOT BE DEFEATED BY THE LIKES OF YOU."

The temperature dropped suddenly, a sense of dread raising gooseflesh on Talius' arms. Red energy exploded from within the

Olympian, forcing Talius back. The god's shadow extended underneath him; glowing red eyes and a vicious maw opening from within it. Talius tried to strike but he could not move, frozen to the spot in fear.

"Come now, Talius!" Ares roared with glee, now back on his feet. "Allow me to introduce you to the power of Deimos. Or in your tongue, Terror. "

Talius began to panic as the shadow creature detached itself from the ground, scuttling towards him on all fours. A large, pink tongue hung limply from the corner of its mouth and the creature giggled.

"What's the matter, Talius?" Ares taunted. "You look as though you are frightened. Surely an *immortal* such as yourself would not freeze with fear in the middle of a fight."

The shadow had reached him now, climbing up his back and wrapping his arms around the Master's neck as though it wanted a piggyback ride. Its tongue lapped at his face, leaving a putrid mucous where it touched. Talius' heart was hammering inside of his chest, trying hard to break free from his ribcage.

Move, a female voice cried out in his head. Try as hard as he might, he could not slow the blood that thrummed through his veins.

Move or die.

The god sauntered toward him, taking his sweet time. Power exuded from him with each step, striking random spots on the ground and turning sand into glass. He raised his sword, pointing it at the Master's heart. The shadow creature giggled directly in his ear at the coming execution.

I did not waste all my time and essence on you, for you to die a coward. MOVE!

The staff in his hand turned hot, searing his flesh, and snapping him out of his fearful stupor. He was drained of energy from the last strike he had delivered and too weak to deal with what was occurring on his own.

With a cry of power mixed with a lot of fear, Talius did the only thing he could think of that would break him from this spell. Gripping the staff on both sides he slammed it down onto his knee, snapping it in half and sending an incredible shockwave of force slamming into Ares.

Deimos, the shadow monster clinging to his back, faded away as its master was once again launched into the side of Petram's wall.

Talius fell to his knees, clutching the broken ends of the staff to his chest. The storm of energy from within the city had also dissipated, blanketing the world in an eerie quietness. Talius could no longer feel the presence of Quinn, indicating the youth had been lost. Talius hung his head.

"I am sorry, Lyssa." He murmured, cradling the wood as though it were a child. "Thank you for saving me, one last time."

A sword punched through his sternum, golden ichor spurting from between his lips. He looked up in shock as Ares sneered down at him. "Who says you are saved?"

Talius coughed, flecking the grey earth with gold. He locked eyes with the Olympian and resigned himself to his defeat. Though the day had been lost, he knew he could not die here. As long as Ashe remained, so too did Clotho's prophecy. He would not, in this condition, be able to interfere in the realm for some time, but that did not mean he could not help when the time came.

With one last act of defiance, he gripped Ares's blade, pulling it from his chest. The god staggered back at the display of strength.

"You have won the day, Ares, but you have not won the war."

He closed his eyes, gathering the essence which still leaked from the ends of the broken staff into himself, and faded away, into the ether.

CHAPTER 21

ANDRA

Andra stood at the forefront of the weary caravan, guiding her people through the desolate Wastes. The scorching heat beat down upon them mercilessly, increasing the difficulty of each step forward. They were not far from the border, proven by the smudge of green along the horizon, yet it felt as though it was still an eternity away.

She thought of the tales of Sisyphus, pushing his rock up the hill for all eternity, only for it to roll back down when it neared the top. Perhaps this was her eternal punishment, she thought to herself. Though life was on the horizon, her steps would bring her no closer to salvation.

Though Andra carried the weight of her people's hopes on her shoulders, a veil of fear and apprehension shrouded her heart. Lately, she had been looked at as a beacon of strength and determination by the Abyssillians, but it had not always been that way. She used to walk through life staring at her feet, young and terrified of what this world held for her.

Until Quinn arrived, she simply drifted through life, fearful that starvation awaited around every corner. She was unable to look anyone in the eye, and would quietly mumble into her sleeve if she had to speak at all.

Quinn was a needed catalyst for change, not only within her own heart but for her people as well. With his guidance, Nes and Sen came out of their shells too. For the first time in ages, the Abyssillian people stopped seeing the Wastes as a prison and instead found hope for the future. Yet now the relentless wasteland was an unyielding adversary, testing not only their endurance but also their spirit.

To make matters worse, Quinn was fighting a god, while Nes and Mallory were off gallivanting after a treasure that may not even exist. She felt as though her friends were in the clutches of the enemy, and it was all on her shoulders to find her people the salvation they deserved. She was not the shy, meek girl she once was, but she felt herself beginning to strain beneath the pressure.

She stroked Horacio, her young black drakon, beneath his chin. The creature rumbled his content, unbothered by their current situation. Horacio came to her during a rare visit from a trader.

The man was selling his wares, unaware the large, black egg in his possession was not, in fact, "a rare stone from the base of the volcano where the Tower had been chained," as he tried to pitch it.

Andra recently retired Marilyn, thanking her for the many years of friendship, freeing her to live out the rest of her days in the mountains to the north. She missed the drakon dearly, but the Wastes were truly no place for a drakon to live.

There was so little food to hunt and the skies were noxious and drab. Though she vowed not to take on another drakon, she couldn't leave the egg in the possession of a man who was clueless as to the value he held. A few months of incubation later, Horacio popped free of his shell—eight pounds of aplomb and spunk.

As she surveyed the weary faces of her people, she saw the toll their journey had taken. They moved with a weariness that seemed to seep into their bones. The glimmers of hope that sustained them through the early stages of their exodus from Pctram were fading, replaced by a sense of uncertainty and doubt.

If they could just reach the border, she thought things would have a chance to improve. For the first time in their lives, they would be in a land filled with life and color. And with the writ of passage,

Cyrus had drawn up for her, all it would take was reaching their destination. Except none of that was true at all.

On the sixth day of their journey, they reached the northern border. Travel to this point from Petram would take someone on their own only a couple of days, but moving an entire people across the Wastes was a slow process. Three days later they made it to the gates of Glenton, a large city in the northwestern region of human civilization.

As they made it to the large stone gates leading into the city proper, Andra noticed they were closed and barred. Fear clouded her thoughts, and she had to actively force it back out. It was likely they were spotted by city scouts some miles out.

Without the understanding of Cyrus' letter, it was surely alarming to these folks to see such a large group of Abyssillians moving toward their land.

"HALT!" A gruff voice yelled from atop the wall. "State your purpose."

The man was rather fat, his beady eyes bulging out from beneath a helm that appeared far too small. Andra wondered if they would have to cut the metal away to free him, or if he simply slept with the thing on. A full, bushy brown mustache made up most of his lower face, hiding what looked to be the edges of a burn scar that poked out from beneath it. He stared at the group of refugees with open hostility.

"Greetings," Andra called back to the man. She still felt a bit of anxiety when speaking, especially from a position of leadership, but her sense of duty and love for her people pushed her forward. "We are refugees from Petram, seeking asylum within your walls. Our home has been set upon by a god."

"HA!" the guard laughed, smacking another guard on the shoulder. "You hear that Gil? A god she says."

Andra stiffened, feeling heat rise into her cheeks.

"It's true," she replied, keeping her tone even and respectful. "I have a missive from Cyrus right here." She held the rolled-up parchment in the air for the man to see. "If you will not believe me, surely you will believe him."

The guard narrowed his eyes suspiciously at the paper.

"I hope you have a good arm young lady, because I'm not

opening the gate and coming down there to read it." He sneered, knowing full well the paper would not make it to the top of the wall.

"Horacio," she spoke softly to the drakon. "Deliver this to the nice man, please."

The drakon stood from his spot curled around her neck. He let out a yawn and stretched his back before unfurling his wings and placing Cyrus' letter in his mouth. Andra watched with silent glee as the guard atop the wall paled and flinched back when he landed, dropping the note at the man's feet before returning to his spot upon her shoulders and going back to sleep.

Mr. Mustache scooped the letter up, gingerly unfurling it as though it would combust, and began to scan its contents. The man must not have known how to read very well because he read it slowly, his eyes bouncing back to the same spot he just read numerous times. When he finished, he snorted air out of his nose before nudging the man he'd called Gil again.

"They must think I'm stupid, Gil. As if a forged letter from Master Cyrus would convince me to open my gates to them."

"Forged?" Andra couldn't believe what she heard. "How could you possibly think that was forged? It has his signature as well as his official seal at the bottom."

The guard spat, twisting his face into an expression of doubt.

"As if Master Cyrus would be slumming it in Petram with the likes of you. Besides, there is no way I believe for even a second a god is walking about in this realm. They haven't been seen in our lands for hundreds of years. I don't blame you for wanting out of that shit stain of a land you call home, but you aren't going to find refuge here."

Anger crept further up Andra's face. She seethed at the complete disdain this man was showing her people, and directly to their faces. A low muttering started behind her, fear and doubt snaking their way amongst them.

"It has only been a few years since the Tower left our land," Andra said, doing everything she could to keep from letting her rage spill over. They had come so far, and could not go home. They could not be turned away now.

"Surely, you have not already forgotten the many monsters who were thought of as 'gone from our lands' that made appearances during that fight."

The guard rolled his eyes, pushing Andra's anger to a boiling point.

"Unless of course," she said, allowing a modicum of venom to enter her words. "You stayed home, safe behind your walls, while countless of your kin fought and died."

The man's face turned a bright scarlet, though whether it was from rage or embarrassment Andra wasn't sure.

"Be gone from my city." He commanded, pointing back toward the Wastes. "You are not now, and never will be, welcome here."

Andra had enough. There were plenty of other towns and even a few other cities further inland. They had already walked this far, what more would a little more traveling hurt?

"We will be gone as soon as we get our missive back," she replied, holding her hand out in the air. "But I hope you have a good arm, as I am not going to come up there to receive it."

The man smiled a smile that did not reach his eyes. It sent shivers down her spine.

"But of course," he said, rearing his arm back as though he were going to chuck it as far into the forest as he could. But as he brought his arm forward, he opened his hand far too early.

"Oh dear," he said with mock sympathy as the scroll fell into the torch beside him. The flames lapped at the dried papyrus, turning it to ash within a matter of seconds. "Sorry about that. Guess you'll just have to make another."

He and Gil howled with laughter, turning their backs to the tired Abyssillians and walking away.

Andra stood still for a moment, fingernails digging into her palms. She would not rise to their bait. They wanted her people to be monsters, and any further display of anger or negative action would only reinforce that idea.

It was all she could do to hold back tears as frustration bubbled deep within her. Horacio perked his head up, lapping up the one that escaped. She took a deep breath, counting to seven before exhaling. Putting on a brave face she turned to her people and smiled her most convincing smile.

"It'll be alright." She tried to reassure them. "There are plenty of other places we can try nearby. Don't lose hope. All we need is one yes."

It wasn't her best speech, that was certain, but her people wanted to believe her and that's what mattered. They turned around and continued marching on towards the next town.

~~~

Three days later and five other denials found Andra sitting beneath a tree in the forest as her people camped a little way away. She came out here to cry, away from the eyes of those who followed her. It wouldn't do to have them break down with her.

The Abyssillian people were running out of options. Food was low, as they packed only the bare necessities in their hurry to flee Petram. Though they were now in a place teeming with life, it was impossible to hunt enough to feed an entire people.

If they did not find a safe haven very soon, she feared what the outcome would be. Morale was low enough already, a single death would likely trigger a landslide Andra was not sure she could recover from.

Horacio did his best to hunt, constantly bringing back little rodents and the occasional hare. He was too small to bring back anything more substantial, but his efforts at the very least cheered her people up. He became somewhat of a celebrity among the Abyssillians, and he in turn seemed to enjoy the praise and attention he received.

Andra unfurled her map beneath the weeping boughs of the tree. It had begun to rain a few hours ago and it showed no sign of letting up. Though she worried it would be another blow to her people's morale, it had the opposite effect.

Most of them had never seen rain before, and the joyous squeals of the children splashing around in this new phenomenon were enough to put smiles on even the greatest doubter's face.

There was nowhere else along this part of the border they could try. Every major settlement had turned them down. Though some were apologetic, citing food shortages or lack of shelter and space, others acted as the first had—open disdain and mistrust plain upon their faces. There was still so much work that needed to be done between their people.

"We'll have to start marching inland," she muttered to Horacio as if the little drakon could understand her. He peered at the map, doing his best to be attentive. "We don't have the resources to turn back, and even if we did, I fear what we might find. At this point, all we can do is move forward until we are accepted somewhere, or die trying."

Horacio squeaked his agreement, drawing a rare smile to Andra's lips. She ruffled the scales between his ears. "Let's see, the closest city to us is Forscha, though I have not heard great things about their treatment of Abyssillians in the past from Quinn.

"Qetzal is smaller but may be more open to us considering how separated they are from the other towns. But smaller means less space...." She sighed, putting her head into her hands.

"Perhaps Stormhaven?" A man's gentle voice spoke to her from the trees across the clearing.

"No, Stormhaven is a pile of rub...." She leaped to her feet, cutting her sentence off and facing the stranger.

He was fairly young and slender, though the bulging beneath his shirt betrayed his strength. His long, black hair was slicked back by the rain, and thrown over his shoulder. He wore no armor, though a sword was belted at his side. He must have seen Andra's eyes fall on it because he held his hands up in a placating gesture.

"Relax, I mean neither you nor your people any harm. Quite the opposite. I have been searching for you. My name is Lend."

Andra wanted so desperately to believe him, but her instincts screamed at her to be cautious. She was in foreign, and semi-hostile territory, and one moment of misplaced trust would spell her people's doom.

"How did you know where to find us? This land is vast." She casually rested her hand on her blade, Horacio alert on her shoulder.

"I received a letter from a man named Bartimaeus." He replied. His hands were still held out in the air, making it very clear he meant her no harm.

"We have been working on a project since the war ended. He made it very clear the time to make contact had come. I have scouts out along the border looking for you, though I assumed you may come this way as it is a route your people have walked once before."

The name Bartimaeus sent a jolt of recognition through her, as he was the one who warned them to leave Petram in the first place.

When he mentioned them having walked this route before, it could only mean one thing, he was there the night the Abyssillians joined the war.

"I want to trust you, Lend," she said, easing her hand off her blade. "But I need more. Prove to me that you are who you say you are."

He looked lost in thought for a moment before nodding at Horacio, and an idea seemed to form in his mind.

"You saved us that night. Had you not come riding in on your large red drakon, things would very likely have ended differently."

Relief flooded into Andra then and she sat back down with a thud, leaning her head back against the trunk of the tree. She didn't know if they were saved. She still had to hear the man out. But right now, she wanted to cry out in exultation.

In this land that had turned her people away time and time again, finally, someone she felt she could trust offered her an olive branch. If nothing else, she could learn what he had come to say. If she didn't like the plan, perhaps he could speak on their behalf somewhere else. Hope began to blossom in her chest again, and this time, she would not let it go.

She looked at the man and patted the ground next to her, inviting him to sit.

"Alright Lend, I'm all ears."

CHAPTER 22

ASHE

The Tower finally made what Clotho knew would be its final appearance. With the help of Talius, they tracked it to the edge of a town known as Stormhaven, a small, but growing village on the eastern side of the continent.

Though Lyssa and Laren wanted to carve a swathe through the horde of monsters it pulled to it, just wide enough for the party to make it to its doors, Talius practically begged Clotho to protect the village first.

"These are good people," *Talius protested, his eyes wide and pleading.* "They will die if we do not defend them. They did not ask for this."

"It's not as though we disagree," *Lyssa said, attempting to calm the young man down.* "However, the mission comes first. If we are quick enough, minimal damage will be inflicted on the town and when the Tower leaves this realm, the rest will be spared."

"And when that time comes, will you two stick around and help drive off the rabble which remains?" *he asked, skeptically.*

"Lord Zeus would not approve," *Laren said, looking to the ground.*

"Lord Zeus is a fool," Talius replied, coldly.

The two guardians' eyes widened at his blasphemy as lightning cracked across the sky.

Clotho watched the lightning flash and break off into a webbed pattern before dissipating, considering for a moment.

"We protect the village," she said finally, squeezing Talius' arm. "It is the least we can do for this realm's people after they have hosted us so graciously these last five years."

Talius grinned, wrapping the immortal in an excited hug. Laren and Lyssa paled.

"Clotho," Laren warned. "Lord Zeus will not like this. He will consider putting mortals ahead of your mission as a slight to him."

"My mission will still be completed." Clotho shrugged. "If he is so insulted by how I choose to do so, then maybe he is a fool as Talius said."

Her guardians gasped in unison.

"We started this together, and I would like to see this journey to its conclusion with both of you as well." Clotho reached her hands out to each of her friends. "Will you do this with me?"

They both stared at her outstretched hands for a few breaths before finding their resolve.

"We will follow you to our deaths if that is what it takes to see this mission through," Lyssa said, taking Clotho's hand.

"Until the end," Laren replied as well.

"Then it is settled." Determination glinted in her eyes. "We stay until the monsters are dealt with, and then we take a throne."

A new plan had been forming in the back of her mind, one that would see the mortal realm change for the better. Zeus would be upset, there was no getting around that.

She wondered if he was already aware of what she hoped to achieve. He was not easy to fool by any means. However, her heart was set on this course, as she knew Talius' was as well. She simply needed to reach the throne.

~~~

A violent rumble shook Ashe out of the memory. She nearly reached the story's conclusion, and no longer held any doubt there was something important, imperative even, that Clotho wanted her to know. The temptation to ignore whatever caused the rumbling and dive back into the memory nearly overwhelmed her, but a second rumble, as well as a darkening of the room, changed her mind.

The sense of dread she felt prior only increased over the days since it first arrived, and she knew her time before something catastrophic occurred was running out. It was no longer a matter of if, but when, she was certain.

It did not take long to find the source of the disturbance. A shadowy, purple energy had engulfed Quinn's orb and everything nearby. The essence was cold and viscous. Large putrid, globs detached from it and plummeted to the floor beneath.

The same energy raced along every string attached to Quinn, infecting the entire Tower, and darkening the room. Another intense rumble shook the Tower, and this time she noticed a flash of blue from up high.

Though she felt certain she knew what she would find, she went to investigate anyway. At the top, the energy slowed its spread. Zeus' orb was glowing bright blue once again, locked in combat with the parasitic essence. Every time the energies collided, they entwined, spitting and sparking, emitting a shockwave that sent more quakes throughout the Tower.

Ashe closed her eyes, grasping at the burning, golden energy at her core. This was her tower, her realm, and she would not let these foreign powers take it over. She let the warm essence spread throughout her, coalescing at her fingertips.

At her command, it released, encompassing the warring energies. Both raged against her, twisting and contorting against the walls of the golden flame, but she held firm against the onslaught until the fire had ensconced both orbs.

She let her power drop away, panting heavily as fatigue washed over her. Her flame would not hold forever, but she hoped it would be enough to learn what it was Clotho wanted her to know.

Drifting back down to her throne, she stared back into the orb, losing herself once more.

~~~

The darkened sky loomed above, heavy with ominous clouds that seemed to devour every ounce of light. Thunder rumbled in the distance, a deep growl that echoed through the hearts of the battle-worn warriors. Rain poured relentlessly, drenching the already muddy ground and turning it into a treacherous quagmire. The air was charged with an electric energy, a palpable anticipation of what was to come.

On the ichor-soaked battlefield, the four warriors fought for their lives against a horde of grotesque monsters. Their armor was battered and scarred, their bodies bruised from countless clashes, yet their spirits burned bright with tenacious resolve.

As they carved their way closer to the Tower, the storm intensified. Wind howled through the torn landscape, tearing at their resolve, and whipping the warriors' cloaks around their bodies. The rain intensified with each step, turning from a downpour into a deluge. Each drop bit against their skin like the fury of a thousand arrows.

Amidst the chaos, a brilliant streak of lightning slashed across the sky, illuminating the battlefield with a blinding flash. The thunder that followed shook the earth; the bellow of an angry Zeus in all its intensity.

The last of the monsters were before them now; the doors of the Tower in the near distance beckoning her forward. In a few more moments it was done. More monsters were likely still being drawn to this spot, but there was nothing that could be done about that. Clotho had kept her promise to Talius; the immediate threat to Stormhaven was gone.

"Hurry!" Laren cried as the group sprinted with all of their might, closing the distance to the doors.

Her sense of urgency was not unfounded. The storm had arrived in an instant, a testament to Zeus' anger. He had likely caught on to what Clotho planned. The god was not stupid.

As if in answer, a blinding flash crashed down from the heavens, knocking them to the ground. The smell of ozone was thick in the air, and a burning taste coated Clotho's mouth. The god stood before them in his purple toga; not even a breastplate graced his body.

It was clear he felt they were no threat to him. A white-hot lightning bolt rested over his shoulder, crackling with a dangerous energy. Anger lit his face, a promise of things to come.

"Lord Zeus," Clotho greeted him, getting to her feet. "To what do we owe the pleasure of your visit so close to my mission's end?"

"Don't play coy with me, girl." Zeus' bassy voice rumbled the earth. "You would have thrown away everything I have worked for. You have the gall to stand here now and act innocent?"

Clotho stepped forward; chin jutted high into the air despite the falling rain.

"I will not allow your reign of terror on these people to continue, Lord Zeus. My entire life I have been taught they are nothing more than puppets for our personal use, but that is wrong. These are people rich in culture, who live their lives to the fullest despite their weakness.

"Immortals have trampled on them for far too long. We have torn their homes apart with our greed and lust for power, and yet they continue to thrive to the best of their abilities regardless. Imagine what we could do if we allowed them to grow, allowed them to truly prosper. We could help them, live side by side with them instead of holding them down."

"Enough!" Zeus boomed, cutting off her speech. "You are a failure Clotho. You sympathize with these mongrels. You even have one as a pet." He nodded at Talius, acknowledging him for the first time. "You need to be taught a lesson."

He lifted his bolt from his chest, pointing the tip towards Talius. Stray bolts of lightning licked the earth around the god, kicking up debris on impact.

"NO!" Clotho screamed, running at the god before she knew what she was doing.

Zeus turned on her, a dangerous light gleaming in his eyes.

"You would dare raise a hand to me for the sake of a mortal? Then you will die with him!"

Time around Clotho seemed to freeze as the god hurled the bolt of lightning toward her. It streaked across the ground, in no more than a flash, yet it felt like an eternity. She thought about how she had ended up in this situation, how she had strayed so far from where she began.

Zeus thought of her as a failure, but she disagreed. Having compassion did not make her weak. Had she just been able to reach the Tower, things could have been so different for the mortal realm. She closed her eyes, waiting for the end to come, wishing she could apologize to Talius for not fulfilling her promise to him.

A force collided with her, throwing her to the side and out of immediate danger. She looked up in horror as Lyssa and Laren took her place, the bolt slamming into them. Their bodies tensed as the torrent of electrical energy coursed through their veins.

Arcs of dazzling blue light exploded from their fingertips, weaving a macabre web of agony and illumination. With each pulse of power, their bodies convulsed in a grotesque display, their muscles contorting against their will.

As soon as it had struck it was over. Both of their bodies fell as one, the flicker of life beginning to wane from their eyes. Zeus shook his head, raising the bolt again.

"This time, it will be you."

Clotho fell to her knees next to her friends, numb to the god's threat. Talius slid to his knees next to her, tears streaming down his face.

"Get out of here." Clotho cried, pushing the man away.

Talius shook his head. "I will not leave you to this fate alone."

"He is going to kill you." Now Clotho was crying. Everything they worked toward came crashing down upon them. Zeus seemed to enjoy her despair as a smug smirk rested upon his face. He took his time delivering the fatal blow.

"Would you look at that, Laren?" A weak voice reached Clotho's ears through the drum of the rain. Lyssa's eyes were half open. Somehow, she found the strength to smile. "A mortal is crying for us. Now I have seen it all."

Laren released a shaky laugh, though it turned to a wheeze by the end. "Despite all we have put him through in training, he still mourns us. Perhaps there is hope for us yet. Give me your hand, boy."

Talius shakily reached out, grasping the warrior's badly burned hand with his tenuous grip.

"I do not know that it will do you any good." She began, looking into the young man's eyes. "But if you intend to die alongside us,

you should at least have a fighting chance."

A golden light began to coalesce on the surface of her skin, overtaking the burnt flesh. A moment later, Talius began to glow as well.

"I grant you my immortal essence, so that you may fight on even terms."

Talius' eyes widened at the gift he had bestowed upon him.

"Laren...." Clotho gasped, unable to believe what she was seeing.

A second hand shot into view, grabbing the oak staff on Talius' side.

"Don't think I'm going to be outdone." Lyssa's smile was pained. "If you're going to try and fight a god, you can't do it with a stick."

A soft blue light ran along the staff, imbuing the wood with a subtle power. Clotho could feel the essence radiate from it in gentle waves.

"There," Lyssa grunted through her pain. "Now it is imbued with my essence. It will not break unless you will it to do so." She let her head fall back next to Laren's, grasping the warrior's hand with her own. "Though I don't think you'll live much longer to appreciate it, I hope it serves you well."

Both sets of eyes fell on Clotho, gentle smiles resting on their faces.

"To the end," they said in unison.

"To the end," Clotho replied, closing their eyes as they exhaled their last breath.

"What a touching display," Zeus mocked with faux sympathy. "Surely you will succeed against me, now that the power of friendship is on your side."

Clotho and Talius stood, hearts heavy, but intent on seeing this through to the end.

"I have had enough of this charade," Zeus bellowed, pulling the bolt back again. "I will have another claim the Tower in my name, even if it takes another thousand years. You will be nothing but ashes upon the earth."

Clotho grabbed Talius' hand, waiting for the end to come; praying it was swift.

"Enough, brother!"

A shining curtain of flame materialized in front of them, parting to reveal a figure cloaked in ethereal fire. Beneath the flaming cloak stood Hestia, goddess of hearth and home, her eyes burned with intense anger as she stepped forward to confront him.

Zeus glared back at Hestia with a mixture of surprise and fury. He would not have expected the normally gentle goddess to challenge his authority. Clotho and Talius, sensing a change in the tides of this fight, stepped to either side of her, their weapons held at the ready.

"Brother, your reign of tyranny over the mortal plane ends here," Hestia declared, her voice resonating with a quiet strength. Raindrops sizzled as they fell against her. "You have abused your power and forgotten the balance that must be maintained in this world."

Zeus scowled; his voice thunderous. "You forget yourself, Sister. I am the ruler of Olympus. You are but a mere flicker of flame compared to my might."

With a wave of his hand, he summoned a new bolt of lightning, hurling it towards the goddess. Hestia raised her arm and the flames around her intensified, shielding her as they absorbed the lightning's power.

Clotho and Talius charged together, their weapons slashing through the air with blinding speed. Zeus parried their blows easily, batting them aside as though they were children. They recovered and advanced again and again, fueled by the righteousness of their shared cause.

Hestia stepped closer while the god was distracted, her tendrils of flame intensifying, wrapping around Zeus and ensnaring him amongst their mighty heat.

"Your reign has been one of fear and domination," She admonished him, pressing her fire ever closer. "You have forgotten your duty to protect humanity. We will no longer stand idly by as you continue to sow chaos and suffering."

With a mighty roar, Zeus unleashed a final surge of power, struggling against the bonds that now held him. Hestia and her allies stood their ground. The goddess' flames surged, forming a vortex of fire that swallowed the lightning, redirecting the combined energy back towards Zeus. It struck him with a thunderous clash, lighting up the night sky.

As the smoke cleared, Zeus found himself battered and weakened, unable to contend with this new threat. He had been completely out-maneuvered and he was furious.

"Very well, Sister." He rasped, his chest heaving from the strain of the fight. "I will retreat just this once, but I will remember this treason. Do not think you will be so lucky as to surprise me a second time. Do not show your face on Olympus again, if you value your life."

He turned then, facing Clotho with a mix of disappointment, and anger. His words came out cool and direct.

"As for you, when your millennium is up, I will see you again, and you will be made to answer for your transgressions. That is a promise. I have a thousand years to prepare for my revenge."

A chilling dread ran down Clotho's spine, but she continued staring into the god's eyes with fierce defiance.

Zeus looked back to Hestia whose flames still coiled around her. Realizing the futility of further resistance, he reluctantly retreated, his form dissolving into a storm cloud that dispersed into the air.

Hestia turned to Talius and Clotho, gratitude shining in her eyes. "Thank you, both of you. Your bravery and ideals have proven invaluable. Now we must look to the future. My brother will not take kindly to this defeat. I can use my essence to keep him from this realm for a time, but eventually, he will break through again."

Talius stepped forward, eager to use his newfound immortality for the good of humanity. "If it is to protect my people, I will do anything."

"I fear a thousand years, though seemingly long, will not be enough time to muster the force it would require to defeat Zeus for good." The goddess said, lost in thought. "We only succeeded today because we caught him by surprise. That will not happen a second time."

"Is there a way we can lock this realm?" Talius asked. "Can we stop them from crossing over for good?"

"Their essence is tied to this place," Clotho said, remembering her studies. "You would have to shut it away, cut them off entirely.

Even then it would be incredibly easy to reopen the way. What we truly need is a way to break the cycle."

Hestia lifted her head, a plan beginning to form in her mind. "As I have already said, I will stay in this realm and use what essence I can to stop my kin from crossing over. In that time Talius, you must gather a group of mortals to our cause. I will instruct you on where to find items of power and we can use my essence to seal them away."

Clotho jumped in then, latching on to Hestia's line of thought. "From within the Tower, I will weave an end to this once and for all. Three heroes with the power to unlock their full potential and face the gods when my cycle ends."

"Why three?" Talius asked.

"Three is the perfect number," she replied, educating him one last time. "It is the number of harmony, wisdom, and understanding." She reached out, embracing Talius.

"I am thankful I met you. Without you, my eyes would have never been opened to the beauty of this realm. I promise I will put my full power into the prophecy I weave. Do your best to prepare my heroes for their trials to come. They may be our last hope to break this chain."

Clotho turned to Hestia then, bowing deeply to show her respect.

"When I started this journey, you warned me to stay true to myself and not to lose my way in Zeus' schemes. Did you know it would play out like this?"

Hestia's smile was sad, her eyes focused on the distant past. "I said the same to every Weaver before you. However, when it came time to claim the throne, none had your courage. Go now, and weave your prophecy. I will see to my part in this tale."

"Will I see you again when my time is up?" Clotho asked, feeling an attachment to the goddess she had not felt before.

"Perhaps," She replied. "Though maybe not in the way you hope. Come, Talius. Let us leave her to her duty. You and I have much to discuss and still more to plan. We can use the nearby town as our base of operations."

Clotho watched as her companions walked over the ridge leading to Stormhaven. Once they were no longer in sight, she turned back to the intricate stone doors that led into Fate's Tower. Despite their size and weight, they opened for her at the slightest push. There was evidence of the last Weaver near the throne in the form of scraps of clothing.

Atropos was her name if Clotho remembered right. She cleared out rather quickly once the doors opened, likely wanting to avoid associating with anybody tied to Zeus' anger. Clotho couldn't say she blamed her.

She sat down upon the throne and was immediately assaulted with power and knowledge. After a moment of feeling utterly overwhelmed, she took a deep breath, collecting herself. She wasn't sure how long it would take to weave enough power into a prophecy to make it hold, but she knew she had to start now if they wanted a chance to save their future from Zeus' wrath.

~~~

900 years passed by during the time Clotho started her weaving. 900 years of draining her power daily, weaving her prophetic net to the point of absolution. With one final stitch, it was complete.

A massive wave of energy flooded over her and every inch of the Tower. Orbs flared to life, flashing bright with the essence of potential. She did not know who her heroes would be—that would be up to Talius and Hestia to decide.

She simply knew when the time came, they would be out there. She sat back on her throne, resting her now wrinkled arms upon the armrests. She knew her time was running short.

In one century, the Tower would be in play again and Zeus would come for her. It would all be worth it, so long as they succeeded with their plan. One more time she read her weaving, committing her words, her legacy to memory.

Heed these words; a prophecy foretold,
Of Valor, Virtue, and Warrior bold.
As Heavens weep, when realms collide;
Three heroes rise to stem the tide.
A sacrifice for all to see;

Embodies hope; forever free.

~~~

The memory orb fell to the ground, shattering. After all this time, everything was beginning to make sense. Ashe had heard a few different people mention a prophecy to her, though nobody ever elaborated further.

Yet now she understood why everyone considered Ashe and her friends so important. They hadn't just been trained for the role of claiming the Tower, that was just the tip of the iceberg. Their true purpose was to have a fated clash with the gods themselves.

They were supposed to usher in a new era for mankind by ending the old regime. For the first time throughout this entire process, Ashe felt angry. She felt used, as though she, Levy, and Quinn were no more than instruments in a grand design in which they had no say.

She wanted what was best for humanity. She didn't even hate that she was chosen to play that role. But the fact everyone who knew about it kept it from them is what upset her. Would Levy have reacted differently to everything had he known the truth?

Would Quinn have more confidence knowing he was not the villain so many of the Masters made him out to be, but instead a hero of prophecy?

Ashe refused to allow more time to pass without this knowledge being shared. When she took the throne, she thought she was part of something greater. She thought with her weaving she could bring peace to her people.

Instead, she was still just a pawn in a greater game.

If they wanted the Tower's cycle broken, she was going to give it to them. It wasn't until she turned towards the orbs that she noticed her guests.

CHAPTER 23

QUINN

Quinn's eyes flickered open, his vision blurry and disoriented. The world around him seemed hazy as if he was viewing it through a foggy lens. As he tried to sit up, an intense pain shot through his chest, leaving him gasping for air. His hand instinctively went to his heart, his fingers coming away wet with blood.

Confusion and panic coursed through him as he struggled to comprehend where he was and what had happened. Memories flooded back to him—his powers out of control, being impaled by a spear, the searing pain, and the feeling of his life force ebbing away. Yet, here he was, awake and breathing. He looked around, trying to make sense of his surroundings.

The air around him sparked with chaotic energy, a tempestuous maelstrom of swirling blues and purples, which tugged at his limbs. The wind howled with an intensity that threatened to sweep him away.

There was no discernable horizon, only an endless expanse of churning clouds that writhed and twisted in an unholy dance. The ground beneath his feet was non-existent, replaced by an abyss that seemed to stretch into infinity. Though it looked vastly different from the last time he was here, the realm's energies were all too familiar to him.

"Welcome back to the Realm of Night, Quinn." A somber, girlish voice said to him.

From out of the nothingness, the slight form of a young girl shimmered into being, mere steps in front of him. Her wide, olive eyes stared into his, as silent and pleading as the day they first met. Her loose, brown pigtails were disheveled and messy. Quinn realized he was staring into the face of his greatest mistake.

"I'm sorry," he whispered. The pain in his chest was replaced with a different kind of burn.

The girl grinned, her smile twisted and grotesque. Her eyes glinted with malice.

"That is right, Quinn. You are sorry. You let me fall. You sacrificed me for power."

"I didn't." Quinn shook his head vigorously, falling to his knees. "I didn't mean to let you fall. I needed to save Ashe. I couldn't...."

"Could not what?" the girl replied, bending down so that they were face to face. Her breath was rotten and cold, as one would expect from the dead.

"Could not find faith in your friend to be able to save herself? Could not turn down the siren song of real power? For all your bluster, and all your lecturing of Levy, you aren't any different than he. One twisted, little vision was all it took for you to forsake your beliefs. And look at where it has gotten you."

He shut his eyes tight, his nails biting the flesh of his palms. Everything the girl was saying was true. It was as though his inner monologue over these last few years had come to life and was now tormenting him with his decisions.

Quinn opened his eyes as a cool, soft touch beneath his chin lifted his face. The girl's features had softened; her eyes were now gentle and consoling.

"You are dead, you know." Her voice was sweet as if she were trying to soothe the wounds she just inflicted. "Levy's spear punched straight through your heart. You only live now thanks to my power, the power of this realm. The moment you leave here, you cease to exist."

Fear jolted through Quinn at the girl's admission. He scrambled backward, putting some distance between them. The girl did not follow, instead appearing amused at his reaction.

"Chaos?" Quinn asked, though he already knew the answer.

"Look at the Realm of Night," Chaos said, ignoring his question. "It is in a state of upheaval. It senses that which does not belong here. You are dead, Quinn, it is as simple as that. If I were not here, holding it at bay, it would have already consumed you; washing over you and dragging you down into the abyss."

"Why save me then?" An overwhelming sense of tiredness flooded through Quinn. He could not remember the last time he had gotten a restful night of sleep. His body was numb, limbs heavy. It was as if the tumultuous state of the Realm of Night reflected his state of mind, frayed and worn.

"I want what I have always wanted."

Though he was still wearing the guise of the girl, his voice changed back to the deep, even cadence Quinn was greeted with on his first visit to the realm.

"There is no future for you, but you need not suffer a painful death. And make no mistake, should you return from this realm, it will be painful. Give me your body so that I may walk amongst the world once again. Fade into the nothingness of this realm. Be at peace, for the first time in a long time."

Quinn's eyes felt heavy. He had to admit, fading into the endless, mind-numbing sleep of nothingness did sound nice. The wind around him calmed slightly as well as if hearing his thoughts and agreeing.

As his eyes began to close, a sudden flash of intense warmth spread through his body. An image of Ashe flooded into his head, alerting him to the presence of Chaos' energy and snapping him out of his stupor.

"Stop that!" Quinn snapped at Chaos. "Your tricks won't work on me again. I will not allow you to wander freely, unchecked."

"That obnoxious girl and her stupid love," Chaos snarled, frustration showing through his calm façade for the first time. "If you will not turn your body over to me, I will simply take it. You are weak and in my domain. It will be as simple as allowing the energy to consume you."

Quinn got back to his feet, resolve steeling his spine. "I will not allow you to run amok in my body, Chaos. Even if that means I am trapped here for the rest of eternity, I will not set you free."

Chaos sneered, twisting the features of the girl's face in an eerie and inhuman way. "We will see about that." He snapped his fingers; the click forceful enough to echo deep into the nothingness around them.

The howling of the wind intensified tenfold as if an invisible barrier muting it vanished. The blues and purples of the swirling energy became shockingly vivid, assaulting Quinn's vision and overloading his senses. Chaos raised his hand, pulling the vibrant energy toward him. It intertwined around his figure in a breathtaking display, fluid and snakelike in its movement.

"Come then, Quinn," Chaos mocked. "Let us see how long you last against the full might of my realm."

He thrust his hand forward, hurling the force at Quinn. He knew he couldn't fight, weakened as he was, but he refused to allow Chaos to take control. As the overwhelming essence streaked toward him, he did the only thing he could think to do. Quinn turned and ran.

The cascading energy surged around him, erupting from the ground, and sending shockwaves rippling across the empty plane, throwing Quinn from his feet. He hit the ground hard, tumbling for a bit before regaining his feet and continuing to sprint as far away from the Primordial as fast as his feet could take him.

The energy continued forward, following close behind. Now and then it crashed into him with the force of a tidal wave. Tendrils lashed out at him, as he had done to Levy, slashing at his arms and legs, and tearing chunks out of his leather armor.

"Where do you think you're going to go?" Chaos asked, floating next to him as he ran. He still wore the guise of the little girl, only now he wore Quinn's old mask upon his face. Now and then he would let loose a tinkling giggle as the energy sent Quinn hurdling to the ground, or tear a fresh strip of leather from his back.

"You cannot escape me, Quinn. You cannot outrun me, or my energy. This is my realm. Where you go, I will follow." His face morphed into that of Levy, though the body stayed the little girl's. "You would have better luck fighting. At least then you would lose yourself in battle rather than running like a coward."

"Shut UP!" Quinn yelled, swiping the air as Chaos chortled, reappearing on his other side.

"So, there is some fight in you after all." The visage of Levy said, shooting Quinn his trademarked sneer. "And here I thought you'd dropped all of your courage into the lava along with me."

Quinn roared, skidding to a stop, and lunging toward Chaos. The Primordial faded away as the blow came down on him, this time reappearing a few feet above Quinn's head.

"You almost had me that time," he taunted, shifting now into the form of Talius. "All you need to do is focus, young Quinn."

He mimicked the Master. "The power is in your grasp if only you can control it." Chaos stroked his beard, cackling as the energy caught up to them, sweeping Quinn off his feet and slamming him into the ground.

"Uh oh," the faux Talius said. "Looks like you let your emotions get the better of you again."

Quinn fought and kicked as the energy pressed in around him, thrashing him repeatedly into the ground. He could feel the air being squeezed from his lungs as the pressure increased; his vision starting to swim.

"Come on now, Quinn." The sweet voice of Ashe called down from above. "Surely you can do better than that. If this is the extent of your strength, maybe I would have been better off with Levy after all."

White-hot anger erupted within Quinn. Chaos could mock him all he wanted. He could use the faces of his friends and past-acquaintances if it tickled him to do so, but Ashe was off limits. She was too good, her heart too pure, for Chaos to make a mockery of her.

Quinn gritted his teeth, fighting against the bonds that held him. He widened his elbows and kicked, attempting to make space for him to move amongst the seething energy.

Why don't I just use my sword? He thought as he made no headway in his escape.

Where was his sword? If he was pulled into the Realm of Night with his armor, surely it would have come too, wouldn't it?

He had certainly been holding it as Levy skewered him. At the thought of the weapon, he felt a familiar weight coalesce in his hand. With the realization he was no longer defenseless, he tightened his grip on the blade's handle, putting as much strength as he could into his swing. The violent energy parted instantly, retreating as though it had been burned.

Chaos stopped laughing, shooting back down to the ground, and examining the blade.

"Curious," he said, circling Quinn. "You should not have been able to call that here."

He shrugged, rising back into the air, though this time with his defenses slightly more raised. "Oh well, it matters not. This is still my domain. Run, fight, it makes no difference. It is only a matter of time until you are ground into nothingness, and when you are, your body will be mine to take."

He thrust out his arm, sending a fresh wave of energy washing over Quinn. It battered him from every side, pushing him to and fro as though he were a piece of flotsam, adrift amid a stormy sea. His sword continuously cut him free of its grasp, offering him a brief respite before it came crashing in again.

Though the weapon offered him a way to fight, Quinn knew he had to think of something quickly. His arms were already feeling the creeping weight of fatigue beginning to settle in, and he knew he couldn't keep this up forever.

An idea struck him then. The shock of it distracted him long enough for a tendril of energy to wrap around his neck. With a swift motion, he swung, cutting the tendril in half. If he could summon his sword to him, did that mean he still had some modicum of control over this realm?

After all, he walked it, commanded it even, for a handful of years. If nothing else, it was worth testing. He turned his brain on auto-pilot, allowing his battle instincts to take over as he focused on the essence of the realm itself.

The energy currently assailing him felt cold and foreign, unwilling to reply to his command. He felt, more than saw, the connection it had to the figure of Chaos watching from up high. Yet, the space around him was filled with fragments of familiar energy. Alone they were too miniscule to be of any help, but if they were brought together....

Quinn grasped at them as he did so many times before, pulling them into himself. Chaos sensed a shift around him, cursed, and doubled the pressure of his assault.

Once Quinn collected enough essence within, he brought it together, before pushing it back out to form a large, cohesive bubble. It wasn't strong enough to stop Chaos altogether, but it would last long enough to buy him some precious time.

Inside the bubble was calm and peaceful. The barrier silenced the howling wind from outside and blocked all but Chaos' threats and curses from entering, and that was music to Quinn's ears.

Knowing his time was short, Quinn walked to the center and sat, legs folded and eyes closed. He let his senses wander out into the realm again, collecting as much of the familiar essence as he could use and began the long process of gathering it together.

He wasn't sure if he would be able to collect enough for it to matter by the time Chaos managed to break through his defenses, but he decided it was better to try and die fighting than it was to simply surrender.

CHAPTER 24

LEVY

Levy wasn't sure what enticed him to come back to the depths of Olympus. It may have been that the grungy squalor of the dungeons was so different as opposed to the serene, almost fake spotlessness of the surface.

Perhaps it was simply the fact he was alone amongst the quiet stone, rather than the opulent marble where there was always an eye or ear intruding upon his business. Whatever it was, he found himself back here again, wandering in the dark.

He and Ares returned from the mortal realm some time ago after demolishing the Abyssillian city. They went to eliminate Quinn and Talius. "Vermin to be culled" as Zeus called them. Despite the Olympian being king amongst the gods, he seemed oddly threatened by the duo. Though Levy succeeded in spearing Quinn, Talius vanished before Ares could finish his side of it which was likely to anger his father.

Levy felt extremely conflicted with how everything had gone. On one hand, he succeeded in his mission and was safe from Zeus' wrath, unlike Ares. On the other, he couldn't shed the guilt he felt at the destruction of Petram.

He meant it when he told Quinn that he felt trapped. The Olympians would tell him he was weak, feeling remorse for mortals, yet he had been brought up to champion them.

The most damning proof of his questionable decisions was that Zeus saw his actions and thought fit to spare him from burning in lava because of them. He still wanted a world where humanity could be free from the powers who would see them suffer. He thought if he could become that power, he could change the narrative and be willing to do whatever it took to achieve his goal.

He realized now how naïve he sounded. It hadn't been long after joining the Olympians to see there was no acceptable future as long as they remained in control. It's not as though he could just walk away though.

Zeus could kill him as he currently was just as easily as he saved him. Any of them could for that matter. Quinn would be thrilled to know his jab of him being a dog and taking commands hit home.

Quinn.

That was the other internal conflict raging within him. He was certain he'd burned his bridges with his former friend. He didn't blame Quinn for letting him fall like he had. If the roles were reversed, he likely would have done the same thing. After his betrayal and stabbing Ashe in the back, immediately followed by his supposed fall to his death, Levy was certain Quinn would have just gone on with his life.

Imagine Levy's surprise when he showed up from the grave, expecting hatred and vitriol, only to see guilt and agony plain upon Quinn's face. It looked as if he hadn't slept a wink for the last three years.

If he didn't know better, Levy was certain he saw a look of relief flash in Quinn's eyes before their fight. Levy wasn't sure what happened with the dark energy and Quinn's disappearance, but he was certain he was dead. His spear went straight through the man's heart, after all. He shouldn't feel guilty for that, given how events unfolded between them, and yet he did.

"If I did not know any better, I would say you have grown since the last time we spoke."

Levy looked up, startled at the old crone's voice. He'd been so lost in thought he didn't realize he wandered back to this place. As with his prior visit, the old woman was still chained to the wall, naked as the day she was born.

She looked to be in even worse shape than before, patches of skin burnt with webbed scarring. A faint smell of ozone lingered in the air, hidden just under the stink of waste and body odor. Levy felt a shiver run down his spine. This was another example of why he couldn't walk away from Zeus.

"Hello, Clotho." He greeted her, surprised he remembered her name. "I don't know that I've grown any. Maybe some muscle perhaps."

"I do not mean physically, boy" She replied, not unkindly. "You appear as though you have found some clarity within yourself."

Levy sighed, sliding his back down the wall until he was seated on the cold, mossy floor. "I don't feel any clarity. If anything, I feel more conflicted now than I ever have."

"Honesty is not always the easiest path to walk, nor the most desirable." Her voice was melancholy, as though she was remembering something from a painful past. "But it is through honesty that we find our true purpose. I will admit it comes easier to some than it does others."

"Is honesty how you ended up in here?" Levy asked, unsure of what to say to that.

"Yes. And I do not regret my choices."

"Did you know?" Levy asked.

"Know what, child?" The woman replied, her eyes kind and attentive, despite the pain she must suffer.

"Did you know your choices would lead you to this point?" He felt as if he were a little kid again, lost in the chaos of the world and trying to find some semblance of stability to grasp onto.

"I spent my youth blissfully unaware of the truth of things." She began, a far-off look in her eyes.

"When I became aware of how our world truly worked, I continued to ignore it as I pressed on with my supposed duty. Were it not for a few very dear friends, I may have allowed my ignorance to dictate my future for the rest of eternity. I certainly would not have ended up where I am now if I had. However, then I would live today filled with regret."

"You would rather live like this, beaten and bloodied, sitting in your waste?" Levy already knew her answer of course, but he wanted her to say otherwise, to justify his actions as he no longer could.

"If I could go back in time, knowing what I know now, I would make the same decision. Sometimes sacrifice is the only way for the world to move forward. I would give up my body time and time again for the benefit of the future." She looked at him then, really looked at him. Not into his eyes, but into his very soul.

Her gaze was filled with a knowing sympathy, and something broke within Levy that he didn't realize he'd been holding onto. Fear, anger, and loneliness were all washed away by her gaze and replaced with a warmth he sorely needed.

"Thank you." His voice rasped, a single tear tracing its way to his chin.

A glow filled the room with light, foreign and nonbelonging in the dark cell. With a start Levy realized it was coming from him. His body was lit up like a beacon, chasing the shadows from the damp enclosure. "What's happening?" he asked, startled.

"You're being summoned by Lord Zeus," The woman replied. "My young hero, I doubt we will see each other again so allow me one final word before you go."

He looked at her, desperate to hear what she had to say. She made him feel more at peace than at any point since he first met Janus all those years ago.

"You know yourself better than any. If you truly believe the path you are on now is right, then walk it proudly. Whatever you decide to do with your power, be confident in your choice. Insecurity will only lead to suffering."

The light flashed bright, carrying him away from Clotho before he could respond. He felt his resolve strengthen thanks to her words, and knew now whatever happened going forward, it would be because he wanted it.

Levy looked around as the light which carried him away subsided. He stood in the center of a grandiose, circular throne room that he'd never before witnessed. The walls were made from cut marble, white as fresh snow.

Soaring pillars, each carved with the likenesses of the gods lined the edges of the room, holding up a domed, transparent ceiling that depicted all manner of constellations. The marble floor beneath his feet was polished to a mirror-like shine, reflecting the splendor of the room, and adding to its magnificence. The air felt charged with an otherworldly energy, the magnitude of which was nearly overwhelming.

At the northernmost point of the room, on an elevated platform, stood the legendary throne of Olympus. It was an imposing structure, crafted from shimmering gold and encrusted with precious gemstones that sparkled like stars.

The throne was adorned with intricate engravings of divine beings and heavenly creatures. Their forms exuded power and wisdom. Zeus sat in his seat of power, looking at Levy with pride in his eyes.

On either side and a level below him sat his brothers, Poseidon and Hades. On the right was Poseidon on a throne of coral, his three-pronged trident strapped at its side. The god's thick, white hair fell freely down his back and sides, mingling with his equally long, white beard. His deep blue eyes were piercing, and a sense of unsteadiness washed over Levy.

To Zeus' left sat Hades, a pale god with deep bags beneath his eyes. His greasy, onyx hair fell to his shoulders, streaked with grey and wild with curls. His throne was made from what looked like a collection of human bones, with a spine for a backrest and femurs for his arms to lay on. The god stared at Levy with open malice.

Ares sat to Levy's immediate right. His throne was a carbon copy of his father's, though smaller in size. A fresh cut ran down the length of his jaw, and he looked at Levy with fury heavy on his brow.

The rest of the Olympians encircled the room, though Levy noticed two of the thrones, those of Athena and Hestia, sat empty. Athena's appeared just as grand and gaudy as the others, though to his surprise Levy noticed Hestia sat in a simple, unadorned marble chair.

"There he is!" Boomed Zeus, a brilliant white smile splitting his face. "The mortal of the hour! Well done, boy. At least one of you managed to eliminate your target."

Levy noticed Ares' scowl at his words. Thunderclouds collected behind his eyes. His face seemed to have lost some color, causing the cut to stand out deep and red upon his face.

"Keep proving your worth and you'll be handsomely rewarded when your realm is securely back within my control."

Levy bowed, keeping his face straight and emotionless. "Thank you, Lord Zeus. It is an honor to serve as you see fit."

If you truly believe the path you are on now is right, then walk it proudly.

Clotho's words were vivid in his head. Whether this was his path or not, insulting the king of the Olympians in the middle of his throne room, flanked by his family, was not the way to continue walking it.

"The boy is a thief." Hades interrupted his thoughts, standing up from his throne. His voice was oily and thick, and it carried with it all the malice his eyes were conveying.

"I agree, Brother." Poseidon's voice was rich and deep, like crashing waves upon the ocean's surface. "Mortals should not be trusted."

Levy was not surprised Hades held a grudge against him. Though he pilfered the god's artifact of power from the vaults of the Masters, releasing a good amount of essence back into the realm and weakening the barrier considerably, he had also allowed the precious orb to be destroyed. It was unlikely such a treasure could be reformed in a short matter of time.

"Silence, Brothers." Zeus' voice trumpeted over their continuing protests. "Were it not for this boy, we would still be fully locked away from the mortal realm. It was because of his actions we were able to strike a blow at all."

Levy grimaced against a fresh wave of guilt at the reminder.

"Yes, and we are all very grateful for his wonderful service," a goddess spoke from his left. The sarcasm in her voice spoke to the true intentions behind the words.

Curly brown hair fell in ringlets around her shoulders, and a leather headband tied tight around her forehead to keep it from her face. Her silver, luminescent eyes carried contempt behind them as she addressed Levy.

"Yet my uncle is correct. You are a mortal *man* and you do not belong here." She said the word man as though she had just taken a sip of a bitter ale.

"Come now, Artemis," Ares' velvety voice cut in. "He is not so much a man as he is a loyal hound, performing father's tasks for scraps." The spite in his gaze as he locked eyes with Levy was intense; gooseflesh rose unwillingly along his arms.

He looked away as a girlish giggle from a couple of thrones to his left pulled his attention. "Well, I think he's cute."

The buxom goddess with thick, auburn hair chimed in, sending Levy a wink. She wore her lavender toga tight to her body which showed off her voluptuous curves. He could smell a pleasant perfume wafting from her direction.

"Of course, ye do, Aphrodite." A burly, red-haired Olympian countered from across the room. He was a mountain of a god, covered in thick muscle and even thicker body hair. "You think anything with a dick is cute."

Aphrodite stood, color rising in her cheeks at the insult. "Not everything, Hephaestus," She said, pointedly. "Some are too...misshapen...for me."

Levy felt as though he was whiplashed as the back and forth continued between the Olympians. Zeus finally had enough and slammed his fist down on the arm of his chair roaring, "ENOUGH!"

The room fell silent, all eyes glued to the floor, fearful of catching Zeus' wrath. "I did not gather us all here so that we may bicker like children. We have a realm to conquer, and fighting amongst ourselves will get us nowhere."

"Apologies, Father," Artemis sniffed, glancing at Levy without an ounce of sorrow in her eyes. A chorus of muttered apologies followed, none of them carrying any weight in the slightest.

"Why did you call us here, Brother?" Poseidon spoke, bringing a modicum of decorum back into the conversation.

"In a matter of days, the barrier barring us from the mortal realm will fall." He looked around the room as an excited buzz began to pick up.

"How?" Hades perked up in his seat, the malice which was so prevalent on his face before was now replaced with an excited curiosity.

"How is of no consequence at the moment," Zeus replied, much to the god of the Underworld's dismay. "The fact is that it will, I have seen to it."

Levy's mind started racing at this news, unsure if he felt elation or terror. Perhaps a mix of both. If the barrier to the mortal realm fell, the gods would undoubtedly storm back into the land. There would likely be Hades to pay for the millennium of defiance, but it would also mean Levy would have upheld his side of his bargain with Zeus.

He was promised godhood if he succeeded, and if he had that power behind him, he might be able to control...

"What about the Tower?" Levy asked suddenly, forgetting himself. Instantly he regretted his interruption as twelve sets of immortal eyes turned on him. "Apologies for interrupting Lord Zeus," he said, shifting his gaze to the ground in deference. "I meant you no disrespect."

To his surprise, the king smiled at him, a knowing twinkle in his eye.

"What of the Tower indeed? So long as fate is not in our control, there will always be a thorn in our side, stopping us from truly ruling humanity. That is where you come in, boy."

"Me?" Levy asked, bewildered. "What can I do?"

"I have *consulted* with the past Weaver." His face took on a dangerous edge as he said this.

Levy shuddered as the battered image of Clotho came to his mind. "She is quite knowledgeable about the workings of the Tower and the Realm of Fate. I believe, with the right...motivation, we might be able to access it."

"Pah!" a voice scoffed two thrones to his right. Hera leaned forward in her chair, arms folded with a visible challenge. Her diadem sat crooked upon her head.

"You rely on a mortal, not once but *twice* now, to find success with your schemes? After being locked out of that realm for so long, have you become so weak as to need help from this boy? I do not know what happened to my husband, but you certainly are not him."

Pressure built within the room, crushing into Levy, and bringing him to his knees. Hera, to her credit, did not back down. Instead, she stood from her throne and pushed back with pressure of her own.

"I will not tolerate having this *creature* live amongst us anymore," Hera continued, walking toward Zeus, one slow step after another.

"Enough," Zeus ordered, narrowing his eyes. "You forget your place." Lightning crackled around the room, raising every hair on Levy's body.

"My place is on Olympus, amongst the *immortals*." She spat, venomously, making a point to glare at Levy as she said the word. "Not watching your newest pet sully our realm."

Anger rose within Levy at her words, though he dared not show it. The rest of the Olympians pressed themselves back against their thrones as if hoping the arguing couple forgot they were there.

Then, as soon as it entered the room, the pressure disappeared, causing Levy's ears to painfully pop. Zeus raised his hands in the air, conceding to his wife.

Hera, seeing she won, dropped her power as well. She wore a sneer on her face as she stared boastfully at the king of the Olympians. "There was a time when you would have smote me where I stood such defiance. How truly soft you have become."

"On the contrary, I am simply willing to do what it takes to reclaim what is rightfully mine," he replied, an edge to his otherwise calmed demeanor. "If that means allowing a mortal into Olympus and using his gifts, then so be it. If you are unconvinced with my methods, then perhaps you would like to accompany us to the gateway so I may show you what I mean."

"I want nothing to do with your schemes, Husband," Hera replied, haughtily.

"I insist," Zeus demanded in a tone that brooked no argument. He turned to Ares then, addressing an Olympian other than Hera for the first time since their outburst. "Come with Levy and meet us in the portal room. Consider this a second chance to make up for your latest failure."

Ares bowed, eyes hardened against his emotion.

~~~

Levy and Ares entered the room holding the gateway behind Hera and Zeus. The walk from the throne room had been tense and uncomfortable. Anger and resentment swirled around the foursome with every step.

As they stood before the obsidian gateway again, Levy

wondered what Zeus had up his sleeve. He hinted they may be able to reach the realm that housed the Tower, though Levy wondered if that were true why they hadn't done so before.

"Now, it is time to link your essence to the portal." Zeus turned to face him.

"My essence?" Levy asked, unsure of how to do so.

"If what Clotho said during my questioning was true, we should be able to find the Realm of Fate through your connection with its current Weaver," Zeus replied.

"My connection with Ashe? I don't know what you mean. We were close once, but..."

"Not your friendship, boy," Zeus said with an air of impatience. "Your essence. You hold part of my sister's essence within you, as does the Weaver. Connect that essence with the gateway so that it may find its other half, and in doing so the Tower should become accessible."

Levy stepped up to the gate, running his hand along the cool, smooth surface of the obsidian. Looking within himself, he located the bit of Hestia he commanded. It was as though it were afraid, cowering in the very recesses of his mind. As he tried to grab it, it bolted away, avoiding his touch at all costs.

"Do it, boy," Zeus growled, growing impatient.

"I'm trying," Levy responded, missing the energy again. "It doesn't want to cooperate."

"This is what you get for relying on a mortal." Hera's voice dripped with venom, angering Levy. "He cannot even control the minuscule amount of power he was given."

"Silent," Zeus commanded. He placed a meaty hand on Levy's shoulder.

Levy couldn't help but feel that it was more of a threat than support.

He allowed the anger he felt at Hera to motivate him, focusing hard on the corner the energy currently hid in. He boxed it in so it was unable to retreat again and lunged for it, grasping it tightly and forcing it out of him and into the gateway.

At first, nothing happened. Levy wondered if perhaps he didn't have enough of Hestia's essence within him to locate anything.

Slowly, foreign golden symbols began appearing along the

obsidian's border. As the final symbol faded into existence, soft, orange energy began to swirl in the center.

As it stabilized, Levy began picking out images on the other side. The sky was colored in all different hues of pinks and purples, oranges, and reds. It was dotted with little pinpricks of light that Levy realized were stars the longer he stared at them.

Large islands of rock floated in the air, disconnected from the main landmass. In the distance, he could see the Tower, standing tall as it had the last time he'd laid eyes upon it. He could feel the sheer amount of power it gave off from where he stood.

Suddenly, the gateway began to flicker, and Levy wondered if he was not strong enough to keep it open.

"Father," Ares dared to speak, his voice small and deferent. "The gateway is not strong enough to step through. Should we try to enter with such a weak portal, we will likely be thrown into some other realm."

"Yes, I feared as much," Zeus replied. His eyes locked on the Tower in the distance. "Without a proper catalyst, this portal will be unusable. Something strong is needed to balance it out. Something primal."

Faster than lightning, he struck out, grabbing Hera around the neck and dragging her in front of the swirling mass of energy. Hera's eyes bulged from her purpling face as she clawed desperately to no avail at the god's large hand.

"Ares," The god spoke calmly, never taking his smoldering eyes from his wife's. "Come here."

Ares approached his father wearily, his face a mask. "Pull your blade, son." Hera's eyes widened as she realized the price she was to pay for her earlier outburst. "We need something powerful to stabilize this portal. Olympian ichor should suffice."

"Father," Ares pleaded, his mask slipping.

"Kill your mother, Ares," Zeus demanded, his voice even and unwavering. "Or there will be two Olympians sacrificed today."

Levy watched in horror as Ares plunged his sword through Hera's breast, spraying the gateway with ichor. Instantly the portal stopped flickering. The images on the other side began to clear, with detail and color showing more prominently with each spurt of ichor that touched it.

As essence leached from Hera, Zeus leaned in, his face just inches from hers. He intimately stroked her hair and spoke softly to her. "Even my queen is not exempt from consequence. May your suffering serve as a reminder to all who dare challenge my authority."

As the final bit of life finished draining from Hera's eyes, Zeus tossed her corpse to the side of the room like a ragdoll. Levy and Ares stood completely still, not daring to move or breathe out of turn.

"Go," Zeus said, not turning to face them. "Kill the Weaver and claim the throne for the Olympians as it should have been a thousand years ago."

Ares stepped through without a second glance, eager to escape his father's wrath. As Levy stepped up to the swirling portal, Zeus reached out, stopping him for a moment longer.

"I feel as though this does not need to be said," he began, a storm raging behind his eyes. "But do not fail me in this."

The monstrous presence Zeus gave off sent fear blossoming throughout Levy's chest. The king of the Olympians did not tell him what would happen if he failed, but he did not need to. Levy had never felt more like prey in his life than he did at that moment. He was fully ensnared by his predator.

"I understand, Lord Zeus." He said, retreating swiftly into the Realm of Fate.

CHAPTER 25

MALLORY

"Um, not to be a killjoy or anything, but are you sure this is your magical temple?" Mallory looked skeptically at Cyrus. The man could barely contain his salivation now that they reached their destination.

Though it had been described as an ancient ruin to her, what Mallory was looking at now was nothing more than a few rocks. Two large, vertical stones stood out of the cracked earth with a flat, horizontal stone bridging between them.

Beyond that, there was nothing more than scattered rubble dotting the barren Wastes. With all the tension and build-up of the trip, Mallory couldn't help but feel disappointed.

"This is most definitely the place," Cyrus responded, running his weathered hands over the smooth stone before him. "The whole area is thrumming with ancient power. The very stones are vibrating with it."

Mallory shot a questioning glance at Nes but he just shrugged in response. She was happy she wasn't the only one unable to feel whatever it was Cyrus felt. He continued running his hands along the stone, eyes shut tight in deep concentration.

"What is it you're looking for?" She asked, reveling in the jolt of frustration the Master showed at being interrupted.

"Some silence would be a good start," Cyrus replied with a quick sideways glance. "This is no simple ruin. With the amount of energy in the air, it appears as though it is the entranceway to a domain. A pocket dimension, if you will, that was created and exists within our realm. The same thing as young Quinn and his friends discovered when they met Hestia. I am looking for the entrance."

Mallory looked up at the darkening sky. It would be night soon and she hoped whatever the Master needed to find would be discovered quickly.

They hadn't even begun to set up any kind of camp, and she didn't relish the thought of trying to do so in the dark. The encounter with the Skorpios had rattled her far more than she cared to admit, and the sooner they were out of the open, the better.

"Aha!" Cyrus called out in triumph. All along the stone, glowing symbols appeared, blinking into existence despite the rock having been blank only moments ago. The symbols glowed golden, lighting up the immediate surroundings in the failing light.

"What do they say?" Nes asked, staring in awe at the foreign symbols.

"It is an ancient language from long ago, when both mortals and immortals walked this realm," Cyrus said, staring at the marvel with wonder in his eyes. "Give me a moment and I will translate."

He went to his bags and pulled several ancient scrolls from a protective wooden case, gingerly opening the first. The papyrus crackled softly as it unfurled, giving away its age.

Cyrus ran his fingers along it, now and then stopping to compare with the glowing symbols upon the stone and mumbling to himself.

"Darrik, fetch me a quill if you would, please."

The grizzled Master grumbled something under his breath before finding Cyrus' writing kit and bringing it to the man enthralled amongst the runes. Cyrus took the kit without so much as a thank you and began hurriedly scribbling notes down upon a blank sheet.

His eyes widened and breathing quickened as he finished transcribing whatever secrets he found amongst the texts. With a deep exhalation, he turned to them, sweaty and excited. Mallory had never seen someone get so hot and bothered over ancient text, and she hoped she never would again.

Cyrus cleared his throat, making a show of his findings, before lifting his writing and reading;

"In stone's embrace, a secret lies,
For those who yearn to claim this prize.
Seek out a child of ancient brew,
And Petram's secrets shall imbue."

All eyes fell on Nes as he finished reciting the text. Though the riddle was gaudy and, in Mallory's opinion, unnecessarily archaic, there were enough keywords in it to make out the gist of what it was trying to say.

"Why is everyone looking at me?" Nes asked, taking a step back.

"Isn't it obvious?" Cyrus asked, agitated. "If we want to open the domain housing the artifact, we need someone with Abyssillian blood to open the gateway."

"You need my blood?!" Nes exclaimed, horrified.

Mallory resisted the urge to shove her palm through her forehead. "No, Nes. We need your essence. Only someone with Abyssillian blood can open the gateway. I think what it is saying is only someone from Petram can imbue the stone with energy to open the domain."

"Precisely." Cyrus gave her an approving nod. "I do not think it will take much. Just run a current of your essence into the stone and the gateway should appear." The Master's eagerness was more and more evident with each word he spoke.

Nes shrugged, walked over to the stone, and placed his hand on its surface. He closed his eyes in concentration, allowing his energy to pool beneath his palm.

Mallory hoped it didn't take too much energy to open the domain, for the sake of his health. Nes was still pale from his fight with the Skorpios. It was miraculous enough he was up and moving on his own, let alone accessing his power once more.

She knew he was in constant pain. He grimaced with each step he took, though he tried his best to hide it. The passion he had for this mission, and the hope it provided him for the future of his people were propelling him forward with sheer grit and determination. Mallory had grown to respect him for it.

"Got it!" he yelled, his bright smile shining back at the party. He was even more pale than a moment ago, but he looked positively alive with his success. Where empty space had existed between the stones only moments prior, now deep green energy swirled in its place.

Cyrus approached the portal with reverence, slowly reaching his hand out before it. Then, as if remembering he was not alone, he snapped his hand back and turned to the group. "Come along, we are so very close now."

"What about our belongings?" Mallory asked, pointing to the mountain of canvas and bags stacked in a pile near the rubble.

"Leave it," Cyrus said, waving at it dismissively. "I do not believe this will take us long. We can set up camp when we return. Come along now."

He placed a hand on Nes' shoulder, guiding him into the swirling energy. They disappeared with a *pop*. The energy distorted as they entered before settling back into its smooth swirl.

A surge of panic hit Mallory as the two disappeared. Something about how Cyrus separated them didn't sit right with her. She quickly ran up to the gateway, attempting to enter after them, but just as she was about to step through, a sword sliced through from the opposite side, severing the portal and shattering the energy within.

"NES!" Mallory cried out, unable to comprehend what had just happened.

Darrik stepped through the now empty gateway, his sword held aloft, its edge glowing with a pale light.

"Oops." He shrugged, sneering at his poor humor.

Around his neck hung a silver talisman which emitted a matching light to his blade. He clutched it with his left hand, transferring its power to himself.

"Why did you do that?" Mallory protested, drawing her sword without thought.

"Your services are no longer required I'm afraid." Derrik walked menacingly toward her, his blade outstretched and humming. "You're just another unfortunate casualty, lost to this hellish landscape. Poor thing."

He lunged forward before she had a chance to respond, whipping his empowered blade in a horizontal strike meant to sever her head from her body. The old man was fast, but thanks to her years on the frontlines, she was able to keep pace and raise her blade, deflecting his strike. She used the momentum to roll backward, opening a small space between them.

"What is your…" He lunged again, refusing to give her a second to speak, or to even think. If it hadn't been for her years of training, allowing her muscles to move on instinct alone, she would already be dead.

Sparks flashed in the air as their blades collided, lighting the Master's twisted face under the now-darkened sky. Mallory was good with her blade, better than most. But against a sword imbued with whatever energy Darrik's talisman was providing, she knew she couldn't hold out forever. She had to end this if she wanted to survive and make it back to Nes.

Using the sandy earth beneath her, she shifted her feet, making it appear as though she was going to turn and run. Darrik fell for the bait, lunging forward eagerly, and opening himself to her true intent.

She used the low traction of the dirt to spin into a crouch and ducked beneath his blow. With all her might, she pushed up with her legs, launching the crown of her head into the old Master's nose with a sickening crunch.

The Master reeled back, clutching at his bloodied face, and cursing at the pain. Seeing her opportunity, she reached out, wrapping her hand around the talisman, and pulled hard, snapping the cord, and freeing it from Darrik's neck. Instantly the glow around his sword faded.

"You damn slip of a girl!" The master howled, spraying blood from between his fingers as he held his broken nose.

"Hey!" Mallory called back in mock affront. She twirled the talisman's cord around her finger, enjoying the burst of energy the trinket was giving her.

"You don't see me insulting your looks, do you? You ancient, crow-nosed, probably impotent, wannabe warrior."

Mallory's jabs hit home as the old man's face turned the same red as the blood that poured from his nose.

"You think I need that to beat you, girl? I'm the Master of Arms for a reason!" He sprinted forward, stabbing his blade toward her sternum.

With the energy that now surged through her thanks to the talisman, it looked as though he were running in slow motion. She stepped smoothly to the side, allowing the point of his sword to slide harmlessly past her. She raised her blade high into the air and brought it down hard, severing the Master's arm at the elbow.

"Now you're the Master of Arm," she smiled, kicking his blade out of reach. She had to give him credit, if she'd lost an arm, she figured the fight would have ended there.

The shock of it, let alone the pain, would have locked her up. Not Darrik, though. He reached down to his thigh, pulling a small blade from a hidden sheath with his one remaining arm, and chucked it at her.

Mallory watched as it twirled in slow motion, end over end. No. She realized that things weren't moving slowly for her, she was just hyper-focused. The night was brighter than it should have been.

She could smell the decay of the Wastes; could hear the loose earth as it was blown across the ground. The energy the talisman provided honed her senses to an extreme degree. Without a second thought, she snagged the knife from the air as easily as if it were lobbed to her.

"This is neat," she smiled, sauntering over to Darrik who was crouched low to the ground, trying to staunch the blood from his stump. "Any other surprises up your sleeves...ah, sleeve...for me?"

Darrik grimaced as she came closer, trying his best to mask the fear his eyes so plainly gave away.

"Do what you will," he jeered. "You won't be able to reach them. You saw yourself that the gateway needed someone with Abyssillian blood."

Panic began to rise as Mallory realized he spoke the truth. Nes went through the gateway, and they saw to it that any other Abyssillian in the area was sent far away. There was always the chance Quinn and Talius would come to find them, assuming they were successful at defeating Petram's intruders. Though even if they did, she doubted they would arrive in time to save Nes from whatever Cyrus had planned.

"What does Cyrus truly want with the artifact?" Mallory asked, trying to push down her rising sense of dread. They never should have split up in the first place. This was all seemingly too connected to be mere coincidence.

Darrik laughed; wheezing and coughing as his lungs ran out of air. "Go to Hades," he grinned, his teeth stained crimson. His eyes closed as he fell unconscious from his blood loss. Seconds later, the old Master's breathing stilled and he was gone.

Mallory let out a cry of frustration as she ran over to Cyrus' bags, ripping through them with reckless abandon in search of a scroll or text that could tell her how to reopen the gateway.

Finding nothing of use, she sprinted back to the stone Nes disappeared through, running her hands over it in the hopes of finding something, anything, that would offer her some help. When that failed, she resorted to hitting it, cursing it, and finally begging for it to open.

After an hour with no progress, she slid to the ground, resting her back against the vertical slab of stone. Her voice was hoarse from screaming; her throat fiery in protest of its rough treatment.

She promised Andra she would keep Nes safe. This was twice now she failed. She could only hope that despite his injuries, he would be able to see through Cyrus' deceit before he fell victim to whatever nefarious plan the Master had cooked up.

She stared up into the night sky, fighting to hold back tears of frustration. It was only then she realized that for the first time in the years since she lived in the Wastes, she could see the moon.

CHAPTER 26

QUINN

"Time is running out, Quinn," Chaos' voice came through the barrier, distorted by the bubble's energy. His tumultuous assault had not relented for even a second as Quinn continued gathering what energy he could from the Realm of Night. Small cracks began to appear along the barrier's surface, proving Chaos' words were not said in bluff.

Quinn knew this wasn't a permanent solution, but at this point, he didn't know what else he could do. The energy he collected wouldn't be enough to defeat the Primordial in his domain, but he had no alternative plan. Plus, the more essence he infused within himself, the more he began to realize just how limited he had been before with his use of it.

When he wore the mask, he only traversed the shadows tying his realm to the Realm of Night, using them as gateways to slip back and forth between the two. He now realized he had only been skimming the surface of this power's true potential.

When he fought with Levy and first lost control, the shadowy tentacles that whipped around him during the fight had been his, despite his lack of control.

Chaos used the same technique when fighting Janus at the base of the Tower. Perhaps he could mold that power into something more, something that could trap the Primordial while he retreated to the mortal realm. He did not see any shadows he could use for such a purpose, though he was starting to think that they weren't necessary, but were instead a simple mechanism Chaos had used to introduce him to his capabilities. If his hypothesis was correct, he wondered if he could open a portal with the use of the realm's energy, guided by his own.

A loud crack indicated he was out of time. A thick glob of Chaos' energy slammed into the top of the barrier, opening a wide fissure at the top which snaked to the very base. The next strike shattered the dome into a thousand crystals of light.

Quinn stood from his trance, took a deep breath, and focused on the new, yet familiar, essence that now coursed through his veins. He felt...powerful. Wild, untamed essence flooded through him, causing every part of his body to tingle.

His eyesight was extremely sharp. Every minute detail around him became clear and vibrant. As he breathed in, power welled within his lungs, dispersing again throughout his extremities with each exhale.

A large wave of energy slammed down upon him, but he saw it coming. Without hesitation he summoned some of the borrowed energy to his hands and struck out with it, splitting the wave in two so that it crashed harmlessly to each side of him.

Focusing on the figure of Chaos floating in the air, he pointed his fingers and pushed out, attempting to hurl his strike at the Primordial, but nothing happened.

"What's the matter?" Chaos called down at him, regathering his essence around him. "Unsure of how to use your stolen power?" He thrust his arms out, dropping another ton of the energy down upon Quinn.

For the second time, Quinn managed to rebuff the attack with ease. He considered why that worked so effortlessly, yet he couldn't seem to strike out with it. He thought back to each time he used this realm's gifts before, and a pattern began to form in his mind.

Whether it buffed his speed and stamina or boosted the strength behind a blow, or even the shadowy tendrils, each time he used it before, it never detached from his body. It seemed as though for the power to work for him, it had to remain a part of him.

Thinking quickly, he gathered the energy into his legs, coiling it tightly and holding it for as long as he could to build tension. When he could hold it back no longer, he pushed off from the ground with all the might he could muster, letting go of the essence as it propelled him forward with great speed.

Chaos' eyes widened as he approached, trying to pull his energy back up to him to use as a shield. Just before Quinn made contact, he shifted the energy into his arm, using the same method to build tension, before throwing his fist into Chaos' astonished face. The power exploded out of him as the punch landed, rocketing Chaos down to the surface.

As Quinn reached the apex of his jump, he started to fall back to the ground, frantically attempting to pull energy into him to shield the blow. Though his attack was effective, he did not have a firm enough grasp over this ability, and he expunged too much at once.

He hit the ground hard, feeling the air leave his lungs upon impact. It took everything he had to roll out of the way as a shadow descended upon him. An exact copy of his blade lodged itself into the ground where his head was only moments before.

He rolled to his feet, summoning his weapon just in time to block another incoming blow. The pressure that exploded forth as the swords crossed sent him flying backward, nearly knocking Quinn off his feet again.

Chaos once again changed his looks, this time copying Quinn to a tee. He wore the same tattered leather, held the same blade, and even mimicked his stance. The only difference was the mask that sat upon his face.

For the first time, Quinn saw what he looked like when he wore that mask, standing with his back straight and his head tilted eerily to the side. He admitted he was not a fan. It was no wonder Ashe wanted him to get rid of it.

Chaos chuckled, though, to Quinn's surprise, there was no malice in it. He did detect a hint of sorrow, which he thought odd. "Even at this moment, with everything happening, you still think of her."

Quinn was taken aback at his words, unsure of how he read that so clearly. It was not an accusation; he could tell by the tone of Chaos' voice. It was just a statement. Yet, it was a statement that held power behind it. He could read Quinn like a book, and he did not try to hide the fact.

"She is in danger again, you know," Chaos continued, cocking his head further as if to gauge Quinn's reaction to his words. "Even now, the enemy closes in around her."

"You're lying," Quinn said. "She's locked away in the Tower. Nobody can reach her there."

"Is that so?" He spoke as though talking to a child who was firm in his belief that he knew how the world worked despite having no exposure to it.

"Then let me show you." He raised his hand, allowing his thick cloud to coalesce in front of him. It began to spin, slowly at first, but quickly picking up speed until the blues and purples began to blend.

The empty space in the middle disappeared as an image began to fade into view. It depicted a long, winding pathway upon a floating island of stone. In the distance, a familiar tower rose from the horizon. Even from this realm, Quinn could feel the radiant energy emanating from it. Walking toward it, to Quinn's horror, were Levy and Ares.

"How did they reach it?" Quinn asked, transfixed upon the image. He wondered if Ashe was aware of the danger she was in, or if they were going to catch her completely off-guard.

Chaos snapped the portal closed, a predatory grin on his face. "How does not matter. If nobody interferes, the Weaver is as good as dead, and the Tower of Fate will fall into Zeus' hands. Give me your body, Quinn, and I will help, as I did the last time."

Quinn scoffed. "What help did you provide last time? I let you take over and you laughed at me as you attempted to let Ashe die anyway. I've learned my lesson."

"Well then, let us test your resolve," Chaos said, raising his sword. The smile was still wide on his face, mocking and unkind.

"Your only hope is to defeat me. Your power is running out though, I can sense it. While I am surrounded by mine. I can draw from an infinite pool of it. At least you can take solace in knowing when you die, your love will not be far behind."

He walked toward Quinn, his blade trailing energy at his side. Quinn lifted his own, prepared to meet the challenge head-on. If the only way he could reach Ashe was by defeating Chaos, then that is what he would do.

How did not matter, because he knew he didn't have a choice. It was either win or die. He summoned everything he had left, the shadowy cloak he had so feared before, now flaring to life at his command.

Chaos, still wearing Quinn's face, matched it with a cloak of his own. Tendrils of energy rushed out toward each other, eager to clash while the two warriors took their time to engage. Quinn knew one way or another, this would be it between them. The air was rife with a finality.

The pressure spiked as the energies of the cloaks collided, each strike like the snap of a whip, pulling and clawing at one another, trying to tear the other apart. The intensity was vicious and primal, as though two mindless beasts fought desperately to prove which was the alpha.

Then their blades met, metal on metal ringing out around them like battle hymns, shrill and energizing. Tendrils of Chaos' power whipped past Quinn's defenses, slicing shallow cuts along his face and arms, but Quinn ignored it, focusing solely on the song their swords created. Back and forth they stepped, locked in a bloody waltz that seemed to drag on for an eternity.

Quinn could feel his reserves fading, but he struggled to care. Years of resentment, fear, and anger washed away from him with each strike, draining his exhausted mind of all the weight he held onto.

Each time their swords crossed, the weight upon his shoulders lightened. Chaos began to give ground beneath the onslaught, his eyes wide at the display of raw power Quinn was putting out. At some point, Quinn realized he was crying, yet the tears felt revitalizing.

His doubts washed away in the heat of the battle, replaced with fierce determination. He didn't know what his plan was, or how he was going to move forward from this point, but for the first time in his life, he didn't care. All that mattered was this moment.

"STOP!" Chaos roared, rivulets of energy slamming down upon

him from above. "YOU WILL NOT PUSH ME BACK INTO MY OWN DOMAIN."

The new downpour of essence spiraled around him, blasting what remained of Quinn's cloak, yet still, he pushed on, striking swiftly and precisely. Chaos' defenses began to grow sluggish, despite the overwhelming presence he exuded, and Quinn struck home more often than not.

Quinn lashed out with the small portion of power he still held, shattering the corner of Chaos' mask. The eye staring back at him was wide and panicked, and for the first time, Quinn saw fear upon the Primordial's face.

His strike froze for a split second as the shock of that realization settled in, and the small window of opportunity was all Chaos needed. Realizing Quinn's mistake, Chaos punched Quinn in the stomach, driving the air out of his lungs and dropping him to his knees. Quinn's vision swam as fresh tears formed at the corners of his eyes.

"You will not defeat me," Chaos muttered, his exposed eye glassy and far away. "This is my realm. This is my power. That is my body. YOU WILL NOT WIN."

He dropped his blade and grabbed his hair with both hands, pulling hard as his eye slammed shut. Quinn's ears popped as he felt pressure like he had never felt before materialize in an instant. The energy coursing across Chaos' body pulsed in an uneven cadence, sending gusts of wind blasting out at Quinn, knocking him onto his back and flattening him.

"YOU WILL NOT SHUT ME AWAY," the Primordial roared, his voice booming and distorted.

His eye flashed purple as a vortex of pure energy erupted around him, engulfing him and towering high into the sky. From the top of the vortex, two massive, glowing eyes emerged, staring down at Quinn with malice.

Slowly, the vortex became more defined, losing its formlessness and growing sleek, until the form of a massive serpent loomed over Quinn. Its body was made of writhing energy, undulating at speeds too fast to keep up with.

A gaping maw ripped open beneath the luminescent eyes as it loosed an ear-splitting screech. Quinn felt warm blood trickle down the side of his neck. He froze in fear, now completely drained, as the serpent locked eyes with him.

"YOUR BODY WILL BE MINE!"

Its words did not come from the serpent itself, but rather from within Quinn's head, as though attempting to split his skull apart. His vision blurred from the internal reverberations and it was all he could do to remain conscious against the mental onslaught. A shadow passed over him then and he looked up in horror as the writhing energy was now directly above him.

"SUBMIT."

The serpent's maw stretched wide, showing nothing but blackness inside. With a whoosh, the energy came crashing down upon him, smashing him into the ground with a force so strong it shattered every bone in his body.

The cold embrace of the abyss washed over him, dulling the pain, and leaving his body numb, both physically and emotionally.

Stay strong, Ashe. He thought before the darkness claimed him.

CHAPTER 27

ANDRA

Andra stared in awe at the high walls of Stormhaven. Never before had she seen a place so bustling and teeming with life. The city was alive with spirited discussion and the heavy sounds of hammers on metal.

Though there were still plenty of half collapsed buildings and piles of rubble thanks to the fallout of Athena's wrath, many more stood strong and proud, and rebuilt with the sweat and hard work of Lend's people.

What captivated Andra even more than the lively city was the immense amount of color this new land held. The sky was cerulean and clear, allowing the yellow of the sun to shine brightly upon the many shades of green plant life that surrounded Stormhaven.

Flowers of every color imaginable cropped up from the grass and bloomed in the trees, accenting the world around them with life. Even if Andra didn't know each and every Abyssillian already, it would be easy to pick them out from the crowd. Every one of them stood and stared at this new world in absolute awe of the beauty they had missed out on for generations.

Better yet was the fact none of the humans Lend brought to Stormhaven with him mistreated any of her people. They did not even shoot them any dirty looks when they thought nobody was watching.

From the moment her ragged group of refugees arrived, the humans here were nothing but kind and welcoming. They did their best to treat any wounds her people received along the journey, fed them hot meals, and welcomed them with open arms into their social circles as though they had known each other their entire lives.

Their children intermingled with not a care in the world, no prejudices present. They taught the Abyssillian children games like tag and hide-and-go-seek, and in turn the Abyssillians taught them their own.

Andra pictured herself and Nes settling down here and truly starting their life together. The sheer positivity and promise Stormhaven held for her people was overwhelming, and for the first time since leaving Petram, Andra felt hope blossoming in her chest.

"I'd like to show you something." Lend's voice drifted into her daydreams, snapping her back to the present.

He wore his long hair tied back into a neat ponytail, falling straight down his back. A small pair of spectacles rested upon the bridge of his nose, framing his brilliant emerald eyes. He switched from his warrior's leathers into a long, thigh-length grey frock as soon as they had reached the city, preferring it to the stiff armor. Though Andra assumed most people would think of it as stuffy, she found it rather dashing.

"Lead the way," she said, trying her best to be cordial. Andra knew she had an edge to her that she tried very hard to not show. It was not that she was ungrateful—quite the opposite. But years of discrimination and a hard life out in the Wastes caused shields to go up, whether willingly or not.

That only intensified once she became responsible for her people's well-being. It was a responsibility that weighed heavily upon her, and even though she decided to trust Lend because of his connections with Quinn, dubious as they were, she was not prepared to drop those shields fully.

They walked deep into the city, through the winding cobbled

streets and half constructed buildings which lined them. Andra wondered if Quinn ever walked this exact path growing up here. It was easy for her to hold some resentment at the fact he'd gotten to live in this wonderful, color-filled city while the rest of the Abyssillians scraped by in the Wastes, but she knew better than that.

Though she was aware that was something he felt guilty about, she also knew his life was harder in many other ways. The world was not black and white and no two people suffered the same.

As they walked further into the heart of Stormhaven, a smaller wall began to rise into view. It rested upon a massive, stone stairway, and encircled what appeared to be a smaller city. The architecture of this new group of buildings looked ancient compared to the construction of the smaller housing and shops Lend's crew had been working on.

"I thought everything fell to rubble when Athena was freed?" Andra asked, unable to tear her eyes away from the piece of history she knew she was looking at.

"We thought so too," Lend replied as he started up the long stairway. "But the Citadel is ancient and likely holds power and secrets that few, if any, still know about. I hoped Commander Ashelia's friend with the mask was with your group since he grew up here. Maybe he could have offered some insight, but alas we will have to make do with the knowledge we have already found within."

As they made it to the top of the stairs, Andra realized despite the Citadel itself having withstood the godly attack, most of the grounds around it had not.

The wall was no longer solid but was instead just slabs of stone with large chunks missing from the sides. The earth inside was scorched, large divots and craters spotting the landscape. It looked as though a war was fought in the enclosed area, though Andra knew that was not true.

"There were bodies strewn all along these grounds and the streets below when we first traveled here," Lend explained with a faraway look in his eyes. "It was ghastly. We moved them of course, gave them proper burials, and saw to it that they were honored as they would have been by their people.

"But the sheer devastation of this place…" He shuddered. "I have fought monsters on the frontlines most of my adult life. I've seen man and woman, friend and foe, ripped to shreds and eaten. We both saw the hoard of the dead as it descended upon us, biting, and clawing and tearing.

"And despite all that, it still paled in comparison to the overwhelming destruction Athena visited upon this place. Children lay broken and burnt in the streets. I do not wish that sight upon anybody. If I had not been sure about the gods before, I was after that. They cannot be allowed to enter this realm again, or I fully believe it will be the end of us."

A cloud passed over the sun as he was speaking, bathing them in a cool shade. Andra felt a chill creep down her spine as she pictured the vivid scenery of Lend's words. She imagined the grounds of the Citadel dotted with the shades of those who had fallen, all staring at her with somber expressions.

She decided long ago the gods were not to be trusted or worshipped, long before even Quinn came home to them. She held no love in her heart for any being of power who allowed them to live as they had.

But Lend's words only solidified that belief further. She imagined Petram, broken and bloodied by whatever god had come their way, had they not left. She pictured her people laying in the streets, slaughtered as the people of Stormhaven had been.

She silently thanked Quinn and Talius for the sacrifice they made, staying to fight while allowing her to lead her people safely away, and hoped desperately that they were okay.

"Come on," Lend said, breaking the silence after some time passed. It seemed as though he needed his own time to think and grieve as well. Andra doubted the sight of what he found here was something easily forgotten.

He led her through a small, wooden doorway and into what appeared to be the remnants of a large mess hall. Though the wooden tables were smashed to pieces, shards of clay bowls and other cutlery were strewn about the room.

Through that room and down another hallway they traveled, passing what looked to be an indoor arena. It was the kind of arena that would have likely been filled with a sand pit, used for training stamina; yet strangely the floor was solid glass, as though it had been struck with immense heat and pressure.

They crossed the threshold of another doorway and stepped back out into the light of the sun. Andra found herself standing in a large, barren courtyard. The stone here was scorched darker than any other part of the Citadel had been, and Andra noticed their steps left footprints in the ashes which littered the ground. Up ahead she noticed a massive pair of doors that looked as though they had been blown off their hinges.

They hung loosely to the wall, blackened by whatever struck them. Inside were steps leading deep down below the earth, but Andra could see nothing more through the darkness.

"What's down there?" she asked, unable to pull her eyes away.

"That is what I wanted to show you," Lend replied.

Andra looked up at him, skeptical of following him alone into the depths of the Citadel. He must have sensed her unease because he held his hands up in a placating gesture.

"You do not need to come if you do not want to. I am certainly not going to force or attempt to coerce you. This is where Athena was held before she was set free. It is here I believe I may have found a way to ensure Stormhaven's safety, but I am unsure how to move forward with it. I was hoping to show it to you and receive your input. Nothing more."

Andra thought about how free she felt since arriving in the city. The happiness of her people was evident; their healing already well on its way. The walls around the city were towering and solid, but she knew that simple stone would not withstand a godly attack, although, throughout her life that was not much of a concern, it was becoming clearer each day that the days of living free from Olympian influence were waning. She nodded her consent to Lend, who looked relieved that she agreed and followed him down into the depths below.

"Have you been down here before?" Andra asked as they made their way into the waiting darkness. Now that they were out of the sun, it became cold. Every few steps her face collided with thick cobwebs, and she frantically brushed them away.

"Twice." He replied, holding a flickering torch out in front of him to light their way. "I first ventured down here in search of any more bodies to bury. The scorching of the Citadel was strongest here so I imagined it would be heavy with casualties.

"To my surprise there were none. The second time was after I did some research in the Citadel's library, trying to find more information on what I found on my first trip. I don't know how that room survived Athena's wrath, though I imagine it was heavily warded.

"This was the center for the war effort to claim the Tower, and I am sure the Masters here wanted to protect their knowledge at all costs."

Andra began to ask him what he found but he cut her off. "It would honestly just be easier to show you than to try and describe it. I realize how suspicious that sounds, but you will see what I mean soon. We are almost there."

Soon after he said those words the corridor they traveled opened into a large chamber. The walls were made from packed earth, as though the room had been carved into the ground itself.

In the center was an onyx altar, large and cylindrical. Long silver chains draped from the top and lay in a tangled pile on the ground. The contrast of black and silver was beautiful, and yet there was something sinister about the shrine.

"What is it?" Andra asked, breathlessly.

"Based on the information I found, this is where they held Athena. Those chains are engraved with powerful runes capable of holding her captive and siphoning her energy into the walls. They are the same style of chain the Masters used to bind the Tower of Fate to our realm when it appeared again."

Lend held one of the chains in his hand as he spoke, running his thumb along the links. "It is my hope that we can find another source to power them again. You saw how the walls still held strong despite Athena's rage. If we can find a way to fill them with essence again, then Stormhaven can weather the Olympians' wrath."

Andra carefully considered his words. There was no malice or threat in them. It didn't appear as though he was making any suggestions, but instead genuinely wanted her input. Even so, she felt it best to set the record straight.

"I do not think there are any among my people strong enough to withstand that kind of task," She said hesitantly, gauging his expression as she spoke. "And even if there was, I would not ask them to subject themselves to something so torturous."

Lend started at her words, a look of genuine shock plain on his face, followed by understanding. "Of course not! I did not mean for you or one of your people to take up such a burden. I would never ask that of you."

Andra let out a breath, relieved to have that out of the way. "I didn't think so, but I had to be sure. Perhaps you can show me to the library where you initially discovered your information. Maybe there's something there that can point us in the right direction?"

"I have scoured the library up and down, though perhaps with a second pair of eyes, we may be able to…" His words cut off as he grabbed Andra's arm, pulling her behind him.

She followed his gaze to the entrance of the room, where a shadow lurked just out of the light of their torch.

"Show yourself," He demanded, a bit of the commander from his time in the army creeping its way into his voice. Andra palmed a knife from her sleeve, ready to throw it at a moment's notice should the newcomer pose a threat to them.

The shadow shifted in the darkness, slowly limping forward as the light washed over his familiar features. His head was still as bald as the last time she'd seen him, though his brown beard held far more grey in it now. The orange Master's robes were tattered, and a large hole was torn in the middle of his chest, showing a large, inflamed scar in the skin beneath it.

"Talius?" Andra ran forward, catching the Master as he stumbled. She saw as she came closer that his robes were not just tattered, but covered in ichor as well. The wound on his chest seemed fresh. "What happened? Where is Quinn?"

The Master looked at her, thinly veiled pain behind his eyes. "I do not know, child. He is not dead, of that much I am certain. But wherever he was taken, he is no longer within this realm."

Andra felt the blood drain from her face as he spoke. Lend walked up beside her, placing a steadying hand on her shoulder.

The master looked at the chains he held and said, "I am not long for this world I'm afraid, but before I go, I believe I may be of assistance one last time."

CHAPTER 28

ASHE

The two men stood before Ashe, radiating a dangerous combination of desperation and fear. She wasn't sure why they were the ones feeling such a way, as it was they who trespassed upon her domain, yet they stank of it. The god stood tall in his radiant armor, his bronzed skin a stark contrast to the elaborate gold. Slightly behind him stood an old friend with whom she held so much history, both good and bad.

"Hello, Levy." She searched his face, trying to find some semblance of the old friend she had known once upon a time.

"Hey, Fire Queen." His voice was small and he refused to look her in the eye, instead focusing intently on the floating orbs above her.

She shifted her gaze to the god beside him. Based on his appearance, she presumed him to be Ares, the god of war. His presence certainly matched his orb. "To what do I owe the pleasure of this intrusion?"

The god drew his sword, a red aura blazing to life around him. "Lord Zeus sends his regards."

"That's it then?" She asked. "Zeus can't handle having lost the Tower for the first time in millennia, so he sends you to kill me and reclaim it?"

The god grunted, taking a heavy step toward her. Levy followed close behind, pulling an ornate spear from his back, though he looked reluctant. Ashe felt a small flame of hope blossom in her chest. Perhaps her friend was not lost just yet.

"It does not have to be this way," she said, gently. Though she spoke to Ares, the words were meant for Levy. "There was a time when man and god walked together; celebrated life and all of its wonders *together*." She emphasized the word, hoping beyond hope her words resonated with him. "There is no reason we can't go back to that."

"Be silent, Weaver," Ares snarled with contempt. "Those days are long past, and good riddance to them. The fact we immortals ever shared anything with the unwashed masses is laughable. If you think such a future exists for your kind, then you have failed in your duty."

Levy looked stricken at Ares' words, his face pale in the whitewashed room. Ashe knew he was many things, but a fool was not one of them. Deep down he had known all along the gods could not help him accomplish what he truly wanted.

He'd lost himself to the siren call of power, but she was certain he still had enough humanity left in him to come back from that cliff. She stared at him, pleading with her eyes to return before he fell so far he could never recover.

"Sorry, Ashe." Were the only words he could muster. And he was right, he did look sorry. The expression he wore on his face was so uncharacteristic, that she was not sure she even recognized him at that moment.

 Her heart shattered for him. Somewhere along his journey, he truly lost himself, and though glimpses of the old Levy were still there, Ashe was unsure he would ever regain his footing.

She was unable to hide her pain, realizing for the first time how hard the choice must have been for Quinn to drop Levy into the lava. Even with the weight of her duty, and what it meant to the mortal realm, there was a part of her that did not want to do the same.

Yet, she knew there were too many innocent lives at stake. The future was a dark one indeed, and no amount of weaving could stop it from wreaking havoc upon humanity. But she could limit its destruction, which is more than she could do if she were dead.

"Then I will do what I must," She whispered, drawing her daggers from their sheaths.

The ground erupted in a blaze of scorching fire, separating Ares from the fight. Ashe sprinted at Levy, hoping to turn the mismatch more in her favor. She did not want to kill him, but if she had to do it, she would rather get it out of the way first so that sentiment would not lead to her downfall. She would grieve after when she knew the future was secure.

Ashe's eyes blazed with determination as she unleashed her power, conjuring torrents of flames that danced around her lithe frame. As she moved, she weaved intricate patterns with the threads of fate, seeking to further change the battlefield to her advantage by harnessing the very essence of destiny itself.

Levy whirled his spear in front of him, slicing through the threads that sought to bind him, and ducked just in time to avoid a blade wreathed in flame from biting into his throat.

From off to the side Ares bellowed his mighty cry, unleashing a torrent of raw power and charging through the fire with unmatched aggression. Ash turned to meet him, kicking Levy back through a wall of flame to avoid a two-on-one scenario.

She turned to meet Ares's blade with her dagger, the explosion of metal-on-metal echoing through the Tower. Ashe unleashed her fiery wrath upon the god, launching a fireball that exploded with devastating force. Flames licked at Ares' formidable armor, but his godly resilience allowed him to withstand the intense heat, pushing forward with an unyielding resolve.

Then Levy returned once more through her curtain of flame, launching attacks of his own. Whenever she attempted to engage with Ares, he continued to deflect her onslaught with precise and powerful strikes.

His spear danced with lethal grace, creating a protective barrier for Ares as he parried and countered Ashe's fiery assaults. The floor shook with the ferocity of their struggle; the clash of their powers reverberating up the very walls of the Tower.

Knowing she needed to do something to turn the fight in her

favor lest she be overpowered, she coiled the threads of fate around her allowing them to entwine with the flames which surrounded her. With deft command, she unleashed them upon her foes, binding Ares and Levy to restrict their movements as they slowly began sapping away the god's divine strength.

She was no longer the girl she once was, mortal and playing with powers she could barely comprehend. This was her tower, and these were her flames. Fate was hers to command and if she had to pump every drop of her essence into draining Ares of his godhood, then so be it.

However, Ares, the embodiment of war and conflict, was not easily subdued. With a surge of godly might, he shredded the fiery threads that ensnared them, breaking free from the blazing bindings. The god unleashed his fury, directing his divine wrath towards Ashe.

It was all she could do to deflect his strikes, though now and again the sword would connect, biting deep into Ashe's shoulders and legs. Despite the fresh wave of pain each new cut sent lancing through her, she continued to push back with her intensity, using her fire to win ground, and her threads to stop a strike here and there; throwing the god out of his rhythm.

And then Levy was back again, like an annoying fly that would not go away. His arms were covered in burns from the fiery restraints that had held him, yet he continued to fight like a demon; despite the pain he surely felt.

Ashe could feel her movements beginning to grow sluggish, her fiery aura flickering and waning. As if he could sense her vulnerability, Levy increased the speed of his strikes, driving her further onto the defensive.

She felt him infuse his weapon with a familiar energy and knew she could not allow him to strike her directly, or the fight would be over. His blows rained down heavily, harder than any mortal should have been able to hit. Each time sapped more of her strength as she struggled to deflect his spear until finally, he succeeded in knocking one of her daggers from her hand.

Ares, sensing victory, seized the opportunity, launching a final, devastating strike. He lunged forward, his sword cleaving through her defenses, and a blast of divine energy sent her sprawling to the ground.

Silence descended upon the battlefield as her flames gradually receded, leaving only the charred remnants of the battle that took place. Ashe lay against the scorched floor, her strength depleted. Levy stood over her, his spear held at the ready, while Ares sheathed his sword with a satisfied smirk.

"I'll give you this," the god rumbled. His voice was gravelly from the heat and smoke. "You fight well for a half-breed."

Ashe gritted her teeth, ignoring the trickle of ichor that traced down her neck as she pressed it against the edge of Levy's spear, the bitter taste of failure heavy in her mouth. "Your superiority complex will be your downfall, Ares."

"My superiority is your downfall." He turned to Levy. "Finish her."

"Me?" Levy asked, eyes widening at the command. "Shouldn't you do it? We wouldn't have won if you hadn't freed us from her thread. This is your victory, so it should be your kill."

He does not want to kill me. Ashe thought to herself as she watched him try to convince the god to claim his prize. *Oh, sweet Levy. Despite all your bluster and posturing, there is still some good inside of you.*

"It is precisely because of your weakness that you will kill her. This is your moment to prove your worth. Up to this point you have yet to do so."

The god spoke down to him as though he were no more than a dog, and she could see that it bristled him. Ashe thought back to the fear that was present in his eyes when they first entered the Tower. She realized that he was caught in a place he did not want to be, angry, resentful, and terrified.

Levy looked back at Ares and started to say, "Perhaps we could take…"

"FINISH HER OR I WILL GUT YOU HERE AND NOW!"

The god pulled his sword free once again as he roared at Levy. The rage and power behind his words caused Ashe to flinch.

He met her eyes again and a fresh wave of sorrow washed through her. They were the eyes of a child, broken and fearful. They reminded her of Quinn's eyes all those years ago when he was mistreated and demonized by the Masters. She could see he felt trapped, bitter at what he had become, yet afraid of the consequences should he refuse.

"Later, Fire Queen." He raised the spear's edge away from her throat, readjusting it so that the tip hovered directly above her; and with one swift, fluid motion, he stabbed.

CHAPTER 29

QUINN

Quinn awoke to blissful nothingness. The world was a void around him; his body was weightless and floating. A wave of confusion washed over his senses. His mind attempted to comprehend this ethereal setting.

As he took a deep breath, he noticed something extraordinary, his thoughts were unusually clear and serene. The usual guilt and restlessness that plagued his mind had vanished, replaced by an overwhelming sense of peace.

In the stillness of the void, Quinn's senses were sharpened, and he became acutely aware of the absence of external distractions. There were no aching muscles, no whirling energies or heart-pumping anxieties. All that remained was an enveloping calmness that soothed his weary soul.

With each passing moment, Quinn felt his muscles unwind, releasing the tension that had built up over years of training and combat, his relentless pursuit of success. The weight of responsibility and the ceaseless chatter of worries and wounds faded away, leaving behind a sense of ease and tranquility.

A familiar mask appeared above him, staring down into his eyes. Images he had seen play out time and time again began to flash through his mind: Levy's panic as he fell to the lava below, Ashe turning away from him as the doors to the Tower of Fate slammed shut, Sen's neck broken and eyes glassy.

Every single choice, every moment of guilt and sorrow; of fear and desperation played for him in one melodramatic slideshow. Moments that had kept Quinn up at night, screaming and crying out for someone, anyone, to pull him from the nightmares that plagued his mind. And yet, he did not feel fear nor anguish at seeing them now.

Not in this peaceful plane. Instead, he felt pity for the creature who wore the mask. Pity for the being before him, so trapped within this never-ending cycle of remorse and shame that he could no longer appreciate life for what it was around him.

Quinn reached up, attempting to pull the mask from the face of this pitiful replica. The being let out a startled cry, lunging back out of his reach. It looked shaken as if it could not believe that Quinn was not affected by the memories which had tormented him for so long.

"Come now," Quinn spoke to it soothingly. "There is no reason to be afraid."

"I will give you this," The creature replied, feigning bravado. "You are resilient for a mortal. Most of your kind would have crumpled by now under the onslaught of my essence."

Quinn smiled at the being's false courage. Though it spoke with an air of confidence, he could read the falseness as easily as he could read himself.

"You can stop pretending to be Chaos," he chided. He made no further attempt to reach up to the being, settling instead for staring at him as he spoke.

"What are you talking about? Perhaps you are closer to death than I thought if you can no longer tell who I am." The being's face was inches from his own now; the hollow eyes of the mask were no longer able to hide what lay behind it.

"Then why are you so afraid?" Quinn asked. The eyes that

stared back at him were wide with panic and fear. The creature's breathing was rapid and heavy, betraying the façade of confidence which masked his terror.

"Why would I be afraid?" it responded, though there was no longer any fire behind its words. It flinched as Quinn sat up, shifting so that he could face the being directly. It mimicked his movements, mirroring his very posture.

"You are not Chaos, just as much as I am not Chaos." Quinn reached out, laying his hand on the side of the being's mask. It winced at the contact but made no effort to pull away from his reach.

"You remember Chaos. You latched onto his energy, wild and unbalanced as it was, because you are wild and unbalanced as well. You feed off it, and I off of you. But Chaos is no more."

Quinn slowly pulled the mask away from the creature's face, careful to avoid any sudden movements. He stared into his own eyes, wild and filled with trepidation. Tears spilled from them, rampant and unquelled, and Quinn noticed he had begun to cry as well.

"Then what am I?" The being whispered, its eyes locked firmly on Quinn's.

Quinn thought of the day he had first gotten the mask in Hestia's domain. He thought of how Hestia had to make the decision for him of which way he would go, how his body locked up at first when Janus dropped the mask and the girl.

"You are my indecision."

He thought of his terror when Levy outed his secret to the Masters, and of how afraid he was of losing Ashe when she discovered it as well.

"You are my fear."

Emotion flooded into him as he remembered Athena laying waste to the Citadel after he escaped with Ashe. He remembered traveling to the Wastes for the first time in his life and seeing the poverty and squalor his people lived in while he grew up with food and comfort readily available to him.

He pictured Levy, standing against him after pilfering the Orb of Hades and lamented at how he could have missed the signs of his best friend's internal battle, wrapped up as he was in his feelings for Ashe,

"You are my guilt."

Quinn touched his forehead to his copy's, closing his eyes as they shared a thousand more memories and emotions between them. He thought about how bitter he felt growing up as Abyssillian in a human city, wishing things were different.

He embraced his self-loathing as he again thought of the girl he let fall the day he grasped for a power he should have never had. He grappled with his insecurity over being unable to control the power he had been left with after Ashe shattered the mask in the fight for the Tower, and with the weight of disappointment that Talius tried so hard to hide at seeing his weakness.

Loneliness crept up within him as he thought of Ashe, no longer within reach of him, and accepted that it was okay to feel the frustration of knowing she picked duty over him. He loved that side of her too.

"You are me," He said, opening his eyes once more to see his mirror image encompassed in a soft light. The terror and sorrow that had been so prevalent had softened now, replaced with a contentedness he had never felt before. "And you are forgiven."

Subtle ripples coursed through the being, causing the essence surrounding it to shimmer with an ethereal radiance. The transformation started at its fingertips; faint trails of essence disengaging and drifting lazily into the air, like fireflies ascending into a starlit sky.

Slowly its entire body began to dissolve, swirling around Quinn in a delicate dance. With a burst of radiant energy, the particles flowed seamlessly back toward Quinn's body. The gentle streams of light cascaded gracefully, interweaving with one another as they found their rightful place.

The luminous particles settled upon Quinn's skin, flowing into every contour, like a million fragments of a beautiful mosaic reassembling. For the first time in his life, Quinn felt complete.

He closed his eyes and took a deep, shuddering breath, allowing his turbulent emotions to settle. A newfound confidence was present within him, like a steady flame burning at his core and spreading its warmth throughout.

When he opened them again, he was back in the Realm of Night, standing in the center of the billowing energy that crashed down upon him. He was not sure whether the whole thing was a hallucination, or if he came close to succumbing to the energy's crushing pressure.

What he did know was it no longer hurt him as it had before. Instead of feeling dangerous and untamed, the energy thrummed with excitement and a recognizable familiarity, as though it were a wild stallion waiting to be reined in by someone skilled enough to ride it.

Quinn raised both hands into the air, grasping at the sides of the turbulent vortex and pulling at the energy, willing it to respond to his touch. At first, it pulled away, hesitant to allow itself to be controlled by just anyone. But Quinn was not just anyone. He pulled at it again, stronger and with more determination, opening himself to it and allowing it to flood every fiber of his being.

Every cell inside of him screamed at the overwhelming intensity of the energy, and for a moment he wondered if he was going to fade away, turning into energy himself and joining it in its feral glory.

He was determined to harness this power. He gritted his teeth and dug his feet into the ground, exerting his will upon it once more, and forcing every last particle within him. It fought back for a moment more, desperate to escape its new confines before finally settling down and accepting Quinn.

Instantly the Realm of Night fell quiet, as if no struggle had ever taken place. Energy the likes of which Quinn had never felt before jolted through him, quickening his breathing, and strengthening all his senses to an unbelievable degree.

He felt as though he could hoist Mount Olympus itself if he so chose to. With a delicate grace, he lifted his hand, summoning the newfound power to his fingertips. Purple energy flickered between them, like lightning jumping back and forth between clouds.

He thought of Petram and pushed the energy from his palm. Instantly the energy shot forth, circling in the air faster and faster until an image formed in the center, and the portal was created. Realizing how easy it was to control, he cut the energy supply off and the portal shattered and faded.

He wondered if it would be as easy to open a portal to a place he had never been before, and with another thought, he pushed more energy out from his fingertips. Though it pushed back a bit at first, he continued to power the portal, picturing the image of the Tower the faux Chaos had shown him before.

It did not surprise him that he struggled more to open this one, as he was doing so based on memory rather than experience. An idea sprung to mind, and he decided to try concentrating on energy rather than image, hoping it may come easier to him.

Locating Ashe's energy was not difficult. He had always had a penchant for feeling the power something emanated, and Ashe's was one he was intimately familiar with. Once he locked onto that, the energy began spinning with an emphatic zeal, opening a portal within moments. The image was the same as he had seen before; a floating island in a twilit sky; the monstrous Tower rising from the horizon in the distance.

Quinn pushed essence into his legs, pride welling up inside him at how swiftly he was managing this new power. It was similar to what he'd been able to do before, only amplified to an insane degree. With this newfound strength, he felt as though he could take on all of the Olympians.

Without wasting another second, he sprinted at the portal with otherworldly speed, leaping through and falling to the rocky pathway below. There was a slight pop of pressure as he stepped between realms, though it was nowhere near as intense as it had been when he had crossed over into Hestia's realm all those years ago.

A wave of Ashe's essence crashed into him, nearly taking him off his feet. He looked up toward the Tower, amazed at the amount of energy given off. If Ashe was throwing around that kind of firepower, Quinn had no doubt she was in trouble. Without another thought he took off in the direction of the blast, hoping he was able to reach her in time.

CHAPTER 30

LEVY

The midday sun cast a blazing heat upon the ancient Citadel, its rays mercilessly seeping into the weathered stones. Levy, young and impetuous as he was, had just finished his morning training and had demanded a mission.

Though still only ten years old, he spent his entire life preparing to be a hero, but he had yet been able to show what he could do in real combat. The Masters always told him he was too young to be sent out into the real world.

It was unfair. He was miles ahead of both Quinn and Ashe; both children late arrivals to the Citadel and therefore behind in their training. It was only fair he be allowed to put his skills to the test against a monster outside the walls. How could he be a hero if he never left the safety of the Masters' watchful eyes?

He wiped the sweat from his brow as he stood before the towering figures who governed his every step within the boundaries of the Citadel. The Masters' faces were stern and bore an air of authority and wisdom that Levy both admired and feared.

"Levy," spoke the eldest of the Masters, his voice carrying over the courtyard like a distant thunderclap. "You have asked for a task, and I have seen fit to grant you one of utmost importance."

Levy's heart quickened. He diligently honed his skills, hoping for a chance to prove his worth. Now, that opportunity had finally presented itself. Quinn was going to be so jealous.

"We dispatched Ashelia to gather supplies this morning," continued a second Master, his voice thin and reedy as if every word was difficult to get out. "She has not returned, and we fear for her safety. It has not been long since the incident in the slums and people are likely still not happy."

Levy could recall overhearing the Masters discuss Ashe in hushed tones a few separate times. She grew up poor in the slums of Stormhaven, directly beneath the shadow of the great walls. They spoke of how she always had a strange love of fire, and one day accidentally set the slums ablaze.

Many families lost their homes in the fire, and many more their lives. Her parents, unable to look at her after the incident, had sold her to the Masters, and in return received enough coin to pay for the damages their daughter caused.

Something about that had never sat right with Levy. The girl he had come to reluctantly know did not seem like the type to set buildings ablaze. She was sweet and loving and she did not seem as if she had any interest in harming even the most annoying of insects, let alone another person.

"Levy, are you listening?" a stern voice cut into his thoughts.

"Apologies Master!" he bowed low, hiding his scarlet face.

"As we were saying, your mission is to find young Ashelia and ensure her safe return to the Citadel."

Levy's mind whirled with a mix of agitation on determination. On one hand, he was thrilled to finally have a mission that took him outside of the Citadel walls, even if it was only down into Stormhaven below.

On the other hand, this was not a mission of danger or heroics, but instead a mission to find Ashe and return. Not the most exciting objective. Ashe was still in the very early stages of her training, so her potential had not yet been fully realized. The thought of the townspeople harming her in any way made his blood boil. Perhaps *there would be some fighting after all.*

He smiled at the thought, bowing again before the Masters. "I will find her and bring her back unharmed."

With their blessing, Levy departed from the sanctuary of the Citadel, stepping into the scorching embrace of the summer day. He was surprised they had asked Levy to fulfill this request and not Quinn.

He and Ashe had become inseparable since she joined their little family. Perhaps he was stuck in one of his classes, though more likely he was being punished in some way by Master Enkar. The little Master certainly had it out for his friend.

He would probably be rather cross that Levy got to play hero for the pretty blonde girl this time. It was rather easy to tell Quinn was smitten with the girl, though to Levy's mild annoyance, she seemed to feel the same.

The streets of Stormhaven sprawled before him, a maze of cobblestones and faded storefronts. His gaze darted from one alleyway to another, searching for any sign of his missing comrade. Stormhaven was relatively safe compared to most other cities.

Poverty was low, which in turn kept the crime rate low as well, but that didn't mean the crime didn't exist, and the darkened alleyways were the perfect place for such misdeeds to occur.

As Levy weaved through the winding streets, he caught the faint echo of laughter and jeers. Curiosity tugged at him like an invisible thread, pulling him toward the commotion. Turning onto a narrow side street, he continued to follow the sound as it grew louder, mingling with the stifled cries of someone in distress.

His heart quickened with a mix of concern and anger as he witnessed a troubling scene. A group of children, only slightly older than Levy himself, formed a circle around a trembling Ashe, their faces twisted with malice. Her eyes were wide with fear and desperation as she had become the target of their merciless bullying.

Without a moment's hesitation, Levy charged forward, his voice ringing out with authority. "Enough!"

The bullies turned to face him, their cruel grins faltering as they assessed the newcomer. Levy stood tall, his jaw set in determination, radiating an unyielding strength that belied his youth.

"Leave her alone," he commanded, his voice filled with a fire

that demanded obedience.

As if compelled by some unspoken force, the children dispersed, their fun abruptly extinguished.

Are you alright?" Levy asked, extending a hand to help her up.

"Thank you," Ashe cried, burying her head in Levy's chest. "It's not true." She muttered; her words muffled as she spoke into his shirt. "I didn't set that fire. I wouldn't."

"I believe you," Levy replied. And he did. Whatever had happened in the slums, there was no way this girl was responsible. She could have fought back against those kids had she chosen to

She may be new, but he was sure she still had more combat training than any of them. Her gentle nature was likely to get her killed someday if that was not something she could break free from.

"Thank you, Levy," she spoke. His heart fluttered as he stared down into her wide, green eyes; eyes filled to the brim with sadness and fear, yet with just a glimmer of hope as well.

It was those same eyes he stared into now, the edge of his spear pressed firmly to the side of her neck. A small trail of blood traced its way down to her collarbone before disappearing beneath her shirt. She gave them one hell of a fight, and though in the end, she lost, he did not think that would be the outcome every time.

"Finish her," Ares commanded, growing impatient at his hesitance. "Be a good dog and listen."

Levy's hands clenched tighter around the shaft of the spear to stop the tip from shaking. This was the moment that would allow him to accomplish everything he hoped for.

They stormed the Realm of Fate thanks to his energy, and defeated the Weaver within the Tower. If he killed her now, control of fate would be the Olympians' once more, and Zeus was bound to reward him with godhood. With the power that came with divinity, he would be strong enough to change his people's lives for the better.

But would Zeus allow that? His conscious screamed at him, staying his hand. Levy was not sure of the answer to that question.

He had been told time and time again if he helped achieve this, he would be free to control the Mortal Realm. All the gods wanted was the freedom to access it again. Yet, he had seen just how poorly Zeus treated those he was supposed to love. What would he do to those he cared nothing for?

We can still stand together; it is not too late. The hope and sadness in Ashe's eyes screamed at him.

Those damn eyes of hers were always filled with love and kindness. How could she look at him like that now, after all he had done to her? She had no right to care about him still.

No, you have no right to be cared for. His conscious butted in again, twisting the dagger deeper.

"What's the matter?" Ares called, his words dripping with derision. "Do you not have the heart to kill your little girlfriend? I told my father you were a waste of time."

"It's fine!" Levy called back, still not breaking from Ashe's eyes. "I can do this."

"You had better!" Ares' voice took on a sharp edge. "Because if you cannot, then becoming one of us will be the least of your worries. We do not allow spineless worms to sit upon Olympus."

Levy was so sick of Ares' contempt. He was tired of being mocked and looked down upon, and treated as though he were nothing more than dirt beneath the feet of the gods for which to walk on. He saw Ashe's eyes widen as he made his choice.

"You want to call me weak? You think I don't have it in me to kill? Then watch carefully Ares."

Levy pulled the edge of the spear away from Ashe's neck and pointed the tip at the middle of her throat. One quick jab was all it would take to sever her spine.

"Later, Fire Queen," he said, watching a tear fall from the corner of her eye, and then he spun, stabbing the tip of the spear directly into Ares' chest.

CHAPTER 31

NES

As Nes stepped through the portal, he was immediately struck by the enchanting sight that unfolded before his eyes. Nature had triumphed over the man-made structure, reclaiming its dominion with an exuberant display of greenery the likes of which he had never seen before.

Vines, thick and sinewy, coiled around ancient stone pillars; their tendrils reaching out at the strange orbs of light that shone down from the ceiling in soft shades of blue and green. They created a web-like tapestry that weaved its way across the ceiling, casting intricate patterns of light and shadow on the floor below. The sound of rushing water roared from deeper within, reverberating across the ancient stone walls.

The air was heavy with the scent of damp earth and the faint aroma of blossoming flowers. A symphony of chirping insects and gently rustling leaves filled the once-silent halls, bringing the space to life. More strange light pierced through the gaps in the vine-laden windows, casting ethereal rays that illuminated the scene like celestial spotlights.

Though partially concealed by a lush carpet of moss and ferns, the floor still bore the remnants of the temple's grandeur, though Nes almost preferred nature to the stone. Mosaic tiles, cracked and weathered, peeked through the verdant carpet, offering glimpses of their former opulence. Delicate flowers in vibrant hues sprang forth from the cracks, adding bursts of color to an otherwise green tableau.

The walls, once adorned with intricate carvings, now provided a backdrop for a riotous display of foliage. Ivy cascaded from alcoves, spilling its cascading leaves in a verdant waterfall. Plants perched precariously on stone ledges, their tendrils trailing down like emerald veins. The faint rays of light caught the leaves, causing them to shimmer in a captivating display.

At the center of the room, a colossal tree had taken root. Its ancient trunk rose tall, gnarled, and imposing, its branches spreading outward like protective arms. Leaves of varying shades of green created a dense canopy, filtering the light and casting a dappled glow upon the ground below. The roots, like serpents, slithered across the marble floor; their power evident as they gripped and reshaped the very foundation of the temple.

The atmosphere within the structure was one of tranquility and harmony. The union of man-made splendor and nature's unyielding spirit created a captivating contrast. It was a place where nature and history intertwined, a sanctuary that served as a testament to the enduring beauty and power of the natural world.

Nes wished Andra, as well as the rest of the Abyssillian people, could be here to witness the sacred beauty of nature the temple held. He needed to succeed here so that they could.

"Beautiful, isn't it?" Cyrus asked, stepping up beside him.

"It's magnificent," Nes replied, breathless. "Never in my life did I think I would see such a thing, let alone within the very Wastes I grew up in."

Behind the two, the portal sputtered; the green glow weakening before disappearing altogether.

"What happened?" Nes asked Cyrus, a hint of worry creeping into his voice.

Cyrus looked unalarmed, shrugging as though he expected it to happen.

"That gateway was ancient, and your power was already weakened thanks to the fight with the Skorpios. Unsurprisingly, the portal was unstable. It likely collapsed in on itself once we stepped through, unable to handle the strain we put on it."

"What about Mallory and Darrik?" he asked, feeling slightly better at the Master's explanation. He was a scholar and knew a lot about the ways of ancient powers. If he was not concerned about the portal snapping closed, then he figured he should not be either.

"Fret not, young Nes. They can set up camp for us while we locate the artifact. If anything, they have an easy job. We are the ones who will have to be vigilant for traps as we make our way into the heart of this place."

The Master produced a crystal from a pocket in his robes, muttering a word beneath his breath and holding it out before them. The crystal gave off a dull purple shine, battling the blue and green hue of the orbs.

"What's that? Nes asked, scooting forward to examine the violet shard.

"Krýstallo Fýlaka" Cyrus replied.

He must have noticed Nes' confusion because he followed with, "Guardian Crystal. It is an artifact we Masters used back in the day when we first stole the Olympians' treasures to lock them away. It will shine brightly as well as vibrate should it detect a trap. Stay close to me while we make our way further within."

Nes nodded, not wishing to fall prey to any of the temple's defenses before he was able to see his mission through to its end. He wished the Master carried a second crystal with him that Nes could use, though he was thankful they had at least one.

It did not take long for the Guardian Crystal to flare to life. They were no more than twenty steps down the dimly lit corridor that connected to the entrance, their senses heightened and eyes scanning for any sign of danger. Suddenly a violet pulse of light expanded out from the Master's hand, catching their attention, and signaling an imminent threat.

Cyrus held out his arm, stopping Nes in his tracks. He tried to silence his heart as it pounded with adrenaline. They glanced at one another, silently acknowledging the gravity of the situation. Gazing ahead, Nes noticed that the floor beneath them was no ordinary surface. Instead, it appeared to be a hidden mechanism, designed to give way under unsuspecting trespassers.

"The trap is likely triggered by the pressure of footsteps, or any other slight disturbance, causing the floor to crumble and give way to whatever lies below," Cyrus noted, focusing on the slight unevenness of the stone compared to the ground they currently stood upon.

The Master motioned for Nes to step back slowly, their movements deliberate and careful. They needed a way to bypass the trap without activating it. As they examined the area, Nes spotted a series of ancient symbols etched onto the walls nearby.

"Can you read those?" Nes asked, pointing them out to Cyrus.

"It may take some time to decipher," the Master said, unfurling the scroll he read earlier to open the gateway. "But it is likely these symbols hold the key to revealing a safe path forward. Excellent eyes." Nes could not help but feel slightly chuffed at the Master's praise.

While Cyrus went to work using his vast knowledge to decipher the ancient runes, Nes remained vigilant, keeping a watchful eye on the floor beneath them. He could sense subtle shifts in the air currents, indicating the intricate mechanism hidden within.

"It's a riddle," Cyrus finally determined after some time.

"What kind of riddle?" Nes asked, hoping the Master already had the answer. Nes was never great with the whole critical thinking part of life. He was great in a fight, but Andra was the one who solved the issues that did not require combat. He wondered if she would have been a better option to come on this mission.

"I am not completely sure yet. I have it written out, but I need more time to interpret what it is saying."

He was glad to have the Master with him, as his knowledge of ancient history was invaluable and without it, Nes would likely already be dead.

After careful consideration, Cyrus felt as though he had properly deciphered the riddle embedded within the symbols. It spoke of balance and harmony, emphasizing the need to distribute weight evenly to navigate this particular trap. Understanding the clue, Cyrus instructed Nes on where to stand and when to move so that they stepped on certain tiles in a specific sequence to bypass the trap unscathed.

Nes and Cyrus synchronized their movements, stepping lightly and deliberately on the designated tiles. Nes did his best to follow Cyrus' instructions. At one point he overshot the tile he was meant to land on, but thankfully he managed to catch the edge with his heels, and with some vigorous windmilling of his arms he managed to stay put.

"Easy, Nes" Cyrus' calming voice reached him from the opposite side of the puzzle.

The ground beneath them creaked and groaned, but with each step, they managed to maintain the equilibrium required to neutralize the trap's trigger.

As they reached the other side of the puzzle, the Guardian Crystal flickered and died out, signaling their successful navigation of the trap. A sense of relief washed over Nes, though he knew without a doubt that more challenges awaited them.

They continued to delve deeper into the depths of the lush temple, their senses remaining sharp and every step cautious. They had surpassed a multitude of traps, each representing its unique danger. One room attempted to skewer them; another to crush them.

In one room, the plant life had all been burned away; the stone beneath was black and scorched. It should have come as no surprise when the flame began spewing from the crevices along the walls.

They barely managed to escape that room thanks to some more quick thinking on Cyrus' part. They made it through unscathed, all things considered, though Nes did have some nasty burns on the palms of his hand as he crawled across the blistering hot floor.

"We're close," Cyrus said, a hungry glint reflecting in his eye.

They traveled down the longest corridor Nes had ever seen. The walls were adorned with fearsome creatures and celestial beings locked in an eternal struggle. A doorway up ahead revealed what somehow looked like sunlight, despite how far down they had delved.

The roaring of the water they had heard as they entered the temple was very loud now; nearly loud enough to drown out their words. As they walked, a thought occurred to Nes.

"Cyrus," he began, "Can you explain something to me?"

"If I am able, I will gladly." He replied cordially, despite not looking over at him. His pace had picked up and he no longer hid his excitement at how close he was to the artifact he sought.

"If the Masters were responsible for locking away the godly artifacts, how is it that something so powerful it turned my home into a wasteland, could have been forgotten about?" He did not want to sound accusatory. He certainly did not mean for it to be.

Cyrus sighed as though he had been caught hiding a dirty secret and was now being forced to tell the world.

"The truth is," he began, "A few hundred years after we formed the Citadel, there was a schism within our ranks, which led to much of our knowledge being lost to time and infighting. Though we all agreed that locking the artifacts away was the best option for humanity, some coveted the very powers we tried to seal."

"You mean there were Masters that wanted to use the artifacts for themselves?" he asked, unsure if he understood.

He certainly did not blame them if that was the case. There was a certain draw to power that if not properly handled, could lead one down a dark road. Quinn's friend Levy was a good example of that.

"Well, no. Funnily enough, the urge to use the artifacts was never something that caused any discord. We all agreed they were not to be trifled with."

"What do you mean then?" Nes asked.

"After we began sealing the Olympians' artifacts away, it came to light that the very man responsible for bringing us together was working hand in hand with one of the Olympians as well as with the former Weaver of Fate. They had come up with a prophecy to prepare the world, not for peace, but for war with the gods themselves." Cyrus looked over at him to gauge his reaction.

"War with the gods?!" Nes could not believe any mortal would believe themselves strong enough to succeed in such a venture. "Why would they do that?"

"Why indeed?" Cyrus said pleased Nes felt that way. "You know the man I speak of by the way. He is the very man young Quinn journeyed to Petram with. His name is Talius.

"As the years went on, he became more and more desperate to find the heroes he believed would fulfill the prophecy. While most of us were content with living under the safety of our barrier, his faction could not fathom a world where the gods still existed. He did heinous things to bring his prophecy to light."

"What kind of things?" Nes asked, transfixed upon the Master's words.

"Things that no man should do if he calls himself good. Now we find ourselves in a world where his war is imminent, and we are woefully unprepared for the consequences."

"Is that why you seek this artifact?" Nes was starting to put the pieces together in his head,

"Would you be against me if I said yes?" Cyrus asked, looking at the youth out of the corner of his eyes. "I do not seek to survive, Nes. I seek to win."

"If what you say is true, then we need all of the help we can get," Nes responded.

He was upset the Master lied to him, but it was not a shocking development. Andra, Mallory, and Quinn had all been screaming at him that this would be the outcome.

"If the barrier is already breaking, and freeing this artifact will provide us the strength we need to combat the Olympians as well as bring life back to the Wastes, then I don't see a reason to stand against you."

"You are wise beyond your years." The Master said to him, his smile flashing bright in the pulsing violet light.

"Thank…" Nes cut off his words as he realized the Guardian Crystal was violently flashing. "CYRUS!"

As they reached the center of the lengthy corridor, the doorway in which they entered slammed shut. Cyrus whipped around, searching for where the trap would spring from. An ominous rumbling filled the air, growing louder with each passing second, shaking the very walls around them.

Nes and Cyrus exchanged a glance and took off sprinting as fast as they could to the doorway on the other side. As they ran, the floor beneath them gave a violent lurch, beginning to fall away and revealing a seemingly bottomless chasm that threatened to engulf them.

Reacting with instinctive agility, Nes leaped forward, reaching the other side just in time. However, as the gap widened further, the older Master found himself stranded on a crumbling precipice. Nes's heart raced as he witnessed fear take over Cyrus' features for the first time. With unwavering resolve, he shouted to the Master, his voice laced with urgency.

"Come on! Reach for my hand and don't let go!"

Summoning every ounce of strength, Cyrus mustered a final burst of energy and sprinted forward. With a desperate lunge, he managed to grasp Nes' outstretched hand, their fingers intertwining in a firm grip. Nes' injuries screamed out in fiery pain as he trembled under the weight of the Master, but he held fast, refusing to let go.

Cyrus dangled precariously, his life hanging in the balance. The chasm seemed to hunger for him, eager to claim him as its victim. Beads of sweat dripped down Nes' forehead as he fought against the pull, his muscles screaming out in protest. The Master's voice grew hoarse as he shouted encouragement to Nes, urging him to find the strength to pull him up.

Gathering everything he had left in his reservoir of determination, Nes mustered a final burst of energy. With a herculean effort, he hoisted Cyrus up, inch by agonizing inch, until finally he was safe, collapsing to the ground beside him. Their breaths came in ragged gasps as they lay side by side, a mixture of exhaustion and relief washing over them.

"You saved my life," Cyrus panted, looking over at the youth beside him.

Nes heaved out large breaths; his eyes shut tight against the pain that lanced through his body. He was sure his stitches had ripped open, as he felt a warmth spreading beneath his tunic.

"Get used to it." He replied, finding the Master's eyes. "If we are going to be a team in what is to come, we are going to have to get used to looking out for one another."

Cyrus looked away, getting back to his feet and brushing debris from his jacket.

"Come on, there's nothing else between us and our prize."

~~~

As they stepped into the treasure room of the temple, Nes was overwhelmed by its awe-inspiring beauty. The vast chamber stretched out before him, adorned with opulent detail. The room was circular, with a high ceiling that seemed as though it vanished into the heavens above.

The walls of the room were lined with intricately carved stone depicting monsters, ancient runes, and scenes from legends long forgotten. Cascading waterfalls flowed down from various points along the walls, creating a symphony of soothing sounds that echoed throughout the chamber. The waterfalls converged into a serene pool at the base of each wall, where aquatic plants flourished, adding a splash of color to the room.

As his gaze moved toward the center of the chamber, he spotted the reason for their voyage- the single pedestal that housed the priceless artifact they had come to find. The pedestal stood atop a small dais made from smooth marble and was inlaid with precious gemstones. It radiated an ethereal glow which drew Nes' gaze in.

Hovering above the pedestal was the most magnificent scythe Nes had ever laid his eyes upon. The weapon was immense, crafted from gleaming silver, and adorned with intricate engravings.

Its curved blade shined like a mirror, reflecting the ambient light that permeated the chamber. Though it was suspended in mid-air, the scythe remained motionless, as though it were awaiting whoever would claim it.

The chamber was bathed in a soft, golden light, reminiscent of a perpetual sunrise. The gentle, artificial light emanated from concealed sources around the room, casting warm hues upon its surroundings. It created an enchanting atmosphere, enhancing the allure of the artifact and infusing the space with a surreal quality.

"The Scythe of Demeter," Cyrus whispered from beside him. The master seemed equally entranced by the beauty of the weapon, slowly stumbling toward it with his hand outstretched as if in a daze.

Nes followed a few steps behind him, taking in the beauty of the wild nature that thrived within the room. The warmth of the artificial sunlight soothed his aching body; the smells of the flowers blooming around the room, calmed his frayed nerves. If this was a glimpse of what was to come for his people, he was ecstatic.

As they reached the pedestal, Cyrus' hand collided with an invisible wall. At his touch, essence coalesced in the air, running up the wall in an intricate pattern, leaving a large green rune glowing in the air before them.

"What is that?" Nes asked the Master. Cyrus seemed annoyed but not overly concerned by the wall's presence.

"That is the seal which protects the scythe and keeps its powers contained within the temple. To get the scythe, as well as return life to the Wastes, it will need to be broken." His eyes were hungry as he stared at the artifact, just out of reach.

How do we do that?"

"WE do not." Cyrus inclined his head toward the boy. "I will be of no use here. I hope you are feeling up to the task with your injuries because you will need to use your power to overwhelm the seal and break it."

"I don't know that in my body's current condition, I will be able to generate enough force," Nes replied, weighing his options.

"We do not have a choice, I'm afraid," Cyrus responded, not unkindly. "It is the only way we will be able to accomplish what we came for. If you cannot do it, then we wasted this trip and your land will never see life again."

"It may kill me," Nes replied, stepping up to the seal.

"Sometimes those of us in power must make sacrifices for a better tomorrow," Cyrus said, laying his hand on Nes' shoulder.

"For what it is worth, if I were in your shoes, I would do it in a heartbeat. I will also do my best to provide whatever medical aid I am able when it is done. I cannot force you to do this, but if you do not, then there was no point in making it this far in the first place."

Nes steeled his resolve, bracing for the pain he knew was about to follow.

"If it is for my people, I will make whatever sacrifices I must."

Nes raised his hands, and a surge of energy emanated from his core. Immediately, the ground began to tremble as white-hot energy ripped through his body and into the seal. Nes could feel his body begin to rip open at his scars; warm blood rushing down his face and arms. Yet still he pushed, throwing as much energy at the seal as he could muster.

The seal began to crack and break under the immense strain of his power. A large fissure ran up the base of the marble dais, rocketing pebbles of debris in every direction, and still Nes pushed. He heard Cyrus yelling encouragements to him, willing him on. He was thankful for the support as it gave him something to focus on while he battled the darkness that swam at the edges of his vision.

Finally, when Nes felt as though he could handle no more, the seal shattered. Large plates of solidified energy crashed to the ground, shattering on impact, and sending shards flying out across the room.

A blast of energy rocketed out from the pedestal like a sonic boom, tearing through the temple at breakneck speed. Nes stumbled to his knees, heaving as he tried desperately to fight off unconsciousness. Seeing Nes momentarily distracted, Cyrus seized the opportunity.

With lightning-fast reflexes, he snatched the Scythe of Demeter from its resting place. The weapon's blade gleamed with otherworldly light, and Nes could feel the power as it coursed down the weapon's shaft and into Cyrus. A deep green aura flared to life around the Master; his eyes disappearing behind a wall of pure green energy.

"I truly must thank you, Nes. Without you, I would have never been able to claim the weapon I sought for so long."

Nes struggled to his feet, unable to understand what the Master was trying to say. "I am more than happy to help you achieve your goal if it means bringing prosperity to my people."

Cyrus laughed a full, lung-bursting laugh. "Yes, they will certainly find peace once they are dead."

Nes stopped in his tracks, the words smacking into him as though they were a physical blow. "What do you mean when they are dead?"

Cyrus stepped toward him; his scythe tucked neatly behind his back. "By breaking this seal and releasing this amount of godly essence back into the mortal realm, the seal is sure to fall within days. Once Lord Zeus leads the Olympians back through it, this realm is in for a cleansing the likes of which it has never seen before. Your people will not be spared."

"LORD Zeus?" Nes asked, dumbfounded. "I thought you wanted to beat the gods."

"On the contrary," Cyrus grinned. "I said I wanted to win. Talius' meddling has made that impossible so I cut a deal. And thanks to you, I now will have the power of a god at my beck and call."

Nes shook with rage at The Master's double-cross. He thought he had already discovered his true intent of wanting the weapon for himself. It was a compromise he was willing to make if it meant prosperity for his people as well as a powerful ally against the gods. Cyrus' words had felt so genuine to him, and he let his passion for his own goals cloud his judgment. Andra and Mallory were right, he truly was too naïve.

"I won't allow you to get away with this." He allowed his rage to energize him, using it to fuel the adrenaline that rushed through his veins.

"Oh?" Cyrus mocked. "And how do you plan on stopping me? You can barely stand. Do you think I truly could not have helped you break that seal? Do not kid yourself. I made sure your body was completely shredded before revealing my motives."

He pulled a long, black whistle from within his robes. "I will admit, I did not expect to lose Enkar to my beast, but it was a sacrifice worth making with the results it procured. You were weakened just enough to still be of use without being a threat. Breaking the seal was just insurance to make sure you were truly tapped."

Nes gritted his teeth, pushing against the strain his body felt. To think the Master had played him so well that even the Skorpios had been planned. "And Mallory?" He asked, fearing the answer.

"Likely dead I would imagine," Cyrus answered nonchalantly. "I doubt the girl is a match for Darrik. He may be dumb as a cyclops but he knows his way around a blade better than most."

"You separated us on purpose." Nes already knew the answer, but he wanted to keep the Master talking. It was true he had used almost all of the remaining energy, but that didn't mean he had none. He gathered it all into one tightly compressed ball within him, condensing it as much as he could so that it built pressure. He knew he was not likely to make it out of this temple alive, but he would be damned if Cyrus did as well.

"Obviously I did," Cyrus answered as though speaking to a child. "That girl never did trust me. She lacked your naivety. I had to get you alone so that she could not whisper in your ear."

Nes laughed then. He was on the brink of unconsciousness, and the pain and exhaustion were making him delirious enough that he just could not help it. "Yeah, I guess I am pretty dumb, eh? Of course, there was always that part of me that doubted your words, but damn if I didn't want to believe them."

"If it is any solace to you, I was not lying about life being returned to the Wastes. For whatever brief time your people have left, they will at least be able to enjoy that."

Nes shook his head, still laughing. "Well, that's good then. At least you weren't a complete snake." The energy at his core was at its limit now, and he was seconds away from unleashing it one final time. "Unfortunately, neither of us are going to get to see that."

"Please, Nes. You are strong, I'll give you that. But in your current state, especially now that I have Demeter's scythe, you cannot defeat me."

Nes smiled then, showing off his bloody teeth. "I don't need to beat you, Cyrus. I need only to stop you from leaving."

"What do you…"

Nes removed all of his constraints upon his energy, allowing it to uncoil within him and burst free from his body in one painful explosion. The essence flooded into the very stone of the temple, shaking the foundation violently and loosening large chunks of debris. The artificial light flickered and went out as giant chunks of rock rained down upon them.

"Fool!" Cyrus roared, his eyes wide in disbelief. "You will kill us both!"

"That's the plan." Nes laughed as he fell onto his back from the pain that lanced through his body. "This will be our tomb to share for all eternity. I hope you're comfy."

Cyrus lashed out in rage, slicing a deep gash in Nes' torso. Nes simply laughed again. That last wave of power had done what he had always been warned would happen if he overused his abilities.

As it tore through him, it killed every nerve, and sliced through every muscle on its way out. He could no longer move; no longer feel. Cyrus could swipe at him all he liked; it would not change anything in the slightest.

Just as Cyrus was about to bury the scythe deep into his stomach, a bright glow outlined his body, replacing the green aura with one of sky blue. The Master's grin became feral as he realized what was happening.

"Lord Zeus calls me, Nes, and when he calls, I must answer."

Nes' eyes widened as he realized his victory was about to be stolen.

"This will be your tomb after all, but not mine. Enjoy a restless eternity, knowing it was through your actions that your people, and all of humanity, will be wiped from the world."

As suddenly as the light had appeared Cyrus was gone, leaving in a bright flash which temporarily lit the crumbling room. Nes could not believe the Master had been pulled free from his final gambit as simply as that.

The exhaustion reached its crescendo and it was all Nes could do to keep his eyes open as debris continued to rain down upon him. He did not want to die, but if he was going to, and he was going to, he felt it was only right he stay awake until the end, as atonement for what his decisions would lead to.

The world was in for a fight it was not prepared for, but he had faith in Quinn. He was not at his full potential yet, but anybody with eyes could see that he had a strength equal to the heroes one read about in the ancient myths. If anybody could save the Abyssillian people, it was him.

When he could no longer keep his eyes open, he let the darkness take him, thinking one last time of Andra, and how he wished he could have seen her, and kissed her, one last time.

CHAPTER 32

MALLORY

A shockwave of essence startled Mallory awake. She had fallen asleep against the onyx gateway, waiting, and hoping that her friend returned to her unharmed. One second, she was dreaming of the time Ashe had woken up to a monster raid upon their camp and showed up to the battle with her armor on backward.

The next she was being propelled forward, her face sliding in the slick mud. She spat it from her mouth, cringing at the gritty dirt as it slid against her teeth. She stood up on the slick grass, making her way over to her bag so she could wash her mouth out with her canteen and- *GRASS?!*

She looked around frantically, wondering if she had somehow been teleported somewhere else while she slept; but no, the pile of rubble was still there, as was the crumbling gateway. She watched in astonishment as a wave of green traveled swiftly across the cracked planes of the Wastes, flooding the dirt with moisture and painting the world a vivid green.

"He did it!" her voice was flush with excitement. She may not have grown up in the Wastes, but she had lived here for the last three years. That was long enough to yearn for the animal and plant life she so desperately missed.

Thick trees sprouted up from the ground instantly; their boughs thick and fruit bountiful. A spring of water burbled nearby as if it had just coalesced into being that exact second. The land was not just healing, it was thriving.

She looked back at the portal, hoping that with Nes' success, she would see him walk through at any moment. Instead, what she saw caused her heart to plummet into her stomach. Nes' body was lying in a heap, bloody and unmoving. Mallory ran up to him, sliding on her knees and lifting his head onto her lap.

She checked for a pulse, finding only a lethargic tremor now and then. Mallory had fought on the frontlines long enough to know what that meant. Her heart shattered to think he had gone through so much and would not even get to see his triumph. And Andra; poor Andra. She would be devastated.

She pulled the cork from her canteen with her teeth, splashing a small trickle of the cold water onto her friend's face. To her surprise, his eyes flickered open, though they seemed clouded.

"Nes? Are you in there?"

Nes gave her a weak smile, though only one side of his face moved with it.

"Hello, Mallory."

Tears spilled down Mallory's face as she clutched him close to her. "What happened?" She asked, her voice hoarse.

"Cyrus got me good. Stole the scythe. He's working with Zeus."

Each statement came out in shallow gasps, the light behind his eyes dulling further as the seconds ticked by.

"I'm sorry, Nes." Mallory cried. "I'm so sorry I wasn't there with you." Tears splashed down onto his face and she hurriedly wiped them away.

"It's not your fault, Mal. I made my choice. I'm sorry I won't be here to face the storm with you all. It's not fair that I caused it and won't be here with you."

Mallory vigorously shook her head. "Don't say that Nes. This isn't your fault. They would have found another way if this hadn't worked for them."

"I'm glad I got to see it at least once." He said, staring at the lush plant life that had overtaken the Wastes.

Mallory did her best to smile through her tears. "You did something amazing for your people, Nes. Be proud."

He said something else but the words were quiet and impossible to make out.

"What?" Mallory asked, lowering her ear to his cracked lips.

"Tell Andra...sorry." His voice was no more than a whisper, and as soon as the words were spoken, he closed his eyes, lying still.

"NES!" she yelled, frantically trying to keep him awake. She splashed some more water on his face, shook him and pried his eyes open, but nothing worked. Her eyes closed tight as her body was wracked with sobs. It was so unfair that he had managed to accomplish his life's goal, only to die before truly getting to enjoy it. She cried as she thought about Andra and what she would feel when she heard the news that her love was gone, so soon after she had lost Sen. She thought of Quinn, wherever he was, and how this would only cut him deeper than he already hurt. Mallory was angry with herself for not being able to do more. She knew the Masters were rotten. If only she had been more insistent that they not follow through with their asinine plan.

There was no way she could return to Petram as she was. Her supplies would be enough to get her there, but she could not leave Nes here. It was not right. She sat down with her back to a thick tree and looked at her fallen friend. In the morning she would bury him, taking something from him for Andra, but she just did not have it in her tonight. She sat back, staring at the moon and stars in the sky, wishing she were not looking at them alone.

CHAPTER 33

LEVY

Ares glanced down at the spear which had gouged deep into his armor, then back up at Levy and grinned. His smile was hungry, his eyes filled with triumph; as if he had been waiting for this moment for a very long time. He batted the shaft aside, dislodging the blade from his chest with a spray of ichor as though it had not just been biting into the skin beneath his battle-marked plate.

"Well would you look at that," he taunted, slowly walking toward Levy with menacing steps. "The pup finally bares his fangs. I have been looking forward to this."

Levy reigned the spear back in, holding it defensively in front of him as though it was a barrier Ares could not pass. Fear lanced through him, though he dared not show it in front of the god.

He knew he was not a match for Ares in his current state, and he understood that by attacking him he had signed his death warrant. But damn if it did not feel free to finally make this choice for himself.

For too long now he had allowed himself to be manipulated by powers stronger than himself. He convinced himself that he was working with those powers to procure the strength he needed to achieve his own goals, but his eyes were finally open to the truth. He had allowed himself to be used, casting aside his ideals for the sake of power. It was just as Quinn had said to him.

Oh gods, Quinn.

Had he really stabbed his friend through the heart? Guilt came crashing down on him so strongly his knees nearly buckled. Here Ashe had been looking at him with those beautiful, hopeful eyes. Despite everything he had done, she still cared about him and still had not given up on him.

How had he repaid that friendship? By killing her boyfriend; his best friend. Perhaps dying to Ares was what he truly deserved. It was better than if Zeus got his hands on him. Turning on Ares meant turning on Zeus, and Levy had seen firsthand what the king of the Olympians was capable of.

Levy looked at Ashe, injured and exhausted on the floor of the Tower behind him. Despite their current predicament and her state of well-being, she looked happier than Levy could remember seeing in a very long time. It was as if his choice to lash out at Ares had healed something inside of her that he could not tell before had been broken.

If this was to be his final fight, he was glad he got to see that smile one last time. She may have never loved him the way he did her, and she was going to be in for a world of hurt when she learned of Quinn, assuming she somehow made it out of this alive, but her light was enough to steel a resolve he had not realized he had been lacking.

He turned back to face the god, squaring off against him and locking eyes, hoping to show Ares he was not afraid. Ares smiled a mischievous grin in response, dropping his sword to the ground with a mocking gesture, choosing to engage Levy with his bare hands instead.

"Go ahead, Levy. Show me just how much time I have wasted on you."

Levy lunged forward, his spear thrusting outwards toward Ares with a precise strike. He was aiming for the same spot he had stuck him before, hoping to take advantage of the flaw in his armor and pierce him through the heart. Ares effortlessly sidestepped the attack, his movement fluid and elusive.

Levy whirled the spear back around, just missing the god's neck as he stepped out of the way again. Ares was toying with Levy, his eyes filled with amusement as he danced around his strikes, taunting him with each dodge.

Frustration burned within Levy's veins, yet he refused to yield. He summoned as much of Hestia's essence as he could muster, hoping that with the enhanced strength behind his strikes, he might land a lucky blow. Though the essence still seemed hesitant to respond to his call, he managed to pull in a good portion of it, increasing the power behind each strike.

He pressed in, launching a series of quick strikes, each aimed at exploiting Ares' defenses; but the god's reflexes were unapparelled. He deflected every blow with ease, his hands and arms moving like lightning.

"Is this all you are capable of, boy?" Ares wore an ugly sneer, plastered across his face. He seemed to be enjoying it as each failed attack shredded Levy's confidence further.

"Three years I spent babysitting you, attempting to turn you into something worth my time. To think that we allowed some bottom-dwelling, mortal leech to walk amongst us for so long. I do not know what my father saw in you, but it sure as Hades is not present now."

Ares closed the distance between them in an instant. His hands became a blur of devastating strikes, each blow landing with tremendous force. Levy did his best to fight back, parrying and blocking, but Ares's strength was overwhelming. It was as if the god's fists were infused with divine power, and Levy could feel the tremors coursing through his body with each impact.

Levy stood in a daze, feeling as though his body was going to shatter into a thousand pieces. The spear hung limply at his side; his arms heavy with bruising from the onslaught. Ares, sensing his victory, pulled his fist back as if to pulverize Levy with one last brutal strike.

"You are a failure to your friends and your people. And it is as a failure I will send you to Hades, where you can spend eternity tormented by the knowledge that you brought nothing but pain to those you claimed to care most about."

He brought his hand down, aiming for the spot right between Levy's eyes. But just as he was about to make contact, his fist abruptly stopped mere centimeters from his face. Levy looked up, startled as the air from the strike contacted his skin. Ares' hand was suspended in the air by a thin, glowing thread. Try as he might to snap it, the thread held strong, refusing to let Ares land his final blow.

"You are not a failure, Levy," Ashe called out to him, her words lit with fiery passion that resonated within his heart, filling him with life. "You are a testament to resilience. You have faced your demons with unwavering strength, and now you have begun to find your way back to the person you truly are. Do not give up just because it seems hopeless. Keep fighting. The light is shining brighter with every step you take. It is not too late to be a hero."

"That is enough out of you, Weaver!" Ares snapped, finally managing to break the thread. He swiped Levy out of the way, throwing him to the side as he lashed out at Ashe, planting his foot into her ribs. She cried out in pain, doubling over against the impact.

Seeing Ashe curled into a ball awakened something primal within Levy, and he launched himself back to his feet, roaring as he barreled into Ares' side, taking them both to the ground. In a desperate attempt to gain an advantage, Levy tried to grapple with Ares, hoping to use his increased strength against him.

Despite the rage and power flowing through him, Ares effortlessly countered, grabbing Levy's arm, and wrenching it with an intensity that threatened to snap bone. Pain surged through Levy's body, his arm on the brink of collapse. The god picked himself up off the ground, panting as he stared down at Levy's pained expression, their noses only inches apart.

"With just a small increase of pressure, I can rip your arm off. If you listen closely, you can probably hear the muscles and tendons beginning to tear." He pushed slightly as if to exemplify his point. Levy cried out in pain as his arm bent back further.

He grasped desperately for more of Hestia's essence, ripping off another bit of it. Through sheer willpower, Levy pushed back, refusing to succumb to the agony. Realizing that if he did not do something drastic, he and Ashe were both dead, he reached out with his free hand, grasping desperately for his spear.

If he could just grab hold of it, he could shove it up through the god's throat before Ares realized what was happening. Levy continued to push back against the god, doing his best to keep Ares' attention on the struggle. His fingers brushed the shaft and with one final bit of effort, he wrapped his hand around it, thrusting it towards Ares' face.

The god's hand lashed out faster than Levy could follow, grasping his wrist like a steel vice, and halting the momentum of his strike before it even started.

"Oh, come now, Levy. Surely you did not think I would drop my guard. What kind of god of war would I be if I was not fully aware of where your weapon was in the heat of combat?"

With a brutal twist, Ares disarmed Levy, snatching the spear from his grasp. Levy's heart sank as he realized his last line of defense had been stolen by his adversary. The god stared at the spear, admiring the craftsmanship.

"Funny," he spoke, as though his mind was suddenly far away. "Everyone who wields this weapon seems to betray us. I wonder if Hestia bewitched it in some way. She was a crafty one, that woman." His eyes refocused on Levy as he sneered triumphantly, holding the spear with malicious intent.

"I did warn you not to fail us, lest you suffer the same fate as its last bearer. Such a shame you did not listen to my sage advice."

In one swift motion, he slashed the weapon across Levy's face; the razor-sharp edge slicing through flesh and tearing apart his eye in a gratuitous spray of blood. From somewhere behind him Ashe cried out, screaming his name. Agonizing pain consumed Levy, his world spiraling into darkness as his blood stained the pristine white floors of the Tower.

Levy collapsed to the ground, his body trembling with exhaustion and his spirit crushed by defeat. Ares stood over him, reveling in his victory. The god of war's laughter echoed through the air, mingling with Ashe's anguished cries. This battle was over, Levy knew. He felt broken and scarred, a stark reminder to the overwhelming might of the Olympians.

Ares raised the spear, ready to plunge it into Levy for the killing blow. A manic smile was spread across his face, his golden eyes wild and bloodshot.

"In the realm of mortals, you were but a fleeting ember. Now embrace the inferno of your insignificance."

Levy heard Ashe gasp as, through the haze of pain and his fading consciousness, a figure shrouded in an ethereal cloak of vibrant, purple energy dashed into view, blocking the oncoming spear with a gleaming silver and black blade of his own. Despite his deteriorating state, Levy had no doubt in his mind that the man standing over him now was Quinn, though he was unsure how that could have been possible. His friend stood tall, exuding an aura of determination.

The cloak of pure energy billowed around him, its tendrils swirling and cracking with raw power. Quinn's eyes were illuminated by the same purple energy that enveloped him, piercing the god with twin beacons of barely contained rage at the scene laid out before him. The swirling aura appeared both dangerous and magnificent, shifting and pulsating in intricate patterns that seemed to dance in harmony with Quinn's movements.

Hope, intermingling with a wave of relief, burst forth within Levy's chest at the presence of his friend. He became acutely aware of the tremendous strength and unwavering resolve Quinn exuded, even in the face of overwhelming odds. As Quinn blocked the spear, shielding Levy from further harm, his fleeting consciousness was filled with a profound sense of gratitude.

This is what a true hero looks like. Levy thought to himself before the strong embrace of darkness grabbed hold of him.

CHAPTER 34

QUINN

The air crackled with tension as Quinn and Ares locked gazes. It appeared as if Quinn had arrived just in the nick of time, though he was surprised it was Levy he was saving rather than Ashe. Quinn was not sure what had transpired before he had arrived, but if it was Levy Ares was trying to kill…

A small ray of hope blossomed within him. Ashe, though battered and bruised, seemed to be in better shape than he expected. Her chest heaved in and out as though she were exhausted from a fight, but she was conscious and breathing.

A fierce smile had found its way to her lips at Quinn's arrival, and he could not help the tingly warmth that spread through him as their eyes briefly met.

"So, you finally claimed the boy, and walk amongst us again." Ares' mused. His chocolatey voice was shockingly soothing, betraying the intense aura that flared out from him. "And now you have set your sights on the power of fate as well. Be gone from here, Primordial. Your time is past, and you stand no chance against my father, nor the rest of us Olympians. Slink back to your shadows and watch as the world turns to ashes."

Quinn flashed his teeth at the god's words, amused that he assumed he was talking to Chaos.

"You couldn't be more wrong, Ares." His voice was steady, despite the storm of emotions raging within him. "I have embraced the power of Chaos, and now I control it. I am still me; still fighting for what is right."

"Bullshit," the god spat. "There is no chance a mortal was able to claim the power of Chaos and keep his mind intact. I do not know what tricks you are trying to play, Primordial, but they hold no merit with me."

"You are wrong, Ares. Ashe shredded what remained of Chaos' consciousness long ago. I have faced the darkness within me. I am nobody's puppet." Quinn's voice was strong with his newfound resolve.

Ares sneered, allowing his words to wash over him. "Then you will be easy to break."

He dashed forward, throwing his fist toward Quinn's stomach with lightning-fast speed. The cloak of energy flared to life around Quinn, reaching out with its shadowy tendrils and wrapping around the god's arm before his fist could make contact, stopping Ares in his tracks. Ares looked up at Quinn, shock plain upon his chiseled features.

Quinn smirked at the god's surprise. "Perhaps not as easy as you may think."

He whirled the Chaos energy around him, pulling the trapped god with it in a vicious cyclone before releasing the energy's grip and hurling the god of war far into the Tower's heights, and away from his fallen friends.

As Ares reached the apex of his ascent, divine energy flared to life around him, halting his fall and holding him in place. Quinn, not wanting to give him even a second to recover, ran to the Tower's wall.

The tendrils of his cloak pierced the sides, ripping chunks of debris free as they gouged out footholds, and he proceeded to scale the Tower; the tendrils pulling him up as though he were a large spider.

Ares sneered as Quinn reached the pinnacle of his climb,

coming face to face with the arrogant deity once more.

"You think your feeble powers can match the might of a god? Let me show you how wrong you are. First, I will kill you. Then, if he has not bled out already, I will finish off that foolish boy below. The Weaver will die third, but I will take my time with that one.

"She has caused me quite a headache after all. I wonder what will break first, her mind or her body? What do you think, boy? You know her well after all." He smiled as he saw Quinn's features change at his words.

With a surge of energy, Quinn unleashed a torrent of chaotic power, engulfing the room in a kaleidoscope of colors. The very air crackled with volatile energy, unsettling the foundation of the Tower.

"You mortals and your emotions. So easy to manipulate. So easy to break."

Ares summoned his sword back to his hand and lunged forward, his blade poised to strike as the divine essence empowered his every move.

Quinn danced nimbly away, the tendrils pushing off from where they clung to the Tower's walls and latching on again a few feet to the side. He channeled essence through his body, enhancing his speed and agility, making him a blur to the mortal eye as he avoided more of Ares' thundering strikes.

Using the moments between the god's bursts of offense, he retaliated with his chaotic barrage of energy, hurling them at Ares with uncanny accuracy.

The clash of swords against energy filled the chamber, creating waves of destructive force that shattered some of the floating orbs around them. Quinn used the orbs to his advantage, grabbing hold of those nearby with his tendrils and chucking them at the god, slowing his attacks and forcing him onto the defensive. Shards of crystal opened shallow cuts along Ares' face as they exploded against the edge of his blade, angering him further.

As his frustration boiled over, Ares tapped into his godly essence, igniting his sword with a crimson ethereal flame, and decimating the remaining orbs surrounding him. The blade became a conduit for his divine fury, slicing through the chaos-infused energy with devastating force. Quinn flattened his body against the wall, his cloak singed and tattered, but his determination unbroken.

With a primal roar, Quinn summoned the full extent of the power he could control, careful not to exceed his limits as he was still learning to harness his abilities. The Tower quaked as reality itself seemed to bend to his will. Swirling rifts appeared floating in the air, tearing the very fabric of existence where they formed. Ares gritted his teeth, his godly essence shielding him from the onslaught, but the strain was evident on his face.

Using this opening, Quinn launched himself from the wall, entering the nearest portal, before re-emerging from one behind the god. With a yell, he pulled his sword from its sheath, swinging at the god's exposed back.

Ares spun around just in time to deflect the blow before Quinn disappeared once more into a portal to his right. Again and again, Quinn emerged from portals all around the room, each time meeting Ares head-on, chaos and war colliding in a cataclysmic clash. Each blow reverberated through the Tower, causing tremors to run through the structure. Sparks of energy danced through the air as their powers clashed with explosive force.

Quinn, fueled by his boundless energy, continued to hammer blows upon the god from every angle, watching with delight as the aura surrounding him flickered, betraying the exhaustion Ares was surely feeling.

Based on the carnage Quinn had entered, it was clear he had already been through at least one fight. If Quinn could just hold out long enough, and wear the god down, he knew he could emerge from this fight victorious.

"ENOUGH," Ares roared as if sensing Quinn's confidence spike.

The ethereal flame around his blade flared brighter, elongating as though the blade were twice its actual size. With a vicious horizontal strike, he sliced through a large amount of the portals surrounding him, shattering the energy, and forcing them to blink out of existence.

Ares swung wildly at Quinn, each time narrowly missing him, but continuing to close more of the hovering portals until none remained. Sensing that Quinn was trapped clinging to the side of the Tower once more, he lunged forward, as if to cut him from the wall.

Quinn, choosing not to end up sliced in half, launched himself over the god, hoping to get a strike in at his head before safely grabbing the wall on the opposite side. But Ares' strike was a feint and Quinn realized in horror that he had fallen for the god's bait. Ares lowered his shoulder, dropping the point of his sword toward the floor so that the edge was angled vertically.

As Quinn crossed immediately above the god, Ares swung the blade up into the air, driving it directly into Quinn's side. It sputtered and spat as his divine essence contacted Quinn's cloak, the two energies locked in a battle of wills. Quinn saw the cloak begin to give way, the white-hot blade sinking deeper into the chaos with each passing moment. He focused as much energy as he could into his defenses, doing all he could to strengthen the cloak and keep the blade from slicing him in twain.

With one final push, Ares finished his swing. Though the blade failed to slice, the momentum of the strike acted as a catapult, scooping Quinn, and flinging him with great force to the base of the Tower.

As the floor rose swiftly up to meet him, Quinn shifted his focus, pouring every ounce of energy he had left into strengthening the cloak and bracing for impact. Within moments Quinn slammed into the ground, his vision momentarily going white as every bit of air was forcibly expelled from his lungs.

As the dust settled, Quinn struggled to his feet, bloodied but unyielding. The cloak had done its job, keeping him from death's embrace for a little longer, but he knew he had only the last remaining dregs of his energy left.

Ares floated down from above, a look of victory lingering on his face. Quinn doubted the god had much remaining energy either, as evidenced by the fact his blade no longer glowed, but the Olympian's false bravado certainly shone through.

"I will admit, I am impressed," Ares said, though contempt coated every word. "It has been quite some time since I have been pushed so far."

Quinn said nothing, focusing only on catching his breath as he watched for an opening that would likely be his final strike. If Ares wanted to posture, he would let him. All Quinn needed was for the god to be distracted enough to land a blow.

"Do not stare at me as though you still think you can win. This fight was over the moment you drew your weapon. What makes you think that you can go blade to blade with the god of war and come out victorious." Ares spat; his face overcome with disdain.

"The fact that you truly believed a mortal could kill a god is the very reason your kind must be razed from existence. You dare to stand here as if you are better than US? You will be returned to the dirt you were formed from."

As Ares spoke, Quinn gathered what little remained of his energy, putting most of it into his legs so that he would be fast enough to reach his target without interruption. He focused on what he decided to be Ares' biggest weak spot, readying himself to plunge the tip of his blade as far as it would go.

He waited patiently, allowing Ares' rant to go in one ear and out the other, steadying his breathing and slowing everything down around him. He felt his muscles tense, twitchy, and ready to spring forth at a moment's notice. Ares barely looked at him as he continued tossing insults out at every mortal who walked the realm.

It was when he finally ran out of air and paused just long enough to suck another lungful in that Quinn struck. He leaped forward, pushing out with everything he had as he closed the distance within a heartbeat. Ares' eyes went wide, first in shock and then rage, as the tip of Quinn's blade streaked directly toward his open mouth.

CHAPTER 35

LEVY

Levy awoke to a feeling of warmth and comfort radiating across his being, a feeling he had not felt in quite some time. It was as if everything were at peace; all of his problems miles away. He stood at the entrance of a familiar scene, though one he did not think he would ever see again.

Before him lay a vast chamber, filled with an otherworldly beauty. The walls of the cave, carved from stone as if crafted by the slow passage of time, bore testament to the ancient history contained within.

The opening to the cavern formed a spacious alcove, its jagged edges giving off an imposing, yet awe-inspiring appearance. Cliffs encircled the entrance, rising majestically upwards; creating an intimate, secluded atmosphere. The sound of distant echoes bounced off the rocky surfaces, lending a mystic aura to the surroundings.

At the center of the opening, a small fire danced gracefully, casting a warm, flickering light over the entirety of the cavern. The walls were adorned with a collection of tapestries, their vibrant colors contrasting against the natural hues of the stone.

These masterpieces depicted scenes from ancient myths, their intricate designs captivating to the eye. As he looked, it appeared as though they came alive, as if the stories they depicted were woven into the very fabric itself.

As it did on his previous visit, a long walkway stretched out along the back of the chamber, gradually ascending into the air. Its surface was smooth and polished, as though countless footsteps had traversed its path.

At the end of the walkway, a grand curtain of shimmering golden flame cascaded down from the ceiling, creating a radiant veil of light. The curtain danced and flickered with a warm, golden glow providing an enchanting spectacle.

The sound of crackling fire was accompanied by a soft, melodic hum, as the young woman tending the hearth shared her beautiful lullaby. She possessed an air of serene elegance and timeless beauty, just as she had the first time he had spoken with her.

Light brown hair cascaded down her back in gentle waves, framing her face with a touch of natural grace. Her eyes gleamed like amber jewels, reflecting wisdom beyond her seemingly youthful years.

Though when last he'd seen them, they looked cold and distant; now they held a gentle flicker of kindness and compassion, mirroring the warmth that emanated from within her.

Draped around her shoulders was a dull, red shawl, its fabric smooth and delicate. The shawl was adorned with intricate golden embroidery, depicting ancient symbols and patterns that danced across the fabric with her movement.

"Hestia," Levy whispered, though it seemed to echo around the walls of the chamber.

"Come, Levy, and sit by my flames." She had turned to him at the mention of her name, her eyes filled with a gentle mirth.

"You did not invite me to sit the last time." He said as he made his way over to a stone that had been carved to resemble a seat.

"You were not yet ready when last we spoke."

"And I am now?" he asked, though he did not put any spirit behind the words. He felt lost as if he were a young kid who had been separated from his parents, with no direction or plan of how to

find safety once more.

Hestia sat across from him, staring at him with understanding, through the crackling flame. *"I do not know, are you?"*

Levy felt the warmth of his tears begin to slide from his eyes as a massive wave of guilt and exhaustion crashed throughout him. He stared deep into the heart of the hearth, thinking back to every decision he had made up to this point.

"I feel lost," he whispered. *"I made bad decisions and hurt people I care for. I doubled down convincing myself I could fix it if I became strong enough, and now, through my bitterness, I have likely brought the two people I care most about in this world down with me."*

He looked into her eyes, trying desperately to latch onto an answer to his problems. The goddess stared back at him, prodding him to continue.

"Am I dead?" he asked, realizing for the first time that it did not make sense for him to have woken up here.

"Not yet," Hestia replied.

"Is this real?" He asked.

She tilted her head as if in thought, before saying, *"This is as real as you wish it to be."*

"What do I do?" He was unsure why he so desperately craved the goddess' approval suddenly. For years he had pushed the thought of her away, wishing only to use her strength for his gain.

It was no wonder her essence had shied away from him so vigorously. Yet, as he sat before her now, staring into the warmth of her amber eyes, he wished desperately for her to share her wisdom with him.

"What is it you seek?" She asked in response. She seemed to be gently prodding him toward a decision, though he was unsure as to what decision that was meant to be.

"I seek what I have always sought," he replied automatically as if the words had been ingrained within him. *"A better future for humanity."*

"No," she replied matter-of-factly. *"That is what Ashelia seeks."*

He began to argue but realized what she spoke was true. There was a time when that was what he truly wished for. He was going to be the hero who saved the world from the tyranny of the gods. That had all changed, however, when Quinn and Ashe had come into his life.

He thought of how his friendship with Quinn had grown from annoyance to a brotherhood within a matter of years, and of his fondness for that soft-hearted girl with the beautiful blonde hair. He recalled the bitterness he felt when they had fallen in love and the guilt that ate at him for feeling such a way.

"I want to be accepted." He replied, though he knew as soon as he said it that was not right either.

"Oh?" Hestia asked, cocking an eyebrow. "So, I am speaking with Quinn now? Be honest with yourself, Levy. Though both of those may be true, what is it that you truly wish for? What drives you?

"You asked earlier if you were dead. If you feel as though your actions have led to that point, then say the word and it will be so. But, if you are not ready to give up yet, then find your purpose to keep on living. What do **you** want?"

Levy closed his eyes against the rush of memories and emotions that flooded through him. He thought about every decision he had made that had brought him to this point and highlighted each regret along the way. He thought of those he loved, and those he had betrayed, and silently sent a prayer for forgiveness to each of them.

When he opened his eyes again, the fire had died down so that only embers remained. The only light left within the cavern came from the golden curtain, shimmering in the darkness. Hestia looked at him intently, ready to reward him with whatever decision he had come to.

"I want to say I'm sorry," he began. Though the words started slowly, they began to tumble out faster and faster as his thoughts rolled out from within his mind. "I want to help create a world where I can stand side-by-side with those that I love. I want to contribute to something more than death and destruction, and leave a legacy that will propel my people into a brighter tomorrow."

He paused for a second, searching for the right words to say. "I want to atone for my sins, and show that I am not the monster I have made myself out to be."

He thought about Zeus and the multitude of terrible things he had done, and all that he still wanted to achieve. He thought of Clotho stripped naked and beaten raw, left to rot in the dungeons of Olympus, and of what Zeus had wanted Levy to do to Ashe, had he gotten his way. "And I want to shove Zeus' lightning bolt up his ass, sideways."

Hestia's smile had split into a wide grin by the time he had finished speaking.

"Though it took you a long time to get there, I am proud of the person who sits before me." She gestured to the curtain of flames, as she had so long ago. "Please, walk through the curtain of my essence, so that it may envelop you fully, as it did once before. Grab hold of your destiny, Levy, and do not let go until you have achieved what you desire."

He walked up the winding path leading to the flame, reaching his hand out to feel the warmth wash over his body.

"How do I face them?" He asked the goddess, looking back in her direction. "After all I have done, all of the pain that I have caused. How do I look them in the eye again?"

"Embrace the remnants of your past choices, Levy, for they hold the seeds of wisdom that will guide you towards a brighter future."

He closed his eyes against his doubts, hoping that when he walked through the flame, he would not find that this had all been a simple hallucination of his mind in its death throes.

"And Levy," Hestia added, no more than a voice now, within the darkened cavern. "Do not be afraid to lean on your friends. There is no shame in showing weakness."

With one final, deep breath, he walked into the curtain's warm embrace.

CHAPTER 36

QUINN

Ares' arms reached out impossibly fast, grabbing Quinn's sword at the base of its blade, and stopping his forward momentum. The god's hands sliced open as they made contact, sliding down the blade's edge before coming to a stop at its hilt, sluicing ichor upon the ground in great splashes as it bit deeply. Ares stared at Quinn with outrage, his life had flashed before his very eyes.

"You absolute worm!" the god bellowed, using all of his remaining strength to keep the sword from skewering him through the head.

Quinn continued to push with everything he had, the last sparks of his energy sputtering and going out. Though he was now completely tapped, he continued to push with every fiber of his being, willing the blade forward with sheer determination and stubbornness.

He thought of Ashe and Levy, injured on the floor, knowing their lives hinged upon his success. He thought of his people and humanity, and what awaited them if he could not stop Ares from stealing the power of fate for Zeus. And so, he pushed harder, his muscles screaming in protest at the abuse he put them through. Though he made no further progress, he gave up no ground either.

"I WILL CRUSH YOU WHERE YOU STAND YOU IMPUDENT-"

Quinn pushed again as the god roared, nearly catching him off guard. The near-death experience shut Ares up and they continued their stalemate. Quinn knew he could not keep this up much longer. Darkness had begun to creep into the edges of his vision, and it felt as though his arms would tear apart at any moment.

Suddenly, the pressure pushing back against him lessened and he made some ground, inching the sword's tip ever closer to the god.

"Don't give up, Quinn!" Ashe yelled from where she crouched. She had managed to force herself back to her knees and had Ares' arms wrapped with thread that gave off a dull glow.

"ENOUGH WITH YOUR TRICKS!" Ares bellowed, turning briefly to shoot Ashe a venomous glare. "YOU CANNOT DEFEAT AN OLYMPIAN!"

Ashe clutched her fingers around the thread, and with a show of effort, she spread her arms out wide, pulling Ares' arms with them as though he were the world's largest marionette. The god's hands were wrenched away from the blade, leaving him wide open to Quinn's strike.

Seeing his target now unguarded, Quinn struck out with renewed energy, driving the sword between Ares' open lips. Just as it seemed his strike would land true, the god, in a last-ditch effort, clamped his teeth down, stopping the blade's progress.

With his life now hanging in the balance, a mighty roar loosed itself from deep within, as once again a divine aura sprung to life around the god. Quinn could not fathom how he had managed to find more energy, but his heart sank as he was once again overpowered by the deity.

Ares pushed forward; his steps slow yet powerful. Despite the predicament he was in, wrapped with the threads of fate, and a sword held between his teeth, he was still able to outclass them both. With each step he managed to take, the ground quaked beneath him.

Ashe pulled back on her threads with all of her remaining strength, yet still, she found herself being dragged along behind the enraged god. Quinn could feel the resistance of Ashe's powerful hold, and it was only thanks to her that he had not been completely overpowered already.

Quinn's muscles strained as he dug his feet into the ground, bracing against Ares' sheer power. He could sense the last vestiges of the Olympian's energy waning, the exhaustion taking its toll, but he knew he could not let up. Ashe had risked everything to give him this opportunity, and he would not let her down. With every ounce of strength he could muster, Quinn pushed against Ares, channeling his frustration through his blade. The clash of wills surged against one another, their struggle becoming a test of endurance and unwavering resolve.

Ashe's fiery control surged once more as she met Quinn's eyes, intensifying the heat and bonds that held Ares captive. Her determination was palpable; her belief in their shared destiny was unwavering. The flames licked at Ares' skin, a reminder of her unyielding spirit.

Yet, still, Ares kept coming, inching forward step by excruciating step. Quinn's arms began to buckle underneath what had started to feel like the opposite of the most painful tug-of-war he had ever experienced.

He doubted a push-of-war was a thing, though if he made it out of this alive, he planned to implement that into his training so that the next time a god bit down on the end of his blade he was ready.

Ares must have sensed Quinn's failing strength, because he began to press even harder, forcing him back three steps in rapid succession. On the third step Quinn faltered; his knee buckling under the immense weight it tried to hold.

Seeing blood in the water, Ares released what remained of his essence, pushing it out in a shockwave that slammed into Quinn, leaving him no time to throw up any kind of guard. The force of the energy felt like a wall of gale-force wind, buffeting him back and throwing one of his hands completely off the hilt of his sword.

Quinn knew as he began to fall backward that he had failed. Within moments Ares would close the distance, finishing him off easily. From there he would go for Ashe, and then with the power of fate at Zeus' command, his realm would be in for pain it was woefully unprepared for. The bitter taste of failure flooded his mouth, and it was all he could do to not spit it out.

As soon as he had begun to fall, his momentum stopped. He felt the warmth of a strong hand between his shoulder blades, stopping him from falling and allowing him to grab his hilt once more.

"Easy, Quinn." Levy's voice came from right beside his ear, "Let's end this together, as it should have been from the start."

A full range of emotions went through Quinn, all at once, but he knew that he did not have time to fully process what this meant. Instead, grateful for his friend's support, he nodded and repeated, "Together."

"Fire Queen!" Levy shouted to Ashe, who stared at them both with fierce pride in her eyes. "When I give the word, pull back on your thread with all of the strength you have left."

Look at this guy, Quinn thought to himself, unable to help the smile that spread across his face. *Wakes up from a nap just in time to save the day, and starts barking orders as if nothing has changed.*

He took a glance behind him and sobered immediately. Levy's face was a mess of blood, both wet and dried. A jagged, diagonal cut had been slashed across his right eye. Quinn doubted an eye even existed under the swollen lid anymore.

Ares, for his part, was red in the face. With his essence now exhausted, and Levy back in the picture, he was fully aware of the predicament he was in. Spittle foamed at the corners of his mouth, flying out into the air as his cheeks puffed and flapped at his heavy breathing combined with the unintelligible insults that spewed from his encumbered mouth.

"What's that?" Levy called out to the god; his words filled with an ire that betrayed his anger. "It's hard to understand you with Quinn's sword between your teeth."

Ares' eyes bulged further, a vein now prominent and pulsing across the god's scarlet face.

"Here," Levy dropped any hint of playfulness in his voice, leaving a calm and steely anger in its place. "Allow me to do something about that."

Quinn felt the energy build from within his friend, flooding into every extremity of his body, before coming to rest within both of his hands and arms. From the hand which propped Quinn up, energy flowed into him, calming his raging muscles, and strengthening his limbs against the pressure the god put on him.

With the influx of energy now empowering him once more, Quinn managed to push back against Ares, driving him back a couple of steps. His eyes widened as he gave up ground, and for the first time in their fight, Quinn saw fear prominent on his face.

"Let's end this," he muttered, and Quinn could feel the remaining energy within Levy gather in his friend's arm.

"NOW, ASHE!" He yelled.

As she did before, Ashe pulled her arms apart, wrenching Ares' arms wide with her and pulling him off balance. The god stumbled backward, his arms flailing against the thread that bound him. With a jarring cry of his own, Levy jammed his hand forward, striking the pommel of Quinn's blade and unleashing a current of his energy as it made contact.

Between Quinn's force and Levy's increased strength, it was too much pressure for Ares' teeth to bear. Enamel shattered under the weight of the strike as Ares' teeth were blown apart. The blade lunged forward, unhindered, and plunged into the back of the god's throat.

A guttural squeal escaped the deity, which turned into a gurgle as the blade protruded forcefully from the other side. Ichor sprayed out from the wound as Ares dropped to his knees, his eyes once filled with vehement anger, now dull, and rolled into the back of his head.

The battlefield descended into a shocked silence at the brutality of what had just occurred, as well as the weight of what the trio had just accomplished. Never before had an Olympian's death been documented in any of their written histories. Though it had been the hardest fight of his life, Quinn felt a twinge of hope at seeing that they could die from a sword.

With a deep breath, he turned around to face his mangled friend. His body was completely drained of energy, his muscles screaming at him from their overuse. So, it was with what little strength he could still muster that he balled his fist, and sent it crashing into Levy's jaw.

"QUINN!" Ashe shouted with surprise.

Levy, for his part, stood completely still; stunned at his friend's outburst.

"Now you hit me," Quinn said, staring at the ground from the corner of his eye.

"I...what?" Levy asked, completely taken aback at this turn of events.

"Hit me," Quinn said again.

Levy thought for a minute more, before shrugging his shoulders and said, "Ok, but you asked for it so don't cry when it hurts."

He balled his fist and pulled his shoulder back, before driving his knuckles into Quinn's stomach. Quinn doubled over with a *whoosh*ing sound, taking a moment to collect himself before straightening and staring back up at Levy. Slowly, a smile began to spread on each of their faces.

At this moment, they were reunited, and the pent-up pressure and weight they carried began to ease as they embraced. But it was only when Ashe came flying in with a hug of her own, sending them all sprawling to the ground, that the three of them could finally laugh together once more.

CHAPTER 37

ASHE

The Tower lay still and quiet sometime later; Ashe, Quinn, and Levy scattered across the cold, hard floor. Though at one time a raging inferno danced along the tile, now it was cool and soothing along their backs.

Despite their bodies being battered and bruised, their spirits were soaring high after the first real taste of victory, as well as their reunion once more. Their battle against Ares had been grueling. They had fought with everything they had, pouring their very souls into each attack, and in the end, it was Levy who had come to their aid, reaffirming his loyalty with one final strike.

Ashe lay on her back, her blonde hair sprawled out across the floor. To her left lay Quinn, his fingers had found her hand some time ago and now lay intertwined with her own. Levy was stretched out across from her, the tops of their heads lightly touching. It was a reminder of simpler times, and Ashe sighed whimsically as a warm wave of nostalgia washed through her.

Her emerald eyes scanned the room, taking in the aftermath of their fight. Broken debris and shattered orbs littered the ground, evidence of the intense battle that had unfolded. The air still crackled with residual energy, a testament to the power that had been wielded by both sides.

Beside her, Quinn groaned, shifting his weight, and wincing at the pain that shot through his body. His jet-black hair was matted with sweat, and his leather armor was shredded to the point that it now limply hung off of his body in tattered strips. He reached out his hand and found Levy's arm, giving it a firm squeeze.

"It's good to have you back, truly, but I think we need to address the elephant in the room." His voice was hoarse, but despite the words, it was also filled with gratitude. He and Ashe both knew that they would not have won that fight if Levy had not come to their aid.

Levy, his dark brown hair plastered to his forehead with sweat and blood, smiled weakly in response. "For what it is worth, I'm sorry for what I did. I let my jealousy be manipulated, and I thought I could find another way, but I was wrong. I should have trusted you both from the beginning."

Ashe watched the exchange, her heart filled with a mixture of relief and admiration. Levy's betrayal had stung deeply. Up until the moment he attacked Ares, she thought she had lost him forever. She saw the conflict in his eyes the second he walked into her Tower, but truly worried that he was no longer able to pull himself back from the ledge.

Seeing him fight alongside them once again, risking his life to defeat Ares, was a testament to the power of redemption. She could not help but rediscover her respect for him.

"You made amends when it mattered most," Ashe said softly, her voice carrying a touch of warmth. "We were once a team, and we can be a team again, Levy, and that means standing beside one another no matter what. We fought together today, and that carries weight."

Levy nodded, his eye glistening with unshed tears. "I won't let you down again. Either of you. I promise."

"It isn't as simple as that." Quinn cut in, though there was no malice behind his words. "If it were up to me, I would gladly have you back, but your actions hurt a lot more than just us."

"Quinn…" Ashe began to protest but he held his hand up. There was a new air of confidence to his every action now, as if a massive weight had been lifted off his shoulders and he was finally able to see the value within himself. Ashe felt a primal mix of pride and attraction course through her at this new version of him.

"I am not suggesting he be cast out or vilified. I am simply pointing out that there are many people whom we will need to work with moving forward who will feel as if they cannot trust him. We have the benefit of having known him before all of this. They do not.

As far as they're concerned, he is the same person who unleashed an army of undead upon them, responsible for the deaths of many of their loved ones. It will not be easy for us to just convince them he has changed."

"He's right, Ashe," Levy said, staring at his hands with his one good eye. "I did a lot of terrible things; Things that I don't know that I'll ever be able to forgive myself of. If I can't forgive myself, how can I expect them to?"

"We will find a way," Ashe said, determination burning bright within her. The three of them were finally back together after so long. She would not let anybody tear that apart again. "Besides, they may not have a choice."

"What do you mean?" Quinn asked, catching onto the hidden meaning in her change of voice. Ashe smiled internally. There was no hiding anything from him, not that she would have chosen to anyway.

"Heed these words, a prophecy foretold, of valor, virtue, and warrior bold. As Heavens weep, when realms collide; Three heroes rise to stem the tide. A sacrifice for all to see embodies hope; forever free."

"Clotho's prophecy?" Levy asked, locking onto Ashe's eyes.

"You know of it?" she asked, surprised.

He shook his head, lost in thought. "I have spoken with her a couple of times while on Olympus and she has mentioned it, though she never told me the exact lines. She called me one of her heroes, though at the time I believed her just mad."

"Someone wants to catch me up?" Quinn asked, looking back

and forth between them both.

"Talius never told you any of this?" Ashe asked, though with what she knew that did not surprise her.

"I get the feeling Talius hasn't told a lot of things," Levy said, a tinge of bitterness has crept into his voice.

"I'm still completely lost," Quinn reminded them, waving his hand to reign their attention back in.

Ashe pushed herself to her feet, wincing as pain shot through her body. She surveyed her companions, seeing the exhaustion etched upon their faces, but also the newfound fire in their eyes that refused to be extinguished.

They had faced down their demons, both internal and external, and had emerged stronger for it. They were ready for the full truth as she had seen it. "Alright, I will tell you what I know."

She spent the next hour recounting the tale of Clotho's journey to claim the Tower. She told them of how Clotho and her companions had met Talius, and of how they trained him along the way.

They listened in awe at how he had changed Clotho's opinion of humanity, and of how the seeds of mistrust for Zeus and the Olympian way of life had started to sprout within her. She recounted the moment they decided to betray him, of the battle that took place the sacrifice of Clotho's guardians so that Talius may live on to stand with her and spread Clotho's will, and of how Hestia had stepped in at the darkest hour to drive Zeus back, sacrificing her seat amongst the Olympians. Their plan was set in motion, and Clotho spent the better part of a millennium weaving her prophecy into being so that future generations may live free from Zeus' influence.

"I don't understand," Quinn said after she had finished her tale. "If she had planned for you to be one of the heroes of her prophecy, why did she want you to take the Tower?"

"I do not believe she ever intended for me to take the Tower, Quinn," Ashe replied. "I think she expected Chaos to claim the throne."

Quinn shuddered at that thought. She knew from his own words and experiences just how afraid he was of the Primordial. "Why would she have ever wanted that?" he asked.

"Because he would have destroyed it." She replied, the meaning behind Clotho's words to her finally beginning to make sense. "With the power of fate no longer in play, Zeus would not be able to control any of the narrative moving forward. The cycle would be broken, and the threat of him ever gaining control of that power again would be lost to him entirely."

"And from those ashes, a new chance at life would be born." Levy finished her thought, sitting up excitedly. "Ashe, we could free you from this! The prophecy says itself that when Heavens collide THREE heroes will rise to stem the tide."

Quinn jumped excitedly to his feet, grabbing her hands in his own. "Is that something you would want? Because that is something I would want, but you have to be okay with it first. I know how important this duty is to you. If you want to stay, I support you. But if not, with a little rest I should be able to summon enough energy to…"

Ashe put her fingers to his lips, smiling softly as his words stopped tumbling from his mouth. The excitement and hope in his eyes were too much for her. Any more and she was afraid she would melt. His features sobered, taking her gesture as though she wanted to stay, and the pain he was unable to hide nearly broke her heart right there.

She leaned forward as if going for a kiss, but instead rested her chin on his shoulder so that her mouth settled directly next to his ear.

"I am way ahead of you." She whispered, pleased at the shudder she felt running down his back as her breath made contact with his skin. She stepped back, staring into his eyes as he connected the dots; his eyes widening in excitement as he realized what her words meant.

His face split into a goofy grin and her heart beat wildly, as if catching up for all of these years apart. She saw that even Levy had a slight grin on his face, though he stared down at the ground. She knew there was a time when he had been in love with her, and though she had always been forthright with her feelings for him, she knew it was something they would need to talk about soon.

She was thrilled to have Levy back and did not want anything to ever jeopardize their friendship again. Though that would be a conversation for another time. For now, she needed to set her plan into motion.

"Come," She said, leading them to the Tower's exit. "Let us take fate into our own hands."

~~~

Ashe stood at the base of the Tower, staring up at the gargantuan structure before her. She had always found it rather spacious inside, though staring up at it now, the throne room seemed cramped. Quinn and Levy stood to either side of her, their hands resting upon her shoulders.

They had spent a little time recovering their lost energy, though it was likely to take days before they were completely recharged; but it was enough to lend what Ashe needed to put her plan into action. She closed her eyes, focusing on the threads she had weaved what felt like a lifetime ago, after having just finished experiencing Clotho's journey and bringing them back into focus.

Wrapped around the Tower, like a shimmering tapestry spun by a celestial spider, were golden webs that glistened in the Realm of Fate's twilit sky. The intricate webbing covered every inch of the Tower, forming a lattice of delicate strands that seemed to defy gravity.

Each thread had been meticulously woven, casting an ethereal barrier that enshrouded the Tower in an otherworldly embrace. The gossamer strands, almost translucent in their golden hue, caught the light and cast a mesmerizing glow. Ashe smiled as he heard a small gasp from behind her as her friends took in the beautiful spectacle.

Ashe held her hands aloft, and it was there that all of the threads converged, as if they were extensions of her very being. Her touch infused the webs with power and purpose, intertwining fate itself with her will.

She moved her hands with graceful precision, her fingers tracing paths in the air visible only to herself. The golden strands responded to her touch, and her touch alone, bending and shifting, creating an intricate network that bound the Tower in its caress.

"Are you sure you want to do this?" Quinn asked once more. He knew better than anybody how important this was to her.

"I am sure." She replied, not losing focus on her weaving. "Once this is done, the power of fate will be no more."

"Though its energy will still exist within you?" Levy asked. "Does that mean you will still be able to weave destiny outside of this realm?"

"No." The power of this realm had been woven into her the moment she sat upon its throne, just as she had woven its power into the world. She did not know why her plan would work; she just knew it would.

"I will take the essence within me, but once the Tower falls, fate will fall with it. The beings of the world, from this moment on, will be the masters of their destiny." Levy nodded, as if satisfied with that outcome.

"Are you both ready?" She asked, tensing her fingers, and pulling the threads tight. They nodded, summoning the energy forth from within them and lending it to Ashe. She drew upon it, drinking it in greedily as she combined it with her own.

With only a thought she ignited the threads, sending an orange flame up toward the Tower. Within moments the structure was engulfed in an inferno, the cocoon of weaving igniting every crevice. After a moment the flame turned bright gold, the momentum of the fire reversing so that it traveled back down into Ashe.

She gasped as power flooded within her, overwhelming her mind with every weaving that had ever been spun. Images flew before her eyes, too numerous to keep track of, and for a moment it felt as though her consciousness would be ripped away, as easily as loose sand caught in a riptide.

She felt Quinn tighten his hand upon her shoulder as if he could sense her beginning to slip, and latched onto his warmth, anchoring herself against the torrent of energy.

Ashe collapsed to the ground as the last of the images ebbed from her mind. Though she felt physically obliterated, her mental state was sharper than ever; energy buzzing throughout her, tumultuous and spirited as though she had kicked a beehive.

"Are you alright?" she heard Quinn ask, swinging her arm around his shoulders and helping her back to her feet. Moments later Levy appeared at her other side, lifting her other arm around his broad shoulders, and helping Quinn hold her up.

"I'll be fine." She spoke. "I just need to rest for a second while my head stops spinning."

She stared up at the Tower of Fate, though she supposed after what she had just accomplished it was merely just a tower now. What once was bright, lustrous stone now appeared scorched and dull. Cracks from the heat of her flame had spread up the foundations, and chunks of rock had already begun to fall from its heights.

"Chaos," she said looking at Quinn with a teasing smile. "Will you do the honors?" She held her hand up, still connected to the thread encasing the Tower.

"Don't call me that," he growled, though there was a playfulness in his words. "Besides, I think Janus over there," he chucked his thumb in Levy's direction, drawing a dramatic eye roll from his friend, "probably wants to finish what he started."

"Cute," Levy said dryly. "How about the three of us do it together?"

They all three grasped Ashe's hand together, tightening her grip upon the last remaining threads of fate. Levy counted to three, and they pulled hard, watching in awe as the crumbling vestiges of the Tower gave in, collapsing in upon itself until only a mountain of rubble remained.

They sat in silence for a bit, staring at what remained of the structure that only three years before had been the focus of their entire lives. Though they all knew that there was a terrible struggle on the horizon, it still felt as if a mammoth weight had been lifted from their shoulders.

Most of their lives had been spent training, at the command of others, to claim something they knew so little about because they were told it was the right thing to do. As they stared now at the smoking remains of that lie, for the first time Ashe truly felt free from its burden.

From here on out, they would do things their way. Zeus was coming for them, but with new determination, and old friendships strengthened from the flames of hardship, they would be ready.

"What now?" Levy asked, breaking the comfortable silence that had settled upon them.

"Now we get answers," Ashe replied, standing up and brushing herself off.

"From who?" Levy stood up himself, reaching out a hand to Quinn and helping him up from the ground. He held his injured eye closed, though whether it was by his own choice or because of the swelling, Ashe did not know. She doubted he would keep the eye, if there was any trace of it left, but she was certain that he needed medical attention.

"From the man who helped set this all into motion."

"Talius is still alive?" Quinn asked, surprised. "I assumed with Ares here it meant he had been lost."

"His orb was still in one piece when Ares breached the Tower." She noticed Levy look away; the corners of his mouth raised at the omission of his name from that sentence.

"If he still lives, I should be able to locate his energy and open a portal to reach him." Quinn closed his eyes, searching for the Master's familiar energy signature. After a moment he opened them again. "I found him, but before we go there, we need to take a quick side errand first."

"Where to?" Ashe asked though she could tell from his expression something was wrong.

"We need to stop and help a friend."

CHAPTER 38

QUINN

Quinn had been able to locate Talius rather quickly in his search. He was not sure if it was strictly because of Chaos' essence he had taken in, or if his ability to sense energies due to his Abyssillian bloodline had been amplified by it, but searching someone out had become second nature to him.

It was only when he had searched for Mallory that he started to get nervous. He found her fairly quickly as well, but to his concern, the energies of Nes and Darrik were nowhere to be found. Cyrus felt as if he were in another realm entirely, which also did not sit well with him.

"Are you guys ready to go?" he asked, opening a portal of swirling purple energy back into the Realm of Night.

"Are we going to be ok in there?" Ashe asked, no doubt remembering the last time she had traveled through it when Quinn had directed her to keep her eyes closed. At the time he had not wanted her to see Chaos, though she was unlikely to know that.

"It will be fine. This realm is mine now. Nothing will hurt you."

He held out his hand, taking hers gently within his own. She looked back at the ruins of the Tower she had spent the last three years of her life in, before taking a deep breath and nodding to him.

"Let's go." She stepped through the portal without a second glance.

Quinn held his hand out to Levy, just as he had Ashe.

"And you, princess?" he asked, smiling to show there was no harm meant behind his words. Levy flashed a smile, smacking him on the shoulder.

He met Quinn's eyes for a brief moment, before briskly looking away and stepping through the portal himself. Quinn could feel the lingering tension between them and knew it was something they would need to work out soon.

Though he was overjoyed to have Levy back on the right side, it did not change the fact that he had done some pretty abhorrent things. The fallout from that would not just go away overnight. There was also the fact that they had both tried to kill one another, each nearly succeeding, multiple times.

There were plenty of wounds that needed to heal and barriers that would need to be torn down, and the fact that they both knew it was the source of their tension. There was also a comfort in knowing that they would succeed in doing so.

Their friendship was more of a brotherhood. Unlike when he had messed up with Ashe, and worried he would never be able to make amends, there was a sort of understanding between him and Levy, though unspoken, that told him everything would be ok.

He stepped into the portal, closing it behind him with a newfound hope for the future. Though he knew there was a rising storm on the horizon, Quinn was happy that it was with the two people he loved most in this world that he got to face it.

~~~

They stepped back through to a lush expanse of untouched, natural beauty. A verdant paradise stretched out before them; wild, fragrant, and packed with vegetation as far as the eyes could see. Running water could be heard trickling in a stream nearby, and the sounds of wildlife echoed off of the trunks of the broad, leafy trees.

"I thought you said we were traveling to the Wastes?" Ashe asked, her eyebrows furrowed together.

"This is the Wastes," Quinn replied, his heart beginning to accelerate. "They did it! Nes and Mallory brought life back to the Wastes!" He closed his eyes, reaching out for Mallory's essence which he had felt nearby before. He still could not feel anybody else, and that worried him, but if Mallory was nearby, that meant answers were as well.

"This way," he called back to his shocked companions, leading them towards a small brook a few yards in the distance.

Quinn's heart sank as he entered the clearing and found Mallory kneeling beside Nes' lifeless body. The sight before him was devastating, and sorrow engulfed him in an instant. He had known Nes for years now; he had practically raised him.

He thought back to his first encounter with his little trio of students when they had been bandits poaching the borders of the Wastes. They had lost Sen in battle against the undead, and now Nes lay before him, broken and bloodied. His heart reached out to Andra, knowing that when she heard the news she would likely break down; the loss was too much to handle on top of the stress of leading their people.

As he approached Mallory, he noticed tears streaming down her face; her grief palpable in the air. Quinn's own eyes welled up with tears, his spirit heavy with an overwhelming sadness. He knelt beside Mallory, his voice choked with emotion, and rested his hand on her shoulder, snapping her out of her stupor.

"Mallory…"

She whipped her head around as though she had only just noticed his presence for the first time. Her eyes were wide with grief and uncertainty, before clearing and seeing Quinn for the first time. With a choked sob she threw her arms around him, burying her head in his shoulder as the sobs came unbidden.

He tried his best to offer her comfort and soothe her pain, though he felt utterly helpless in the face of such a profound loss. The weight of the moment was unmeasurable, and Quinn's mind raced with memories of their adventures, their laughter, and the bond they had shared.

He recalled Nes' infectious smile and the way he always

brought a ray of sunshine into their lives. Nes was the one who had a knack for making everyone in a room laugh, even in the darkest of times. And now, the light had been extinguished, leaving a void that could never be filled.

"It's all my fault," Mallory sobbed between shuttering breaths. "I knew the Masters couldn't be trusted. I let my guard down and he paid the price. I promised Andra I'd look after him."

As Quinn looked at Nes' lifeless form, he knew there was a time not so long ago when he would have been like her; beating himself up, wracked with guilt over this outcome. He knew how bitter those feelings tasted, and how dark of a place that could drag one's mind, kicking and screaming against the sharp embrace of failure.

"You cannot blame yourself, Mallory." He said, wiping a tear from her eye. "Nes knew the risks of this plan, and he gladly accepted them, because the rewards were worth it. Look around us," he said, gesturing to the life that had taken root in the previously inhospitable land. "He did not die in vain. Thanks to you, he got to see his dreams come to life."

Mallory shook her head, a look of disappointment plain upon her face. "I did not do anything, Quinn. He saved my life and then was ported away before I knew what was happening. I was useless."

"You were a friend when he needed it, Mallory. Do you think he would have been comfortable traveling with people he did not fully trust on his own? You once told me not to shoulder everything on my own and to accept the help of my friends because it was important. Don't devalue those words now."

"But, Andra…" She started, but Quinn gently interrupted her.

"Andra is going to need us now more than ever. We all need to be strong for what is to come, and we can do that together. Nes would want that."

Mallory sighed, wiping her eyes with the back of her hand. "Well, I guess one of us needs to be strong, eh? Can't have us both screaming in the middle of the night and waking the entire complex." She hugged Quinn again before getting back to her feet, reaching out a hand to help him up as well. "Thanks, Quinn."

"You know I always have your back, Mal. Now come with me for a second. We will get Nes' body transported shortly, but first I have a surprise for you; a familiar face you'll be happy to see.

As they made their way back towards the shaded line of trees, Levy stepped out into the light of the moon, calling out to him.

"Quinn, you've got to come see this."

"Quinn, what the fuck?!" Mallory stopped in her tracks, unsheathing her sword with trained speed.

Levy's eye widened, but thankfully he made no move to reach for a weapon of his own, instead opting to throw his hands up in a placating gesture.

Quinn stepped between them, holding his hand out to Mallory's shoulder so that she could not advance further.

"That's my bad." He said, pulling his mouth back with a look of contrition. "That was not the face I was implying, and honestly I probably would have reacted that way too."

"Why is he here?" She asked, her grief momentarily forgotten; replaced instead by a seething rage.

"There is a lot I need to catch you up on."

"Gee, ya think?!" She said, though thankfully she sheathed her sword.

"Long story short, Levy is with us again. I know that may be hard to accept, given everything you have been through involving him, but without him, Ares would still be alive and I would not be here." She looked around Quinn, locking eyes with her one-time foe.

"What happened to your eye?" She asked, squinting as though if she focused it would reappear.

"Lost it to the edge of a spear," Levy answered, unsure of the sudden, random line of questioning.

Mallory nodded once as if that made everything better. "Good, if you so much as look at me funny, you'll lose the other one."

Quinn stifled a snort, knowing that the threat was more than just bravado. Mallory was a firecracker on a good day. When she held a grudge, all bets were off.

"Look," Levy began, "I'm sorry for what I have done. I remember you from that night; how valiantly you fought beside Ashe. I..."

"Oooooh no, bud. Honey-dipped words won't get you out of this. The only reason I'm not ripping your throat out right now is because Quinn vouched for you. Even then I don't know that his word is enough to hold me back."

"And how about mine?" Ashe spoke, stepping out from the shadows. Quinn shot her a thankful look, knowing that if he had to break up a fight, he was likely to lose a finger. It would have been like trying to pull a badger away from a snake.

Mallory fell completely still, her eyes snapping to Ashe as though she had seen a ghost. Then, as if the tension from a slingshot pulled tight was suddenly released, she shot toward the woman, leaping from her feet when she was near enough and flying into Ashe's outstretched arms.

"AAAAASSSSHHHEE," Mallory wailed, half sobbing and half joyful.

Levy sidled up to Quinn as the two women hugged and talked in excited, hushed tones. His face was pale, and a thin sheen of sweat was present on his forehead under the pale moonlight.

"That one is certainly something," Levy said, swallowing audibly. "I thought I was going to die."

"Give her some time," Quinn smiled, staring at the friends laughing in the distance. "She's worth it. And what do you mean by die? Are you telling me you wouldn't have fought back had push come to shove?"

"No, I would not have. It's like you said, I need to face my sins head-on. There is going to be a whole lot more of that, but my time of hurting these people is over. Whatever is decided, I'll accept it."

Quinn clapped his friend on the back, warmed to hear his words. "And Ashe and I will have your back the entire way. It's going to be a long road, but you will never walk it alone again. I promise."

Levy nodded his thanks, before changing the subject. There was still a lot of turmoil behind his eyes, and Quinn knew it made him uncomfortable.

"I was going to tell you before she flipped out, Darrik is dead over there." He pointed to a small pile of rubble in the distance where the shadow of a body could just be made out in the minuscule light.

"That was likely Mallory," Quinn replied. He had not gotten the full story out of her back by Nes' body, but she had confirmed the Masters' betrayal. Levy gave him a genuine smile then, his eyes glittering at the news.

"Well then, perhaps you're right, Quinn. Maybe she isn't so bad after all."

After allowing Ashe and Mallory some time to catch up, the group reconvened around Nes' body. Upon his request, Ashe had wrapped Nes in a blanket of golden thread, leaving his head uncovered.

"Andra will want to see him one last time," Mallory explained, her mirth once again quelled for the time being.

With that task taken care of, everyone gathered around Quinn, ready to cross back into the Realm of Night, and then onto their next destination.

"Everyone ready?" Quinn asked as he opened the portal, taking in the scenery one last time before they left it behind.

No matter what lies on the horizon for us, Nes, he silently promised, picturing the look of excitement upon his friend's face at the news that life could once again be brought to the Wastes, *I swear to you, our people will come back here. They will see what you have sacrificed for, and they will sing your name for lifetimes to come.*

As the portal swirled to life, he locked eyes with Mallory, and they nodded at one another, no doubt sharing a similar thought.

"Where are we heading?" Ashe asked, stepping up to the purple glob of energy before them.

"Back to where it all began," Quinn replied, looking at each of his friends. "Brace yourselves, we're going home."

CHAPTER 39

QUINN

Four jaws hit the floor in unison as they stepped into the bustling city of Stormhaven. Quinn had expected to find Talius amongst the smoldering ruins of a city untouched since Athena had visited her wrath upon it. Instead, the night was alive with a cacophony of music and boisterous shouts from the many taverns that lined the lively streets.

Though construction was still well underway, a good portion of Stormhaven had been rebuilt; the buildings appearing sturdier than ever. The party picked their way toward the Citadel in silence, taking in the mirthful cries and tantalizing mix of scents that wafted out into the warm night air.

Despite the ominous tidings they carried with them, Quinn could not help the joy he felt at seeing so many Abyssillian faces amongst the crowds. Ashe slipped her hand into his, sending him a warm smile as if he knew what was on his mind. Mallory quickly stepped between them, breaking their hold, and taking Ashe's hand within her own, sticking her tongue out at Quinn and pulling Ashe ahead.

"You can hold my hand if you'd like," Levy said from behind him, shooting him a quick grin at the venomous look Quinn returned his way.

Seeing Stormhaven thriving had helped lift their spirits, but a somber weight settled back upon the group as they reached the wall of the Citadel. The guards stepped up to meet them, likely having seen the party advancing up the steps before they had even gotten halfway.

It looked as if they were going to question them, but recognition dawned in their eyes as they saw Quinn and Mallory. Shock, followed swiftly by sorrow, took root in their expressions as they laid eyes upon Nes, carried gently in the arms of Levy.

Though Mallory had initially protested to Levy carrying him, his strength made transporting the body up the multitude of steps easier than any other solution she had suggested.

Inside the inner walls, the Citadel was a hive of activity. Human and Abyssillian builders alike bustled back and forth, despite the late hour, setting lumber and stone and hammering supports for tomorrow's work. Quinn could not believe how far along a rebuilding effort had already come in the wake of such utter devastation.

"Quinn! Mallory!"

They turned towards the voice, seeing Andra come bounding in their direction. A tall, slender man followed closely behind; his eyes filled with delight upon seeing Ashe. Quinn remembered seeing the man in Ashe's camp the day after the attack from the undead. Though he could not remember the man's name, he did remember his attitude towards his people, and a slight amount of mistrust settled amongst his shoulders.

"Lady Ashelia!" The man bowed, though the quickness of it betrayed his excitement. "I thought you lost to the Tower. What a wonderful surprise."

"Lend!" Ashe smiled. "How wonderful it is to see you! Are you responsible for all of this?"

"Myself and Bartimaeus, aye." Lend replied. "Though I fear he may be lost to us now."

Quinn noticed Levy shrink at his words; as though he hoped he could hide himself from the conversation. Quinn reached out to him, taking Nes from his arms and nodding towards the wall, giving his friend a chance to quietly remove himself from the situation. The topic of Levy would have to come up soon, but for now, it was unnecessary fuel to add to the fire.

"Andra," Mallory said quietly, tears once again falling freely from her eyes.

Even in the moonlight, Quinn could see the young woman's face go pale. Andra was incredibly sharp, so it would not have taken her long to notice Nes was not standing with them. Quinn slowly walked up to the pair, gently placing Nes' wrapped body upon the stones at her feet. Softly, she knelt, reaching out and brushing a strand of blonde from his face.

"I'm so sorry, Andra," Mallory said, shaking her head. "It was exactly as we had feared. As soon as they had the chance, the Masters turned on us. I broke my promise."

"Hush now, Mal," Andra said, standing up and embracing her friend. "I believe you. I know that you would have done all that you could." She held Mallory out at arm-length, staring at her with glistening eyes. "We were both prepared for this when we went our separate ways."

Quinn stepped up, a knowing look on his face. For a moment he and Andra locked eyes, and an entire conversation passed between them within a matter of moments. He knew they would talk later, but for now, Andra needed to process everything, so instead he offered her the only good news he could.

"He succeeded, Andra. The Wastes are no longer a land of death and decay. When this is all over, our people will have a home, and the ability to thrive."

Her smile was bittersweet, but there was a small bit of genuine joy behind it. With a quick gesture, she summoned a couple of men over to her.

"Please take Nes to the inner sanctuary," She said, staring at the passive expression resting upon Nes' face. If they had not known better, he looked as though he could be peacefully sleeping. "Tomorrow we will celebrate his life. Tell the people if you would be so kind."

The men reached down, lifting Nes between them, and hustled

him away. When they were out of sight she turned back to Mallory, offering her one more hug before saying to the group, "I am sure there is a lot we need to discuss, but I hope you understand if I ask that we wait a bit longer." When they all agreed, she bowed stiffly before wishing them a good night and heading inside.

Lend attempted to halt Mallory as she swiftly followed, but Quinn reached out, stopping him before he had the chance.

"Let her go." He said, staring after her as she ducked into the doorway and out of sight. "Andra is strong, but right now they could both use the comfort of a friend."

Lend sighed, but did not argue, instead turning back to Ashe as Levy returned to the group. The pair locked eyes, and though Quinn noticed the man's hand twitch toward his blade, he thankfully did not draw it.

"I assume there is a good reason for his presence here." Lend said. "So, I will not question you on it just yet."

Ashe smiled her thanks. "There is good reason indeed, Lend. For now, just know he is on our side. I know that is not a good enough explanation, and I promise you a much more detailed debriefing after tomorrow's funeral."

"Very well, but for the sake of everyone here, please just... hide him away for now. These people have all been through a lot, much of it at his hands. Until we know more, they shouldn't see him walking the grounds freely."

Quinn was impressed at Levy's restraint throughout the conversation. If people were speaking negatively about him as if he were not present, he did not think he would be able to just sit back and not interject; and he knew for certain the old Levy would not have. To his surprise, as Lend finished speaking, Levy simply bowed his head and said, "I will stay out of the way, thank you."

"Lend?" Ashe asked, drawing the man's attention once more. "Could you point us toward Talius? We have some questions we would like to ask him."

Lend cocked an eyebrow, though he did not appear eager to offer the information. After a moment though he relented. "I can tell you where to find him, but be warned. He may not be able to answer you very well, if at all."

Quinn had his suspicions when they had first entered the city as he felt the energy humming through the towering stone walls, but once Lend pointed them in his direction, it had all but confirmed it. There was only one reason Talius would be so far below the surface of the Citadel.

CHAPTER 40

LEVY

The smell of sweat mingled with the taste of stale apprehension, thick upon Levy's tongue. Memories came unbidden to his mind as he and his friends walked down the narrow corridor that led beneath the Citadel, much as they had the last time all three had walked this path.

"Anybody else feeling some intense déjà vu?" Quinn asked, breaking the uncomfortable silence.

Levy chuckled, though the mixture of nerves and amusement was evenly split. They all knew this trip into the depths was different from their previous visit, but this was where everything had truly started to fall apart for the three of them, and though they were united once again, that wound still existed, scarred over as it was.

A tawny glow lit the cavern ahead, and the soft sounds of grunts highlighted a secret struggle that took place. Though Levy was well aware of the purpose of this chamber, he was somewhat surprised the Master would have decided to take up such a burden.

He half expected to enter through the little doorway ahead and see Talius lording over another, forced to bear the burden of powering Stormhaven's walls. Though he had not gotten confirmation of his doubts about the Master, Levy felt as though he had enough evidence to pull the truth from the man, and he most certainly intended to do just that.

As the trio reached the end of the corridor, Ashe pulled them to a stop, gathering each of their hands together with her own. Her golden eyes glimmered in the soft amber glow; confident, yet gentle. Levy felt a soothing wave of warmth spread through him, fighting away the anxiety that had started to overtake him as they arrived closer to the chamber.

"Nothing is as it was." She spoke softly, looking both Quinn and Levy in the eye. "Before we enter, we must let go of any remaining animosities. We cannot let bad memories of this place, nor any other, cloud our friendship ever again.

"We cannot win this war if we are not united. Take a deep breath, and quiet your mind. Talius holds no sway over us. Hestia has no power over us.

"Not even Clotho nor her prophecy control our fate. From this moment forward, we are in control." They nodded at her words, allowing her essence to calm their racing hearts. Pushing the doubts from his mind, Levy turned and entered the chamber, Quinn and Ashe following closely behind.

In the center of the room, a familiar onyx altar rose from the cold earthen floor, standing tall and majestic like an obsidian monolith. Its polished surface glistened with an otherworldly sheen, drawing Levy's eye with an irresistible allure, just as it had the first time he had witnessed it. The chamber itself was bathed in an eerie, ethereal glow, emanating with siphoned energy.

Shackled to the center of the pillar stood a man whose presence exuded both agony and resilience. Beads of sweat lined the Master's face; his mouth shut tight in an eternal grimace as his immortal essence was leached from his being.

The chains that bound him were intricately crafted, their links forged and engraved with an ancient power. They wrapped tightly around his limbs, constricting his movement and leaving crimson imprints upon his pale flesh. Yet, despite his torment, his eyes still held a glimmer of unwavering determination.

Though the last time Levy had seen Talius outside the gates of Petram he had not looked young, the man before him looked positively old. His body now wore the marks of relentless suffering; his once brown beard was now a muddle of greys and white.

His lean physique had withered to the point of being gaunt; no doubt the toll of this unceasing torment. Every breath came labored and his body trembled as the chains mercilessly feasted upon his immortal essence.

"I did not wish for you three to see me like this."

His voice, strained and weary, emerged no stronger than a whisper, ladencd with pain. He managed to lift his head and meet each of his young charges with a strength his voice betrayed.

"You do not seem surprised to see me here," Levy responded. Though his words were filled with no venom, the accusation hung in the air between them.

"Should I be?" Talius replied. "I trust Clotho's weaving implicitly. Though you may have lost your way, I had no doubts that in the end, you would return to us."

"And me?" Quinn asked, drawing even with Levy. "The last you saw of me I was lost to the Realm of Night. Was that intended in your prophecy as well?"

"I do not know the exact meaning of prophecy, young Quinn. Anybody who pretends to understand it is a liar or a fool. I put my faith in Clotho and Hestia. So no, I am not surprised to see you here. I am proud of you for overcoming your faults." The Master's eyes settled on Ashe and widened a fraction. "Ashelia, why are you not in the Tower?"

Ashe stepped past them, drawing up so that she was face-to-face with Talius. She searched his eyes for a brief moment, allowing her essence to come forth and wrap around the chains that bound the master. Her eyes widened and she immediately cut her power; her energy dissolving into the links of the chain.

"Who forged these evil chains, Talius?" She asked, her voice firmer than Levy had ever heard it before.

Talius' face split into a grin as a weak laugh escaped from between his lips, which quickly turned into a wracking cough.

"You need not look at me so coldly, Ashelia. I did not have them forged if that is what you think. These chains are far more ancient than I. Their first purpose was one similar to this. They are the chains that held Atlas in place so that he would not abandon his charge of holding up the world."

"Then why are they here?" She asked, backing up so that Quinn was able to wrap his arm around her.

"Hestia was able to find an alternative for Atlas, and in doing so, she brought them to me so that we could trap Athena. I am certain you know the prophecy now, do you not? When Zeus breaches this realm, humanity will need a place safe from his wrath. A haven against the storm, so to speak." He smiled as though he had told them a very clever joke.

"But those chains are awful." Ashe shivered, burying deeper into Quinn's embrace.

"I do not disagree," Talius confirmed. "Which is why I have chosen to bear the brunt of them. I will do what it takes to win, even if it means enduring this torture until it is over. So now you three must do the same.

"When Hestia came to me three years ago, I warned her you were not ready. Now, as you stand here before me, I can see that you are. The future of humanity lies upon your shoulders, and you must do anything you can to succeed."

"The three of us together will defeat Zeus, just as we did Ares," Quinn responded, straightening his back, and meeting the Master's eyes. "Thank you for bearing this burden in the meantime."

Levy noticed that something Talius said had irked his friend. Though he did not give away that he was upset, the way Quinn had just spoken was not typical. It was formal and concise but did not hold the genuine emotion he typically showed to those he cared for.

Talius' eyes softened. "I am truly proud of you all. You will be heroes the likes of which have not been seen since the ancient mythologies."

Quinn nodded and began to turn away, leading a shaken Ashe back toward the corridor that led to the surface.

"If you would do me one last favor when you go," Talius began, pausing for a moment as a particularly strong pain wracked his body. "Please, reseal this chamber when you leave. I do not wish for anybody else to find me here. The walls must stay powered, and I fear Lend may try to 'rescue' me from this fate. He was not particularly pleased when he witnessed the effects."

"It will be done," Quinn responded without sparing him a

second glance.

As his friends were halfway to the door Levy called out to them. "I'll meet you guys up on the surface in a minute. I have something else I'd like to speak with Talius about before we seal him away."

Quinn raised his free hand to signify that he understood and exited into the shadows of the corridor, out of sight.

Talius raised an eyebrow as Levy turned back to the master, his mask of civility dropped entirely, replaced by skepticism.

"I have a couple of questions for you, and I want you to answer them truthfully."

"I may have kept to the shadows for the entirety of your training and upbringing, young Levy, but I have never once been dishonest with you. Whatever you wish to know, so long as I can answer, I will do so."

"How long have you known about the prophecy?" he asked, giving the Master a soft question to start with so he could gauge his honesty.

"I was part of the plan to create it," he replied, matter-of-factly. "Though I did not know its contents until the last fifty years or so."

Levy nodded, content with his answer. "And how did you learn of the exact words, if Clotho was locked within the tower?"

Talius tilted his head, unsure of the direction of this questioning. "When the Weaver wants a message delivered, she needs only weave it into being. Any number of methods could be used to reach me. In this case, we had a goddess working with us."

"Did you choose your heroes for it, or was that part of the weaving also?"

Finally, Talius began to understand the direction in which Levy was leading him. A serious expression settled upon the Master's face as he stood tall against the chains.

"Are you sure you wish to go further with this?" Talius asked his words carrying a slight edge to them.

"Answer the question," Levy replied, unflinching.

"Yes, I chose the heroes."

"Ashe never set fire to the slums." Levy accused, feeling heat creep up the back of his neck.

"No, she did not. Ashelia showed potential as a young child, carrying a sense of compassion that was unrivaled by you or Quinn.

She complimented the two of you perfectly, so I deemed it necessary. I had those fires set, and paid her parents' debts when it was their only way out."

"And Quinn?" Levy's voice was low now, steely anger laced into every word. "You said his parents had come to Stormhaven to procure needed goods for the Abyssillians."

"They came at my behest," Talius replied. "I wanted an Abyssillian child with strong bloodlines I could mold into a hero. When his parents would not sell him to me, I had them murdered."

Levy stared at the man in disgust. "And me?"

Talius shook his head, knowing his next words would twist a dagger inside Levy he did not wish to twist. "There was naught special about you, I am afraid. You were simply an orphan within Stormhaven. I chose you because you were taller and stronger than the other children."

To Levy's surprise, the Master looked genuinely contrite at his own words.

"I am not proud of the actions I have taken, Levy. You are free to look at me with all of the disgust you would like. The truth is, I did what I had to do. I would sacrifice as many lives as it took to preserve life for humanity in this realm. You may think me harsh, or even evil if you wish. So long as we win, that is all that matters."

Levy chuckled then, drawing a surprised look from Talius. "You are saying the same bullshit I used to spout not so long ago. I'll be honest, Talius, I want to kill you for what you just admitted to. The old me probably would have."

His expression turned serious again, and he brought his mouth next to the Master's ear, speaking low. "We will win your war for you. When we do, if you still live and have not wasted away to nothing from these chains, you will admit this to Ashe and Quinn.

"And if they do not kill you, I will. You will live just long enough to see the world you wish for, and then you will be gone from it, as you should have been a thousand years ago."

He patted the side of the Master's face, not hard, but with just enough force to sting.

"Thank you for powering our walls, Talius." He said, before exiting into the corridor and climbing back to the surface without another look back.

CHAPTER 41

MALLORY

Mallory managed little sleep, electing to stay with Andra as they shared their favorite memories of Nes, laughing and crying until the early rays of dawn poked through the window. To Mallory's surprise, Ashe had poked her head in at one point, meeting with Andra to pay her respects as well as organize the pyre for the next day's funeral. Mallory was happy to see a quick friendship begin to bloom between her two friends.

Nothing brings strangers together faster than loss, her mother used to tell her growing up. Mallory never really thought much about it until she joined the army. As she began to experience loss in her everyday life, her mother's words resonated with her more and more.

Andra seemed to be taking the loss of Nes in stride, showing a strength Mallory respected. They had said their goodbyes when they split from one another, and a part of Andra had felt as though she would never see Nes again. Though Mallory could tell his loss wounded her deeply, she held her chin high, proud of what he had accomplished for their people.

She knew Andra would miss him dearly, but her ability to shoulder the burden and keep moving forward spoke to her strength as a leader in ways similar to Ashe's. Mallory had no doubts the two would become fast friends.

As for Cyrus, Mallory did not envy the fate that awaited him. Though she hoped to be there when he showed his face again, and Mallory had no doubts that they had not seen the last of him, the things Andra said she would do to him made Malloy's skin crawl. Horacio would eat well the next time they clashed.

As the morning sun cast its golden rays upon the towering walls of Stormhaven, signaling the beginning of a day both somber and poignant, a funeral procession emerged from the heart of the Citadel, winding its way through the cobbled streets of the city.

The air stirred with a delicate blend of sorrow and celebration as the people of Stormhaven, both Abyssillian and human alike, bid farewell to a young hero, taken too soon.

At the forefront of the procession walked Andra, Quinn, and Mallory, dressed in fine, black velvet. Behind them marched a contingent of Abyssillian warriors, clad in sparkling silver armor that glistened in the soft light; the people of Stormhaven's contribution to their fallen leader.

They carried Nes, wrapped head to toe in the finest thread Ashe could spin, upon a simple wooden bier as they made their way out towards the walls. The rhythmic beat of a single drum reverberated through the hushed streets, setting the tone for the solemn march.

Mourners emerged from every rebuilt corner of the city as they passed, drawn together by a shared grief that transcended race. Merchants abandoned their stalls, artisans set aside their tools, and even the children paused their games, their youth temporarily subdued by the weight of loss.

The streets came alive with a tapestry of lament. Colorful banners and shimmering drapes adorned shops and houses along the cortège's path, as if the entire city had draped itself in sorrowful splendor. As the procession made its way through the winding streets, mourners stepped forward, their hands cradling bouquets of fragrant wildflowers.

They cast the petals into the air, releasing a cascade of life and color. The flowers mingled with the soft rain of tears, symbolizing both sorrows as well as celebration for the life Nes lived.

They reached the open fields just outside of the towering walls, where Ashe stood waiting at a grand pyre. She wore deep, black robes laced with gold, matching the engravings carved upon the wood that would be Nes' final resting place.

As they placed the bier upon the pyre, Andra stepped up to the crowd which had gathered to give her final eulogy. Though her eyes were red from crying, her voice was strong, carrying easily across the throngs of people.

"Today, we gather to bid farewell to a remarkable soul, whose life was a testament to the power of redemption and the unyielding spirit of a leader. Born into a world ravaged by greed and prejudice, he found himself drawn to a life many of us knew at one point; that of thievery and banditry.

"However, fate had other plans for Nes. Quinn recognized the untapped potential within, and it is thanks to him that all of our lives began to change for the better."

"Through rigorous training, Nes honed his skills. Not only did his strength as a warrior grow, but his compassion and understanding of the world around him grew as well. He understood that strength was not defined by the might of one's axe, but also by the ability to inspire and protect those who needed it most. He stood tall, reminding us that our past need not define our future."

"It was this unwavering resolve that led him to take on his greatest quest—to restore life to our home. Where others saw bareness and despair, Nes envisioned a land teeming with vitality and possibility.

"His determination knew no bounds, fighting not only for himself but for every one of us still yearning for a better life. Through his actions he gave us a second chance, reminding us of the incredible power we possess when we stand united."

"Though we mourn the loss of our beloved leader, we must also celebrate the triumph of his legacy. Nes fulfilled his promise. He breathed life into the Wastes, turning it into a vibrant oasis; a testament to the enduring power of his spirit."

Andra turned then, looking down at the wrapped, still form of Nes as tears began to run down her face.

"You were more than just a warrior; you were a guiding light for us all. Your unwavering commitment to our people will forever be etched into our hearts. Rest in peace, dear Nes. May your spirit soar free, forever guiding us towards a brighter future, and protecting us for the storm that is to come."

Cheers erupted from the gathered crowd as Andra finished her emotional speech; their spirits resonating with every word she had spoken. Mallory nodded to Ashe as Andra stepped back, and with a flick of her fingers the pyre was lit; golden flames burning high into the air.

The flames danced and crackled from day into night, transforming the sky into a celestial theater. Stars, like radiant spectators, twinkled above, bearing witness to the celebration of life that had touched so many, forever preserving the memory of the fallen hero.

~~~

The next day, Mallory was summoned to meet with a group of prominent figures within Stormhaven to discuss the elephant in the room; that being the presence of Levy. The assembled company was comprised of Lend as well as a youthful man known as Avery, who served as Lend's trusted right hand.

Alongside them were Ashe, Quinn, Andra, a formidable individual named Kael, the new leader of the Abyssillan warriors now that Nes had passed, and Mallory herself. They met within the Masters' old mess hall, the tables having all been pushed to the sides of the room so that only one remained within the center.

On one end sat Lend and Avery, and upon the other sat Quinn and Ashe. Andra, Kael, and Mallory all sat along the side, leaving the last side open for Levy, though the warrior declined to sit, rather choosing to stand against the wall.

"We should stick his head on a spike and be done with it," Kael said for the third time. They had been discussing Levy's fate as though he were on trial for the last hour with little progress made.

On one side were Avery and Kael, calling for the young warrior's death as reparation for the damages he had caused. Avery was calm and collected, his neat, brown eyebrows scrunched together in thought every time he spoke.

Kael was all fire and emotion, his face matching the red of his hair as he pounded the table. On the other side sat Quinn and Ashe, both calm but insistent that they allow their friend leniency. Mallory knew that Lend leaned against him, and though she had plenty of distrust and anger towards the cocky man herself, she trusted Ashe and Quinn's judgment on the matter.

That left Andra as a deciding voice, who had reason to be on either side. Mallory knew she too, trusted Quinn, but she was also aware of the losses her people had endured, including her friend Sen, to Levy's attack.

"Please, just hear us out," Ashe said, her voice calm but assertive. "We do not wish to cheapen the pain you have felt due to his actions. What Levy has done should not be forgotten. But killing him will not soothe your wounded heart, nor will it bring those you have lost back.

"The fact is the Olympians are coming, whether you want to think about it or not. When Zeus breaks back through, we will need all of the help we can get. Levy is one of the strongest people alive.

"He has the power to help us weather Zeus' assault, and without him, we are weakened. Do not forget the pain he has caused you, but allow him to use his strengths for us so that you do not need to feel the pains of loss again."

Lend grunted, pulling all eyes in the room to him. "Commander, you know I trust you implicitly."

Ashe smiled at the man. "Lend, you do not have to call me commander anymore. We may be fighting a battle, but we are not on the frontlines."

"Nevertheless," he replied, "I was there the night that man sent a horde of undead to attack us. I fought that battle, and I witnessed many of our men and women fall. It seems unwise to allow him back into our good graces."

Just as it seemed unwise to allow the Abyssillians into your good graces after the fact?" Quinn asked, meeting Lend's challenge with one of his own.

Lend looked back at Quinn and sighed. "My words to you that day are words that I regret, and now wholly reject. Surely you can see that by what I have done here in Stormhaven."

Quinn nodded back at him. "I do not say those words in challenge, but simply to show you that your judgment is not always correct."

Quinn stood up from the table, meeting the eyes of all who sat around it. Mallory felt a shiver run down her spine as his gaze drifted across her own. Gone was the meek, self-doubting man she had spoken to last in Petram. In his place stood a man filled with confidence and self-assurance; someone who could lead a group into a storm they could not survive, and still come out the other side.

"When we were initially betrayed by Levy, I allowed my judgment to falter and dropped him to his perceived death. For years after, that decision haunted me. I will not allow that to happen again.

"It is easy to look at what he has done and take the easy way out, killing him before he can do more. But you did not see what Ashe and I saw inside the Tower of Fate. Had Levy not stood against Ares with us, none of us would be here right now.

"First, he sacrificed his eye, and then what should have been his life. It was Levy who landed the killing blow upon the Olympian. I understand how hard forgiveness can be, but Ashe and I have forgiven him.

"And now I will stake my life on his change. Grant him time to show what he says is true. If it is not to your liking, then I will accept whatever punishment you grant him upon myself as well."

A shocked silence fell over the room as Quinn regained his seat. Mallory noticed Levy staring at his friend with a look of surprise, though he quickly wiped his face clean of emotion when he noticed Mallory's stare. *He broods as Quinn used to,* Mallory thought to herself, smiling internally.

"I would like to hear what he has to say," Andra spoke for the first time, gesturing towards Levy.

"My lady-" Kael began to protest but Andra silenced him with a look.

"As far as I can tell, we currently have a split vote." She looked toward Levy, raising her chin in challenge. "I have lost many of my people to your antics," she continued. "Including my friend, Sen. Though I highly value the opinion of Quinn and owe him a great debt, I would like you to convince me why I should not cut the infection from the wound now rather than risk its spread."

After a moment of thought, Levy stepped forward and into the light.

"I am sorry about your people, and about your friend. I am sorry to everyone at this table, and to everyone outside of it, who has been wounded by my decisions. I could stand here now and claim that I had a god whispering in my ear, or that I was lost but now am found, but I will not.

"The truth is, I chose the path I went down. I allowed my anger and my lust for power to cloud my judgment, and for that, I am sorry as well. I can sit here and apologize for everything I have done if you'd like, but I don't think that's what you wish to hear from me. The truth is, you have every right to despise me."

He looked over to Kael and said, "I do not blame you for calling for my head. If that is the answer you come to today, I will accept it. I simply ask that you give me the chance to prove that I am not what I was. I would like nothing more than to repair the damage I have caused."

After a brief pause, he turned back to Andra, meeting her gaze with a look of genuine contrition. "To quote your own words back to you, our past does not define our future."

Andra sat up in her seat; a fire kindled behind her eyes. "You would repeat my eulogy for the man I loved back at me in your defense?" She hissed.

"I do not do so to save my own life, and I certainly do not intend to cheapen your words in such a way. I did not know Nes, but I wish I had. He died for what he believed in and saw to it that his people could prosper in return. I simply wish for a chance to do the same."

"Andra," Mallory spoke, drawing the woman's attention. "Nes fought to the very end to bring his goals to life." Andra shook her head, her eyes glistening with barely contained tears. "If he heard Levy's plea here now, and knew Quinn stood behind him fully, he would want to give him a chance to show it."

"I know he would," she whispered. "And he wound up dead because of those ideals." She turned back to Levy, staring deeply into his eyes. Levy stared back; the strength of his words still strong upon his features.

"I will honor Nes' memory," she decided, a tear finally slipping free from her eye. "I truly hope you mean what you say, because if you betray us in any way, I will make it my life's mission, before I die, to make sure you suffer the consequences."

Levy released a long, shuddering breath as if he had been holding it for the duration of her decision. For the first time since he had come back, it looked to Mallory as if a massive weight had been lifted from his shoulders. His eyes gleamed within the dimly lit room, and Mallory was surprised to see the relief on his face. *He was truly prepared to die,* she thought, surprised at the sympathy she felt for him.

"I suppose that's settled then," Lend said, cutting into her reverie. "From here on out, Levy will be welcomed within Stormhaven, until such a time our judgment has been proven to have been made in error." He looked at Levy as he said, "Hopefully that time never comes."

The group dispersed to go their separate ways, each with a laundry list of tasks to get done for the day. Running Stormhaven was taxing, and this delay would likely have already put everyone behind on their duties.

Mallory ducked out into the sunny courtyard, allowing Ashe and Quinn to speak privately with their newly exonerated friend. Though she would have loved to be a fly on the wall of their conversation, she knew they would want time together, freshly reunited as they were.

"Mallory," Andra called out to her, beckoning her over to a bench beside a row of purple and white lilies. As Mallory approached, Andra held a silver talisman out to her. The metal was shaped into the form of an axe, its shaft engraved with a series of familiar crisscrossing lines.

"What is this?" Mallory asked, holding the talisman up into the light.

"It was modeled after Nes' axe," Andra explained. The lines are his scars, signifying that even the greatest hardships can be brought back together.

"You never intended to side against Levy," Mallory said, handing the metal back to Andra. She shook her head, pushing Mallory's hand back.

"I wanted to hear what he had to say. I wanted to see if he would fight for his ideals, as Nes did, or if his fire had been extinguished."

She sighed. "It's as you said, Nes would have agreed to give him a chance. What kind of hypocrite would I be to cite his words and then reject them at the first opportunity?" She shook her head.

"Anyways, I was not just giving you that to look at. It's for you if you will have it. When this is all over, I'll bring my people back to the Wastes and rebuild. Though I suppose it can't be called the Wastes anymore. I can't do it alone though. Without Nes, I could use some help." She looked at Mallory expectantly.

Mallory connected the dots in her head and gasped. "Andra, I'm not Abyssillian."

"It doesn't matter. You have lived amongst us longer than any human ever has. The people love you. They will accept it. I understand if you do not wish to tie your life to Petram, but if there is even the chance of you saying yes, I must ask. Be my right hand and help me lead my people into prosperity."

Mallory stared in awe at the significance of the axe within her hand. To ask someone who was not Abyssillian to help lead her people was unheard of. However, perhaps this was exactly what was needed to finally bridge the gap between their peoples. Stormhaven was a good start, and proof that it could be done on a larger scale. Mallory looked up to Andra and smiled. Andra matched her smile immediately, knowing what her words would be before she spoke them.

"Yes, Andra. I accept."

CHAPTER 42

ASHE

Ashe traced little circles along Quinn's chest with her finger, her head resting comfortably upon his shoulder. He bulked up some since the last time she had seen him, much to her delight. Much had happened in the short amount of time since they had been reunited, and it was not until now that the two had had a chance to celebrate their reunion.

The hand-holding and lingering gazes had been nice; his little touches on the small of her back now and then sent electricity racing through her. But it was nothing compared to truly being able to reconnect behind a closed door after years of longing for one another.

Now they rested content within one another's embrace. She took in his scent with each breath, sandalwood and sweat mixing in an intoxicating way.

"I should probably get going," Quinn said, making no move to rise from the bed. "I promised Kael I would help train the new guard."

"Yes, you probably should," Ashe replied, knowing full well

she would not remove her head from his chest even had he tried. Quinn chuckled, leaning down to lay a gentle kiss upon the crown of her head.

"Have you asked Levy to join you?" she asked as he finally extracted himself from her grasp, slipping his shirt on over his head.

"He said he would be happy to join, but he wants to make sure the men expect his presence first. He may be allowed to move freely around Stormhaven, but he still feels like he has to walk on eggshells. It will take time for the people here to truly accept him."

Ashe sighed, sitting up and swinging her legs over the side of their bed. "I know their perception of him will not change overnight, but I hope they can find it in their hearts to accept him soon."

She looked up at him, her lower lip poking out in a slight pout. She knew Quinn melted beneath that face, and she enjoyed pushing his buttons immensely.

Quinn smiled, cupping her face within his hand. "Until they do, we will be there with him every step of the way. He won't feel alone here."

"Good," Ashe stood up and began throwing her clothing on. "Everything we do from here on out, we will include him also; whether it be planning, fighting, etc."

"Fine." Quinn said, "But I am not doing to him what I just did to you."

Ashe snorted, lightly slapping the back of his head. "You know what I meant."

Just then a knock sounded from the entrance to the room. Quinn made his way over, unlatching the bolt and pulling the wooden door open to see Levy standing on the other side. He looked his friend up and down.

"Is this a bad time?"

"Not at all," Quinn replied, clapping Levy on his back as he walked past. "I was just heading out to join the guard in their training exercises. Are you sure you don't want to come along? They're pretty green and I could use the extra help."

"Next time," Levy said. "I promise."

Quinn nodded, looking back at Ashe. "See you later."

Ashe beckoned Levy inside, gesturing to a wooden chair in the corner of the room. He sat down, collecting his thoughts for a minute.

"You will have to get involved sooner or later, Levy," Ashe said gently, sitting on the edge of her bed. "I know it will be difficult at first, but eventually they will come to see you for who you are."

A slight grin came to rest upon Levy's face.

"I know. It's funny, I spent my whole life telling Quinn to be more confident and to care less about the looks thrown his way. Now he has found himself, and it's me walking around with my head down beneath the piercing glares of the people.

"It's not even so much them that I care about, as much as it is myself." He stared at the floor, his mask of confidence no longer on his face as it always had been. "I hate what I have done, Ashe. I know I talked a big game to Andra about being better, and I meant those words.

"Yet, every opportunity I get to get involved and prove it I freeze. Quinn stuck his neck out for me, despite everything I have done to him, and so far, I have repaid him with cowardice."

"Levy, look at me," Ashe directed, firmly but with kindness lacing each word. He looked up instantly. "Do you remember when I first came to the Citadel? The people of this city hated me for burning down so much of the slums."

Levy shifted uncomfortably as she spoke, but did not break eye contact.

"Do you remember how many times you had to come to my rescue before I learned how to fight? And then once I did start to learn, do you remember how you took time out of each of your days off, teaching me tricks to protect myself?

"Because I remember. Not once, despite everything that has happened, have I forgotten who the real Levy Sylva is. Soon, every single person out there is going to know as well. You have the heart of a hero, Levy, and I will burn away anybody who tries to tear that part of you down."

Levy's grin had turned into a full smile, his eyes alight with a confidence Ashe had not seen since they had returned here together.

"I don't know if it is because you absorbed fate, or if it is just your personality shining through, but your words carry so much weight, Ashe. It's like you speak, and your words fill me with courage. I may have to start calling you Fire Witch."

Ashe sniffed, turning up her nose at him. "Queen will suffice, thank you. I have started to rather like that moniker." Levy laughed, and Ashe quickly joined him.

"This feels nice," he said, staring into the flickering flame of a candle. "It feels like it has been so long since we last spoke together like this."

"The hot springs we found after we left Hestia," Ashe replied, her eyes distant.

"I'm happy for you two, you know." Levy cut in, pulling her out of the memory. "I know my feelings have been a point of contention between us in the past."

"Thank you, Levy" Ashe said, "I am as well. I know we did not exactly make it easy for you, and I am sorry for that."

Levy laughed. "You don't need to be sorry for being in love, Ashe. And I mean it when I say I am happy for you both. These last few years have opened my eyes to so much. Please, don't feel like you have to walk on pins and needles around me. I'll be ok, I promise."

"If you ever want to talk," Ashe said, standing from her spot on the edge of her bed and walking over to him, "please do not hesitate to find us. Quinn and I are so happy to have you back."

Levy stood as well; his shoulders held back in a way that signified the weight that had been removed from his chest. "I am happy to be back. Thanks, Ashe."

She wrapped him in a brief hug before pointing to the door with her thumb. "I have to go meet with Lend about some city planning for the rest of the repairs. Want to come with?"

Levy shook his head, staring out through the door in the direction Quinn had gone.

"I was thinking I'd take Quinn up on his offer after all. I just had an idea that I'd like to run by him. Meet you in the mess hall for dinner after?"

Ashe smiled, happy to see some of Levy's confidence back where it belonged. "I wouldn't miss it."

EPILOGUE

Cyrus sat upon his very own throne within the gleaming throne room of Olympus. For his efforts in acquiring the Scythe of Demeter and bringing the barrier crashing down once and for all, Zeus had seen fit to grant him godhood, a reward rarely given out.

He could feel the immortal essence flowing through him, his power crackling at his fingertips whenever he pleased. Had he known immortality felt this good, he would have made his move years ago.

"I do not understand why we sit here and squabble amongst ourselves, Father." The whiney voice of Dionysus spoke from Cyrus' right.

Though previously he was the youngest of the gods granted a place upon Olympus, thanks to the addition of Cyrus he moved up a spot. The promotion had gone to his head because he had just openly spoken against their king, much to Cyrus' disbelief. Though he had not been on Olympus long, even he knew better than to question the word of Zeus. Rumor was that Hera had recently paid the process for doing just that.

The throne room fell deathly silent as Zeus met Dionysus' gaze; electricity crackling at the edges of his vision.

"Speak your piece, but speak carefully, son." Zeus rumbled, his voice shaking the very foundations of the room. Levy's betrayal culminating in the death of his son Ares had left his patience stretched very thin as of late.

"If the barrier is down, why have we not already crossed over and exacted revenge for the millennium we have been kept out? Are we not Olympians? Surely we do not cower simply because of a couple of mortals with powers they do not yet fully understand how to wield."

Dionysus was standing by the end of his speech, his hand balled into a fist and held out in front of him. All eyes turned to Zeus, awaiting his response to the god's audacity. Though it was a common question Cyrus had heard many times outside of the king of the Olympian's earshot, nobody had dared voice it in his presence up until now.

"Sit," Zeus commanded, the word leaving his mouth with the intensity of a crack of thunder. Dionysius, having come to his senses, complied without restraint, sitting back down upon his throne so hard Cyrus wondered if the marble base had cracked beneath the pressure.

"Our vengeance will come soon," Zeus continued, boring holes into each of them with the intensity of his gaze. "But I do not wish to simply win. We will raze and salt the very ground the mortals walk on so that no life will take hold ever again."

"What are your orders, Lord Zeus?" Cyrus felt himself saying before he could hold his tongue. Every set of eyes found him in unison, some hostile, others worried. A few of the Olympians even looked impressed at the fact he dared speak directly to their king.

Zeus, for his part, simply smiled; his brilliant white teeth putting the throne room's marble to shame. "It is time we reclaim what is ours."

~~~

Quinn found Levy waiting for him outside the gates of Stormhaven before the sun fully climbed above the horizon. The grass was slick with morning dew, crystalizing cobwebs that hung between the branches of trees. There was a slight bite in the air, the chill of Autumn settling upon the world as the heat of summer gradually died off.

Levy was dressed in a fine, black cloak, its silver trimming undoubtedly identified it as something Ashe had made. A black eyepatch covered his missing eye, though the diagonal scar still poked out from either end, only adding to his already handsome face.

Quinn raised an eyebrow as he looked his friend up and down. "You trying to look like me?" he asked, lifting his arms to show off his matching cloak. "First the scar and now the color scheme. You may as well have raided my closet. You even have my sword."

Levy laughed as he drew a gleaming blade from the scabbard on his back. Much like Quinn's, the blade was adorned with black and silver, though it was far wider and heavier than anything Quinn would have used.

The Abyssillians had made it for him in thanks for helping train their warriors for the fight to come. Though forgiveness was still a long way off, the people of Stormhaven had begun to show Levy more trust over the last few months as he became more involved with planning for the Olympian incursion.

Nobody was sure why it had not come yet, though because of the delay, Ashe was hard at work, attempting to weave a new barrier around their realm. It would not have the strength to stop the Olympians from entering, but it would alert them when and where it happened, giving Quinn and their allies enough time to react.

"You sure you want to do this?" Quinn asked as he drew even with his friend. "It isn't too late to change your mind."

"I'm sure, Quinn," Levy responded, resheathing his blade. "I cannot stand against the might of the Olympians as I am. You have the power of Chaos at your command, and Ashe the power of fate. A small amount of Hestia's essence will allow me to stand with you both, but not to win."

Quinn raised his eyebrows at his friend's words, though Levy caught his meaning.

"It is not like it was before, I promise. I do not seek power for my gain. If I can pull this off, it will benefit all of us. Besides, you'll be with me the whole time."

"I know," Quinn replied. "I just wanted to make sure you understood how it sounded. Ashe agreed to this plan, so I have no doubts either. I feel as though I should point out that we do not even know that it will work, however. It has only ever been done once before, and even then, we only know about it through myth. Who's to say that carries any accuracy with it?"

Levy shrugged. "We will only know by attempting it. If it works, then we have another powerful defense against Zeus and his offspring. And if it doesn't, then no harm done."

Quinn sighed, but raised his hand, summoning the power of Chaos to his fingertips. Instantly a glowing portal spun to life, its essence beckoning them forward as if eager to allow them through and close once more. As Levy stepped up to it, Quinn reached out, stopping him in his tracks.

"Just so you are aware, if something happens to you when you try this, there is plenty of harm that can occur. You are important, Levy, whether you attain this power or not. Don't forget that, please."

Levy smiled. "Relax, Quinn. It will be alright. And hey," he said as he lifted one leg into the portal. "At least I already took care of the guard dog."

ABOUT THE AUTHOR

Brian has dreamed of being an author since his early days in high school. He used to sit in the school library whenever he had the chance, soaking up as many tales from Greek Mythology as he could get his hands on; fascinated by the stories of gods and heroes. After stumbling upon the Percy Jackson series in his school's library, he began reading at a feverish pace and never looked back.

Realm Walker marks his second novel as an author, as well as the second book of an Epic Series; Wrath of Olympus.

www.ingramcontent.com/pod-product-compliance
Lightning Source LLC
Chambersburg PA
CBHW030651260626
47157CB00007B/2593